A
Date
Which
Will
Live
in Infamy

AN ANTHOLOGY OF PEARL HARBOR
STORIES THAT MIGHT HAVE BEEN

A Date Which Will Live in Infamy

EDITED BY
Brian M. Thomsen & Martin H. Greenberg

CUMBERLAND HOUSE
NASHVILLE, TENNESSEE

Published by
CUMBERLAND HOUSE PUBLISHING, INC.
431 Harding Industrial Drive
Nashville, Tennessee 37211
www.cumberlandhouse.com

All photographs courtesy of the U.S. Naval Historical Center.

Cover design by Unlikely Suburban Design, Nashville, Tennessee.

Library of Congress Cataloging-in-Publication Data

A date which will live in infamy : an anthology of Pearl Harbor stories that might have been / edited by Brian M. Thomsen & Martin H. Greenberg.

p. cm.

Includes bibliographical references.

ISBN 1-58182-222-7 (alk. paper)

1. World War, 1939–1945—Hawaii—Fiction. 2. Pearl Harbor (Hawaii), Attack on, 1941—Fiction. 3. War stories, American. I. Thomsen, Brian. II. Greenberg, Martin Harry.

PS648.W65 D38 2001   2001037133

Printed in the United States of America.

1 2 3 4 5 6 7 8 9 10—05 04 03 02 01

To the brave men and women of our nation's
armed forces who defended not only Pearl Harbor
but the liberty of America and the world

Contents

APPENDIXES

Introduction

When Interesting History Makes Bad Hollywood

BRIAN M. THOMSEN

While putting this volume together I had a discussion with my brother the historian. As I bounced various scenarios emanating from that day which will live in infamy, he seemed to take insidious delight in shooting down each one with remarks like "things just don't work that way," "they would never do something like that," and "not in a million years."

Historians like facts that are carved in stone. If it didn't happen that way, well, then it didn't happen that way.

Now I like history, but I prefer fiction (it has a certain amount of elasticity), but even I have to admit that certain plot twists are beyond the bounds of credibility.

Imagine an attack that manages to precede the delivery of the last-chance ultimatum that could have prevented it.

Imagine a Japanese attack designed by an American-educated admiral based on a previous attack designed by the British.

Imagine that the first warning of the attack in process is disregarded and the pertinent targets are all aligned in the manner most favorable to the bombers.

Imagine the attackers, having met with little resistance so far, declining a third round to put the final nail in the coffin by taking out all available fuel reserves and shipyards.

Now let's add a few miscellaneous details, like having all the authorities on hand who had any suspicion of an attack being dead sure that it was going to be Singapore (which actually took place a day later). Throw in some dumb luck, like having the most desirable targets (the aircraft carriers) otherwise engaged and out to sea. Add a bit of comic relief and human interest like having a female flight instructor trying to give a lesson during the attack. Pick two or three of the above, put them in a movie, and let the groans begin.

Of course we would let Hollywood get away with it. We'll enjoy the movie but then make fun of it, relegating such nonsense to the ranks of bad moviemaking that gives us scenes with Roman soldiers wearing wristwatches or cowboys with six-shooters that can fire nonstop.

Just like my brother, we all sit back and enjoy, deride and dismiss, because things just don't happen that way in real life. But at Pearl Harbor on December 7, 1941, all of the above actually happened and more. We believe it, because it was history (as fiction it would strain credibility).

This collection of stories is devoted to looking at some of these historically less-than-credible alternatives to the events of December 7 or their cause or outcome.

One case in point is the issue of whom to blame for the attack. Well, the Japanese, of course . . . but what about Hitler or Churchill or maybe even good old FDR. All equally far-fetched? Well, at least one of them receives the mantle of blame in a well-reviewed book entitled *Day of Deceit*, and it has been universally designated as nonfiction, so who is to say? The authors herein make all three credible.

Other stories deal with different attacks with different outcomes, each episode well reasoned if not necessarily historically vetted. There are even stories that wave the flag with tales of action and intrigue, heroes and spies, that allow us to win on that seventh of December or lose even more horribly, only to rebound in a bitter blaze of redemptive glory. As a fan of fiction, anything is possible.

Part of the ingenuity in these stories lies in the authors' abilities to deal with the historical actualities involved, the history so to speak. To enhance your enjoyment, a historical appendix has been included that provides an overview of the actual events of that day, a background piece on the diplomatic subtext involved, and an examination of the thematic concept of an alternate Pearl Harbor from a historian's point of view.

It is always better to know what actually happened before pondering what might haven been. And remember, truth can be stranger than fiction, and sometimes good history can make bad Hollywood.

A
Date
Which
Will
Live
in Infamy

Part 1

Alternate
Architects

Undeniably, Adm. Isoroku Yamamoto was the chief architect of Japan's attack on Pearl Harbor.

But nothing happens in a vacuum.

The battle plan alone was not enough to christen that date in infamy.

Some others had to be involved in the planning. If not in the attack itself, definitely in the resultant actions and situations.

The Sumter Scenario
A Time Wars Story

SIMON HAWKE

Brig. Gen. Lucas Priest glanced around briefly as he entered the First Division lounge. There were a few soldiers seated here and there around the room, some dressed in crisp, black base fatigues, others in various field uniforms. Two Roman centurions, their plumed helmets resting on the table before them, sat chatting over drinks with a couple of Green Berets in jungle camo. Several tables over, a nearly naked, heavily tattooed Pict warrior was engaged in conversation with an armored samurai and a female Israeli commando freshly clocked in from the Six-Day War. Nearby, a French musketeer in a royal blue surplice emblazoned with a fleur-de-lis was enjoying a pitcher of martinis with a couple of World War I doughboys.

Someone spotted Priest and immediately called out, "Ten-*HUT!*"

Chairs scraped suddenly as everyone rose to their feet at once and snapped to attention.

"As you were," said Priest, nodding to them in acknowledgment.

Under most circumstances, rank was not observed within the lounge. The one exception was when the director entered. Except that no one ever called him the director. To everyone under his command, he was simply "the General" or, on occasion, "the Old Man," though he was hardly old. His blond hair was cropped short and showed no signs of gray. His posture was ramrod straight, and his skin was unblemished by age. He was in peak physical condition from a regular fitness regimen, which included running, weightlifting, cycling, and various forms of martial arts training. He looked years younger than most men his age, though in part, that was due to the special life-extending treatments he had received on entering the service. Nevertheless, he knew he would continue to be referred to as "the Old Man," just as Moses Forrester had been before him. It was less a question of age than of seniority.

It was late, but like most of the facilities at Pendleton Base, the lounge never closed. It was about the size of a large briefing room, with a long bar against one wall and round tables with comfortable chairs placed all around. Other than that, the First Division lounge did not really have much of the ambiance of a bar. There were no hanging ferns or potted plants, no dim lighting, and there was little in the way of decor.

The entire far wall was a huge floor-to-ceiling window looking out over the sprawling base from sixty stories up. In the distance, the glittering lights of the Los Angeles megaplex were visible, stretching out to the north all the way to San Francisco. Upon one wall of the lounge hung a large plaque of the division insignia, a gold number one bisected by the symbol for infinity, which resembled a slightly stretched-out, horizontal figure eight. Next to it was another large plaque, solid gold mounted on mahogany. It was a smaller replica of the Wall of Honor downstairs in the lobby of the building. On it were listed the names of the members of the First Division who had died in action throughout time. There was another plaque flanking that one, about the same size as the divisional insignia. It was the symbol π, which represented an infinitely repeating number. It was also the insignia of the Temporal Intelligence Agency.

As the insignia suggested, the resources of the TIA did indeed seem infinite, as did the number of its personnel. Its budget, one of the government's most closely guarded secrets, had been staggering from the days of its inception, and until only a few years ago, the highly classified nature of the work the agency performed was such that its section chiefs had never been required to justify their budgetary requisitions or fully document their subsidiary personnel.

When Priest's predecessor, Gen. Moses Forrester, had assumed the directorship of the agency following its merging with the First Division of the Temporal Army Corps, he had discovered to his chagrin that the agency was like an octopus that had lost count of the number of its tentacles and, as a result, no longer had the real ability to control them.

Section chiefs in the field had often recruited from among locals in their temporal sectors, none of whom, for obvious reasons, knew who their employers really were. As a result, the section chiefs would not cooperate with any attempts to obtain accurate listings of all their field personnel, citing the necessity for temporal security. Past directors had essentially allowed the agency to operate almost completely on its own, without any great concern for regulations. Abuses had been both flagrant and frequent. And highly dangerous, as well, considering the possibilities for temporal interference.

Sometimes, it seemed difficult to believe that the threat of temporal disruption had existed for almost two hundred years. Ever since the invention of the chronoplate by Dr. Wolfgang Mensinger in 2425, ironically on April Fools' Day, people had been traveling through time. For the next fifty years, temporal research expeditions had been carried out on a limited scale and under strictly controlled conditions, following long-accepted principles of scientific method. However, when Dr. Albrecht Mensinger lost control of his father's discovery and his laboratories were seized by troops of the Transatlantic Treaty Organization, the threat of temporal disruption escalated dramatically.

In June 2497 the newly formed Referee Corps began presiding over the first temporal arbitration campaigns as a way of resolving international conflicts. In a world where increasing technological complexity and the devastating efficiency of weapons systems made even the possibility of war unthinkable, sending cybernetically conditioned troops through time to participate in armed conflicts of the past seemed an elegant solution. No one had believed that the past could be affected by temporal voyagers. Despite impassioned arguments to the contrary by Albrecht Mensinger, prevailing scientific testimony had reinforced the conventional wisdom that time was an immutable absolute. As time had often demonstrated, however, this conventional wisdom turned out to be completely wrong.

By the time even the most recalcitrant skeptics were convinced that temporal disruption was not only a very real but a potentially eschatonic threat, the massive support industry that had grown up around the temporal arbitration conflicts—or the Time Wars, as they became popularly known—had become so entrenched and so firmly a part of the modern economy and bureaucracy that any legislator arguing for the suspension of the conflicts would be committing political suicide. And so the Time Wars had continued: the threat of temporal disruption had become a new paradigm in temporal physics, and the First Division of the Temporal Army Corps was tasked with the express mission to conduct temporal adjustments in order to preserve the undisrupted continuity of the timeline. In essence, their mission was to conduct covert operations in the past so as to preserve the future.

In support of this imperative, the TIA, which had grown or, as Priest would often say, metastasized from Albrecht Mensinger's research organization, the Committee for Temporal Intelligence, was assigned the pivotal role of monitoring history for potential temporal disruptions. Needless to say, the task required an organization that was *very* large. One of the greatest secrets of the TIA was that it was, in fact, larger and possessed more resources than most nations. And in any organization of that size, holding so much power, corruption was inevitable.

After he took the helm of the TIA, Forrester had recruited soldiers from his own elite First Division to form the Internal Security Division in an attempt to bring things under control and, at the same time, weed out the corruption. Functioning as the agency's internal police force, the ISD had not taken very long to uncover evidence of corruption in the TIA. In the process, they also uncovered the existence of a secret agency *within* the agency, a deeply clandestine and complex transtemporal organization known as "the Network."

The Network's primary concern was profit, and in that regard the renegade organization made up its own rules and was accountable to no one. Forrester discovered that the Network was like a multinational corporation whose influence transcended the boundaries of time. The ISD had uncovered evidence of Network involvement in industrial conglomerates of the twenty-first century as well as in the African slave trade of the eighteenth century. They were active in seventeenth-century piracy on the Spanish Main and in the colonial empire of ancient Rome. In short, the Network was practically everywhere.

Profits skimmed from the Dutch West India Company in the 1600s were converted into gold and used to finance commodities transactions in the bear markets of the twentieth century, using the knowledge gained from time travel to pull off the ultimate in insider-trading operations. That money was used to finance even further profits taken from twentieth-century gambling casinos in Monte Carlo, Las Vegas, and Atlantic City. Those profits could in turn be laundered through transactions that were nearly impossible to trace, because the trail would lead from one time period to another, from bootlegging in the 1940s to arms trading in the 1980s to real estate investments in the early 1900s to corporate takeovers in the late twenty-first century. It was, in a way, the penultimate form of investment banking, with virtually unlimited potential for profit, because the Network had actually turned time into a commodity that could be successfully manipulated.

Forrester had set out to break the Network, but years of entrenched and unfettered operations had made the clandestine organization vast and powerful. Even when Network operatives were captured and interrogated, the closed-cell system that the Network used to structure its complex operations had made it nearly impossible to compromise its infrastructure. And since they were all seasoned operatives of Temporal Intelligence, they were highly trained and dangerous antagonists, as they had proved when they assassinated the first commander of the ISD. Forrester himself had survived several Network assassination attempts before retiring to an undisclosed location. Since Lucas had assumed the directorship, he had felt the pressure, too. At first, they had tried to feel him out discreetly to see if he was corruptible. When they found that he wasn't and that he was cut from the same cloth as Moses Forrester, the Network targeted him for elimination.

Forrester had never backed down from anyone or anything. Lucas Priest had served under him for many years in the legendary First Division, the elite Time Commandos of the Temporal Army Corps. He had always respected Forrester above all other men and was determined to finish the job that he had started. Priest didn't care how impossible it seemed or how long it would take. After all, in the Temporal Corps, time was a flexible commodity.

He spotted Col. Finn Delaney seated at the far end of the lounge, having a beer at a table by the window. The general smiled and headed over. Delaney stood as he approached. To look at him, no one would have guessed he was a division commander, much less the leader of the most honored division in the Temporal Corps. He looked less like an army officer than an amiable longshoreman, and as usual, he pushed uniform standards about as far as possible without actually dressing in civilian clothes. His one-piece black base fatigues were rumpled and open at the collar about two buttons too low, revealing a nonregulation red T-shirt. He had his sleeves unbuttoned and rolled up, displaying his muscular forearms, and instead of a web belt, he wore a wide, nonregulation, black leather garrison belt with a nickel-plated buckle. Attached to his belt was an equally nonregulation leather holster, holding a highly nonregulation lead-projectile sidearm—a twentieth-century-vintage Glock .45, which he had obtained brand-new on an assignment in the field and smuggled back with him.

"General," Delaney said.

"Colonel." They shook hands and sat down, both of them ignoring the black-clad ISD agents who had quietly entered the lounge and took up positions nearby, their eyes alert, their hands close to their plasma sidearms. They had the unenviable job of being the director's bodyguards. Assassins capable of time travel could strike literally out of nowhere.

"How the hell are ya, Finn?" asked Lucas, leaning back in his chair. A waiter appeared beside him almost immediately, with the general's usual drink, mineral water with lime.

Delaney shrugged and ran his hand through his thick, dark red hair. "Hangin' in there. Though I gotta say that flyin' a desk is even more boring than I ever imagined it would be, and that's going some."

"Not like the old days, eh?"

"Not even close. In fact, while you were walking over here, I was thinking about maybe haulin' off and poppin' you one, so I could get busted for striking a superior officer and then go back to field duty."

"So what's stopping you?" Priest asked.

"Well, knowing you, you probably wouldn't press charges, and then I'd only feel bad about breaking your jaw for nothing."

Priest smiled. "Come on, it's not really all that bad, is it?"

"How many times have we had this conversation?" asked Delaney.

"I don't know. A bunch of times, I guess."

"And does my answer ever change?"

Priest looked down and shook his head. "No."

"And now you're gonna tell me that you understand how I must feel, but that you really need me here and blah blah blah. Then we'll talk about old times a bit, and then we'll finally get down to what you really wanted to see me about, and then you'll go back to your office and I'll go back to my office and we'll send staff memos back and forth and won't see each other for another few weeks, and then we'll do this whole damn thing all over again. Christ, Lucas, what's happened to us? We're like a couple of old ladies gettin' together to talk about our grandchildren, except we ain't got grandchildren."

"Well, we're not exactly kids anymore, Finn."

"And we're not exactly dead, either. So how come we're actin' like it?"

"Well, I don't really think we are, Finn. What we're doing now may not seem as glamorous or exciting as conducting temporal adjustment missions in the field, but it's just as important, if not more so."

"Lucas, I swear to God, if you give me that speech about the big picture again, I'm gonna puke, so help me."

Priest frowned. "It's a speech?"

"It's a speech. You do it with some minor variations every time, but it's still a goddamn speech."

"I see. I hadn't realized that."

Delaney sighed. "Lucas, we've got too much history under our belts to BS one another, no pun intended. I love you like a brother, but we're just not the same. We never have been. You've always been the model officer, while I've always been the maverick who detested officers. Every time I ever got promoted, I always managed to get myself busted down again, because I just felt more comfortable as an enlisted man. And then Forrester had to screw everything up by putting me in for the MOH. Nobody wants to bust a Medal of Honor winner. The fact that I'm now commanding the division is truly the supreme irony. I'm just no good at it."

"Actually, Finn, you're very good at it. You may not *like* it, but that's another story. The fact is that I can't think of anyone else I'd rather—"

"I'm putting in for retirement, Lucas."

Priest was brought up short. *"Retirement?"*

"As you just said yourself, we're not exactly kids anymore. Besides, I'm a soldier, Lucas, not a goddamn bureaucrat. I've stuck it out this long for your sake, but I'm sick and tired of it. I've had enough. I can give you a short list of officers who are qualified and capable of taking over for me. I'll stick around 'til you find a suitable replacement, but I'd appreciate it if you didn't drag your heels about it."

"I see," said Priest. "Is that your final decision? There's nothing I can do to change your mind?"

"Not unless you want to put me back on active duty in the field again," Delaney said.

Priest pursed his lips and nodded. "Okay."

"Well, then . . . I've enjoyed serving with you, sir," Delaney said, getting up.

"I haven't dismissed you yet," said Priest.

Delaney gave him a look but sat back down.

"I meant, okay, I'll put you back on field duty," the general said.

Delaney raised his eyebrows. "You serious?"

"If that's what you really want. I hate to lose you as commander of the First, but if it's a choice between a transfer and losing you altogether, then I suppose it'll have to be a transfer."

Deleany frowned. *"Transfer?* Who the hell said anything about a transfer?"

"Well, I can't simply reduce you in grade and have you step down to do field duty in the First," said Priest. "For one thing, you're too old. And for another, you're headquarters command staff. It would be awkward, and I wouldn't want to set that kind of precedent. I'm not even sure I can, as far as regulations are concerned. So if you want active field duty, you'll just have to accept a transfer."

"To *where?*"

"Why, the agency, of course. Where else? It's not as if you have a lot of options."

Delaney grimaced. "Look, don't get me wrong, Lucas, I appreciate what you're trying to do, but intelligence wasn't exactly what I had in mind. As I said, I'm a soldier, not a bureaucrat. I don't think my personality is suited to being a section chief in Minus Time."

"I agree with you. Actually, I was thinking ISD," said Priest. "With your experience on temporal adjustment missions, you'd be an excellent choice to head up a special ops unit I'm putting together. In fact, that's what I was going to discuss with you. I wanted your help to recruit some talent from the First for a special mission, but why not just put you in charge of the entire operation? Having you transferred to the ISD to head up a special ops unit wouldn't be hard for me to justify at all. In fact, I wouldn't have to, since the ISD is under direct agency authority and technically separate from TAC-COM. We could process your retirement from the army, then I'd simply have the agency hire you as a civilian. You'd have the best of both worlds, active duty *and* your army pension. That is, assuming you're interested. I can have it expedited, and you can clock out on your first ISD assignment by tomorrow morning."

Delaney raised an eyebrow. "We *are* talking about a field mission?"

"How much do you know about Pearl Harbor, circa 1941?"

"World War II," Delaney said. "Japan's surprise attack on the U.S. Pacific Fleet at the Hawaiian naval base. It was called 'a day which will live in infamy.' It brought about America's involvement in the war by galvanizing public opinion against Japan and the Axis powers, thereby ending isolationism."

Priest nodded. "A very good textbook response," he said. "But as we know, textbooks are very often wrong."

"The attack on Pearl Harbor *didn't* result in the United States' entering World War II?"

"Oh, it did that, all right," said Priest. "But it wasn't much of a surprise."

Delaney frowned. "You saying they knew the attack was coming?"

"They not only knew about it, they practically engineered it. What Roosevelt did with Pearl Harbor was, in essence, the same thing Lincoln did with Fort Sumter. In fact, it wouldn't even surprise me if that particular historical scenario was what gave FDR the idea in the first place."

"Really? How's that?"

"Well, in 1861 Lincoln wanted to force the seceded Southern states back into the Union and was trying to stir up public support in favor of a war. The problem was, the support just wasn't out there. So he dragged his heels and pretty much did nothing while he tried to figure out some way to make the South fire the first shot and start the war he wanted. He got that opportunity when the South demanded the surrender of Fort Sumter, a relatively insignificant Federal garrison in Charleston Harbor. Up until that point, no one had made any big deal about the South taking over Federal facilities within their territories. But Lincoln refused to turn over Fort Sumter. The South made repeated demands that he turn over the fort, but instead he very publicly had it resupplied and thereby baited the South into officially opening hostilities."

"So you're saying that Roosevelt *baited* the Japanese into attacking Pearl Harbor?" asked Delaney.

"Pretty much."

"That's not the way I learned it," said Delaney.

"That's not the way it's taught," replied Priest with a shrug. "The truth wouldn't be very politically correct, even today. Japan didn't really have anything to gain by attacking the United States. In fact, it was the last thing they wanted to do. Communications from Tokyo to their embassy in Washington during November 1941 were particularly frantic in their urgency to have Ambassadors Kurusu and Nomura successfully conclude their negotiations, which were aimed toward a diplomatic resolution of the issues between Japan and the United States. The official version of the story has it that the Japanese were continuing the pretext of negotiations to lull the American government into a false sense of security that some diplomatic resolution was still possible, and that while all this was going on, they hit Pearl Harbor with a sneak attack. But if there was a pretext of anything, it was on the part of Washington. Roosevelt never wanted any diplomatic settlement with Japan and in fact did everything he could to make such a settlement impossible. He knew that without American intervention in the war, England was almost certainly doomed."

"That much I know," Delaney said. "Churchill did just about everything short of falling on his knees to plead with Washington for help. But at that time, most Americans didn't give a damn about what Hitler was doing in Europe. It wasn't their fight. And aside from that, Hitler also had his share of admirers in the United States back then. It was not one of our better moments."

"No, it wasn't," said Priest. "But Roosevelt had no illusions about Hitler. He knew exactly what he was. His problem was convincing the rest of the country. If you look at what actually happened, from the summer of 1940 to December 1941, the United States repeatedly violated its supposed neutrality in the war by such actions as sending war materiel to England and its allied nations, establishing military bases in British territory, and then freezing German and Italian assets in the U.S. But the Germans didn't take the bait. They still remembered World War I and how American intervention had turned the tide back then, so Hitler refrained from breaking off diplomatic relations, even after naval hostilities occurred between American ships and German submarines. So if Roosevelt couldn't get Germany to declare war on the United States, he had to shift gears and concentrate on Hitler's Japanese allies."

"Interesting," Delaney said. "Go on."

"I've got a detailed download you can access, complete with the intelligence reports. In brief, however, the U.S. had steadily applied political and economic pressure to Japan. Progressive trade sanctions were applied. Military aid was given to China, Japan's enemy. When Japan occupied French Indochina, the United States, Great Britain, and the Netherlands acted in concert to freeze all Japanese assets in those countries and cut off all trade with Japan. Negotiations with Japan continued, but in September 1941 the U.S. set conditions for further talks, among which were demands that Japan respect the sovereignty of all nations, refrain from interference in the internal affairs of other nations, and accept equality of trade. The Japanese agreed to withdraw their troops from French Indochina upon restoration of peace between them and China or the establishment of an equitable peace in the Pacific, provided that the United States unfreeze their assets and restore trade, especially in oil, which they needed very badly, and accept a mutual agreement not to advance troops into Southeast Asia or the South Pacific. The secretary of state responded in November to the Japanese ambassadors with a letter containing conditions that Japan could not possibly agree to, because accepting them would have required complete surrender. It wasn't diplomacy, it was an ultimatum. There was no opportunity for them to 'save face.' There were only two options. Surrender or declare war."

"Okay, so Roosevelt was playing hardball," said Delaney. "But that still doesn't prove he knew the sneak attack was coming."

"There's more," said Priest. "The Japanese used cipher encryptions for all their top-secret communications back then. Their so-called Purple Code had been broken by American cryptologists well before the outbreak of hostilities. Tokyo's communications to their embassy in Washington were all decoded, as were their communications to their consul general in Honolulu. Washington knew that they were very interested in the fleet dispositions at Pearl Harbor and wanted regular reports concerning the movements of all military vessels. The War Department had decoded messages along those lines in October 1941, *two months* prior to the attack. And the American ambassador in Tokyo had informed the State Department that he'd heard from several sources, including Japanese contacts, that if trouble broke out between the U.S. and Japan, the Japanese would make a surprise attack against Pearl Harbor 'with all their strength and employing all their equipment.' That was in a message from Ambassador Grew in Tokyo to Washington, dated January 27, 1941, almost a full year prior to the attack. Add to that the fact that it was well known that the Japanese began all their previous wars with sneak attacks against key enemy targets or positions. And the only available target for such an attack in the Pacific, with the possible exception of the Panama Canal, was the U.S. naval base at Pearl Harbor."

Delaney nodded. "Makes sense," he said.

"Here's the clincher," Priest said, leaning forward. "The code word that was used to refer to the decoded Japanese transmissions was 'Magic.' Both the War Department and the Navy Department were tasked with processing Magic, which they did on alternate days to avoid duplication of effort. The Communications Intelligence Unit handled Magic for the navy, the Signal Intelligence Unit processed it for the army. Each department had a distribution list for Magic. Among the people on those two lists were the president of the

United States, the secretary of state, the secretary of war, the secretary of the navy, the chief of naval operations, the army chief of staff, the director of naval communications, the director of naval intelligence, and others. The decoded dispatches were all hand delivered to their recipients by special couriers who carried locked pouches. The commander in chief of the Pacific Fleet, Admiral Kimmel, was not on the list. Neither he nor General Short, the commanding general of the Hawaiian Department, were given any access to Magic.

"Early in 1941," Priest went on, "cipher machines that were duplicates of the Japanese encrypting units were constructed and shipped to various locations, enabling them to decode Japanese transmissions that they intercepted. One or more were sent to London. Two went to the Navy Department's Communications Intelligence Unit. Two went to Signal Intelligence. One was sent to the Philippines, accompanied by support personnel to establish a decrypting unit on Corregidor. None were sent to Hawaii, which meant intelligence units there could not decode any intercepted Japanese transmissions. And they were not on a list to receive decoded Magic, either. So the prime target for the Japanese in the Pacific was essentially left out in the cold when it came to access to intelligence. And both the army and the navy commanders in Hawaii were specifically denied access to intelligence directly concerning their commands.

"In 1940 the commander of the Pacific Fleet, who was then Admiral Richardson, went to Washington on two separate occasions to urge that the fleet be withdrawn to the West Coast because the ships were inadequately manned, the area was too exposed, especially considering international tensions at the time, and the defenses against both air and submarine attack were below required standards. In January 1941 he was suddenly relieved of command and Kimmel was appointed in his place. The Pacific Fleet was retained in Hawaii on the orders of the president. And in the month prior to the attack, a number of Magic transmissions from Tokyo to the Washington embassy were decoded in which the ambassadors were urged repeatedly to conclude their negotiations and do everything in their power to reach an agreement with the United States by November 25, a deadline they referred to as 'immovable.' You can draw your own conclusions."

Delaney sat silent for a few moments, his arms folded. He nodded. "Okay. So Roosevelt wanted Japan to attack Pearl Harbor so that he could get America into the war. . . ." He paused. "How many casualties were there?"

"Nearly forty-six hundred killed or wounded. Two battleships, two destroyers, and a target ship were a total loss. The other damaged ships were all repaired and returned to active service. None of the three aircraft carriers in the fleet were in the harbor at the time."

"Convenient," said Delaney with a grimace. "Well, with the perfect hindsight that history affords, America needed to get into the war, because Hitler needed to be stopped and Japan's hegemony was maybe getting out of hand, though one can argue whether or not that was truly any of our business. But I can't say I like the way Roosevelt went about it."

"Soldiers rarely like the way that politicians do things," Priest replied.

"Because soldiers are usually the ones who have to pay for it," said Delaney.

"Comes with the job."

"Yeah. Comes with the job. But sometimes the job sucks. Which brings me to my most important question . . . where does our mission fit in with all of this?"

"ISD has discovered a Network plot to alter the history of the Peal Harbor attack," said Priest. "They're going to make sure that Kimmel knows it's coming."

"Whoa," Delaney said. "Back up a minute. The *Network* is going to try to alter history? That's crazy. Why the hell would they want to do that? Their operations are illegal, but they still require temporal continuity. A timestream split would affect them just as it would everybody else."

"Apparently, they don't believe that it would bring about a timestream split," said Priest. "A temporal disruption, yes, but not a full-scale timestream split. It would affect the future—in other words, our present—but it would not disrupt the basic continuity of the timeline. We'd simply wake up one day and things would just be . . . a little different."

"You're talking about a time wave," said Delaney, softly.

Priest nodded. "Yeah."

Delaney exhaled heavily. "But . . . how can they be sure? What gives them the idea that it's going to be a time wave, which could have some disastrous consequences all by itself, rather than a full-on timestream split? Temporal physics just isn't that exact a science. Who the hell worked all that out?"

"The Japanese, apparently," said Priest.

Delaney stared at him. "You're kidding."

"I wish I was."

"You mean the *modern* Japanese? The NCE?"

Priest nodded. "I don't know if it's actually an official arm of the Nippon Conglomerate Empire," he said, "or if it's just some wild-haired, independent business faction, but either way, it seems that somebody's worked it out, and they've done their homework well enough to convince some people in the Network."

"You're sure about this?" said Delaney. "There's no mistake?"

Priest shook his head. "The intelligence is solid. Straight from the horse's mouth."

"Somebody came in?"

Priest nodded. "Only a few hours ago," he said. "I've authorized ISD to cut a deal with him and it's being worked out as we speak."

"How do you know it's on the level?"

"Because we scanned him. He's scared, Finn. He doesn't buy it. He thinks it's going to bring about a timestream split. He knew exactly what was going to happen when he came in. He knew there weren't going to be any calls to any lawyers. He knew we'd turn him inside out and by the time we were done with him, his entire personality might be erased. Or worse, if we decided not to be too gentle. He came in, anyway."

"And you're working out a *deal* with him? One of your own people who went bad? For God's sake, why?"

"Because I wanted to. It's a judgment call. I want his cooperation without having to compel him or risk damaging him. I want him to work with you on this. I think it's our best chance."

"You want me to work with a traitor?"

"Not a traitor so much as a crook. It's a fine distinction perhaps, but a significant one. He *did* come in on his own. I want you to meet him."

Delaney grimaced. "When?"

"Right now."

THE ROOM was stark and white. Several concealed video cameras monitored its contents, which on this occasion consisted of a young male in his late twenties who was secured to a contoured white reclining couch with a system of restraints. On the other side of a thick window in the wall was a control room with banks of sophisticated computer equipment, video monitors, and readout screens. Priest nodded to an operator in the control room as he and Delaney entered, and the couch swiveled up from a horizontal position to nearly vertical. The face and head of the man strapped to the couch were almost completely covered by a cybernetic helmet. Priest nodded once more, and the helmet came up and pulled back, revealing the man's face.

"*Neilson!*" Delaney exclaimed. "Jesus Christ."

The young man smiled wanly. "Hello, Colonel. It's been a while."

"Yeah," said Delaney tensely. "It has."

"Just like old times," said Neilson. "You, me, the general here . . . except he wasn't a general back then. And you weren't a colonel."

"And you weren't a goddamn traitor."

"Well, now, that's a little harsh, don't you think?"

"Finn . . . ," said Priest.

"Yeah, yeah, I know. He's not a traitor so much as a crook. Well, maybe you see it your way and I see it mine. Goddammit, Scott. You were one of the best. What made you go over to the Network? Was it just the money?"

Neilson moistened his lips and swallowed hard. "No . . . not exactly. Although I guess the money didn't hurt any."

"So why, then?"

"You remember that mission back in Tombstone?" Neilson said.

Delaney gave a small snort. "The gunfight at the O.K. Corral. Who the hell could ever forget it? That's where we almost lost it. The whole time continuum just about came apart."

"Yeah, well . . . so did I, I guess," said Neilson softly.

Delaney remembered. "That girl . . . the one who died."

"Her name was Jenny," Neilson said. His mouth twitched. "Jenny Riley. The very least you could do is remember her name, Delaney. I mean, considering you killed her."

Delaney glanced at Priest. "You can't possibly be serious about me going out in the field with him."

"I'm afraid we have no choice, Finn."

"This guy's not only a traitor, he's got issues," Delaney replied. "He's got all sorts of unresolved conflicts. With me. With you. With the service. . . . How the hell am I supposed to work with him? Neither of us can trust him."

"Except he's all we've got," said Priest.

"And you believe him?"

"Come on, Finn. What the hell do you think we've been doing here? You know better than that."

Delaney took a deep breath and let it out slowly. "Yes, I do, goddammit."

"I don't have any issues with you, Delaney," Neilson said. "I understand you had to kill her. She was planted in that time period to change history, and you had no other choice. I don't hold that against you, really. She had to die. But unfortunately, I fell in love with her. And I guess I never quite got over that."

"The Network got to him while he was vulnerable," said Priest. "He made a mistake. And then it was too late to back out."

"Yeah, well, people who do what we do can't afford mistakes," Delaney said.

"And nobody's going to forgive him his," Priest replied. "But he wants to make up for it. He scans out. He's telling the truth." He paused. "Of course, I can find someone else to take this mission if you don't feel confident."

Delaney looked at him. "When do we leave?"

"0600 tomorrow."

☆ ☆ ☆

THE AFTEREFFECTS of time travel, known as "warp lag" to the soldiers of the Temporal Corps, could make even veterans double over and puke their guts out. Knowing that it had been a while since he had clocked out to Minus Time, Delaney had purposely avoided breakfast, but the dry heaves were just as bad.

"A little out of practice, huh?" said Neilson with a grin.

"Up yours, kid."

Neilson chuckled. "It gets to me as well, just not as bad. I guess it must be an age thing."

Delaney got up off his knees, wiping the drool from his mouth. "All right, so I'm older and I'm a little out of shape," he said. "But there's still enough here to take you down if I have to, and don't you forget it." He glanced around. They were in a nondescript room with a tiled floor and no furniture. The paint on the walls was faded and there were cobwebs in the corners. The setting sun was sending its last rays of light through the grimy, shadeless window. "Where the hell are we?" asked Delaney, his stomach still in knots from the transition.

"We're in an office building on Hotel Street in Honolulu," Neilson said. He went over to the window and looked out at the city. "December 6, 1941. Just about sunset."

Delaney remained silent. He was watching Neilson.

"Looks peaceful out there, doesn't it? Hard to believe that a world war is going to break out in only a few hours."

Delaney came up behind him. "I think they've actually been fighting it for a while by now," he said. "I mean, if you asked anyone from Poland or Britain or Russia, for example."

"Yeah, but for us arrogant Americans, it doesn't really matter unless we're in it," Neilson said. "It's kinda like the World Series. We're the only ones who play in it because nobody else counts."

They were both dressed in U.S. naval uniforms, the better to blend in on the streets of Honolulu, if necessary.

"You guys could've picked a more comfortable room," Delaney said, glancing around. "Or at least one with some chairs."

"It's just a safe transition point, that's all," said Neilson, turning from the window.

"Safe for whom?" Delaney asked. "How do we know some Network agents aren't going to be clocking in right on top of us at any moment?"

Neilson shrugged. "I suppose they might."

"You *suppose?*"

"Relax. We're not expecting anybody. At least, not for a while."
He looked out the window once more at the streets. "Doesn't look
like much out there right now, does it? Nothing like the crowded,
bustling city it's going to become after the war." He paused reflec-
tively. "In just a few hours, the Japanese are going to start dropping
their bombs. Only on military targets, not that anybody's going to
appreciate that fine distinction. There's going to be some damage in
the city, but for the most part that will result from American antiaircraft shells; the widespread perception will be that Japan bombed
Pearl Harbor and attacked civilian targets, too. The result will be a
xenophobic reaction on the part of the American people that they
won't get over for years. Thousands of Asian-Americans will be
rounded up and sent to concentration camps. Except, of course,
they won't be called concentration camps. Internment camps
sounds much more palatable. But at least we didn't have any gas
chambers, like Hitler did. I suppose that counts for something."

Delaney listened to him tensely. Neilson's manner seemed
relaxed, as if he were just making casual conversation, but the bitterness was coming through loud and clear. Bitterness, resentment
. . . and something else. Delaney let him talk.

"It's almost over now. The waiting, I mean," said Neilson, still
staring out the window. "By now, the Japanese have destroyed all of
their codes and ciphering machines in their embassies. The order for
that went out about a week ago, on the first. The dispatches were
decoded, so Washington knew all about that. What do you suppose
it means when a country sends out word to all its embassies to burn
their codebooks, especially when you know that your relations with
that country are strained to the breaking point? Between the third
and the fifth, word was sent out from Tokyo to have key intelligence
and embassy personnel leave the country immediately. Washington
knew about that, too. Except they didn't bother to inform the commanders in Hawaii. And a message went out today, the sixth, from
the U.S. Office of Naval Operations to all diplomatic posts in Japan
and Japanese-held territories, ordering the destruction of all secret
codes. The message that went out to the commander in chief of the
Pacific Fleet originally had the wording 'in view of the imminence
of war.' But that line was deleted at the last minute and changed to
'in view of the international situation,' and the message was released

to be transmitted 'with deferred precedence.' In other words, not urgent. No big deal. Send it whenever it's convenient. And, 'in view of the international situation,' the most urgent thing most people paid attention to today in Honolulu was the Shrine football game between Willamette University and the University of Hawaii."

Delaney felt a knot forming in his stomach that had nothing to do with the aftereffects of temporal transition. He had served with Neilson in the past, quite literally, and knew him to be a brave and capable young officer. But something had happened to him. He never should have been allowed to remain on active duty. He needed help. But somehow his crisis had been overlooked, and he had slipped through the cracks and the Network found him and discovered that he was vulnerable and took advantage of it. He looked calm standing over there, staring out the window into the distance. But inside, he was hurting.

"Sometime around 2100 tonight the president will receive a message delivered in a locked pouch by a special courier," Neilson continued as he glanced at his watch, which contained the complex chronocircuitry for his warp disk. If he were captured and anyone opened the watch, they wouldn't even see it. In the 1940s nobody would know what microchips were, much less chips designed on the particle level. "It's going to be thirteen parts of a fourteen-part decoded message intercepted from the Japanese, from Tokyo to their embassy in Washington, their official reply to what amounted to the American ultimatum. The final part is scheduled for transmission tomorrow morning, the idea being to synchronize its delivery as nearly as possible with the actual attack at 1300. But the thirteen parts are going to be enough to convince Roosevelt, because when he reads the message a couple of hours from now, he's going to say, 'This means war.' Something that he knew all along. After all, it was what he wanted. But as he put it, 'We are a democracy and a peaceful people,' so we couldn't strike the first blow."

"Scott . . . ," Delaney said.

Neilson went on as if he hadn't heard him. "Washington received the final part of the intercepted Japanese message between 0400 and 0600 on the morning of the seventh. And they had decoded Tokyo's instructions to their embassy to deliver it at precisely one o'clock, Washington time. That means the president knew a state of war existed between the U.S. and Japan the night before the attack, and everyone else involved with the decoding and reception of Magic knew about it by about 6 A.M. on the morning of the seventh. Nobody bothered to inform the Pacific Fleet. Imagine the difference even three or four hours' warning would have made. But nobody even bothered to pick up a phone."

"Scott . . . ," Delaney said again. "You *have* to let this go."

"Well, it's the economics of the thing, you know," Neilson replied, a distant look in his eyes. "The Network understands economics. The NCE, or at least some people high up in the NCE, presented a proposal to some people high up in the Network that looked pretty good on paper, I guess. You know how these things are handled, Finn. Important matters, the big picture . . . all that stuff we little people aren't supposed to understand. Don't ask me how they did it, but they convinced the Network that a timestream split ain't gonna happen if Japan fails to attack Pearl Harbor by surprise on December 7. Oh, there's still going to be a war, but it will be done properly, with a declaration submitted in advance, the way these things are supposed to be handled in polite society.

"That will change everything, of course," Neilson went on. "The Pacific Fleet will receive a warning, supposedly transmitted from Washington, though it will actually come from right here in this room. They'll have time to put the ships out and get the planes up, and Vice Admiral Nagumo, in command of the attacking fleet, will receive signals from his agents in Hawaii that the element of surprise has been lost. At that point, he will follow the prearranged plan and cancel the attack. Instead, the Japanese will shift their focus to targets in Indochina. They war-gamed the whole thing in Tokyo. Back in our own time, that is. The Asian-Americans are still going to be rounded up and sent off to internment camps, and they're still going to drop atomic bombs on Hiroshima and Nagasaki, but the key difference, apparently, is that without the dastardly sneak attack on Pearl Harbor that started the war against Japan, American guilt over the bombing of Hiroshima and Nagasaki in the years after the war is going to be a significant factor in the rebuilding of Japan. There is going to be an honorable armistice and in the aftermath, we're going to give them lots of help in rebuilding their industrial infrastructure, and we're not going to prevent them from achieving a nuclear capability. They're going to become a world power much sooner, not just economically, but militarily as well. And when we start having trouble with China in the twenty-first century, we're going to form an alliance with Japan, Russia, and Tibet, led by the exiled Dalai Lama, and there's going to be a holy war. World War III, in other words. It's going to be dicey, but Japan figures they're going to come out on top. And there will be lots of opportunities for profit while it lasts. Of course, a lot of ordinary people are going to be killed, but hey, we've got to look at the big picture, right?"

"Scott, this isn't about Pearl Harbor for you, is it?" said Delaney. "It's not even about a timestream split. It's still about Jenny."

Neilson turned back from the window, and Delaney stiffened when he saw the stubby black disrupter in his hand. "It's always the ordinary people that get hurt," said Neilson. "The little people don't matter when it comes to the big picture. They're just expendable. Like you and me, Delaney."

"I did what I had to do, Scott," Delaney said in a calm and level tone. "I had no choice. Ever since people started traveling through time, the genie was out of the bottle and somebody had to make sure that temporal continuity got preserved. Jenny was a little person, as you put it, just like you and me. But she was a plant in that time period. She did not belong there, and she was about to do something that would have affected history. Our mission was to stop that. Not just my mission, Scott, *our* mission, because we're soldiers. That's what we do. We knew what the job was when we signed on for it. We knew the risks. We knew that other people would be making decisions about the big picture and those decisions would affect us. We took the job, Scott, you and me. It was our responsibility. It was just my bad luck to have to pull the trigger. I'm sorry."

"I know," said Neilson. "I don't hold it against you. It just sucks that it had to happen, that's all. Like what's going to happen out there in a few hours. I know it has to happen. But it still sucks."

He fired. The disrupter blast went past Delaney and struck two men who appeared out of nowhere in the center of the room, along with some communications equipment. The plasma blast struck them as they materialized and bathed them in the bright blue glow of Cerenkov radiation. In an instant they were gone.

Delaney held his breath. For a moment, he thought he'd had it.

"Well, I guess that does it," Neilson said. "Mission accomplished, Colonel. I did the job."

And then he stuck the disrupter in his mouth and fired.

"*SCOTT!*" Delaney shouted, but it was too late. There was a brief, bright blue flash, and he was gone.

☆ ☆ ☆

"Lemme have another one," Delaney slurred, but the bartender shook his head as he cut him off.

"I'm sorry, sir," he said. "You've had enough."

"Come on, dammit. Gimme another one."

"Nothing doing," said the bartender. "Look, I shouldn't even be serving you right now. It's past closing time and I need to be getting home. I got a life, too, y'know. I cut you a break because you're in the service and you looked like you could use it, but hell, whatever it is, it just can't be that bad. Tomorrow morning everything is going to look different."

"Brother, you don't know the half of it," Delaney said. He threw some bills down on the bar and lurched out the door. Out in the street, several women walking by on their way home from the late shift gave him disgusted looks. Yeah, disgraceful, thought Delaney, a naval officer staggering around drunk on the streets of Honolulu. But he didn't feel nearly drunk enough.

The Network wouldn't try doing it again. Their operation had been compromised; they wouldn't risk it twice. And whoever had come up with the scheme in the first place would probably not pursue it now, because if they did, it could get ugly. Not good for the big political picture.

Priest came to him for a reason, Delaney realized. Part of it was that Priest knew his old friend wanted to go back on active duty because he simply wasn't comfortable sitting behind a desk and sending other people out to take the risks. And part of it was because Priest knew that he would be the best one to send out to Minus Time with Neilson, because they had a history and because there needed to be closure. Priest had to know what Neilson would do. They had put him through the wringer; they had scanned him and they had to know exactly what was on his mind. Delaney knew that he was going to be violently ill when he clocked back, because of the effects of all the alcohol combined with the lag of temporal transition. He was going to be so sick, they'd have to carry him away. But that was just as well.

As he got ready to activate his warp disk, he looked up at the sky. It was going to be dawn soon. He thought, for a moment, that he could hear the sound of planes in the distance, but it was still too early. And, at the same time, it was much too late.

"Goddammit," he said and clocked out.

The Secret History of
Mr. Churchill's Revenge

TONY GERAGHTY

THIS IS JAARMANY CALLING . . . Jaarmany calling. Do you hear me, Mr. Churchill? Do you feel nervous this evening? You should, you know. The Luftwaffe is on its way with a nice big bomb with your name on it. And where are your allies now? Where are the French, Mr. Churchill? Where are the Americans, Mr. Churchill?"

"Switch off the wireless, will you?" the prime minister said. His bodyguard, clumsy, well-meaning Murray, almost knocked over the port as he struggled for the off switch. "When the war is over I will have that man hanged."

"Who, sir?" asked Murray.

"Why, Lord Haw-Haw, of course. William Joyce. Claims he was born in New York . . . We'll have him, all the same, in due time."

Oh, America! Churchill blew a plume of cigar smoke toward the ceiling. If only America would come in. . . . He could send another cable to Roosevelt, of course, but to what effect? Like those letters he had written to his American mother, from boarding school and desolate, lonely holidays alike: "Do come and see me soon . . . Will you come and see me?" He was just ten then and already used to the floggings the English upper classes handed out at one remove, through the muscle of a teacher, to their offspring. His mother, Lady

Randolph, the society beauty daughter of the New York stockbroker Leonard Jerome, had sent a governess instead. Again Winston wrote: "The governess is very unkind . . . I am not enjoying myself at all."

Two years later, having survived a near fatal fever, he found the governess, Miss Thomson, blocking every hope of seeing his mother. He wrote:

"My dear Mamma—Miss Thomson doesn't want me to go home for the Jubilee of Queen Victoria because she says I shall have no place in Westminster Abbey. . . . Also that you will be very busy and unable to be with me much. Now you know that is not the case. I want to see Buffalo Bill and the play as you promised me."

He was dozing now, head drooping forward over his unfinished port, black satin eye band askew on his forehead. But those close to him knew that Churchill never quite slept.

"Sir?"

One eye opened. "What is it, Murray?"

"Sir, the siren has started. The air raid warning. I've got the shelter warmed up with a paraffin heater for you down below."

"You have, have you, Murray? And have you brought my Thompson gun? We are going up, man, not down."

From the roof of Number 10 Downing Street, the official home and office of the British prime minister, there was a grandstand view of the nightly battle during that autumn and winter of 1940 between the aerial raiders of the Luftwaffe and the antiaircraft gunners on the ground. The Luftwaffe came in disciplined waves of twin-engined Heinkel He-111s and Dornier Do-17s, their deep engines beating like war drums in a Wagnerian Reichvolks drama, veritable angels of death. From the ground, searchlights stretched like fingers out of the graves of the unquiet dead. The big guns, some on railway bogies on the line from Victoria Station or dug into Battersea Park just south of the river, bellowed defiance like cattle in an abattoir.

Then there were the bombs you heard—high explosive bombs, shrieking ever louder in free fall until the ground shook under their anger—and those you did not . . . the tinkling, 18-inch incendiaries . . . the silent, massively destructive land mines, swinging down under green parachutes to take out entire streets in one massive götterdämmerung of a bang. In that sort of blitzkrieg, people on their way home from the pub were vaporized. They simply vanished.

Amid the fires, the smoke, shouted orders, screams of the dying, the clanging bells, the wheeling circus of firefighters atop spindly ladders that came under low-level strafing as the second Luftwaffe wave came in, Churchill's own gun, his Thompson, his "Chicago Piano," would have gone unnoticed by everyone except Murray. Churchill, firing from the hip, punctuated each burst with the speech with which he had rallied the British (with some help from a professional actor who had imitated him on the wireless): "We shall fight them on the beaches . . ."

Rat-tat-tat!

"We shall fight them in the fields and in the streets . . . the hills . . ."

Rat-tat-tat!

"We shall never surrender!"

Click. Magazine empty.

Murray peered out of the skylight that gave access to the roof and exposed the top of his steel helmet. "Sir, for heaven's sake come down! The shrapnel will get you!"

Even Churchill had to admit that Murray had a point. After each salvo from the guns, the streets rattled to a different tune as brass shell caps and hot metal fragments, big enough to decapitate a horse, rained on the streets of Westminster.

"One more magazine, Murray," the prime minister replied.

"Sir . . . we have no more. The ammunition—caliber .45—comes from America. You have used it all. There is none left."

Now, more than ever, Churchill knew that by fair means or foul he had to induce the Americans to join the fight. As he curled up to sleep under his desk in the war room, he brought to bear the one weapon he knew was invincible. The floggings, the neglect, the cruelties had not been wasted. Churchill's greatest talent, and the most secret, was his capacity for sustained, intelligent revenge.

For that to work, he needed sleep. His subconscious would do the rest. He had arrived at a place appointed by destiny. The journey had been long, wearisome. He was happy to have arrived at his rendezvous with fate at last. For the next day or so, the war could run itself.

☆ ☆ ☆

NEXT DAY, after a late breakfast of brandy and raw egg, Churchill summoned the head of his counterintelligence service, Col. Malcolm Fell. On the street they were still sweeping away the glass and pouring sand over the blood. Fell, dapper in pinstriped suit, shoes polished, arrived by bicycle. He looked uncomfortable beneath the steel helmet, his body constrained by the gas mask in its container, as the latest wartime regulations required.

"Fell, what are you people doing about the Japanese?"

"The embassy is watched, sir."

"Don't you tap their telephone lines, man? Listen to their wireless signals?"

"Sir . . . that's a question of resources. London is full of aliens from occupied Europe. One in three is probably a spy. . . . We do our best."

"Humph. . . . Is that naval attaché of theirs still here? 'Poisonus' . . . some name like that. Met him at a Royal Navy reception just before hostilities."

"You mean Commander Minoru Koizumi, Prime Minister. One of the Kodo-ha wing."

"The Kodo-ha wing?"

"A sort of military freemasonry, sir. I'm told 'Kodo-ha' means 'the Imperial Way.' It takes action without bothering to get permission from the emperor."

"Hmmm. . . . And he is here to spy on us, I suppose."

"Very likely, sir."

"Then p'raps we should give him something to think about. . . . Keep him out of trouble. Where does he dine? Does Poisooni womanize?"

"He lives quietly at Princes Gate, sir, round the corner from the embassy with his wife and baby son. His only recreation, out of doors, seems to be to cross the street to Kensington Gardens every Sunday morning. He sails a model boat across the pond, and one of his friends turns it round and sends it back again. They do that for an hour or so, then go their separate ways."

"Tomorrow is Sunday. Let us watch these Japanese naval maneuvers together, Fell."

☆ ☆ ☆

IN A GESTURE toward anonymity, Churchill wore a straw hat and dark glasses. There were no air alerts, either because the Germans still treated the sabbath as a day of peace, or because their air crews were resting. The sun shone. By 10 A.M. a multitude of sailing craft were being urged on by boys and girls and men of a certain age who took their hobby seriously. For them, the Round Pond was second only to that other pond, the Atlantic.

"Isn't that Mr. Churchill, Mummy?" one asked.

"No, dahling. London is full of people who look like him so as to frighten the Germans."

At 11 A.M. exactly, Koizumi arrived. He wore a black suit with waistcoat, gold watch and chain in the pockets, and black shoes with yellow spats. His tie, bearing the red orb of Japan, was neatly held down by a large ruby tie pin. He carried his vessel. This was a perfect scale version of *Akagi*, an aircraft carrier adapted from the hull of a battleship as a response to limitations on Japanese naval strength imposed by the Washington Naval Treaty of 1922. More than twenty years later it was still an affront to Japanese naval pride. Tokyo's response to a limit on battleship numbers was to convert some of them into aircraft carriers, with the thought that, at some future time, they could be reconstructed as battleships once more.

Koizumi was greeted respectfully enough by his fellow pond sailors, the bowler-hatted gents and the flat-capped Cockneys alike.

"Mornin', Commander," they chorused.

They did not quite salute, but he bowed politely then unfolded a small canvas chair on which to sit while he nursed his ship and prepared her for sea. This *Akagi*, in context, outsized everything else on the pond. Churchill, a former navy minister (1911–15), naval aviator, and torpedo expert, guessed it would be at least four feet in length. It was powered by a clockwork engine that, when wound, turned two screws. Koizumi flipped open the flight deck, hinged on one side, and wound up the engine.

He closed the flight deck and attached several small aircraft to it with the help of tiny magnets. Next he produced from his top pocket a miniature flag, the flag of Japan, and held it aloft. The other sailors, smiling at the spectacle, did their best to give him the right of way, but in all the circumstances, this was an uncertain process. Like all warlike maneuvers, the outcome could not be predicted.

Frowning in concentration—for this was the point of no return—the Japanese naval attaché now reached forward, placed his ship in the water, and pointed her toward the opposite shore. She moved with smooth efficiency, leaving only the faintest wake, two-thirds of the way across the pond, then coasted the remaining distance. An assistant—a neat figure in ceremonial kimono—retrieved the vessel. Churchill noted that her nimble fingers operated some concealed mechanism, a button perhaps, to release the flight deck. She was about to send the *Akagi* back to home waters when Churchill stepped forward.

"Allow me, madam," he said. She turned, surprised. He used his bulk unobtrusively, yet leaving no doubt as to his intention, to remove the ship from her grasp. He then placed on the flight deck a miniature Rising Sun, weighed down by a gold sovereign, placed the ship back in the water, and returned it to the commander, bowing as he did so. (His politeness was not always what it seemed. A month or so later, when he formally declared war against Japan, he signed the letter: "I beg to remain your humble servant, Winston Churchill." As he told some of his British critics: "That I intend to kill a man does not require me to be impolite to him as well." His critics, not understanding the devious nature of their leader, took that as a joke.)

By the time Koizumi had the *Akagi* safely back in port, Churchill had vanished. The Rising Sun contained an unsigned note, written in impeccable Japanese: "I have the honor to inform you that the larger model of the *Akagi,* now serving with the Imperial Japanese Navy, will not be in a position to put to sea unless you act swiftly. Following the oil sanctions recently imposed upon your country by President Roosevelt the IJN is using 400 tons of oil every hour, or so Admiral Yamamoto says. Your fleet cannot cross the Pacific on clockwork. It is bleeding to death. What should you do? The answer is to be found in Taranto."

Koizumi sat on his little canvas chair, his hands shaking. Only yesterday he had received the encrypted message from Yamamoto, requiring proposals for "positive measures" if he was to avoid "disgrace." "Disgrace," according to the warrior code, had only one remedy: hara-kiri. Now the breakdown in the security of his personal communications could strip him of all face, even posthumously. He read the note again, carefully: "The answer is to be found in Taranto." And suddenly he smiled, stood, bowed to the onlookers as usual, and marched jauntily out of the park.

HIS ENCRYPTED message, intercepted and decoded by American codebreakers using the latest Magic technology, smoothly combined serious analysis with what he knew Yamamoto wanted to hear. Against the orthodoxy of submarine and battleship assault, Yamamoto was much taken with the possibilities of naval air power.

> Excellency. I have the honor to report that the British recently destroyed most of the Italian fleet at anchor in the port of Taranto. The assault was made by twenty-four aircraft launched from the carrier *Illustrious*. Within half an hour three battleships and four other warships were sunk. Only two aircraft were lost. The surprise nature of the attack was total.
>
> This success also relied on the key fact that the Italian ships were destroyed not by aerial bombs but with torpedoes dropped from low level. Our Imperial Navy has the carriers. It has the aircraft. It has a clear target. As you warned us, the movement of an American fleet from West Coast USA to Hawaii is tantamount to a dagger pointed at our sacred homeland. But do we have the right torpedoes?
>
> If we remove the American threat we will claim the oil of Sumatra by right of conquest. The Pacific zone will then truly be the Great East-Asian Co-prosperity Sphere.

CHURCHILL WAS also pleased with the results of his exercise in the park. Back in his war room, many feet below Whitehall, he scripted an urgent message to Washington:

> Mr President, greetings! My intelligence service informs me that a Japanese fleet will endeavour to mount a surprise attack upon the U.S. anchorage at Pearl Harbor in the near future. You will make your own

dispositions. In your shoes I would preempt this aggression with a surprise attack of my own.

Like Hitler, the Japanese high command takes pride in striking the first blow. Should we not strike first for a change?

ROOSEVELT, SIPPING lemon tea, did not rise to meet his visitor in the Blue Room on the second floor of the White House. He nodded a courteous-enough nod to his erstwhile ambassador to London. Joseph Kennedy's hasty flight from the front line of the British capital had not impressed Roosevelt. Back in New York's Hyde Park, they had discussed the matter vigorously. Time had passed since then, and the president had to remind himself that Kennedy's continuing influence with Wall Street made it desirable—to understate the case—to keep the banker from Boston on board.

"Sit, Joe . . . Drink? Rye?"

Kennedy, whose principal hobby was bashing the Brits, smiled owlishly behind heavy spectacles and freckles. "An Irish, if your stock runs to that, Mr. President." As a prominent contributor to Roosevelt's campaign, Kennedy knew well enough what the stocks were.

"You've seen Churchill's cable. Whaddya think?"

"Like our pilots say of those weather forecasters: 'We don't believe this guy even when he says "Good morning."'"

Roosevelt nodded, his eyes guarded. "We all know your views about the Brits, Joe. You know my attitude toward the Japanese. Same story. But I have to know if the Japs are playing poker and, if so, if it is with a gun up their sleeve. So let's take a cool, detached look at this thing. Could Churchill be right? We had this policy of containment and deterrence. Could it provoke the problem it is meant to contain?"

"Sir, Churchill wants to drag us into a war with him, that's all," Kennedy replied. His clipped Bostonian accent sounded almost English. "I tell you, if he can't do that, this pygmy and his miserable little island will bow the knee to Hitler."

"He says he'll fight to the last bottle of ketchup."

Kennedy, ignoring the joke, snapped, "Then some other Brit will collaborate. There's that ex-king of theirs, running Bermuda.

Wallis Simpson's latest client. The Duke of Windsor. He's a big friend of Hitler. There are plenty more of them. We don't need to get into a war with anyone. Let the Europeans make a bonfire of their economies while we warm our hands. Let the British Empire bleed to death. I'll drink to that."

"But if the Japs come at us? Did you hear about this Taranto thing? The Brits wiped out half the Italian fleet in half an hour. Churchill cabled me about that. And when I asked Navy Secretary Knox—Frank Knox, remember him?—what he thought, he said Pearl would be next. Here's his brief: 'The greatest danger will come from aerial torpedoes.'"

Kennedy held up his glass, admiring the sunlight as it picked up the smooth glycerine trace of good Irish whiskey. Fleetingly, fondly, he recalled the palmy days of Prohibition when—by way of a change from regular banking—a man could brew the stuff at arm's length and earn money the taxman could never trace . . . but that was before he had taken over the Securities and Exchange Commission and turned sheriff.

"Brit propaganda, sir. There's no way the Japanese could invade this continent. And anything else, even Pearl Harbor, would be a gnat's bite on an elephant's arse."

Roosevelt hedged his bets, as any wise leader must sometimes. The Brits wanted fifty laid-up World War I–vintage American destroyers to escort their convoys. They could have them—at a price. What they would not get would be America in the war. This time there would be no replay of the *Lusitania*. Joe had a point. If Churchill wanted to get into another scrap, okay. He'd hold the guy's coat for him. Nothing more.

Late that night, long after the staff had gone, Roosevelt added one more presidential executive order to his labors:

To: Adm. Thomas Husband E. Kimmel/Gen. Walter Short:
  The War Department has drawn my attention to the practice of the Pacific Fleet under your command to put into the Oahu facility each weekend and there to drop anchor. Henceforth, you will ensure that one element of the fleet is at sea at all times including weekends. The details I leave to you. However, you might consider it prudent to ensure that your carrier force is at sea if your capital warships—particularly your battleships—are in port; and vice versa.

Of course, Roosevelt told himself as he prepared to sleep, Churchill's belief in an imminent Japanese blitzkrieg against the might of America was insane. But then, Winston was a man under stress. Give any man enough pressure and he would likely jump at shadows. Still, it paid to keep a few ships out of harm's way, just in case. After all, some smart people, including Harry Hopkins and Henry Morgenthau, shared his conviction that in Japan's bottom drawer, ever since 1889, there lurked a hundred-year "plan of conquest." Then again, America had not had to go to war in the Pacific since 1898.

Churchill the nighthawk was not sleeping. He was reading the personnel file of Britain's best intelligence agent in Tokyo. Richard Sorge—trusted insider at the German embassy; lover to the ambassador's wife, head of Moscow's "Japan Unit"—had been on the books of London's Secret Intelligence Service since 1918. Bon viveur, partygoer, and Japan correspondent for *Die Welt*, he was flamboyant, clever, and dangerous to know. Very much my sort of man, Churchill reflected. He will know . . .

Sorge's sake parties were famous. His latest was aboard a hired fishing boat on the calm waters of Tokyo Bay. They were a mixed bunch: the multilingual Hozumi Osaki, scholar, dilettante, and cornerstone of the old Japanese establishment; the communist American journalist Agnes Smedley, whose battle chic included a threat to "take the uniform off" of Gen. Douglas MacArthur; and Adm. Isoroku Yamamoto. He, like others, had arrived at the embarkation point on horseback, to save petrol.

No one asked out loud where Sorge got the fuel for this trip. Sorge was an unkempt giant whose bulk could often be seen looming among the paper lanterns of the geisha quarter like a letching, leering parody of Orson Welles. His contempt for the "clotheshorses" of polite society was notorious. He commanded his own squad of assassins. He was not the sort of person of whom such questions were asked.

The joke that night, before many of the guests dived below into the depths of the comfort women hired by Sorge, was about the U.S. ambassador, Joe Grew, and it was not kind.

"Imagine!" Sorge told the semicircle of Japanese officers around him. "It is the daily liaison conference. Your emperor, the Tenno Hirohito, is on his throne, sitting before the golden screen, his gold seal ready to signify 'Yes' or 'No.' The sacred incense burns to his left and right. I dare not tell you exactly who said what, but there, on the side, stood the American ambassador. Now, as we all know, poor Mr. Grew is deaf. And as we all know, no one may speak above a whisper in the presence of the Tenno and that is proper. . . . But America does not even hear the whisper of the translator. Isn't that perfect? America is deaf!"

He deliberately failed to mention Grew's lip-reading skills or the fact that the ambassador's wife spoke perfect Japanese. He waited. His audience, tense with anxiety at Sorge's near-heresy in joking about the god-emperor, got the point but only slowly. Then it dawned. The target of the joke was the United States. Laughter broke like an uncontrolled fart. No one would be guilty of subversion after all. No heads would roll. In spite of the sense of relief it was many hours, and after much more sake, before Sorge's friend Ozaki got the information they wanted.

In one month, as negotiations with Washington about the oil embargo dragged on, the fleet would sail for the secluded waters of Hitokappu Bay, far away in the Kuril Islands, to test Yamamoto's latest concept: an aerial attack on a fleet at anchor, using torpedoes as the instrument of destruction. Already the elders of the Imperial Japanese Navy were shaking their heads at the futility of such an idea. The IJN, faithful to bushido, saw the battleship as its sword, not something that could, in a certain light, pass for a large, edible fish.

To his Soviet paymasters, Sorge was "Agent Pushkin." To London, he was "Diamond." Washington knew him as "Dalliance." Pushkin, Diamond, and Dalliance sent the same basic signal, through different Morse operators and separate codebooks. The key to a successful trial of Yamamoto's concept, it said, was a low-wing monoplane known as "Kate," with a radial engine of 770-brake horsepower and delivering a single torpedo of 1,764 pounds. Pushkin received only an acknowledgment. Diamond's controller avidly wanted the results of the trial as soon as possible. Dalliance was told he would receive technical advice within forty-eight hours.

Acting on that advice, distributing bribes that even surprised Sorge himself, he was able to report the outcome of Yamamoto's experiment: "The approach phase on the target vessels went according to plan, but the torpedoes, once launched, turned away from the targets and back toward the carriers, one of which (used by the VIP observation team, with the emperor onboard) was struck.

"Fortunately for the emperor, the warheads were inert. The torpedo designer was beheaded on board the same ship an hour later."

ROOSEVELT AND his navy secretary studied the Dalliance report in a spirit of cautious optimism.

"I know it looks good, Mr. Per-resident," Knox spluttered, "but I'd still sleep easier if we had torpedo nets deployed at Pearl. That's still the lesson of Port Arthur."

"You know, Frank, you can be too careful in this life," Roosevelt replied. He hated pessimists. The New Deal would have gotten nowhere without a little faith. But then, he had to remind himself, Knox was a Republican. "Port Arthur's half a century away, for heaven's sake," he said, suddenly irritated. It was one of those days when the pain in his back did not respond to medication. "And in any case, the Japanese could not have won that little war without advice from Britain."

He was also now certain that Joe Kennedy was right. The Japanese threat—so-called threat—was growing out of control; a monster "Made in the USA" with which to frighten ourselves. Not even the orthodox Japanese military minds believed in Yamamoto's scheme after the torpedo trials disaster. "I'll leave that little detail of torpedo nets to Kimmel and Short," he snapped. "You may now leave, Mr. Secretary."

THAT SAME day Churchill made an unannounced trip to the Royal Navy's torpedo school at Gosport, on the English south coast. It was very much a homecoming. Long before—in November 1911

to be exact—as navy minister (or "First Lord of the Admiralty," as the Brits, with their love of archaic titles, described the job), his first action was to correct "the disconcerting fact of a shortage of 120 21-inch torpedoes." He was still preoccupied with this weapon the following year. As he wrote to his wife, Clementine, in September 1912: "This afternoon I studied the torpedo again under my young officer. It is a tangle of complications & the 2d lesson opens up all sorts of vistas of which I never dreamed. I could write ten pages on the 'Valve group.'" His passion for torpedoes at this time was equalled only by his addiction to flying seaplanes, which usually crashed a few days after he had been at the controls. Now, thirty years later, another young officer found himself in the presence of Churchill's omnivorous mind.

"How did you get on with the prime minister," they asked in the officers' mess that night.

"Like being locked up in a small box with a hungry animal," he replied.

Churchill, as usual, got what he wanted.

"Sir, if a torpedo veers off course to the extent you say, I think we must be looking at dihedral flex."

"Meaning?"

"Meaning that under some impact—say, being dropped from an aircraft—the fins are too malleable. They get distorted."

"Solution?"

"No big mystery, sir. You stiffen 'em. Any good ship's carpenter would fix up a bodice out of good hard wood. Lignam vitae is best. But oak would do almost as well."

"What about Japanese flowering cherry?"

"Don't know about that, sir."

THE LONG black American limousine, its headlights extinguished in accord with blackout regulations, the Stars and Stripes fluttering from a spike on the bonnet, glided to a halt outside 10 Downing Street at 7:30 P.M. on the evening of 7 December. The driver, a plump figure in a dark blue uniform, black peaked cap pulled forward, remained at the wheel as his passengers disembarked.

"Wait for us, Sergeant Spengler," said one of them. The bobby at the front door was struck by the driver's remarkable resemblance to his own prime minister.

☆ ☆ ☆

ENTER LAUREL AND HARDY? Churchill did not say it out loud, but his distinguished American dinner guests were an ill-assorted pair. Averell Harriman, the hustling, open-faced railway tycoon—as naive, sometimes, as he seemed behind those Santa Claus eyebrows and loud check tie—was Mr. Happy, the embodiment of American can-do optimism. He had undertaken a dangerous voyage to be present as Roosevelt's personal envoy.

The other man—the gaunt J. G. O'Donnell—was the acting U.S. ambassador to London, but in spite of the conceit of the George Washington walking stick he so treasured, he still carried the careworn aspect of the schoolteacher he had once been. Churchill sensed that here was a man who could do himself a mischief if the going got tough. He hoped he could stomach snoek, a fish of uncertain provenance and now part of Britain's rationed wartime diet.

The party began well. News from the eastern front was excellent. Stalin, in an inspired stroke, had pulled twenty divisions out of its Far East frontline so as to defend Moscow. The Red Army had counterattacked. The Wehrmacht advance to the Moscow suburbs was now bogged down in snow and a lethal temperature of minus thirty-seven degrees. In Washington, two Japanese diplomats were still talking peace.

"But can you believe them, gentlemen?" Churchill asked, passing the decanter to the left. Harriman waited for O'Donnell to speak. O'Donnell waited for Harriman. "Oh come," said their host. "Thanks to FDR we see the Magic decodes also. It is clear, is it not, that the Japanese mean further harm? First, Indochina; then the Dutch islands . . . who knows, perhaps our own colonies of Malaya and Singapore?"

Harriman responded. "Okay, Winston, we'll square with you. We read it this way: Russia has been tipped the wink from some quarter—maybe from an agent they code-name 'Pushkin'—that the Japs who advocate a northern expansion into Russia have lost the big argument in Tokyo. The 'southerners' have it. That means a maritime campaign. You should indeed check your fences around the Malay Peninsula."

"And what about America's fences?"

"Such as where, Prime Minister?"

"Well, worst case I suppose, there could be a surprise attack on the Panama Locks. Then there is your base at Pearl Harbor."

O'Donnell looked more anxious than Stan Laurel after getting Ollie into another fine mess, but Harriman leaned back magisterially, fingertips touching, a chess master who has just identified checkmate.

"Panama is out of Japanese range for all practical purposes," he said. "And Pearl Harbor is impregnable. General Marshall says so. So do all our military. So does our Navy Secretary Knox, and he was one of the doubters a month or so back."

"Not everyone agrees with them," Churchill said. "Four months ago didn't your own ambassador to Tokyo—Mr. Grew, isn't it?—say something about an attack on Pearl Harbor?"

"Oh, that. . . . A rumor he picked up from the Peruvians. There's a lot of hogwash speculation of that sort. Anyways, FDR seems to think that even if they did try something of that sort, it wouldn't work out."

"Perhaps," Churchill murmured Delphically through the cigar smoke, "we should both keep in mind St. Matthew's advice: 'Why beholdest thou the mote that is in thy brother's eye, but considerest not the beam that is in thine own eye?' Now, I acknowledge that the Dutch East Indies as well as our colonies are at risk in this devilish game of Japanese roulette. But I have also said publicly, as you both know, that an attack by Japan on the U.S. in the Pacific would mean war with Britain also. So we have a keen interest in the outcome."

"And an equal interest in torpedoes, Prime Minister?"

Churchill frowned a bulldog frown. "I'm not sure to what you allude, Averell."

"The Japs got the message from Taranto. So did we. The difference is that your torpedoes worked just fine. The Japanese will discover—how should I put this without compromising some 'Nofor' material?—they will discover that a torpedo, in some circumstances, has much in common with a boomerang."

"Have a glass of Scotch," Churchill suggested. His smile filled the room. "And let us hear the nine o'clock news."

"This is the BBC Home Service: the nine o'clock news read by Alvar Liddell. The Soviet Red Army continues to repel German troops on the outskirts of Moscow. In Libya, the Eighth Army—known as 'the Desert Rats'—under General Auckinleck have broken enemy lines toward the besieged port of Tobruk. There has been an attack by forces believed to be Japanese against American shipping at Hawaii and on British vessels in the Dutch East Indies."

Churchill rose abruptly, walked out of the room, and lifted a red scrambler telephone on the desk in the adjoining lobby. "Get me the White House," he said. Harriman and O'Donnell followed.

"It'll be breakfast time in Hawaii," O'Donnell murmured mournfully. "Sunday morning. They'll all be in church."

"You are connected," said an American voice.

Employing his usual pseudonym for such occasions, Churchill said: "This is John Martin. What's this about Japan?"

"It is quite true, Winston," Roosevelt replied. "They have attacked us at Pearl Harbor. We are all in the same boat now."

"Except that one of us is already at war with Germany."

"Well that's kinda difficult. It's little more'n six weeks since I stood up in Philadelphia and denied those Republican fantasies about having some secret agreement with you to go to war. Our public won't stand for it. There's a world of difference between a maritime war and a rerun of the First World War. A naval campaign is one thing. An expeditionary force on dry land is a much bigger commitment."

"Your people will come round to it," Churchill said. "They will have to now. Good luck."

"Is Harriman with you? I'd like a word with him . . ."

"Mr. President, sir?"

"Averell. How's the weather in London?"

"Fine, sir. And in Washington?"

"Clear. Very clear. Good luck."

As Harriman replaced the telephone on its cradle, the air raid siren crooned its deadly overture. Churchill, face flushed, handed steel helmets to his guests. "Come, gentlemen," he said. "Let's go to war!"

Harriman and O'Donnell looked at one another, sharing the same thought, but they followed their host all the same. He took them along an underground passage that led across Whitehall to the Air Ministry building. From there an elevator moved them slowly to the top floor. Their journey was not over. As Harriman later described it: "We went on a fantastic climb up ladders and a long circular stairway to a tiny manhole right at the top of a tower." On the way, Churchill paused occasionally, breathing hard, his posterior heaving at them.

"Ah . . . here we are. Best seats in the house," he said when he had recovered his breath. They were on a dangerously constricted, flat surface.

☆ ☆ ☆

THIS NIGHT it seemed that the Luftwaffe came from every direction at once to swamp the defenders with fire. It was a night that another five hundred Londoners would not survive. At least four incendiaries—silver-colored cylinders with round fin tails—clattered onto the roof around them, magnesium spurting flame. Churchill, whooping with excitement, kicked them over the unguarded edge into the street 120 feet below. Then he turned toward his guests, arms raised, doing a war dance.

"We are all in the same boat now!" he triumphed. Again Harriman and O'Donnell looked searchingly at him and at one another. Harriman's eyebrows were raised in a silent question. O'Donnell nodded, affirmative. They advanced on Churchill. Each took one arm, joining in, whirling the prime minister in an accelerating circle. The edge of the roof was a mere six inches away.

"One, two, three!" Harriman shouted.

"Go!" O'Donnell responded.

Churchill's last words, as they let him fly, were: "We won, after all!"

☆ ☆ ☆

THE BODY found on the street after daylight, in a one-piece siren suit, carried no identity documents. It was unrecognizable. In the darkness, several vehicles, headlights extinguished, had driven over it. It was just one of hundreds of anonymous victims of enemy action, hastily buried before the next air raid struck. By then, Harriman and O'Donnell had made their way unescorted back to Downing Street, pausing only to allow O'Donnell to throw up in a trash bin. Harriman knew that his companion was not cut out for this sort of thing. He was no soldier. All due credit to him then, Harriman felt, for doing his duty.

Spengler was waiting, as instructed, in the back of the limousine, puffing on a cigar and studying a file of official British documents taken from a red box on the seat beside him. Harriman, opening the door, said: "Sorry to have kept you waiting, Prime Minister."

"Not as long as last time," said the new Churchill. "In the Great War we had to wait three years for you to arrive. This time it is not so long."

The voice, the sentiment, were vintage Winston. So was the declaration of war against Japan later that day, hours ahead of a similar decision by the U.S. Congress. If Murray, Churchill's bodyguard, sensed that his boss "wasn't quite himself" that day, then it was no surprise. They were all unnaturally elated by the prospect of a war with America alongside.

It was some time before even the most sophisticated Churchill-watchers detected a growing willingness (to which some attached the word "statesmanlike") on the part of the great man to listen to advice, particularly if it came from Washington, and to be less headstrong. This new Churchill did not even complain much when Roosevelt still declined to declare war on Germany. It was a surprise to both men, however, when the American chargé in Berlin, Leland Morris, was summoned before Foreign Minister Joachim von Ribbentrop four days after Pearl Harbor. In the style of his Führer, Ribbentrop berated Morris: *"Ihr Präsident diesen Kreig gewolt; jetzt hat her ihn!"* (Your president wanted this war; now he has it!)

So it was that America was in, after all. But Harriman asked Roosevelt one day four years later, as they prepared for Yalta, didn't

Hitler's declaration nullify the high-risk strategy of substituting Sgt. Hiram Spengler Jr. for Winston Churchill?

"Spengler," said Roosevelt affectionately, "is a consummate actor. That was his profession you know, in the thirties. Small-time. They still remember his Hamlet in Zephyr Hills, Florida. Now, not only has he grown into the part, he has been completely taken over by his new personality. Believes he is Churchill. He overdoes it a little sometimes. The British will not reelect him once the war is over. . . . But to answer your question . . . okay, we were drawn in, just as Winston wanted. But we emerged with our economy intact and—thanks to British research at the very outset—we got the atomic bomb first.

"The Brits became a second-rate, regional power forever, though we don't say so out loud. You could say it all turned out for the best. I'm sure Winston would understand. He might even approve. After all, his mother was American."

3

Cain

JIM DEFELICE

STEPPING FROM THE PACKARD in front of the White House, Louis Erhard smelled roses. It was October, and by rights there shouldn't be roses here, but he smelled them nonetheless. The scent was so powerful that despite the setting, despite his nervousness at meeting the president and the gravity of what they were to discuss, it evoked a distant memory: a day in the garden with his mother. He was five or six, alone with her as she worked, basking in the sun if not her attention, for his mother always cared considerably more for her flowers than for either of her sons, not even William, whom Louis knew she would prefer until the day of her death. In his reverie, she plucked a tiny pink rose and turned toward him with it, holding out a trophy for him to sniff but not possess—like all her roses, it was destined for a garden club display. Its scent consumed him, becoming hers; the memory blocked everything else out, as if she were with him now, walking at his side over the carpeting of the West Wing hallway toward the most important meeting of his life.

It wasn't until he stopped behind the general at the doorway that he realized the scent came not from roses but from a woman's perfume. The woman had come from one of the other cars and now stood a few feet away, next to the marine guard at the door.

Her thick glasses and severe frown were camouflage, he decided, just as her stiff gray suit hid a soft pinkness that would give itself up willingly at the first caress. He imagined his thumbs curling into the waistband of her skirt, jerking it downward, her body falling beneath his; the scent grew so thick he could feel it massaging his skin.

The door opened abruptly. Framed between the guards stood George Marshall, chief of staff and head of the army.

"Gentlemen." The general nodded but said nothing else, expecting them to follow him inside.

War Secretary Henry Stimson, Harry Hopkins, and two men Erhard didn't recognize sat in chairs parallel to the far wall. The president sat behind his desk, a thick weave of cigarette smoke around his head, reading glasses perched on the bridge of his nose. He was in shirtsleeves—that, not the wheelchair nor the whiteness of his face, shocked Louis.

Erhard knew, as most higher-ranking members of Army G-2 knew, that Roosevelt could not walk. He also knew that for the last few days he had not been feeling particularly well, or so said the rumors. But to see him without a coat was like seeing a tank shorn of its armor, suddenly mortal and infinitely vulnerable.

"Lieutenant Colonel Erhard, Mr. President," said Louis's boss, nodding as he introduced the rest of his staff.

"Colonel. I hear you're from Long Island." Roosevelt's smile flashed like an old-fashioned photographer's store of powder.

"Yes sir."

"North Shore or South?"

"North, sir," said Louis.

"Far from where that scoundrel Moses ran his roads, I hope."

"Yes sir."

Roosevelt pushed his wheelchair forward, leaning toward Erhard. "Voted for Tuttle, I suppose."

Roosevelt was referring to his second election for governor, in 1930, which he'd won in a landslide; Tuttle was the Republican candidate. Erhard had never, in fact, voted for a Democrat in his life. But he had enough wits about him now to say, "Greatest mistake of my life, sir."

Everyone laughed heartily, FDR leading the way.

"Tell me your theory, son," said the president.

"The Japanese wish to guarantee their—"

"Hold." Roosevelt abruptly put up his hand, then pressed a button on his intercom. The side door opened and several naval officers entered. Louis thought he recognized two of them, though he wasn't sure whether he had met them because of his brother, who was a navy lieutenant commander and aviator, or at some still-born intelligence exchange conference with the Office of Naval Intelligence, or ONI.

Louis's boss bristled, though he had warned that this might happen. Louis himself felt somewhat reassured that what he had to say was in fact important.

And correct.

Roosevelt nodded at him.

"The Japanese wish to secure their prosperity and domination in Asia by controlling sufficient resources, such as petroleum," said Erhard. "To do so, they must neutralize the Pacific Fleet."

Even though the statement was self-evident, the navy men all shifted their shoulders as if they were bulls reacting to a wrangler stepping into their coral.

"They will use airpower to strike a devastating blow," Louis said, turning to the meat of what he had come to say. "They are aiming at Hawaii—our capital ships."

"Capital ships, my ass," said one of the admirals. "What do you know about naval strategy, son?"

"I know intelligence. My sources are impeccable. I've also been able to analyze certain documents pertaining to deployment and training patterns. In the past two months—"

"We've seen the same intelligence as you," said one of the others. "They're aiming at the Philippines."

Erhard glanced at his boss. They had gone over the parameters of what he was to reveal of his sources very carefully, even if provoked.

"I do have some unique contacts," Erhard said.

"Sources on Churchill's payroll, no doubt," sneered one of the navy people.

"We all know the prime minister's prejudices," said the president. He grinned toward Louis. "Anyone from Long Island would have factored that in."

"German sources," suggested the ONI officer, his tone sliding into a sneer. "Hitler selling out his slant-eyed allies."

"What difference would it make if the devil himself told me?" sputtered Louis.

"I'd be interested in the devil's motivation," said FDR. He glanced up toward Marshall. "Of course, we're not fighting the devil."

"The devil would be easier," said the general.

"The Germans would try and confuse us," said the ONI man. "As for the English or French—"

"The source is impeccable," said Louis.

Erhard's general took up the argument, again carefully protecting their sources and the actual documents they had supplied. But the discussion degenerated along predictable lines. Even if the Japanese did intend war—which they all agreed was likely though not absolutely certain—a long-range attack against the Pacific Fleet would be nearly impossible to pull off. The Philippines, yes. But sending carriers to bomb battleships in American waters, as Louis suggested, was far too great a risk for the ordinarily cautious Japanese.

To Erhard, striking the Philippines without neutralizing the American fleet would be much more of a gamble. But as the argument continued he wondered how he might react if the navy experts laid out intelligence indicating a vast army of armor would attack through heavy forest.

Which, of course, the Germans had done to rout France.

"Good intelligence work and an interesting theory," said the president finally. He pressed his intercom again. The scent of roses returned as the door opened. Secretary of State Cordell Hull entered, followed by the woman and some of the others from the hallway. The president glanced at both Marshall and the admirals. "I don't believe we need the staffs. A cabinet discussion, gentlemen," he added, turning to the rest and fixing his gaze on Erhard. "Thank you for your time. Say hello to your family for me."

"Yes sir. You know them?"

"Perhaps not personally." Roosevelt's grin was full force. "But sooner or later, everyone in New York bumps into everyone else."

"Yes sir."

Later, in the Packard, the general turned to Louis. "We tried."

"Yes," said Erhard, thinking again of his mother.

A PINK BAND of light sifted upward from the edge of the ocean to Lt. Comdr. William Erhard's right, dotting the horizon with the silver speckles of a salmon's skin. The sun remained just out of view behind the clouds, in the direction of Pearl, lurking there, waiting for the right moment to leap.

William felt a burst of cold air through his thick leather gear. His fingers cramped. He'd reached the point of every flight he dreaded—the long, wasted middle. The drone of the SBD's big Wright Cyclone engine had worked its way into his cheekbones more than an hour ago, and the numbness that had begun there now extended all the way to his toes. The terror-driven adrenaline of takeoff from the carrier had given way to elation when he cleared his gear; both emotions were now distant memories. He flew only because he had to, fulfilling his duty as squadron commander, as a navy officer, as a man determined to do his duty despite fatigue and cold.

But when he turned his head back to the front of the plane, the adrenaline returned. A silver dagger floated through the air five thousand feet below, a mile ahead. It slit the dim twilight in half, its clean cut revealing deep eddies in the blue ocean ahead. A bank of clouds obscured the vision temporarily; by the time they cleared, William had already clicked his microphone to alert the rest of his flight.

"East wind," he said.

The words ran through the squadron like ten thousand lightning strikes. They had found the Japanese fleet.

William felt it himself, hunkering forward against the Dauntless's stick, heart pounding faster than at any takeoff, even his first. He stared down at the pink-rippled ocean until a thin splinter appeared at the bottom of his windscreen. He thought it was a battleship and began to tip forward, finger edging against the transmit button, but then he saw something much larger ahead, a misshapen bar of soap floating in a bath. He held back, realizing the splinter was only a destroyer.

The bar of soap grew larger quickly. He knew the shape intimately; it was one of the carriers, *Soryu* he thought. The actual identity was irrelevant, for he could see the others, all of them stretching across the distance, arcing against the color-dappled waves. He wanted the third, if possible, leaving the closer ships for the flight behind them. But in truth he would settle for whatever he could get.

"Bogeys! Twelve o'clock!" screamed his wingman. His gunner began rumbling behind him.

It was too late to worry about the enemy fighters. William pitched left, sliding down to lead the echelon of navy dive-bombers toward the waves. He passed quickly into a scattered deck of clouds.

As he cleared the clouds, fear surged into his chest. Erhard felt convinced he'd made some mistake, gotten blown off course and confused—that was *Lady Lex* he was diving on, his own flattop he was hitting.

No, far different, filled with planes being readied for launch, organizing—it would be the second strike by now.

Kaga, the biggest carrier in the Japanese fleet.

The Dauntless fell at seventy degrees. His gunner kept at it behind him. Tracers flashed by from above, but William steadied his hand on the control column, all of his attention on the target. He had to squint to see it through the light fog on the bombing telescope, the changing temperature of the air layers kicking up condensation.

The carrier's forecastle sat in the middle of his cross hairs. William wanted the fat part of the deck, the part where men moved now, planes and snakes wrapping around them.

He saw it very clearly now and knew it wasn't *Lexington* or *Enterprise* or any American ship. But there had been no signal, no confirmation of an attack. His orders had been to wait for a signal—they weren't supposed to be the ones guilty of starting a war.

What were the carriers doing here, if not attacking Pearl? It was too late to wait for a signal, far too late.

A red ribbon fluttered before his wing. The ribbon became a white stream. The wings began to shudder.

William would not pull away. Dark bees flashed in front of him, then boards of wood flying all around. One of the CAP planes, attempting to break up the attack, flung itself into the thick of the bombing run and was slashed to pieces by the gunners.

The scream broke his eardrums. The rear of the plane rumbled and the tail began to slip toward his right shoulder. A Zero crossed over it.

The target had slipped beneath his scope. He needed more angle. His viewer fogged gray. William's chest thumped with the rapid beat of a thoroughbred's heart, and he felt a sharp pain in his lower stomach above his groin.

He looked away from the scope, down to the red button with its *B* at the top of the stick. He glanced back, saw the fog thick on his glass. The middle of the carrier was square in his windshield.

Now, he thought, and in an instant the Dauntless began to drift upward, caught in the eddy of an angel's thought, set free from gravity.

Then thunder rumbled and hell returned and William lost the adrenaline; his arms turned to rubber as he threw his weight on the stick, trying to fight through the curtain of flak. The world became an endless run of volcanoes, flames everywhere. The SBD stuttered sideways. Wind ripped across her canopy so hard that it shattered, glass splintering in thick shards. Bits of the rudder's skin ripped back. The perforated dive brake on the starboard wing pulled half out of its hinges. A fire began in her rear compartment; William threw off his headset as the wires shrieked. He felt the heat, then nothing but cold. Erhard thought of throwing open the canopy and bailing but quickly realized that would be foolhardy.

And then he was clear. William took a breath and turned around, not to survey the damage to his plane but to see the Japanese fleet. Eight or nine tight curls of black smoke rose from the center of the enemy task force, thick typhoons of black carbon—a dark, elongated hole in the middle of a donut. Flames splattered in the smoke. A wave of planes disappeared behind them, preparing to drop more bombs and torpedoes.

Only after seeing all this did William feel strong enough to twist back and look at the compartment behind him. Wide swaths of red crisscrossed the blackened metal; he saw, or thought he saw, a mangled stump where Jacky's head should be.

He turned back quickly. Two planes appeared off his right wing. William froze for an instant, thinking they were Zeros before seeing they were much too large for that. They were SBDs, members of his squadron—Tinfisher and Scully. He gave Scully a thumbs-up and pointed at him, indicating he had the lead now; the squadron's executive officer wagged his wings slightly to show he understood.

William turned his eyes back to the horizon. The sun had pulled itself full over the edge of the water. It was going to be a beautiful day.

THE BREATHLESS radio report took him by surprise as he pulled up a seat against the bar.

"Pearl—Pearl Harbor," stuttered the announcer, "has been attacked. The Japanese—great loss of life. Battleships lost. A counterattack is under way. *Arizona,* down, sunk—"

The patter in the bar ceased. The bartender turned back to raise the volume. Someone dropped a glass as the announcer repeated the bulletin with even less coherence. Someone said "fuck" behind him.

Louis thought of his brother.

"What? What happened?" asked Vivian, returning from the ladies' room.

Louis glanced toward her, but it was the bartender who answered. "The Japs bombed Pearl Harbor."

She said nothing. Louis noticed that she'd freshened her perfume and glanced at the smooth line of her skirt at her hips. He thought of the last time they were here together and wondered if, like then, she'd removed her panties in the ladies' room.

Suddenly she began to crumble. He jumped up, grabbed her in his arms, then carried her out to the car. People stood like statues, dazed by the news; he had to worm his way around them as the broadcast continued.

The radio in the car repeated the bulletin, adding no details the whole way to her house. Only later, much later, after they had made love and he went out to the living room, did a newscaster start adding real details: three, perhaps four American battleships sunk at Pearl, several hundred if not a thousand people dead.

Details of the counterpunch were sketchy. An unconfirmed report said several Japanese ships had been sunk or at least attacked.

Louis wondered if perhaps the navy had listened to him after all.

He could, of course, find out much of what had happened with a single phone call. But making that phone call would put him under an obligation he did not, at that instant, desire—he would be ordered to report immediately for duty, despite the fact that his leave had just begun.

He might already be legally AWOL. The radio said the army and navy were ordering everyone to report. The country was at war, or would be shortly.

He went to the liquor cabinet and took out a bottle of gin, pouring it high in a thick tumbler. He savored a long sip—Vivian's husband bought only the best—then stepped out through the French doors onto the patio that overlooked a dock and the ocean.

It reminded him of his mother's home on Long Island. He thought of her as she would be now, huddled in her bedclothes. He thought of calling her but knew it would be pointless; he wouldn't have any answers for her and couldn't take her silence or her complaints.

Worse, she would answer the phone not with "hello" but with "William?" Even though she knew it couldn't possibly be her other son, her favorite son.

Night had already set, but it seemed to Louis that if he stared long enough, he'd make out the shadows of Europe and Africa in the distance.

"A penny for your thoughts," said Viv, slipping her hand over his shoulder and then wrapping her body around him. He let her slide around his side and took her kiss passively.

"Not worth a penny," he said.

"You're not thinking of me."

"Thinking of war, I guess."

"Yes." Vivian pouted, her hands working around his back. "I suppose you have to go and report."

"I have business," he said.

"Your mother."

That surprised him, and while ordinarily he might have tried to hide it, he found himself powerless now. He felt anger welling inside him—he always did when anyone mentioned her.

"She'd said you were going there," explained Vivian.

"You talk to her?"

"Well, I am her daughter-in-law," said Vivian.

"I meant about me."

"Of course not." Viv slipped back from him. She'd put on a chemise but was otherwise naked; the cold air made her nipples large against the green silk. He felt desire rushing back to him.

But he'd felt that way earlier, too, only to find making love almost perfunctory. Was it the attack and the war, what was to come tomorrow in New York, or simply familiarity? He had a theory that if you made love to the same woman more than four times in a row, boredom set in. He and Viv had been seeing each other now for nearly a decade, though always in bits and pieces; the excitement ebbed and flowed.

"Are you worried about William?" he asked.

"He takes care of himself. Are you?"

Louis shrugged. He thought of his meeting with the president, then sipped his drink.

Vivian crossed her arms. "If you're drinking, so will I."

"Go ahead."

"Fine."

She disappeared inside. He took another glance toward the water then went to test his theory.

☆ ☆ ☆

WILLIAM ERHARD paced the length of the ready room in the bowels of the *Lex,* continuing his briefing for the other Dauntless squadron commanders. Ten days of nearly nonstop missions had left him feeling as if his chest were pressed against a grindstone; he'd caught maybe three hours of sleep in the past week. His head buzzed with coffee and the strong cigars the head of maintenance smoked.

The success of the past few days didn't necessarily mean there would be a rest. The Japanese were still a serious threat, and in fact the last remnants of the force that had attempted to take the Philippines were regrouping somewhere to the west, perhaps near Hong Kong, which a separate Japanese group was already pressing. As William had just finished explaining, they had to expect a cat-fight in the next few days.

"The next week, maybe two, may be the difference," William told the others. "Now that *Saratoga*'s here, things will go down easier. If we can get them here, while they're down, we can bottle up the home islands. I know a lot of you need replacements. I'm in the same boat—my squadron's below 50 percent."

He glanced around the room. The others were shrugging. Jake Fitch had told William to give a full-bore rah-rah speech, maybe say something about wanting to "clear the decks" before the *Hornet* joined them next week, but clearly it wasn't needed.

Just as well. He cut himself short.

"I guess I'll turn it back to Jack for the operational details," he said abruptly, taking a seat.

As he did, he noticed that the admiral had appeared at the door. A shadow aged his face but added a golden glow, as if the carrier were adding its accolades to those of the fleet and the country. As the leader of the counterattack that had struck back at Japan minutes after the attack on Pearl, Husband E. Kimmel, commander in chief of the U.S. Pacific Fleet, was now arguably the single most important American warrior in the world.

The admiral stepped back from the hatchway slowly, returning to the shadows like a ghost. But William found him there when the meeting broke up, saw the grim expression and the subtle head nod indicating he must follow. The admiral was a difficult read—most likely he was inviting him to a late-night bull session, but he'd had the same grim face when delivering the details of the Japanese raid on Pearl when William returned December 7.

Kimmel stopped a few feet from the squadron room, turning abruptly and making sure they were alone in the passage.

"Admiral?"

"You boys sound well prepared," said Kimmel.

"Yes sir."

"Orders for you have arrived direct from Washington, on the highest authority—the absolute highest."

"I don't understand," said William.

"You're being reassigned stateside. You're to leave immediately."

"Wait—I'm being pulled off the ship now? I don't understand. That's not possible."

Kimmel nodded. "Unless we've made contact with the enemy, you'll leave at first light."

"But Admiral—"

"This is something even I can't override. Your squadron's going to be joined with VB-2. It makes sense; replacements won't reach us for some time. Dixon will be in charge."

"He's a good man."

"I did a little checking," the admiral added. He put his hand out, resting it momentarily on one of *Lex*'s large run of pipes. A seaman appeared at the far end of the passage then abruptly turned back. "I was wondering why I was losing my best squadron commander so abruptly."

William felt the deck below him starting to give way. The fatigue had finally caught up to him; his head felt sweaty suddenly. But it was just an immense swell catching the ship unawares. The flattop steadied herself quickly, and Erhard waited for the admiral to go on.

"It's difficult to get details while we're at sea, as you can imagine," said Kimmel finally. "You have had some dealings with ONI?"

The reference to the Office of Naval Intelligence felt like a kidney punch. He nodded weakly.

"There's something about your brother?"

"My brother?"

"You have a brother, Louis."

Ordinarily, William would have made some deprecating joke about his older brother and the fact that he had chosen the army rather than the navy. But this didn't seem like the time or place to joke.

"He's in the army."

"There's an FBI officer in my quarters waiting to question you. Apparently there are some questions about your brother. His loyalty," said the admiral.

Kimmel stared at him, but William couldn't think of anything to say.

"Go ahead," said Kimmel finally. William nodded and started to pass by him. The admiral touched his shoulder. "We couldn't have done all this without you. Everyone knows that. Jake Fitch says you're our top commander, and that's high praise. You're still on the promotion list. The commendations will come through. I promise. This won't harm you."

Erhard managed to nod, but walking to the admiral's quarters was like plunging through a never-ending fog. Half a dozen men greeted him; the marine guards—two—posted at the hatchway snapped to attention, but if he saluted or nodded to any of them he wasn't aware of it.

The FBI agent stood at the far end of the small cabin. His green wool suit not only looked out of place here, but also seemed wet, as if he'd swum half the way.

"Lieutenant Commander Erhard." The agent didn't offer his hand. "My name is Fischer. I have some questions."

William shrugged. The fog circled thick around his head.

"Your brother visited Germany in 1937?"

"He may have."

"And 1939."

"I don't know." William noticed the heavy lines at the corners of the agent's eyes; he didn't seem to have slept. "My brother and I sometimes don't get along." He felt for a moment as if he were in his Dauntless, taking fire from a Japanese battleship.

As he had yesterday. And the day before.

They'd sunk it the second time. During the first, he'd lost Scully.

Tinfisher had gone down yesterday.

"What did he do in Berlin?"

"I'm not sure I even knew he was in Berlin," said William. "I'm not my brother's keeper. I mean, I don't know. He traveled on work a lot."

"Yes, he did," said the G-man. "Did he favor the Germans?"

"In what sense?"

"Oh, I don't know." Fischer made an obvious effort to seem conversational. "Did he admire Hitler?"

"A lot of people do. We're not at war with Germany."

"No, we're not." He hitched his thumbs in his pants. He seemed to have exhausted his knowledge, which obviously was extremely limited. William's heart stopped pounding, and he began thinking of getting some sleep.

"You're a hero," said Fischer, catching him by surprise.

"Excuse me?"

"The admiral says you bombed *Kaga* the morning of the seventh and turned around and sank *Soryu* that afternoon."

"It was more like evening," said William. Then, more modestly, "At least eight guys got bombs on that ship. I was just one of the first."

He shrugged, remembering the sight of his plane being pushed off the edge of the carrier after he landed. He grabbed Riley's for the second wave, pulling rank. By then word of the devastation at Pearl had reached the ships. The deaths of so many friends had chilled and enraged the men on the carriers, even led to fistfights between pilots who wanted revenge against the stricken Jap task force.

Five enemy carriers, three cruisers, one destroyer in eight hours, with a loss of only twenty-two planes. The second biggest bag in naval history.

The Japs' own attack at Pearl was the first.

Fischer sighed, giving up his tough-guy routine completely. He reached into a pocket and pulled out a pipe, fingering it. "Thing is, Commander, your brother, well, there are some questions about him. And he's AWOL."

"AWOL? Louis?"

The FBI man shrugged. "There's a theory he was working with the Germans. You'll come back with me, won't you?"

"The admiral ordered me to."

"I'm sorry about this."

"Me, too," said William, not knowing what else to say.

THE STORM had passed northeastward, but the Atlantic continued to swell, blue-green waves frothing against the planks of the small dock Louis had built years before. The small boat pitched wildly, one moment straining its ropes and the next threatening to heave over the walkway. There was no question of putting out, though Louis wanted to in the worst way, wanted to get in the boat and just keep going.

Where would he go? Europe?

His grandfather had come from Germany and supposedly never once talked of going back. He'd made his fortune here, after all. And his father—however much he didn't know or understand about his father, Louis knew that regrets were not part of his makeup.

Louis was now older than his father had been when he died. It felt odd to think of that. Perhaps if he had children of his own, he might feel older.

He'd never have kids now.

He heard the sound of a car on the gravel behind him, back at the house. For a moment he felt an impulse to jump into the boat, but he'd never been a good fatalist—he turned, saw a man in an woolen army-issue overcoat descending the steps toward him. Two burly fellows, sergeants, shadowed him.

"Colonel?"

"You're Johnson," he said, recognizing the captain. He held a staff position under the general; they'd worked together a few times.

"Sir, you're AWOL."

"What? No," said Louis. "My leave was approved. It runs through tomorrow."

As Louis reached into his jacket to get the paper, one of the sergeants dropped to his knee, reaching for his holster.

Louis held out his hands. "Whoa. Slow down there. Hold it, Jack." He laughed a little. "I don't know what you guys think is up. I'm just getting the telegram. The general approved my leave. My mother was sick and she—passed, passed over."

He couldn't even say it.

The man who had dropped to his knee remained there, training his weapon on Louis. The other sergeant had also unholstered his gun.

"Sir, I'm afraid you're under arrest," said Johnson.

Two other cars pulled in above. One was a marked police car; the other probably a detective's. The occupants quickly began double-timing down the steps. Louis stared at them.

"Look, Captain, my mother passed away," said Louis, concentrating on the words. His throat hitched and his lip quivered, but he managed it. "She died. What's going on?"

"We can discuss it in the car, if you'd like."

"We'll discuss it here." The ocean swelled beneath the boards so severely he had to take a step sideways to keep his balance.

"You want to make a statement?" asked Johnson.

"I want to know what the hell's going on," said Erhard. He shifted again, but stubbornly held his ground on the floating dock, as if to go forward would be a surrender.

He'd felt that way at the funeral, refusing to touch the casket. He'd stood over it at the cemetery, after it was lowered, and thrown in the dirt—that was his duty.

Why didn't you love me? he'd thought. *Why William, not me?*

"Did you take a trip to Berlin in 1937?" asked Johnson.

"Berlin?"

"You've heard of it."

"Don't be a wise guy."

"Did you meet or have contact with the German ambassador's staff?"

"Of course. That's part of my job. What's this about? We're not at war with Germany. They're negotiating with Churchill. They'll be at peace any day."

"How do you know that?"

Louis would have laughed, except that the ocean nearly knocked him off his feet. "Long Island isn't that far from civilization. Germany's taking care of the commies. That should be good enough for all of us."

"Did you have unauthorized contacts?" asked Johnson.

"What do you mean, unauthorized contacts? What are you driving at here?"

"Berlin, 1937. You were there and you never reported it."

"I wasn't." Louis shifted his feet as the waves pushed up from beneath him.

"I have a receipt," said Johnson. The MPs behind him edged closer. "When you got your information about Japanese plans to attack Pearl Harbor—"

"Leave me alone," Louis told him.

Johnson glanced toward the house before continuing. "How did your mother die?"

He saw her hunched on her side in the bed, slipping away in agony.

Asking for William.

"Did you kill her?"

Rage leaped in Louis's chest and he stepped forward, hands rising to throttle the scrawny bastard. But the waves beneath the dock swelled and he lost his balance, falling and almost diving toward the water. He saw the boat bobbing to his right, saw one of the MPs ducking, heard something, a shout, a long, long shout that tunneled into something larger, became not a noise but a physical thing pushing his head into blackness.

Louis thought again of the roses and the nearby garden. He saw his mother smile and felt her pat him on the cheek. Then Louis Erhard felt an incredible coldness take him by the neck and he plunged into unending darkness.

"Sorry we had to make you work on a Sunday, Commander."

"Not a problem," William told Lieutenant Rosen. He pointed toward the road. "You're going to miss the turn though."

"Oops."

Rosen veered his Chevy off the highway and onto the narrow back road that led to William's house. He didn't slow down; that was just like Rosen, just as it was like the lieutenant to apologize for his boss's decision to call William in. Both personality traits would undoubtedly take the young man far.

"The president seemed very friendly. I didn't realize you'd met him before."

"One of his great knacks, putting people at ease," said William. "I met him for a few minutes back in the fall, before shipping out to the *Lex*."

The meeting had come as a surprise to William. He had only the vaguest notion of the larger picture, though it had been his idea to use his brother. The Germans, of course, didn't know about his motive.

Or perhaps they did and didn't care. His implicating Louis only enhanced the credibility of the information that was passed on. He'd spoken with the Office of Naval Intelligence people and given them the information to check out. By that time, things were evidently greatly advanced—which was why, he imagined, he was taken to meet the president himself.

Until the moment he entered the building where the president was appearing in Texas, William had been convinced it was an elaborate rouse. But his ONI escort explained later that the president liked to get a feel for things himself, and this was an unusual situation, after all.

The betrayal of a brother.

Better a brother, he said, than a country.

FDR had exchanged pleasantries, asked him about Hawaii and flying, said nothing about Europe or Germany, much less Louis. The meeting lasted no more than two minutes, ending with an odd look from Roosevelt, a penetrating stare an opponent might give someone over a chessboard.

He'd looked at him the same way today but then laughed.

"Sorry about your mother," said Rosen.

"She was getting old," William said. "I hardly ever saw her."

"Tough to lose a mother."

William shrugged. She'd always been so swarmy with her flowers and her parties, smothering him since he was little. Half the reason he'd joined the navy was to get away. The funny thing was that Louis had always been a little jealous of her attention—maybe a lot jealous.

They drove on in an awkward silence until William pointed to the dirt road ahead. Rosen took this turnoff a little more gently, though he still managed to kick up enough dirt and dust to obscure the low-slung sun.

"Nice, for March," said Rosen. "This is a great place out here."

"My father left a bit of money when he passed away," William told him. "I put it in the house. Our family has always liked being near the water."

"You have a boat?"

"I'm going to get one," he said.

The trees parted and the house appeared on the right. Smoke poured from the chimney—Vivian had obviously stoked the fire.

"My wife," Erhard said. "She can't stand the cold."

"It has to be at least seventy," said the lieutenant.

"Women." William shook his head and grabbed his briefcase. "Hit the Japs hard while I'm away."

"We'll be in Tokyo by the time you come back," said Rosen. "We'll be planning to help the Jerries mop up the commies."

"That'll be fun. Leave a few for me."

William put a jaunty bounce into his step as he walked up the path to the house. Vivian sat in the living room, listening to the radio.

"The Japanese negotiators have already agreed on a timetable for withdrawal from Hong Kong and China," droned the announcer as

William came through the door. "With the collapse of their navy, the emperor has apparently recognized the inevitable and is prepared to return to the status quo."

"As long as we have them cornered," said William sardonically.

Vivian got up from the couch and kissed him on the cheek. He dropped his briefcase and grabbed her arm as she started to turn away, pulling her close to him. The rubbery, cosmetic scent of her lipstick mingled with the sweeter aroma of gin; she folded into him, a warm, soft mass. Slipping his hands down her back, he felt for a moment as he had the first night they'd made love on their honeymoon, ten years before. He'd been so naive then, still a mama's boy. So much had changed.

William saw a folded yellow paper on the side table as their lips finally parted. He recognized the tight typescript immediately—it was a carbon of his mother's autopsy, outlining the case for long-term arsenic poisoning, administered, more than likely, under the guise of stomach medicine.

"I'd like to try the new boat," he said, slipping toward the bedroom to change, "see if all my cash was worth it. Then we can go over to Bayside for dinner. We can do both. We'll take the boat and dock there."

"Maybe we should just stay home," said Vivian. "You haven't kissed me like that in years."

"I haven't?" William shed his uniform, leaving it in a heap on the bed. She came and placed her arms around him; her hands soon slipped toward his groin.

He was tempted, very tempted, but in the end discipline prevailed.

"Later," he said gently, turning around and giving her a consolation kiss.

Vivian began to pout.

"We'll have that lobster you like," he told her before she could say anything else. "And some champagne. Come on. I barely drove it last night. I have to break it in."

"Champagne would be nice."

"Come on. Get your coat. I'll lock up and meet you in the boat."

"Lock up?"

"Don't want to be robbed, do we?"

He ignored her stare, pulling on a shirt and then tending to the rest of the house. The last thing he did before coming out the door was to throw fresh wood on the fire and turn up the heat.

"You didn't lock the front door," she said as he got into the car.

"Sure I did."

"No you didn't."

She started to get out. He grabbed her wrist, pressing a bit too hard.

"I'll get it, honey," he said. William smiled at her, then let her hand drop. He ran back to the house, pretended to lock the front door, and came back. He walked as deliberately as he could.

The Chrysler took three tries before it started.

"Admiral wanted to know what I thought of Churchill's agreeing to peace with the Germans," he told Vivian, who was staring at him from the side. She could be an absolute sphinx at times, keeping everything to herself. Still, part of him loved her, despite everything.

He abruptly turned off the engine.

"It's such a great night," he told her, "why don't we walk down to the boat?"

"Walk?"

"Come on." He slid out and went around the side. She took his hand reluctantly, tensing as he folded his arm around her shoulder. They began the long walk down the winding gravel road tentatively.

"So I told the admiral I was shocked, but I guess I always knew it would come to that if we stayed out of it. The Russians are the real problem," he said, picking up where he'd left off in the car as the dock came in sight. "Hitler's doing us a favor, kicking the commies' butts. If Roosevelt were smart, he'd attack the bastards once Japan comes to heel."

"I'm cold," she said as he stopped. "Let's go by car."

"Come on. It's a beautiful night. Hey." He took her into his arms, felt the spark from before. "I love you. Do you love me?"

"Of course I do," she said.

"Maybe we should make love right here," he told her.

Now it was Vivian who demurred. "Let's have dinner first."

"Come on, then."

He led her to the boat, helped her in, cast off quickly. The unusually warm day had given way to an equally warm evening; the sun was just setting behind them, casting long shadows across the water.

He stopped across from Proudman's Point. She didn't seem surprised as he killed the engine.

"Let's make love," he told her.

"Now?"

"Yes."

"Your mother was poisoned," she said.

William sighed. "The DA suspected Louis, but of course, since he died—"

"Louis would never kill her."

"Who else could it be?"

Vivian said nothing.

"Unless it was you," added William, his hand still back on the wheel of the boat as he faced her. "You did see her a few weeks earlier. And you brought her medicine."

"I always brought the medicine. I wasn't the one who bought it," she said sharply.

There was no reason to hold back now. "When did you first sleep with Louis? Was it really right after our honeymoon?" William said.

He took a step toward her—he hadn't planned on the confrontation, hadn't thought he'd feel the anger welling inside him. His fingers trembled.

"I never slept with your brother."

He slapped her hard across the face. She tried to duck away, but he grabbed her, pulling her across the deck.

"Don't William, don't—"

"Don't what, Vivian? Don't hit you? Don't ask you about Louis?"

"Don't kill me."

The hard pump of her heart shook the boat. He had her by the lapels of her blouse; he felt an urge to have her then, lay her down, and screw her damn, cheating brains out.

But he held back, his rational mind returning.

"Do you remember Berlin, darling?" he asked.

"Berlin? You and I? Four years ago?"

"It was warm, wasn't it? Warmer than today," he said.

"Oh, William, don't kill me," she said. "Let's make love. Please. Take me."

When Vivian's fingers touched his pants, the fire ignited; he couldn't hold himself back anymore, couldn't be rational—passion and anger and hatred and loathing exploded. He threw her on the deck and tore down her skirt, ripping her underthings, plunging into her as blood began to drip from her mouth. She sobbed but he didn't hear it, heard nothing more, not even the splash when he finally dropped her limp body into the still water nearly an hour later.

By then he'd bound and locked her in the heavy chains he'd stowed. Sure she was already dead, he took the time to check the charts and his position, making sure he was over a deep canyon where there was no possibility of her being discovered. He cleaned the boat carefully, then disposed of the rags as well, taking care to inspect every inch of the floor. William added the old clothes he'd worn to the anchored bag as well. Only after the last ripple smoothed from the water did he restart the engine and head back south.

He had drawn parallel to the dock when the house exploded. Once more he cut the engine and began to drift. Spectacular flames shot high into the darkened sky.

Twenty miles out to sea, a German U-boat was surfacing, waiting to make contact with a man they knew only as E.

It would be a long wait. William did not trust the Germans, much less their Führer, to keep their bargain in its entirety, though they had made their first two payments of diamonds exactly as agreed. But he had no illusions that he was now both unnecessary and a potential liability; it was very possible that the U-boat captain was under orders to sink his boat and drown him at sea.

The Third Reich had gone to enormous lengths to make sure that the Americans knew that their erstwhile Asian allies were planning an attack.

They surely wouldn't care to leave a witness, even one so deeply implicated in murders of his own.

Revenge against Louis wasn't all of it, of course. It certainly hadn't been on his mind in 1937. William had admired Hitler since Austria was annexed. He agreed with his strong hand toward the Jews and the mongrel nations of Central Europe—even the French.

Most of all, he agreed with the Nazi approach to commies—kill the bastards before they kill you. Meeting with the German attaché and then traveling to Berlin with his brother's civilian passport had later turned out to be fortunate, but in the beginning William had been motivated only by a sincere admiration for a strong leader with a vision of the future.

But the Führer was best admired from afar. It was not wise to count on him as an ally or friend for very long—just ask the Japanese, who had been condemned by the Führer in a three-hour tirade on December 8. In the course of the same speech he offered assistance to the Americans and suspended submarine operations in the Atlantic.

U.S. opinion had made Roosevelt temper his plan to send more assistance to Churchill, but that was nothing compared to the sensation the following week, when Hitler declared unilateral peace toward the British and voluntarily restored her colonial territories.

Peace in our time. Perhaps only until the Bolsheviks were defeated, but still, who could turn it down?

Churchill.

But the pressure against his party in Parliament continued to build. The lack of U.S. supplies crimped his ability to make war, which he wasn't doing much of at the moment anyway, according to the newspapers.

If France was reunited and the Low Countries restored—they had discussed the rumors this afternoon—how long could Churchill last? Even if the governments of those countries were essentially Nazi puppet regimes, how could the British prime minister hold out alone?

Was it treason to assist a country you were not at war with? If it helped your own country?

Louis's superiors had seemed to think it was. William himself wasn't sure, though he didn't intend to debate the question with his own admirals.

What was the nature of treason, anyway? What was your exact responsibility to a brother or a countryman or an ally or an enemy? If you were at war or at peace, if you might be harmed or not harmed, if you crippled your enemy a few minutes after he struck you—what was the right thing to do?

Ham Fish and some other congressmen were planning hearings on why so much of the fleet had been at anchor when the Japanese attacked. The hearings would be a problem for Admiral Kimmel, but even more so for Roosevelt, their real aim.

Another storm for FDR to weather. The fox was on the run. Already he'd had to stop the shipments to the Soviets. But he'd winked this afternoon; he was in control.

With luck, Roosevelt might even declare war on the commies when this was all over. Perhaps American and German troops would converge on Stalingrad next spring, if the USSR held out that long.

By then, Erhard would be in Switzerland. A fresh passport and tickets waited for him in Toronto.

His brother's death had been an unplanned bonus. The best William had hoped for was twenty years of hard labor at Leavenworth as a spy.

This was infinitely better. Now he had all of his mother's money, not merely half. Between that and the diamonds, life would not be terrible, even in peace.

There were sirens on the shore. He turned the engine over. It caught immediately, and William pressed the throttle to full, aiming toward the jetty a few miles away where a new car and a new identity awaited.

Pariah

ED GORMAN

EVERY SO OFTEN, FRANK Stover would let himself go and take the chance of relaxing. Of enjoying himself. Of forgetting for the moment his dirty little secret.

Take today, May 16, 1951. How could a man not enjoy a summer's afternoon of flawless blue sky, babies in strollers pushed by young pretty moms, the Andrews Sisters on the radio of his yellow Plymouth convertible, butterflies, furiously gorgeous summer flowers, and the prospect of going home to the perfect wife and the perfect eleven-year-old son?

Maybe he'd finally found the right town. Maybe his days of running, of hiding, were finally over. He hoped so. It was hard enough on him. But on Mary and Tommy . . . he didn't know how much more they could endure.

THE HOUSE was one of those prefab jobs going up all across the country now that the war was over and all the soldiers were back home. Nineteen forty-nine had been a terrible year for the economy, but fortunately it was now doing cartwheels. Everybody was buying washers and dryers and automobiles and that latest and greatest must-have of all, television sets. Oh, yes, and starting families. There were now as many diaper services as there were corner grocery stores.

His own little domicile was bursting with all of these blessings, too. He'd made an awful lot of money with his book and most of it was still in the bank. He was a sensible man.

He drove ten miles an hour through the streets of the housing development. You had to be ever alert for kids dashing in front of your car, on foot or bicycle.

His own house was on a corner lot. A sunny yellow house to match his sunny yellow convertible. They'd lived here five months now. Tommy was just starting to adjust to school, and Mary was just starting to make some coffee-klatch-type friends. Both of them were shy. He'd been forced to give up his shyness the day he went to work for the *Washington Courier* in 1939. He'd avoided being drafted because of a trick knee, the result of a basketball injury.

He'd been at the library. The town wasn't big enough to have branches. You had to drive down to the main library. He was working on a new book, a novel this time, a suspense thriller set in Washington about the housing shortage during the war and how a Nazi spy and an American spy (unknown to each other at first) came to stay in the same boarding house. His publisher loved it. They both agreed that it would be published under a pseudonym. People still remembered the name Dick Reynolds (his real name) all too well. There would be no author photo or any biographical information in the book.

Effie ran around in merry circles as he walked from the carport to the side door of the house. She was a Border collie with a face so sweet, she forced you to smile no matter what kind of mood you were in. She perched up on her hind legs as he'd trained her, and he gave her a kiss on the head.

The first thing he noticed as he stood among all the shiny new appliances in the kitchen was the silence. Tommy should be home by now. Which meant the television should be on and western movie gunfire and cattle stampedes should be making noise in the living room.

He'd tried to train himself not to surmise the worst. Many times, there were perfectly ordinary reasons for things seeming strange.

He started walking toward the east part of the house. The living room was empty. He followed the carpeted hallway to the bathroom and peeked in. Tommy's buff blue school shirt hung from the shower door. It had obviously just been washed. But there were dark spatters on the front of it. Stover had no doubt what the spatters were.

Voices. Soft, muffled. Tommy's room.

He paused at the door before knocking. Crying. Tommy was crying.

"I'm so sorry, honey," Mary said.

"It's just like every other place we've lived," Tommy said. "They find out who Dad is and—"

He knocked. Opened the door. Tommy's walls were covered with photos of Roy Rogers, Gene Autry, and Captain Midnight. His bureau and desk also held other hero treasures, including a small statue of Superman and a framed, autographed photo of Batman. Tommy had expressed the vague disbelief that Batman himself had signed it.

"Hey, slugger," he said, knowing how foolish he sounded, not knowing what else to say. "How you doing?"

They both watched him with pity filling their eyes, and that's what he couldn't take. They should feel sorry for themselves, not for him. But they did. Because they loved him. And knowing how his past crushed them time and time again, he felt ashamed and helpless.

"They found out," Mary said softly.

"I got in a fight," Tommy said.

He went to his son and set him on his lap. Sitting there on Tommy's bed, he knew that the days of holding Tommy like this were fading fast. Tommy was getting to be a big kid. He'd easily exceed his father's five-eleven by the time he stopped growing.

"Did you get hurt?"

"Bloody nose. But I gave him a black eye."

"God, Tommy—"

A paralysis always came over him at this point. There was nothing to do or say to help those he loved. Many times he'd suggested that they split up, that Mary and Tommy move somewhere else and start again. And he was serious. But they always said no. They were a family, Mary said. Families didn't split up. Not loving families.

"Maybe it won't get so bad this time," Mary said. "Maybe these are nicer people than we've run into before."

But all three of them knew better than that. Once people found out that their real name was Stover, and Frank Stover was the husband and father—

Frank Stover . . .

If only he hadn't been working late that night eight years ago . . .

HURRY, NOW. Nearly eleven o'clock. Mary's always nervous when he gets home so late. The war news takes a toll on everybody. Makes them edgy.

The city room behind him for the night. The madness of typewriters and telegraphs and telephones and reporters shouting for copyboys.

The night steamy-hot. Nearly ninety degrees. A citywide blackout earlier in the evening. Air raid sirens shrieking. A bomber's moon as Edward R. Murrow so aptly described a full moon. Could it actually happen here? Could Nazi bombers actually get here?

The real threat, as he sees it, is sabotage. Terrorism. Assassination. That, both the Germans and the Japanese are capable of. To hear J. Edgar tell it, their spies and minions are everywhere.

The night smells of cigarette smoke, heat, and deep July.

He is halfway down the parking lot when he hears something to his right. There. In the shadows between to parked cars. Something—

By stopping, squinting, he makes out two figures. Men. They're fighting. Drunks? A mugging in progress? A jealous husband beating up his wife's lover?

Common sense says to stay out of it. Common sense says, if you want to get involved, Frank old boy, walk around to the front of the building and grab one of the security men who guard the front door, snoops and fanatics and crackpots having made the newspaper offices a target lately. Common sense says best of all, get in your nice little car and drive home to your nice little family and leave these two, whoever they are, way the hell alone.

But Stover doesn't take time to use common sense.

He gives in to his reporter's curiosity.

He turns toward the two men and says, "Hey, stop that!"

One man is now getting the best of the other. Has him propped up against the side of the car door and is pounding him in his stomach and face.

"Hey!" Stover shouts again.

And then the blaze and bark of a handgun.

Out of nowhere. Cry and moan of man against the car. Slumping suddenly.

Man with the gun—eyes glowing a filthy white beneath the wing of his wide Fedora—turning and firing on Stover. Not meaning to hit him, just clearing a path for his escape.

Another shot. This one close enough for Stover to feel its heat. He retreats to the far side of the nearest car. Huddles down.

Man jumps into a coupe and bursts away, headlights alive now, toward the front of the parking lot. Mud covering his license plate. No hope of reading the numbers.

Stover bolts from his hiding place. Runs to the wounded man.

Hard to see him. And what he *can* see is pretty nondescript. Inexpensive gray suit now blood-soaked. Long, solemn face. Balding. Fortyish, maybe. Breath coming in explosions that are partly sobs.

Then up at the front of the lot—gunfire. Easy enough to picture. The guard on the front door hears the gunplay back here. Tries to stop the escaping man. Then they shoot it out. A scream. The shooter or the guard?

"Why did he shoot you?" Stover says.

The reporter in him has taken over completely. He should be muttering meaningless assurances. You'll be fine. A doc is on the way. Instead, a hard-ass, he wants the story.

"Was gonna tell somebody at your paper what I find out. That's where I was headed." The man gasps out each word, convulses every thirty seconds or so. Is dying fast.

"And he didn't want you to tell us?"

The man nods and says, "Shoe. Right one."

Man fouls himself then. Looks plaintively up at Stover. "Oh. God, the smell. I'm sorry."

Guy is dying and he's apologizing.

Sirens. Three or four black-and-white Ford fastback cop cars converging all at once . . . but before the men in blue can quite reach Stover and the dying man, Stover whips off the man's right black loafer. A ticket stub of some kind falls out.

Then the man convulses so violently that he cracks his head against the running board.

Just as the man is taking his last breath, the cops appear, guns and flashlights busy on the steamy night air.

Stover slides the ticket stub into the pocket of his suit jacket . . .

MARY DECIDED it would be better if they all ate in the living room on TV trays. And let Tommy have one of those TV dinners that neither of them could gag down. And let him watch Hopalong Cassiday, even though they find Hoppy interminable.

They both kept checking out Tommy's face. Looking for signs. Was he going to get through this one all right?

Tommy laughed whenever Hop's sidekick did something funny. Andy Clyde, the actor's name. An old sourdough type. Nothing graced the ears like Tommy's laughter.

Around 7:30, deciding the worst of the evening had been gotten through, planning to put Tommy lovingly to bed and then decide how they're going to handle the school situation, the phone rang.

Stover was half-expecting the call. Not that he knew who was calling. But that was the pattern. The sudden exposure—people in a given town finding out who Frank Stover really was—and then the incidents began.

Starting with the phone call.

"We don't want you in our town," the voice said. Middle-aged woman. Angry. They always were. "You're a disgrace. My husband said to tell you that you'd better move before something happens to you or your family."

"Tell him next time to call me himself. If he has the guts."

Slammed the phone down. He'd taken it in the spare bedroom he used as his office. The door closed. That way neither Tommy nor Mary had heard.

In bed, after Tommy was asleep in the next room, Mary said, "It was one of those calls, wasn't it?"

"Huh?"

"C'mon, Frank. You hurried down the hall to your office. You must've sensed what it was. Then when you came back you hardly said a word all night. You were brooding."

He sighed. "Yeah. One of those calls."

"We'll have to move."

"No!" he said, so angrily he scared her. He swung his legs out of bed. Grappled with his package of Lucky Strikes. Got one lit finally. Exhaled a stream of smoke that was a lovely blue in the moonlight through the window. "We're not moving. We're going to stay here. No more running."

"Is that fair to Bobby?"

"Is it fair to teach him to run every time somebody confronts him? He'll never learn to stick up for himself if we don't stick up for *our*-selves." He turned around, facing her. "I told the truth, Mary. That's what this is all about. I told the truth. A lot of people said it wasn't the truth, but they knew better. They just couldn't handle it, that was the problem. I mean, I don't hate the guy. He was a remarkable man. But we have to admit what he did. And maybe he was right to do it. I never said it wasn't. That's not for me to judge. All I was doing was presenting the facts, Mary. And letting other people decide."

She reached across the dark gulf between them and took his hand. Her tenderness always calmed him down immediately. "Maybe you're right, Frank. About setting an example for Tommy. Maybe it's not good to always run away."

"He needs to be strong to survive this world, Mary. He'll never *get* strong if we keep moving every time—"

"Put the cigarette out and c'mere. I don't know about you, but I need a hug."

He smiled. "Yeah, I guess I do, too."

THE DEAD guy's name turned out to be Todd Whitman. The killer—who also killed the security guard—was never apprehended, though eventually Stover came to devise a theory as to who the killer had been working for.

Todd Whitman's ticket stub belonged to a savings bank. Safe-deposit box. Stover had decided to pursue the story himself rather than bring in the police at this point. He knew the risks he was taking. But if he turned up a strong story—and instinct told him something serious and major was going on here—he could get the raise he needed to take care of his family better. The mortgage payment on their very small house had left them virtually penniless halfway through every month.

Turns out Whitman had worked for the government as a decoder. He was pretty far down the ladder. But he'd bowled once a week with a decoder who worked with the director of the entire department. And one night, when both Whitman and this man had had one too many beers, the man told him about a message he'd decoded between two foreign spies.

Their reaction was Stover's reaction. Disbelief. It had been rumored, of course, but none but the fanatics gave it any kind of credence. The two decoders even speculated that maybe it was a plant on the part of this foreign power to stir up trouble in the United States government.

Whitman didn't really think about it after that night, not in any serious way. Then his bowling friend was found with his throat cut in the alley of a bar. The police wrote it off as a mugging. He'd clearly been robbed. Whitman wondered if the murder had anything to do with the story his friend had told him—but no. That was crazy thinking.

Then his friend's assistant was drowned. Good swimmer. Clear day. No alcohol. Drowned. Inexplicable.

And Whitman knew. The decoded message was true. And anybody who knew about it was being eliminated. And by the American government.

Six nights later, Whitman was killed in the parking lot of the *Washington Courier.* But not before writing down everything he knew and stashing it in the safe-deposit box.

Stover knew, too, especially after he'd checked everything he could in Whitman's terse letter, that he'd been planning to hand it over to one of the paper's reporters.

The trouble was, what was Stover going to do with it? It was clear that the government wanted the story kept secret. They'd already murdered at least three people.

Stover was understandably scared.

☆ ☆ ☆

THE PRINCIPAL was a portly man named LaPierre, Donald K. LaPierre. He wore a blue gabardine suit, a yellow bow tie, a white shirt, and a pair of gleaming white store-boughts that clicked every once in a while when he confronted a consonant. His office was large, tidy, and smelled of sweet floor wax.

He didn't work very hard at hiding his disdain for Stover. "It would have been better if you'd told us who you really were."

"And you would have done what, exactly, to protect Tommy?"

"We could have taken precautions."

"And which precautions would those have been?"

LaPierre waved a dismissive hand. He spent his days with grade-schoolers. He was not used to being questioned. "Honesty is always the best policy."

In turn, Stover didn't work very hard at hiding his disdain for LaPierre. Or his sarcasm. "Sounds like something I should memorize."

"So now what, Mr. Stover?"

"That's what I want you to tell me. I pay taxes. I'm a citizen. My son deserves to be safe in his school."

"I agree. Or shall we say, I would *normally* agree." He leaned back in his chair and stared at Stover a long minute. "Do you have any idea how much most people despise you?"

His candor jarred Stover. "I think so."

"When you called me at home this morning and asked for this meeting, my wife started talking as if I was going to meet Satan himself."

The words hurt. Stover didn't have to be reminded of how much the average American loathed him. Hatred, scorn, even humorous radio skits about him. Humorous if you weren't Frank Stover.

"I guess you didn't know how much people loved him? He was like God to them."

"Yes, he was."

"And you took that away. There are so few people to really admire and cherish these days. That's important to a society, Mr. Stover."

"I agree."

"But we'll never look at him the same way. Not ever." LaPierre paused. "Because of what you did. If you'd cared for this country at all, you never would've let your secret out, Mr. Stover."

Stover's depression was starting to turn into cold anger. "So you're saying you can't help my son?"

LaPierre leaned forward, planting his folded hands on his desk. "What can I do, Mr. Stover? He's the son of the most hated man in America. Even if I could protect him from fists and name-calling, he'd still be a pariah. Just as you and your wife are pariahs, Mr. Stover. I couldn't change the hearts and minds of the students. And that's really what you're asking me to do. Is it fair for them to take their hatred out on your son and your wife? No, of course it isn't. But it's human nature. And it's not going to change. I can't change it, anyway. I'm just a small-town grade school principal. I don't have any wisdom on something like this." Another pause. "If you really love your son, Mr. Stover, I'd take him out of this school as soon as you can. In fact, I wouldn't even let him come back here to pick up his things. We'll mail them to you if you like. Though if I were you—and this really is friendly advice—I'd leave this town as soon as you can. Pack up and get out. Before something terrible happens."

And exactly what did you do in the face of an admonition like that? You did what Frank Stover did. You lifted yourself out of the chair, you walked to the door, and you left Principal LaPierre's office forever.

ENEMIES.

Any man so beloved had enemies. Stover couldn't go to the man's friends—it was the man's friends who were having all these people killed and were doing everything they could to keep the secret a secret—so he went to the man's enemies.

They treated him like the prodigal son come home at last.

A reporter for a newspaper that had supported the man all these years . . . a reporter who had proof that the rumors were true . . . and a reporter who knew firsthand that there was a government conspiracy to keep a certain coded communiqué hidden from the public.

These were powerful and wealthy men, yet even they knew they had reason to fear not only for their reputations but for their lives. They had to be careful.

They hid Stover and his family in a safe house in Phoenix, Arizona, while he wrote the book. Had to be done quickly. They copyedited and typeset chapters as soon as he finished them. The publisher was a small place called Patriot Press. A printer was selected who was in great sympathy with their cause. The book was bound and shipped in secret. Key newspapers received—without any advance publicity—copies of the book. As did key radio commentators.

There had been no news story like it ever before in the history of the country. It was a bigger story than even the war itself.

People chose sides quickly. And, for the most part, predictably.

That portion of the press favorable to the man began proclaiming that author Frank Stover was in fact a foreign agent, a psychotic who had recently been treated in a mental hospital, a drug addict, a homosexual with brutal tastes, a seditionist, a publicity monger, and a lifelong enemy of the man.

That portion of the press that had always despised the man began proclaiming that author Frank Stover was a patriot, a hero, a model husband and father and citizen, a devout Christian, a man who had begged to serve his country, and, ironically, a lifelong *admirer* of the man, who was just as shocked by what he'd learned as everybody else.

Three attempts were made on his life in the first month following publication of the book, but in each case the culprit proved to be an inept/insane amateur who just couldn't live with the fact that the name of their idol had been dirtied in this fashion.

Another safe house. Another town. Frank Stover was rich now—twenty-one printings in nine weeks, radios and newspapers filled with it—but he was also a scourge. No matter how he disguised himself, somebody found him out.

Many other safe houses. Many other towns.

And always, always, somehow, somebody found out who he was.

And if they couldn't find Frank, they'd find Tommy. Or they'd find Mary. And humiliate them. And sometimes inflict physical harm.

And it would become the summary judgment of whatever community they were living in that the Stovers were not welcome here.

Were not welcome anywhere, in fact, in the entire country.

☆ ☆ ☆

He was half a block away from his house when he saw them in the street. No guns. No knives. No clubs. Not even any overt threats. Not yet, anyway.

There were maybe a dozen of them, men and women alike. Nicely dressed, middle-class folks just like Stover and his family.

A woman spotted him first and then said something to the others. Then they were all watching him.

Sweat. Heart pounding. Hands gripping the steering wheel so hard in anger and frustration he nearly snapped it in half.

Damn them. Damn all of them. Everywhere. Would have been different if he'd told a lie. But he'd told the truth. That was his sin. *He'd told the truth.*

They watched him. Didn't shout. Didn't raise fists. Didn't acknowledge him in any way that he could see. They just watched him. This was how it started. By nightfall, it would be different. People would start drinking. Rocks and bottles would be thrown through windows. Taunts would be shrieked into the night. In a couple of towns, men had even tried to storm the house, get inside. God knows what would have happened if Stover hadn't turned them back with his shotgun.

He pulled into his driveway and as he did so, he saw Mary peeking around the curtain at the group in the street. The look of fear was back in her eyes and it broke his heart. She deserved one whole hell of a lot better life than this.

He closed the garage and hurried into the house through the side door.

He went straight to the living room. She came quickly into his arms. He held her, all the aspects of her—friend, wife, lover. There was nothing to say. It had all been said so many, many times before. This town or that town. Before they'd started running again.

"How's Tommy?"

"Scared. He's getting those cramps again."

Kid was going to have an ulcer before he was fifteen, Stover thought bitterly. And there wasn't a thing he could do about it.

"Maybe I should call the moving van people," she said softly.

He held her away from him. "We're not moving."

"But Frank—"

"Where to this time? West? East? South? It doesn't make any difference. It's always the same. Don't you see that, honey? There's no place we *can* run unless it's—"

She shook her head. "Don't even say it. Out of the question."

Overseas, he'd been going to say. But he hadn't meant it. He was like she was. Wouldn't give up on his country no matter how bad it got.

"I'll go see Tommy."

RED RYDER, *The Durango Kid,* and *Captain Marvel* were the comic books of the day for Tommy. He obviously derived not only pleasure but a sense of well-being from them. Like a security blanket. Even when he slept, he liked to have comic books scattered across his bed. His escape from the cruelties of the outside world.

"How you doing?" Stover asked, sitting down on the edge of the bed.

Tommy looked up from *Captain Marvel.* "This is a good one. There's lots of Billy Batson in this one." Billy Batson was the teenage alter ego of Captain Marvel. It was easier for Tommy to identify with a teenager than a guy in long red underwear with a golden cape and a bolt of lightning sewn on his chest.

"Yeah, I like Billy, too."

Tommy put his comic book down. "You see them out there?"

Stover nodded.

"You think they'll try to get inside again, like those people did that one time?"

Tommy's right eye had begun to tic. And every so often, he'd flinch from the pain in his stomach.

"I'm sorry about this, son."

"I know you are, Dad. It's not your fault."

That was the worst thing of all. Neither Mary nor Tommy blamed him. Maybe it would have been easier if they did.

☆ ☆ ☆

THE FIRST rock hit the front door around nine o'clock. By that time, the crowd was maybe fifty deep. Mary had called the police a couple of times. They'd promised to get right out there. Somehow, they hadn't made it yet.

Stover had his shotgun ready and loaded and standing just inside the front door. Ready if he needed it.

They'd fixed up the couch in the basement for Tommy. It was cool and quiet down there. They'd also let him take his radio along. He got to listen to all the crime story programs he normally couldn't stay up for.

They sat in darkness.

"I shouldn't have done it," he said. They sat on the couch, holding hands. "I should have seen where it would all lead. I should've just kept my damned mouth shut."

"You couldn't have lived with yourself, Frank," she said. "And I couldn't have lived with you, either. You're an honest man. You had to tell the truth."

"Yeah, and look what we got for it."

"I just wish you'd reconsider moving. There's a nice suburb of Minneapolis I've been wanting to try. I always keep a place in the back of my mind and then write the chamber of commerce and ask for pamphlets and things about the town. It's a real nice place, Frank. Real nice. We could go on ahead, the three of us, and then have the moving company bring our things later."

"We're not moving," he said. "Not this time. Not anymore."

THE KNOCK surprised them.

This was just after ten o'clock.

A couple of things had happened.

Tommy had fallen asleep. They'd switched off the radio and pulled his covers up good and tight.

And a white-haired man they recognized as Dr. Stuart from the end of the street had shown up suddenly and begun giving everybody hell for carrying on like the KKK. That's just what he'd said, too, the KKK. He told them to go home and leave these people alone. And in twos and threes and fours, over a period of ten sullen minutes, they started drifting back to their houses like children who'd been chastised with especial harshness. They didn't like being treated this way or being compared to the KKK, but every block had an icon, and Dr. Stuart was the icon for this block.

And so they left, disappearing into the shadows around the streetlights, fireflies darting at their heads as they walked up sweet-smelling newly mown lawns and headed inside to have a nightcap beer and a couple more cigarettes and maybe another little rant about that bastard Frank Stover.

You just never knew who was living in your neighborhood . . .

Mary opened the door.

Stover stood behind her, his shotgun pointed directly in the center of the doorway.

Dr. Bill Stuart said, "Sure hope that thing isn't loaded, Stover. Guns make me nervous."

"What do you want?" Stover said.

"To talk. To apologize. To explain."

"I've heard it all before," Stover said.

"Frank," Mary said. "Come in, Dr. Stuart. I'll get some lights on. And Frank, put that shotgun away. It makes me nervous, too."

She put a table lamp on, and the three of them sat down.

"I'd take a beer if anybody'd offer it," Dr. Stuart, a hefty but not fat man, said. His white hair and large blue eyes and hard face gave him a granite authority, even while he was wearing walking shorts and a Hawaiian shirt.

"Of course," Mary said. "Frank?"

"Please."

They sat and stared at each other while Mary was gone. She returned with three bottles of Pabst Blue Ribbon and their pilsner beer glasses.

After they were all wearing foam mustaches, Dr. Stuart said, "First of all, let me apologize for the neighborhood here. There are a couple of bad ones in the bushel—about the same number of bad ones you'd find in any bushel—and they spoil everything. They've always got some angry cause they're promoting. This teacher is a communist, this city councilman is a queer, or this new businessman may be part of organized crime. Nothing pleases them more than to make trouble. And the men are just as guilty as the women, in case you think it's only women who like to gossip. They've driven people out of this town before, and they'll drive them out again."

He took some more beer.

"My husband told the truth," Mary said. "That's why they hate us."

Dr. Stuart smiled sadly. "That isn't why they hate you, Mrs. Stover. They hate you because you told them there was no God. That the man we thought was God was just as weak and conniving and dishonest as every other human being. That he could be good—just as most of us are most of the time—but that he could also be bad. Very bad, in fact."

Mary glanced at Stover. "It wasn't Frank's intention to—"

"I'm sure it wasn't, Mrs. Stover. And as far as I'm concerned, your husband *did* tell the truth. Franklin Roosevelt—as that coded message proved—did know about Pearl Harbor in advance. He could've saved all those lives and all those ships. But he saw a way of getting us into the war and he took it." More beer. "I lost two sons in the war. And I'm damned proud of them because if they hadn't given their lives along with all the other boys, Germany and Japan would have won. I don't even hate Roosevelt for what he did at Pearl Harbor. We should've gotten in the war even earlier than we did. Maybe this was the only alternative he had. But when your book came out, Mr. Stover, Roosevelt's enemies ganged up on him and made him out to be the most treacherous man in our history. All those boys killed at Pearl that morning. And all that blood on his hands.

"And you have to remember how the majority of people saw FDR. He was God. He created Social Security for the old folks; he got the farmers back on their feet; he started fixing up cities and building national parks and even helping colored people. He was God. People had that kind of faith in him. It really was religious, the way they saw that. And your book destroyed that faith. Even the people who called you a liar knew that you were telling the truth. In their hearts, they did. But they'll always hate you for making them face up to it." He smiled his sad smile again. "I even hate you a little bit, Mr. Stover. I sort of looked up to him as a God myself. I was really shocked when he committed suicide. I guess he couldn't face up to the truth of what he'd done, either."

A rational, not unkind, very articulate man had just explained to Frank Stover why he was a pariah. It had never been put so simply, so compellingly to him before.

Mary took his hand. Gripped it tight.

"Frank's a good man, Doctor."

"I don't doubt that he is, Mrs. Stover. But I'm not sure most people are ready to believe that."

The medical man had drained his bottle of beer and now put big hands on big white knees and levered himself up from his chair. "I wish I could tell you that things'll get better here for you. But I'm afraid they won't. Well, good night now."

FIVE DAYS later, in sunny Timberlake, Minnesota, Mary Stover stood on the edge of the driveway watching the moving van back in. She slid her arm around her husband's waist and gave him a hug. "Things'll be better here for us, Frank. I just know they will. Can't you just feel it?"

He leaned down and gave her a kiss. "Sure I can, honey. Sure I can."

Sixteen days later a local reporter recognized Frank's face.

Their next destination was Hastings, Maine.

Part 2

Alternate Actions

In war, things don't always go according to plan.

As the poem cast into metaphor, "because of a nail" a war can be lost.

Whether it's a change in weather, a change in location, or just a change in the amount of warning or information at hand, alternate situations can lead to alternate actions (and reactions).

5

Green Zeros

R. J. PINEIRO

In the year of our Lord 1940, French Canadians, unwilling to sacrifice themselves to defend England following the fall of France, rally alongside Canadian separatists for an independent Canada and vote to keep their troops home. As a result of the lost Canadian support, the British are forced to keep more of their forces home to defend their nation against the growing Nazi threat, thus failing to keep Italy at bay in the Mediterranean. Consequently, the British never launch an air strike against the Italian port of Taranto.

Adm. Isoroku Yamamoto is never inspired to attack Pearl Harbor.

In response to a plea from Japanese emperor Hirohito in 1941, Adolf Hitler halts his plans to invade the Soviet Union, opting instead for sending Gen. Friedrich von Paulus's Sixth Army to the Middle East in an effort to secure oil resources for his Far East ally, which is suffering a U.S. oil embargo in retaliation for its Manchurian campaign.

The United States and the Soviet Union remain out of the war . . .

I T'S THE HEAT, YOU know. It really gets to you on days like today, spending hour after hour under a scorching sun in the

Arabian Sea and hauling bombs, torpedoes, depth charges, and rockets across the wooden flight deck to ready the next group of Hellcats—all under the impatient stare of the pilots, who don't have an appreciation for how damned backbreaking our job is.

But then again, they too have their own bag of shit to worry about.

Poor bastards. Most of them have less than fifty hours in the Hellcat and already are being catapulted off to fight against seasoned Jap pilots in Zeros. Half of them won't last a week. Only 10 percent will make the first month.

But, hey, that's what happens when the bureaucrats in Washington decide to sit on their thumbs for two years under the pretext of giving embargoes and diplomacy time to work. While America was busy watching the 1942 and 1943 World Series, pretending nothing was wrong, Germany, Italy, and Japan conquered half of the world. Germany and Italy secured Europe and Northern Africa with an eye toward the oil-rich nations of the Middle East while Japan raced across Indochina, the Malay Peninsula, Singapore, Thailand, Burma, and India, sending British forces in the region running for cover. Russia joined the fight in late 1942, when the Germans violated their nonaggression pact and threatened the Soviets' supply of oil from the Black Sea region.

For the United States, it wasn't until the threat of losing access to Middle Eastern oil in 1943 became a reality that we finally declared war on the Axis, deploying our mighty navy across the Atlantic to assist a decimated Great Britain and toward the Middle East to protect our regional interests, also joining forces with Russia. I guess it was fine by us if the Axis raped, pillaged, and slaughtered half the world. But don't fuck with our oil.

My friend Chico Martinez once told me that there's nothing like a good old war to nurture progress and innovation. Well, for the past few years Japan and Germany have certainly leaped forward in technology, designing and mass-producing amazing machines of destruction, from aircraft and tanks to ships. There's even rumors out there about a fighter without propellers that can fly twice as fast as anything ever built. And, of course, don't forget about those incredible V-1 and V-2 rockets that have turned London inside out, as well as the new V-3s, with three times the range of their predecessor, which has caused so much havoc in Moscow. There's even word out there about a prototype V-4 with a range capable of reaching America. We, on the other hand, enjoyed our World Series and now find ourselves the underdog in a new kind of ball game.

A young pilot straps on his helmet, climbs up the side of his Hellcat, goes through his checklist, and moments later cranks up the engine. The fighter belches inky smoke and rumbles as the large propeller begins to whirl, disappearing in a shiny disk as he advances the throttle. He taxies into position, gets the signal, and off he goes, racing down the deck. The plane takes off as expected, shortly before reaching the forward edge of the carrier, and starts to climb while the next fighter taxies into position. A moment later the Hellcat's engine sputters and quits. We all turn our heads toward the bow and watch the frozen propeller. The pilot banks the fighter-bomber to the right, getting it out of the way of the carrier while trying to restart the engine. The propeller begins to turn. Smoke puffs off the side, but the needed thrust comes too late. The Hellcat plunges into the sea, its propeller momentarily hammering the swells. Escorts from our task force steer into position for a rescue, but the pilot apparently can't cut himself loose from his straps and sinks with his plane seconds later.

Shit. You feel bad, but after a year of this crap, every disaster is taken in stride, with a sad glance before moving on. I guess that's war, and as Chico says, it also means that every weapon at our disposal was made in a rush and by the lowest bidder.

Now, don't get Chico wrong. The Hellcat is a fine enough plane, certainly an improvement from the smaller Wildcats, which could barely keep up with the Zeros, but he's right about the unfortunate fact that it's still machinery designed and manufactured in a hurry by a government subcontractor before all of its systems have been properly wrung out, leaving it up to us to shake out the last few kinks.

We're not just at war with the Japs, the Germans, and the Italians, but also with our own equipment.

Two years late, with poorly trained personnel and flawed hardware—not the ideal way to prevail against such formidable opponents. But we chose to wait, not relishing the thought of sending our young generation to fight a distant war. Now we're paying the price. A year into this, and we're still barely containing the Axis, which continues to be on the offensive.

I don't even remember anymore who won the darned Series back in '43. The sun must have fried my brain cells this past year.

Irony aside, we're actually the first real opposition the Axis has had since this whole thing blew up in 1940, unless you want to count England's refusal to surrender and Russia's modest victories in the Caucasus Mountains and the Ukrainian plains. Our navy gained control of both the Arabian and Mediterranean Seas, securing the Suez Canal while sinking a number of enemy ships, including two Japanese carriers and a few Italian and German surface vessels and submarines. Meanwhile, Douglas MacArthur's armies engaged the Japanese in India with the assistance of any British forces that had managed to survive the Japanese onslaught of '42 and '43. George S. Patton focused his forces on the northern front, trying to halt the German advance from Turkey. He's being assisted by Russian troops under the command of some general whose name I can't pronounce. Over in England, Dwight D. Eisenhower has been working on something with the Brits to keep Hitler busy on that front. There's even a rumor of an impending continental invasion somewhere along the French coast. But that's supposed to be hush-hush.

So here we are, the so-called Allied Forces, stuck in the middle of nowhere, thousands of miles from home, sandwiched between two advancing armies, and *always* short of everything, from ammunition to carriers to destroyers. And it's not that we can't manufacture them. Our factories back home are surely cranking out all of the hardware that we need. The trick is getting it past those sneaky German U-boats, which have sunk so many of our convoys in the Atlantic and the Mediterranean.

I frown. Nazi bastards.

The other day, in spite of recent improvements in naval countermeasures to protect our ships from submarine attacks, we got word that they had torpedoed a clearly marked hospital ship packed with wounded GIs, sinking it before the doctors and nurses could get a tenth of the patients out. So much for honor in battle.

Although that episode really hurt, don't expect sympathy from the world. Remember that we chose to play the isolationist card, turning a blind eye while that same world was being looted and murdered.

Guess now it's our turn to suffer. It's time for the sons of America to step forward and join in the pain and hardship alongside Britain and Russia to stop the Axis. And the sons of America are definitely here. There's guys from every corner of America; from Maine to Texas; from California to Florida; from sea to shining sea—though lately the sea seems more gloomy than shiny. The latest statistics—if you choose to believe them—indicate that anywhere from four to five thousand of our boys die each day in the frontlines, and that number seems to grow every day. I tell you, we'd better win this thing soon or we'll be out of soldiers in another year.

Unfortunately, there is no end to the struggle. Germany, Japan, and Italy are incredibly powerful, even with their oil shortages, and they have dug themselves pretty deep in all of their controlled territories, making us pay dearly for every square inch of soil we take back. There's blood from Idaho, Wisconsin, New York, Utah, Arizona, and the rest of the Union spilled all across India and Turkey.

But we're holding the line.

How do I know so much for being just a lowly ensign? My dad's a radio aficionado and taught me everything he knew about them. By the time of my fifteenth birthday I could disassemble and reassemble just about anything with tubes. The recruiter back in Houston quickly latched on to that skill, and next thing I knew I had become a radio technician for the United States Navy. As one of a dozen assistant chief radiomen aboard the USS *Sargent Bay* (CVE 83), I get to listen in on many ongoing operations, keeping abreast of the rapidly developing situations on all fronts. The radio room is next door to the CIC—that's the Combat Information Center—where technicians plot all airborne planes and surrounding vessels on a clear plastic wall according to the information fed to them by the radar operators, whose equipment picks up anything that moves in our area of interest. Unidentified blips on the radar screen are plotted and their coordinates fed to our aircraft to go out and intercept. Our radio room receives encrypted transmissions, which we decode and run over to the CIC. In some cases, the commanding officer (CO) will confer with his executive officer (XO) and formulate a reply, which one of us would have to encrypt before transmitting it back to the original sender.

Another reason I know more than I should is because I have to repair those damned radar units all the time. Their tubes never seem to last more than a few weeks, and since spares are slow coming—just as everything else around here—I find myself cannibalizing old systems with the help of my trusty soldering iron, a gift from Dad before I sailed away.

We're part of the largest naval task force ever deployed by the United States, with the aircraft carriers *Lexington, Enterprise,* and *Yorktown* as centerpieces, along with tons of support ships, from the mighty battleships *Arizona, Oklahoma,* and *California,* to destroyers, cruisers, light cruisers, submarines, minesweepers, oilers, and, of course, a number of escort carriers, like the *Sargent Bay,* roughly half the size of the *Enterprise.* There's a second task force patrolling the Mediterranean, though not as large as this one.

Our job is to keep at least a dozen planes stationed at ten thousand feet covering this side of the task force, plus as many Hellcats providing air support to the ground troops hammering the Japs in India, over a hundred miles away. For the *Sargent Bay* that means maintaining a twenty-four-by-seven operation to keep the fighters airborne, which for us means nonstop action as planes are constantly taking off and landing.

But why is a radio technician hauling explosives across the controlled chaos of a flight deck you ask?

As fate would have it, eighty-two of our guys bought it last month when the tailhook of a landing Hellcat, weakened by antiaircraft fire during a raid north of Bombay, broke off as it snagged one of the arresting wires stretched across the deck. The plane proceeded to plunge into the barrier cable that snapped up a moment later, but the fighter's momentum was such that it simply tumbled past the cable and into fully fueled and armed planes. The large explosion that followed pretty much vaporized the entire day shift operating the flight deck—along with several planes and their pilots.

But a carrier is built to take it, and our beloved *Sargent Bay* took the punishment quite well. Another crew extinguished the flames within the hour, and the next day, following a burial at sea of all the charred body parts we could find, we were back in business—with a number of us pulling double duty.

I'm now a deckhand by day and a radioman by night. I sleep, eat, and take a crap somewhere in between. About seventy new sailors arrived last week, supposedly to replace those we lost. In reality though, the new guys are just that: new, rookies. It will probably take us six months to whip them into shape. Meanwhile, seasoned guys like Chico and me have to hold the fort.

"Marshall!"

I glance behind me. It's Master Chief Rollings, a real son of a bitch who became even meaner after the incident a month ago. The man's over six-feet-five and probably exceeds 350 pounds of tanned muscle in spite of his middle age. Really, the guy is a gorilla, making my 200 pounds look as intimidating as a light cruiser in the presence of the *Arizona*. Sometimes I wonder if we belong to the same species.

"Sir!"

The chief gets an inch from my face. I can smell coffee on his breath as he sprays me with spit while shouting: "I thought I told you to get those damned bombs over to the fucking fighters! What have you been doing? Playing with yourself? Son, we've got a war to fight around here! We've got troops in India counting on our ability to deliver air cover all day long. We ain't got time to screw around!"

I'm overworked, sleep-deprived, sunburned, sweaty, and down-right tired of this double-duty shit plus this ape's verbal abuse. I've been lugging bombs without a break for six straight hours, just barely keeping up with the fighters, and given the recent Japanese advances toward our task force, there is no break in sight. Every part of my anatomy hurts, and I'm in no mood for this man, but I still manage to control the urge to tell him where to shove his atti-tude. Chief Rollings lost his oldest son in that explosion last month and just last week his second boy, a Hellcat pilot, didn't come back from a sortie over southern India. He either died or bailed over enemy lines, which is probably worse. The Japs ain't nice to POWs. The man's earned the right to be a first-class asshole—though sometimes he abuses this unspoken privilege.

"Sorry, sir. I'll try to go faster."

"Don't try, son! Do, dammit! Do! Or in six months you'll be eating sushi and speaking Jap like the rest of Asia!"

"Aye Master Chief!"

He marches on to scream at the next guy.

Wiping the spit off my face, I roll the cart over to one of the Hellcats crowding the starboard side of the flight deck, out of the way from most of the action—though last month's incident taught me that *any* portion of the deck can be dangerous with so much movement amid so many explosives and high-octane fuel.

Despite the master chief's warning about screwing off, I take a moment to admire this stubby-looking fighter currently being fueled and prepped by the ground crew. The Hellcat's definitely an oddity among American warplanes. Grumman designed it specifically to fight Zeros, and it is one of the slowest fighters in the war, but it is a damned maneuverable one. The Hellcat has huge fuel tanks, which is a definite plus when fighting sorties in India, but they affect its ability to turn when fully fueled. However, the fighter has a phenomenal air brake capability, meaning it can slow down so fast during a dogfight that a pilot could almost swear the plane had just deployed a tail parachute, thus allowing for sudden tight turns and the ability to stay on the enemy's tail without the fear of flying by. Although the plane lacks the streamlined looks of a P-51 Mustang, it outclimbs both the Mustang and the Zero. Its heavy armor allows it to take an awful lot of punishment and still keep on fighting, which the Hellcat does quite well with its six .50-caliber machine guns and a capacity of twenty-four hundred rounds for plenty of Jap spraying.

The crew takes my bomb, and I start to haul the empty cart back to the stack of bombs. On the way I spot Chico Martinez. The master chief's got him hauling belts of .50-cal ammo.

"Hey, Ray!" Chico calls out, rushing over to me while pushing his cart. A small crucifix dangling at the end of a chain rattles against his dog tags.

"Yeah?"

The native of Los Angeles, California, is sweating profusely, like the rest of us. But *unlike* the rest of us, Chico's brown skin seems to soak up the sun without burning. A bright-red bandanna wrapped around his forehead, his dark eyes glinting with excitement, he says, "Just heard from one of my pals in Battle Ops that the Japs have launched a massive counteroffensive against MacArthur, including an all-out naval and aerial assault on his supporting navy—that's us, *amigo*. Would you believe that shit? Looks like the little bastards just can't get enough of us."

I suppress a laugh. Chico's calling the Japs little bastards when he's barely five feet four inches and weighs less than 110 pounds soaked and wet.

Humor aside though, I simply shrug off the possible threat. Had I heard that a year ago, soon after I was shipped over here, anxiety would have instantly wormed through my intestines, wondering if I would make it through a large-scale Japanese attack. For the first few months here, I had lived with such fear, always concerned that something terrible was just about to happen, having heard one too many stories about Japanese brutality and their borderline suicide tactics. And many exciting things did happen, including a number of intense battles against Japanese planes trying to pierce the task force and come after their preferred targets: aircraft carriers. But our Hellcats plus tons of AA fire pushed them back every time, preventing a single hit to our ships, boosting our confidence that we could actually beat these guys. Just last week, two flights of Jap bombers made a desperate attempt to break through the destroyers' shield and once again failed. We roasted them.

Having survived so many attacks unscathed—although not without a couple of close calls—I came to the conclusion that if I eliminated that terrible fear, life aboard the *Sargent Bay* would not be nearly so bad. To my pleasant surprise, bravery filled the void left behind when I managed to shove anxiety aside. I realized that being brave was easy once you got the hang of it. Chico, who arrived on the *Sargent Bay* at the same time I did, has also learned to play brave.

"Right on, pal," I finally say. "Let those bastards come back. We'll give them some more."

A couple of rookies nearby hear us talk and shoot us the new guy stare. They simply can't believe we can be so cool about such matters.

I just wink at them and get on with my job.

21 November 1944
USS SARGENT BAY
ASTF

Dear Dad:

Once again I am able to tell you that I am very much OK. Not even a scratch after almost a whole year in combat. Your prayers are certainly working. Ironically, our carrier has had more casualties because of our own mistakes, like the explosion I told you about a month ago, than at the hand of the Japs.

However, that could change. The word here is that the Japs are mounting a very large counteroffensive against the ASTF. They want our oil, Dad, and they want it bad. Last week the Japs tried once again to breach our defenses in an effort to kill our carriers, which provide the air support for our land forces. Before the destroyers and cruisers were through with them, they must have thought that they had flown into Hell itself, because not a single one of them made it through the AA shield. In a way the battle was like watching one big show where none of our guys got hurt. It was kind of a high-altitude "turkey shoot."

I continue to learn a lot about radios. I'm thinking that maybe when I get back I can go to college and get a degree in electronics. Kind of hard to imagine me in college, but the idea has been floating in my head for a while now. Chico told me the other day that there's a new bill being passed in Congress to fund the college education of all the men who served in the war. Could you check if that's real? I sure hope so, because the navy is really working me hard. Aside from the radio work, I have been pulling double duty five times a week after the explosion a month ago. It's hard work, Dad, but I'm looking pretty lean and mean (although a bit sunburned) after hauling around so much gear all day long.

Well, give Mom a hug for me, tell all of my buddies hello around there, and also tell Jennifer that I think about her every day. Her picture is always in my wallet. And above all: DON'T WORRY!

Forever yours,

Your son,

Raymond Marshall Jr.

I FOLD THE letter, shove it in an envelope, jot my parents' address across the front, and make a mental note to drop it off in the morning by the ship's censoring department, which checks our outgoing correspondence for any unintended information leaks before taking it to the day's mail plane. The navy has been pretty good at keeping the mail service running for us, and that's a good thing because nothing short of going home lifts our spirits more than a letter from home.

I write a letter a day, usually between dinner and my evening radio shift, which runs from seven until one in the morning. Then I get to catch a few Zs before Rollings kicks me out of bed at dawn for another day in paradise.

Yesterday I wrote to Mom. Today is Dad's turn. Tomorrow is Jenny's. Did I tell you that I'm engaged? I popped the question a week before heading over here, and she said yes on the spot. I'm now using part of my navy pay to make the monthly payments on the ring I slipped on her finger, but Jenny's worth it. We've been dating since junior high. She's a gorgeous brunette whose picture has gotten me through more than a few rough nights, especially during the early months, when I got really homesick. Now I get to watch the rookies go through that painful phase and on occasion take the time to pat them on the back and encourage them that the feeling will soon pass.

"Writing to Jenny, *amigo?*"

Chico is looking down from the bunk above mine.

I shake my head. "Dad's turn today, buddy. He was pretty worried in his last letter. He said he saw a clip last week at the movie house, and it showed the hospital ship sinking. Got everybody back home all upset."

"Yeah," he says. "Same with me. Looks like that one made news all over the barrio."

I lean back on the bed, resting my head on a hard pillow, hands behind my head, fingers interlocked. I stare at the bottom of Chico's mattress and yawn. I'm sunburned and tired, feeling I could sleep straight through tomorrow. But I have to report to duty in the radio room in twenty minutes. A short nap seems appealing at the moment, but Chico is in one of his *rare* talkative moods.

"Hey, Ray?"

"Yeah?"

"How long do you think we're going to be in this shit?"

Great. My body's screaming for rest and this guy wants to philosophize about the war. I make a face and shrug. I heard the XO commenting the other day that the war would last at least a couple more years, but the truth is that no one knows for sure. I can't imagine fighting for that long, though. But then again, a whole year has gone by already, and it really feels like only yesterday when Mom and Dad drove me to the base. Time sure flies around here, but we're certainly NOT having fun.

He frowns at my silence then says, "That long, huh?"

"We waited too long, buddy."

"No shit, *amigo*. But that's in our nature."

"What do you mean?"

He narrows his eyes. "You ever heard the one about the French, the Brit, and the Gringo in a German POW camp?"

As tired as I am, I can't help but smile. "No, Chico, but I get the feeling I'm about to."

"Well," he starts. "These three guys share a prison cell in this POW camp. Every night the guard who brings their food kicks the Frenchy in the ass. When the Brit stands up to protest, the German also kicks him in the butt. The Gringo just sits in the corner and eats his food, minding his own business. This goes on for six months. Then one night, the guard decides to kick the Gringo, who proceeds to kill the German and his buddies outside the cell, before leading an escape. When they reach safety, his former cellmates ask him why he'd waited so long to act when he could have obviously done it much sooner. Do you know what the Gringo said in reply?"

I know where this is heading but shake my head.

Chico says, "'The German didn't bother me until tonight.'"

"Are you trying to make a point there, buddy?"

"I wish someone like the Japs or the Germans would have kicked us in the ass a few years back, Ray. You know, done something to piss us off. Maybe then we would have gotten our shit together and joined the fight before the bastards got so damned strong."

Chico loves to get into these discussions, and usually I just nod him off, but tonight he has brought forth a compelling thought. When you think about it, the Axis was very careful to steer clear of our forces while raping the rest of the world. They didn't want to provoke us until *after* they had entrenched themselves across Europe and Asia.

"You're right," I say. "I wish someone *had* kicked us in the ass back in '41. Maybe we wouldn't be in the shit we're in today."

"You bet your ass we wouldn't be. We would have entered the war right away and clipped their wings before they got a chance to fly out of control."

I let out a heavy sigh, trying not to worry about the future, wondering if I'm ever going to see my parents again, or Jenny.

Oh, well. We are where we are. No sense in beating ourselves silly with what-ifs. We just need to plow ahead, inch after agonizing inch. We need to stay the course, stay alive until the winds of this damned war start blowing in our favor.

We have good allies, and God Almighty is on our side.

THE WAITING is probably worse than the heat. The encrypted messages started flowing about eight hours ago. A few of them were from Adm. Chester Nimitz, commander of the Arabian Sea Task Force. It looked as if the Japs were going to attack our side of the task force first, eliminating the escort carriers before going for the big boys in the center. Our radars had detected a large strike force of around ninety planes seventy miles away and closing. That's by far the largest one they have thrown at us. Of course, to get to the *Sargent Bay* and the other escort carriers, they first have to get past our own flights of Hellcats meeting them halfway. Anything that sneaks through this first line of defense would then have to survive the intense AA fire of the destroyers and battleships forming the outer ring and the cruisers forming the inner ring of our shield, plus our own planes stationed overhead. Of course, all it takes is one or two torpedoes or a well-placed bomb to send us all into kingdom come.

But, hey, I'm brave, right?

Right.

Because of all the activity, I remain in the radio room until around six, when Chief Rollings storms in and drags me to the flight deck to haul explosives instead of letting me stay and listen to the pilot frequency for updates on the upcoming air battle.

Chico and I are assisting a crew loading up Hellcats with .50-caliber ammo when the general quarters alarm goes off, followed by the XO's voice on the PA system.

"Now hear this . . . Now hear this. We're under attack. Repeat. The carrier fleet is under attack. Battle stations. Battle stations."

His voice is almost drowned out by the distant rumbling of the antiaircraft batteries from the destroyers. We all put on our life vests.

I grab a pair of binoculars from a nearby rookie and turn toward the havoc while fingering the adjusting wheel, bringing into focus a group of incoming bombers—Japanese Betties—at our seven o'clock, amid puffs of black smoke from the AA guns. Around the bombers, like buzzing flies, are silvery Zeros and our dark-colored Hellcats entwined in multiple dogfights.

Damn, that's a sight to see. The escort vessels are really unloading, peppering the sapphire sky. But what happened to the interceptors that catapulted off before dawn? Did they miss the incoming Japs? Or worse, did the Japs overrun them? I'm sure we'll find out soon enough, but we now have more immediate problems, like getting this Hellcat and as many others like it as we can on their merry way to keep those bombers from taking a crap on us.

Ignoring the battle in the skies, we finish loading up the Hellcat, and the pilot cranks up the engine. Smoke puffs off the side before the propeller creates enough thrust to get the fighter rolling.

A moment later, as he taxies into position for his takeoff run, our own AA batteries begin to pound the skies. Everyone is looking up at the flights of Betties. The majority vanish in the heavy escort fire, either exploding in midair or dropping like flaming meteors. But a few are getting through and coming our way.

The *Sargent Bay*'s AA guns are so loud that I begin to get nauseous. But I don't have time to worry about that. There's another Hellcat waiting for ammo, and there's little .50-cal left on deck, probably for no more than a couple of Hellcats.

"Marshall! Martinez!"

It's the master chief.

"Aye sir!" we reply in unison.

"Jesus Christ, men! How in the *hell* are we supposed to fight this damned war without ammunition?"

It's not our job to get the ammo from the hangar deck, but we dare not reply. Excuses ignite this man like high-octane fuel.

"You are the sorriest and dumbest pair of assholes I've ever seen! Did your mamas drop you on your heads when you were babies?"

We, of course, say nothing.

"Follow me below!" he barks.

"Aye Master Chief!"

Rollings grabs a couple of rookies lingering about, looking scared, and the five of us run toward the nearest stairs, by the stern of the ship. The chief never stops screaming at us. The man has got an incredible lung capacity and a never-ending repertoire of insults.

Along the way I spot a Betty at around a thousand feet high coming straight for us. The *Sargent Bay*'s gunners are hammering the sky in front of the Jap bomber, creating a wall of AA fire. For a moment everyone looks up, even the master chief. The lone bomber approaches us beneath a spotted sky. The guns drown the Betty's engines. Its bomb-bay doors swing open.

Rats!

I cringe, hoping for a miracle.

One of our gunners gets lucky. A 5-inch round punches through the left wing's aluminum skin as the light bomber gets within a thousand feet of our stern, hitting the fuel tank, which, lacking self-sealing capability, ignites moments later. Fire erupts across the wing, devouring it, exposing the framework beneath as flames rapidly propagate toward the main fuselage. We call the Betties "Flying Zippos" because of the way they blow up with just a single well-placed round. And this Betty is no exception. The wing collapses, ripping off in the slipstream, sending the bomber into a downward spiral.

It crashes into the sea less than a hundred feet from where I'm standing, totally stupefied. I had seen the face of the Japanese pilot, a leer frozen on his face, just before water swallowed the cockpit. I had locked eyes with him for no more than a second or two. A year in this war and I had not seen the enemy eye to eye until just now.

A creepy feeling inches up my spine.

A huge column of water rises up to the dotted heavens when the Betty's bombs and fuel detonate on impact. The ensuing splash, like a tidal wave, collides against the hull of the carrier, water against metal, clashing in a cloud of foam and mist, splashing over the edge, washing everyone but Rollings across the flight deck. The bastard's just too massive and holds his ground.

"Up!" Rollings shouts, standing ramrod straight while Chico and I stagger to our feet, thoroughly soaked. "Move it, girls! We ain't got time to play in the surf!"

Son of a bitch.

The two rookies look about them, confused, the wide-eyed stare of fear glinting in their eyes. But they obey, getting up, following Rollings, Chico, and me down to the hangar deck, where we scramble to load boxes of .50-cal belts onto a pair of carts.

AA fire gets much worse, rattling the carrier's structure, as well as every bone in my body, its tempo increasing as more bombers get past the escort shield.

"Faster! Faster!" Rollings shouts over the soul-numbing pounding. "My little sister can load up ammo quicker than you girls!"

We move faster. The boxes are damned heavy, and my back and shoulders are screaming bloody murder, but I keep pushing myself.

Sailors are running all around us on the hangar deck, but there's purpose to the apparent madness. The skipper has taken us through enough drills, and everyone's pretty much following their training, save for the usual lost rookie here and there. Of course, the near miss—plus the chief's encouraging words—magnifies the sense of urgency in our movements.

The AA batteries aboard the *Sargent Bay* continue firing away at the heavens, at an enemy I can no longer see while one level below—though my mind keeps superimposing the grinning face of that Japanese pilot. I can see his eyes glinting with anger, with hatred. But if it was anger, why was he smiling at me in the face of death?

And it's at this moment, in the middle of what could turn out to be the worst attack yet on our fleet, that I truly realize that the mysterious Japanese, conquerors of Asia, aren't afraid of dying, of sacrificing themselves, of going up against our mighty fleet. I have seen the determination in the eye of the enemy, and that knowledge has made him seem more threatening.

"Dios mio!" Chico hisses as a nearby explosion rumbles the ship; another Betty missing its bombing run. He grabs his small crucifix and makes the sign of the cross with it.

"Relax, buddy," I find myself saying when Rollings stomps away to scream at a rookie crying beneath a parked Hellcat. "This goes to show how damned desperate the Japs are, coming at us in those flimsy bombers. Just plain suicidal."

The words have the desired effect. Chico relaxes, and so do the other guys. Ironically, I'm the one having a hard time believing my own pep talk. The expression on the face of that Jap pilot has rattled me. I begin to wonder if we can actually beat—

An incredibly loud explosion hammers the ship. In the same instance, an invisible force sends everyone tumbling about the hangar deck like rag dolls. The floor, ceiling, planes, and supporting equipment swap places as I roll out of control, until something hard breaks my momentum, a landing gear. It crashes into my torso, stabbing my ribs. I cringe in pain while clutching my side and squinting, looking around me.

Tongues of fire pulsate within billowing smoke at the other end of the hangar deck, propagating in our direction like an apocalyptic beast, swallowing machinery and men alike. Agonizing screams echo across the cavernous room; men set ablaze by the inferno heading my way.

Shit!

Having learned a while back that incoming fire has the right of way, I stand, ignoring my throbbing torso, quickly looking about me as I make a run for the nearest service platform, which has a direct opening to the sea. I'd rather chance sharks or drowning than burning alive. Those sailors back there weren't screaming for nothing.

Along the way, I spot Chico sprawled on the deck and grab him by the top of his vest, lifting him to his feet.

"Let's go, man!" I shout, watching his legs kicking into action before I release him.

I fail to see anyone else through the thickening haze traveling ahead of the flames, which are almost on top of us as we dash out of the way as fast as our legs will let us.

Jesus, it's hot!

The platform has no guardrail, just a straight drop for about six stories to swells the size of my parents' ranch house.

Chico pauses next to me. "Too high up, man! We ain't making that!" he shouts.

For a moment I also wonder if we'll actually survive the fall. The heat singeing the hair on the back of my head makes up my mind for me. As orange flames threaten to engulf me, I jump while shouting at Chico to do the same. He hesitates, remaining at the edge as I drop out of the way of the gushing hell shooting straight out of the wide opening.

I glance up in midair, watch a fist of crimson flames punching Chico off the ledge. He screams as the fire swallows him.

I hit the water feet first, the impact knocking the wind out of me. Fortunately, my life jacket pulls me back to the surface quickly. I breathe with my mouth open, trying to force air into my lungs.

Blinking rapidly to clear my vision, I spot Chico's head surrounded by his vest floating about a dozen feet away. He isn't moving. I swim faster than I have ever swam, reaching him in seconds.

I fight the sinking feeling that twists my guts. He's unconscious. Most of his hair is burned and his face is the color of charcoal, but at least he's breathing and the vest's keeping his head above water. I kick off my shoes and use my belt to tie his vest to mine.

I begin to look about me, and I'm suddenly in awe at the sight of the *Sargent Bay,* smoke and flames covering the entire flight deck, boiling up to the blue heavens like a colossal bonfire. I can't even see the bridge through the dense haze, but the vessel is listing toward the bow, where the explosion occurred.

I begin to swim away, towing Chico along, rising and falling in the waves, looking about me for other survivors, constantly getting my bearings to keep moving in the right direction—away from the carrier. You don't want to be anywhere near a sinking vessel this size, unless you have a strong desire to be pulled under by it, even with a life vest.

A couple of screaming sailors are jumping overboard near the bow, in flames, dropping to the water like fallen stars. The explosion was too massive and has expanded far too quickly for our emergency procedures to work. Right now it's every man for himself.

My shoulders are hurting, as well as my legs, but I don't let up, kicking and stroking. I need to get away, need to increase the gap. Several minutes later I'm roughly five hundred feet away from the carrier, which continues to float in spite of the fire aboard. The ship is barely hanging in there. Though I doubt anyone on the flight deck or the hangar deck is alive, given the intense fire and smoke, I'm pretty sure there's men trapped below. The carrier is very compartmentalized. If the ship sinks before the fires above can be put out, those men will surely drown.

Shit.

As the realization hits that I have just lost the place I've called home for a year— along with most of its inhabitants—another realization strikes me with the force of a hundred Japanese bombs: there are other vessels on fire. I can see the columns of smoke rising in the distance, amid the shapes of Hellcats, Betties, Zeros, and clouds of AA fire.

Damn. How did things get so bad so quickly? What happened to the Hellcats sent to intercept? How did the Betties get through? Our gunners were nailing them.

I get my answer a moment later, as I pull Chico next to me and check that he's still breathing.

A light engine noise looms behind me, at first like a mere whisper, growing to a light rumble. A Japanese Zero suddenly zooms right over our heads, flying so low that I feel a rush of air from its propeller as it passes me by, its green paint blending in with the surrounding sea. A dark cylindrical shape strapped to its belly gets released into the water just a hundred feet beyond me.

A torpedo.

Sons of bitches!

As the well-camouflaged Zero banks hard right, the torpedo scurries beneath the surface toward the wounded carrier.

I curse out loud at the departing plane, which continues to hug the swells.

The torpedo scores a direct hit just forward of the stern, sealing the carrier's fate in a massive explosion. I shield my eyes as a blinding sheet of orange and yellow-gold surges up to the checkered sky, followed by more smoke. Moments later the *Sargent Bay* starts to capsize.

I clench my teeth in anger, my eyes filling as I see the green Zero flying away. Then, just as sudden, a Hellcat drops right over the Japanese plane like an angry bird of prey, its .50-caliber machine guns alive with fire, the tracers filling the gap between the fighters, turning the Zero into a hunk of twisted metal in seconds.

The Jap plane disappears into the water as the Hellcat resumes its hunt.

But it's too little, too late.

The trick worked brilliantly. While the flight of bombers and its escort of Zeros came at us from a height of a thousand feet—thus *diverting* our attention—a second flight of Zeros, camouflaged to blend in with the sea, came in from below, fooling our radar as well as our gunners, sneaking in close enough to drop their deadly cargoes in the water.

The *Sargent Bay* makes horrendous noises that sound like an out-of-tune tuba as it rolls over, as it bellows the dying sounds of a dying ship, the twin screws flanking its rudder rising up to the sky as the bow sinks first, exposing the gaping hole blown by the last torpedo.

Alone with Chico, riding the waves of this sea so far away from home, I now understand the grin on the face of that Japanese pilot. I understand his snickering expression, which also makes me realize that this will be a very, *very* long war, contrary to what was first advertised to our armed forces. The Japanese are determined to push their line in the sand, to fight back, to reach the coveted Persian oil, to feed their hungry war machine. They are willing to make whatever sacrifice is necessary to win, even if that means sending pilots to their deaths as decoys, using them to draw the full anger of our navy to give a handful of camouflaged Zeros the precious minutes needed to drop their torpedoes in the water.

Anger, frustration, and desperation all collide inside of me as my ship disappears beneath the torrid, bubbling surface of the Arabian Sea, as other vessels burn on the horizon, as the navy I've grown to know and love vanishes before my eyes. Battleships, destroyers, cruisers, and carriers, their distant trails of smoke coiling up to the heavens, are the silent testimonies of just how much we have yet to learn about modern-day warfare, about an enemy that has a big lead on us in the art of waging war. We've gotten too far behind, gotten too complacent, ignored this problem for so long that it now threatens our very existence, our way of life. Catching up will mean far more sacrifice than we have ever imagined. It will mean becoming more dangerous than the enemy itself.

I close my eyes and pray for the souls of the sailors who have just perished, for their families, for our nation, for the rough road ahead.

I silently pray for our world.

6

The East Wind Caper

JAMES REASONER

So I SAY TO her, how does a guy get a lei around here—l-e-i, you get it?—and she socks me! I ask you, is that any way to treat a nice Hawaiian boy?"

The audience laughed and applauded, and Johnny grinned that big toothy grin of his and did a little mock hula and got even more applause. The crowd loved him, all right.

I turned to the bartender and said, "Schlitz." He picked up a tall glass from a row of glasses turned upside down on a towel and drew the beer from the tap. As the bartender put the glass in front of me, up on the stage Johnny said, "Now, I know you folks are anxious to see the real thing, so here they are—the Volcano Room dancers!"

With a swish of grass skirts, the hula girls came onstage and launched into their hip-shaking routine while Johnny went behind the curtain. The girls were the real thing: I had been in Honolulu long enough to know that. But the sailors who made up most of the clientele of the Volcano Room neither knew nor cared how authentic the dances were. The girls were sexy. That was all that mattered to the gobs.

I took my beer and went backstage. The muscle whose job it was to keep the sailors away from the dancers knew me and passed me on without any trouble. I found Johnny in the wings, mopping sweat off his face with a handkerchief. This was December, but it was also the tropics, and it was hot backstage.

"Hi, Nick," Johnny said. He wore a shirt with a bright flower pattern on it and white duck trousers. "How's tricks?"

"Got a job for you," I said.

"Yeah, it's good to see you, too. And I don't want a job. I've got a job."

"Being a comic in a Hotel Street dive like this isn't a job. It's a punishment from God."

"Screw you, Lake. Where else is a guy like me gonna get work, unless I go to Hollywood and try out for the part of Charlie Chan's number four son. And how long are they even gonna keep making those movies if we go to war with the Japs?"

"Charlie Chan's not Japanese."

Johnny put the tips of his index fingers on the folds of his eyes and pushed them up, making their slant even more pronounced. "Evil Celestials allee same, don't you know that?"

Maybe some people thought so, but I didn't. And Johnny Fung was different from all the other Asians I knew. He'd been born in Honolulu to a Chinese father and a Polynesian mother, which wasn't unusual in this polyglot society. But he had decided early in life that he was going to be a vaudeville comic. He listened to all of them on the radio: Benny, Berle, Fred Allen. When he was still a teenager, he finagled one of the local stations, KGMB, to put him on the air. He called himself Aloha Jones. From there he'd been able to get some jobs at places like the Volcano Room, cracking jokes and introducing the band or the dancers. To make ends meet, he drove a cab, and he was one of the best men behind a wheel I'd ever seen. He knew Honolulu as only someone who had grown up here could.

"Knock off the comedy," I told him. "I just need you for tonight, and the job pays twenty bucks."

"How much are you making? A hundred?"

"I wish. Don't worry about my end of it. Are you in or not?"

He jerked a thumb toward the stage, where the hula dancers were still shimmying. "I gotta do another spiel when the girls get done."

I looked at my watch and said, "No problem. It's early yet. I need you to be in position by eight."

"Divorce work?"

"What else?"

Johnny shook his head. "You private peepers."

"You got your nerve, you baggy-pantsed refugee from the Catskills."

"Hey, we can forget about the whole deal—"

"No, no," I told him. "That's all right. I'll just go nurse this beer until the show's done."

"Cheap chiseler," he muttered as he turned away, but I let it pass.

Because to tell the truth, I guess I *was* a cheap chiseler. I left the cops and hung out my own shingle because there wasn't enough money in carrying a badge, little knowing that I was getting into a racket that paid even worse most of the time. But at least I was my own boss now. I answered to nobody but Nick Lake.

But one of these days, there would be a big payoff. I knew it in my bones. Maybe tonight, I told myself as I went back out front and watched the hula girls. Maybe tonight.

THE NAVY captain's name was Worrell, Jerome P. That was the way he introduced himself, anyway, when he came into my office late that afternoon bearing the same tale of woe I'd heard a hundred times before. His little wifey was stepping out on him, and he wanted to find out with who. He wanted all the details, with pictures if possible.

Despite the fact that I needed the money, I tried to talk him out of it. "An ugly divorce won't help your career in the navy, Captain. Things are tense enough these days over at Pearl."

He paced back and forth in front of my scarred desk, spiffy in his white dress uniform. "I can't help it. I have to know who Sue is seeing. I just have to."

There was nothing I could do except shrug and say, "You're the boss, Captain. I'll find out for you. You got a photo of the little woman?"

He put one of their wedding shots on the desk. He'd been an ensign then, all fresh-faced and eager, and Sue Worrell was young and blonde and cute.

"That was five years ago, but Sue hasn't changed much since then. Her hair is a little longer now. That's about the only difference I can think of."

I nodded, put the photo in an envelope and the envelope in my coat pocket. "Fifty bucks will do for a retainer."

He dropped four tens and a pair of fives on the desk. They went in my pocket with the envelope.

"Where do I find her?"

"She's supposed to be going to a movie with a friend of hers tonight, the wife of another officer. But I'm sure she's meeting her lover. She'll take a taxi to the Waikiki Theater and then go on to her rendezvous from there."

Probably in another taxi, I thought. That meant Johnny Fung.

"I'm on it," I told Worrell. "How do I get the report to you?"

"Can you come out to Pearl Harbor in the morning? I'll be on duty at CINCPAC HQ, but I can get away for a few minutes and meet you."

"On Sunday morning?" I tried not to groan. Thinking about the tens and fives in my pocket made it easier. "Okay. But fix it with the guards, will you? Everybody's on edge these days, and I don't want to get shot."

Worrell nodded. "All right. I'll tell them you're my cousin from the States."

Wouldn't want to tell them that I'm a cheap private eye you hired to follow your cheating wife and get some snapshots of her humping her boyfriend, would you, Captain?

I thought it, but I didn't say it.

Before we left the Volcano Room, I gave Johnny the photograph of Captain and Mrs. Worrell. He looked at it, grunted, and said, "Pretty girl."

"Take a good enough look so you'll be able to recognize her. Pick her up at the Waikiki at eight and go wherever she says. I'll be behind you in my car, so be sure you don't lose me. But just in case you do, meet me at the Black Cat so you can tell me where you took her. Got it?"

He nodded. "Sure, I got it. It's nothing fancy, Nick."

"No, but it pays the bills."

Johnny went to get his cab while I sat in my Ford and had a smoke. When I saw him drive past, I started the engine and followed him.

We were ready by seven-forty-five. I hoped Mrs. Worrell hadn't been early. Johnny sat in his cab at the curb, the flag on the meter down. Several sailors approached him, then went away, and I knew he had told them he was waiting for a fare. I was parked on the other side of the street, half a block back, with the window down. I heard the surf hissing on the white sand beach a couple of blocks away.

At five minutes of eight, a nice-looking brunette came along the sidewalk and paused under the brightly lit marquee of the movie theater. She looked around like she was expecting somebody, and a minute later a cab pulled up and a blonde in a blue hat and yellow dress got out. Bingo. Sue Worrell. She spoke to the brunette, who looked worried and a little mad. Probably she was getting tired of covering for Sue. Finally the brunette shrugged and nodded. Sue patted her arm, then turned back to the curb.

Johnny pulled forward and slid his cab to a stop before Sue could even raise her hand. He hopped out, wearing a big grin, and opened the back door for her. Sue got in, Johnny closed the door, slid behind the wheel, and they were off.

So was I.

☆ ☆ ☆

JOHNNY WAS good, timing things so that I wouldn't get caught at any traffic lights behind him. I had the radio on, soft, as I drove, listening to KGMB. Normally the station didn't broadcast at night, but for some reason it was on the air tonight. An announcer talked about the annual Shrine football game, which had been played that afternoon. The University of Hawaii had defeated Willamette by a score of 20-6. I didn't care about football and was glad when the station started playing music. I hummed along with Glenn Miller.

The cab climbed into the hills above Honolulu. There were some ritzy houses up there, along with some more modest neighborhoods. Brake lights flared up ahead. I made a right into a side street, cut my lights and engine, coasted to a stop in the thick shadows of a palm tree. I got out and walked back to the corner to wait.

A minute later the cab swung around and came down the hill toward me. I stepped out where the edge of the headlight wash would catch me. Johnny brought the cab to a stop beside me and said through the open window, "She's up there in a bungalow. There's something weird going on, though, Nick."

"What's weird about cheating? Everybody does it, sooner or later."

"I'm not talking about that—and good Lord, that's a cynical outlook on life."

"What *are* you talking about?"

"About the guy she's cheating with."

"You saw him?"

Johnny shook his head. "No, but I got a gander at his car parked in the drive next to the bungalow. I can't be sure because it was so dark, but I think it had diplomatic plates on it."

"So? There are diplomats all over these islands."

"*Japanese* diplomatic plates."

That was a little strange, all right. Why would some Jap diplomat be carrying on with the wife of a navy officer—

I actually formed that question in my mind, then my eyes got wide and I said, "Oh, shit."

"Where does the lady's husband work, Nick?"

"Navy HQ. For Kimmel, I'll bet."

Johnny scrubbed a hand over his face. "He's a spy. He's gotta be."

"Nice work if you can get it, sleeping with an officer's wife to get military secrets out of her."

"You're not going to bust in there with your camera, are you?"

"I don't see that I have any choice. Espionage doesn't have anything to do with infidelity. Besides, how do we *know* the guy's a spy? Maybe he just likes going to bed with Mrs. Worrell."

Johnny gave me a look. I couldn't see it too well in the shadows, but I knew he wasn't convinced.

"I took the captain's money," I said. "I gotta do it."

"All right, but you're not going in by yourself. Gimme your gun."

I handed him the .38 from my shoulder holster and then got the flash camera out of my car. We started up the hill toward the bungalow. There were no sidewalks, only paths made out of crushed shell, the same as the driveways. Johnny pointed to one of the bungalows without saying anything. The front of the little house was dark, but a small light glowed in the rear.

I paused beside the car in the drive and leaned over to take a look at the plates. Enough moonlight came through the trees for me to see that Johnny was right: the crate had Japanese diplomatic plates on it. I wasn't sure why the government allowed the Japanese embassy in Honolulu to remain open, the way the big shots back in the Land of the Rising Sun were rattling their sabers, but let's face it: FDR didn't ask my opinion on that or anything else. I straightened, gestured toward the back of the bungalow.

We catfooted around to the back door. I reached for the knob, hoping it was unlocked. I could jimmy it if it wasn't, but why make things any more difficult than they had to be?

The knob turned. I started to ease the door open.

That's when a couple of shots blasted somewhere inside the bungalow, making an unholy racket in the warm, quiet night.

☆ ☆ ☆

TWO POSSIBILITIES flashed through my mind. Either Mrs. Worrell had shot the Jap, or the Jap had shot Mrs. Worrell. Both shots had come from the same gun, very close together. Either way, I didn't want any part of it. I turned around as fast as I could and gave Johnny a shove. "Let's get the hell out of here!"

Before we could even take a step, though, a couple of figures loomed up from the thick shrubbery that grew close to the side of the bungalow. "Hold it!" somebody yelled.

I lowered my shoulder and plowed into one of the guys as they tried to block us in. I twisted my body a little as I did so, trying to protect the camera I was holding. Good flash cameras are expensive.

The guy staggered but was able to grab hold of me. I rapped him in the nose with a short right. A couple of feet away, Johnny and the other guy were waltzing around.

The back door slammed open as the guy I was fighting with looped a punch that caught me on the button. I went down, knocked silly for a couple of seconds.

The silliness went away in a hurry. An orange glare split the night as whoever bolted from the house fired twice more. In the flash, I saw the guy who'd punched me flung backward by the bullets. I rolled over, trying to get out of the way of the gunman so he wouldn't shoot me, too.

Unfortunately, I rolled right under his feet and he fell on top of me. Johnny still had my .38, so I used the only weapon I had: I smashed the camera against what I hoped was the guy's head.

Then his knee dug into my groin and I went away for a second into a land of dark red pain. When I came out of it and lifted my head, I caught a glimpse of the guy scrambling to his feet and racing toward the front of the bungalow. A second later, as I tried to push myself to my feet, somebody grabbed my arm, and Johnny said, "Nick! Nick, are you all right?" In front of the bungalow, a motor raced and tires squealed as a car took off.

"I'm okay." In disgust, I dropped what little was left of the busted camera. "What happened to your guy?"

"I got lucky and knocked him out. What about the one who jumped you?"

"The Jap shot him when he came running out."

Even in my addled state, I knew I hadn't been wrestling with a woman. That meant the guy who had come out of the bungalow shooting had to be the Japanese diplomat. Which meant, in turn, that Mrs. Worrell probably was still inside and had been the recipient of those first two shots. I cursed at the thought.

Johnny went to a knee beside the guy who'd been gunned down. He checked for a pulse, then said in a shaky voice, "This guy's dead, Nick."

"See if he's got a wallet on him, so we can find out who he is."

Johnny reached inside the corpse's coat and dug around, came out with a small leather folder instead of a wallet. He opened it, then dropped it like a hot potato as the moonlight reflected off something shiny inside.

I bent over and picked up the folder, held it at an angle so I could read what was written on the badge. It said *Federal Bureau of Investigation.* I said, "Hell, this guy was a Fed!"

"Oh, my God, Nick, what've we got ourselves mixed up in?" Johnny asked. He was almost moaning.

I was pretty upset myself. I closed the folder with the FBI badge in it and stuck it in my hip pocket without thinking. "Gimme my gun," I said. "We got to go inside and take a look around."

"I thought you wanted to get out of here."

"That was before one of J. Edgar's bloodhounds got himself bumped off. I want to know what's going on here. No Federal boy's gonna railroad me for something I didn't do."

I stuck the .38 back in its holster, picked up the ruined camera I had dropped earlier. I didn't want to leave any evidence behind. Somebody would have heard those shots and called the cops by now. Johnny and I had to hurry.

I used my handkerchief to give the doorknob a quick polish, then went inside. The lights were on in a room to the right, spilling into the hallway. I gave the busted camera to Johnny and took out the little revolver again. "Anybody in there?" I called, ready to jump if somebody took a shot at me.

A woman moaned.

I thought about it, hunched my shoulders a couple of times, shook my head. Part of me wanted to take a powder, but part of me wanted to know what had happened here—and why. Besides, if Sue Worrell was in there, sooner or later her husband would be notified that she'd been shot, and then he would most likely tell the cops that I'd been trailing Sue tonight, and I'd be up to my elbows in this mess anyway. Might as well try to get a jump on the trouble, I decided.

I stepped into the doorway, the .38 leveled.

SUE WORRELL was in the bedroom, all right. She had taken off the floppy-brimmed hat she'd been wearing earlier when I saw her at the Waikiki Theater, but she still wore the stylish yellow frock. Only now there were red splashes on the front of her frock, ruining the color.

I hurried across the room, dropped to a knee beside her. She'd been hit once in the left shoulder and once in the midsection. I'm no doctor, didn't know how serious the wounds were. But she had already lost enough blood for that to be worrisome by itself.

"Mrs. Worrell?" I said.

She was alive, her chest rising and falling rapidly. Her eyelids fluttered open, and blue eyes awash in a sea of pain looked up at me. "Agent . . . Agent Carr?" she said in a hoarse whisper.

She was mistaking me for one of the FBI guys. So she knew they'd been hiding in the bushes. Which meant that maybe she'd been working for the FBI, too, I thought. And here her husband had thought she just had the hots for another guy.

"Take it easy," I told her. "Help's on the way."

"East . . . wind . . . ," she said. "Know what it means . . . now . . . east wind . . . rain."

I didn't have a clue what she was talking about.

"Hakashi . . ." She turned her head, and with an effort, moved her hand so that she was reaching under a brown leather ottoman a couple of feet away. She brought out a small black book. "Got this . . . from him . . . east wind . . . saw what it meant . . . he caught me . . . reading it . . . sh-shot me . . ."

She tried to press the book into my hand. I didn't want it, but I couldn't bring myself to argue with her. She was badly wounded, but I thought she might live if she got medical attention in time.

And as I heard the faint, distant whine of a siren climbing into the hills, I knew that attention was on the way.

"Don't worry," I told her. "We'll take care of it." I tucked the book away in my pocket with the FBI badge. I was putting together quite a collection tonight.

Sue Worrell's eyes closed, and she let out a long sigh. Johnny asked, "Is she . . . ?"

She was still breathing. "She's out of it, but she's alive," I said. "But we may not be if we don't get the hell out of here."

I hated leaving her there, but there was nothing else we could do about it. If the cops caught us on the scene, we'd get the blame for everything. We had to stay a couple of jumps ahead of them until I had a chance to figure out what to do.

We went out the back door. The FBI agent Johnny had clouted was still out cold. "You sure your name's not really John L. Sullivan?" I asked him.

"Funny. What are we going to do, Nick?"

"I don't know yet. But we'll do something. Right now we just gotta keep moving."

We hurried down the hill to the side street where we'd left the cars. I started toward my Ford while Johnny got into his taxi. "I'm going home," he said. "I wash my hands of this whole deal."

"You can't do that," I told him, stopping and resting my hands on the sill of the cab's open window. "Somebody might've seen you pick up Mrs. Worrell at the Waikiki. They might've even got your hack number."

He put his face in his hands. "Why do I ever listen to you? I could be back at the Volcano Room right now, watching the girls dance."

I ignored his complaints and said, "Meet me at the Black Cat. That place is so busy nobody will notice us."

"Sure, sure," he muttered. He put the cab in gear and rolled away so fast I had to jerk my hands back from the window.

I hoped he would do like I told him. I had a hunch it would take both of us to sort out this mess.

A police car passed me, lights flashing and siren wailing, as I drove sedately down the hill toward the main part of town, like I didn't have a care in the world.

THE BLACK CAT Café was across the street from the YMCA, which was also the main bus stop in downtown Honolulu. The sailors from Pearl Harbor and the soldiers from Hickam Field and Schofield Barracks usually got off the bus there and stopped in at the Black Cat for a drink before heading for the fleshpots of Hotel Street. So the place was busy, and Johnny and I were inconspicuous as we settled into a booth and ordered coffee.

I took the little book I'd gotten from Sue Worrell out of my pocket and slid it across the table to Johnny. "Take a look at that," I said. "I don't read Jap."

"You're lucky I do." He opened the book and scanned the markings inside. They looked like hen scratchings to me. As Johnny flipped the pages, he leaned forward, his expression growing more intense.

The waitress brought our coffee and set the cups on the table. I said, "Thanks," and dumped cream and sugar in mine. A shot of brandy in it would have tasted even better, but I figured I needed to keep a clear head right now.

"Do you know what this is?" Johnny's voice shook a little as he asked the question.

"No, that's why I gave it to you. I told you, I don't read Jap."

He looked around the crowded room, like he was worried that somebody might be trying to listen in. Hell, considering everything else we had already run across, I suppose it was possible.

"This is the Japanese attack plan," he said at last.

"What Japanese attack plan?"

"The one they're going to use when they bomb Pearl Harbor tomorrow morning."

I looked at him like he was crazy. Sure, the situation was tense, and there were rumblings out of Washington that war might be imminent, but nobody expected the Japanese to hit Pearl Harbor. All the war talk centered around the Philippines, Borneo, and places like that.

But not Pearl Harbor. Not American territory.

Johnny's finger jabbed at some of the chicken scratching in the book. "East wind, rain," he said. "That's the signal for all the Japanese agents here in Hawaii. When they hear it over the short wave in the weather forecast for Tokyo, they know the attack is about to be launched. And according to what this Hakashi guy wrote, the signal came through yesterday. The Jap planes should be here early tomorrow morning. They're going to try to destroy the Pacific Fleet."

And they might do it, too, I thought. The Honolulu papers had mentioned that most of the fleet was anchored at Pearl, including all the battleships. Only the carriers and a few destroyers were out at sea.

Johnny let out a little moan. "What are we gonna do, Nick? We can't sit on this."

I didn't like it, but I knew he was right. Going to the authorities would land us in hot water, but this business was more important now than a second-rate private gumshoe and a would-be Hawaiian comic.

"Look, the FBI must've been suspicious of this guy Hakashi," I said. "That's why they sicced Mrs. Worrell on him. So if we get the book to them, they'll know what to do with it."

"I thought you were worried we might get blamed for those shootings."

I shrugged. "That's a chance we'll have to take." I reached across the table. "Gimme the book. I'll hang on to it for now."

Johnny didn't argue. He handed the book back to me like it was a snake. I put it away, sucked down the last of my coffee, and we left the Black Cat.

I didn't know any of the local FBI agents, but some of my pals from the police department probably would, I decided. I figured we'd go down to headquarters, spill our story, and let the experts take over from there. "We can take my car," I said to Johnny.

But as I stepped up to the door of the Ford where it was parked down the block from the café, somebody came up behind me and jabbed something hard and round into my back. "Please don't move," a voice said in my ear, "or I will shoot you. And right now I would enjoy doing so."

☆ ☆ ☆

IT WAS Hakashi. I turned my head enough to see him from the corner of my eye. What the hell was he doing here? The answer came to me. He had to have hung around and followed Johnny and me from the bungalow in the hills, and the only reason he would have done that was if he'd realized he had lost the package of dynamite in the shape of a little book. We had taken off from there, and Hakashi took a chance that we had what he was after.

Johnny was on the other side of the Ford. He'd been going around to the passenger door when Hakashi stepped up behind me. He looked across the roof of the car and said, "Nick?"

"Everybody just take it easy," I said. "Nobody has to get hurt."

"You have something of mine," Hakashi said. "I want it back."

"Sure, buddy. Just let me reach inside my coat and get it . . ."

I moved my hand, but Hakashi was faster, reaching around me with his free hand to dig inside my coat, just in case I was going for a gun instead of his book. He couldn't do that, though, without taking the gun out of my back, and as soon as the hard pressure of the barrel went away, I twisted, turning toward him and throwing out an elbow. It sank into his gut and knocked him back. My coat tore as his hand pulled away from it.

I was counting on the fact that he wouldn't want to shoot me on the sidewalk of a busy street in downtown Honolulu. I was wrong.

The gun cracked, sending a slug screaming off the hood of my Ford. I looped a punch into Hakashi's jaw and yelled at Johnny, "Get in the car!" As Hakashi staggered, I chopped down on his wrist and knocked the gun loose. A kick of my foot sent it skittering away down the sidewalk.

Then he took me by surprise again by shouting, "Help! Help! Police! I'm being robbed!"

I snarled a curse, jerked the car door open, and dived inside. He was a quick-thinking son of a bitch. Since he was attached to the Japanese embassy, he had diplomatic immunity and a considerable amount of pull with the cops. He could pretend to be the injured party and keep us tied up with questioning all night. All he had to do was stall until early the next morning. But the book would prove who was really the bad guy here—

I slapped at my coat. The book was gone. It must have fallen out when Hakashi tore my coat, I realized. And he was already scrambling after the gun I'd kicked away.

Without the book, we couldn't turn to the cops or the FBI for help. There was only one thing left to do. I kicked the starter and sent the Ford screeching away from the curb. Hakashi must've gotten his hands on the gun again, because the back window shattered as a bullet punched through it. Johnny ducked for the floorboard on the passenger side.

"You hit?" I yelled at him as I floored the gas pedal.

"No, I don't think so. What're we gonna do now, Nick?"

"The only thing we can do," I said as an idea came to me. "It's up to us to save Pearl Harbor, pal."

The radio was still on in the car. The strains of Hawaiian songs floated from the speaker. I said, "What's KGMB doing on the air tonight?" I figured Johnny might know, since he worked at the station part of the time.

"The army requested that Mr. Edwards stay on," Johnny said as he straightened from his crouching position in the passenger seat.

"That usually means there's a flight of planes coming in from the States. They use the signal like a homing beacon."

"I'll bet they're not the only ones." The Japanese bombers and fighters could home in on KGMB's signal just as easily as any Army Air Corps planes could.

"What's that got to do with us saving Pearl Harbor?"

I kept one hand on the wheel as I sent the Ford rocketing around a corner into Kapiolani Street. With the other hand I reached inside my coat. Hakashi had ripped out most of the inner pocket, but the small leather folder containing the FBI badge was still there, even though the book was gone.

My lips pulled back in a grin. "You're about to make the most important broadcast of your life, Johnny. No more Aloha Jones for you. You're the next Edward R. Murrow."

"What? You're crazy, Nick!"

"Hakashi got the book. It'd be our word against his if we went to the cops. Mrs. Worrell got shot up, and that Fed got killed. It's a mess, Johnny. It'd take all night and all day tomorrow to straighten it out. And we don't have that much time."

He ran his fingers through his hair, but at least he didn't start pulling out clumps of it. After a few seconds, he said, "You're right. We have to spread the word, and the radio station's the best way. But how are we going to get on the air?"

I took the folder out of my coat and held it up. "I'm sure your boss would be willing to cooperate with the FBI."

He stared at me and made a noise, but he didn't argue.

KGMB had started out broadcasting from the Royal Hawaiian Hotel in Waikiki, but the station had its own building now at the corner of Kapiolani and Amana. We headed for it as fast as the old jalopy would carry us. It was a little after ten o'clock when we got there.

The guard at the door let us in when I flashed the badge at him. I'd pulled my fedora down and wore the sort of grim, businesslike expression that the Feds favored. The guard recognized Johnny and asked, "What's going on here, Aloha?"

"Mr. Edwards is up in the studio, isn't he?" Johnny said. "I heard him on the air a minute ago."

The guard nodded. "Yeah, he's doing a special edition of *Hawaii Calls.*" He looked at me. "Is the station in trouble?"

"Not at all," I told him. "I'm here to ask your boss to do a special broadcast on behalf of the government."

"Go right on up," the guard said. "Mr. Jones knows the way."

Johnny took me to the elevator. No operator was on duty at this hour, but he knew how to run it. We rose smoothly toward the rooftop broadcasting studio where Webley Edwards, the general manager and star attraction of KGMB, was doing his show.

The place was mostly deserted, which gave it a sort of eerie feel as we hurried along a corridor. Big windows on the sides of the hallway showed darkened recording studios full of equipment that cast odd shadows and looked somehow alive. I shivered a little and told myself I just had the fantods because I knew what was going to happen if Johnny and I didn't manage to stop it.

A small red light was burning over a door ahead of us. Johnny turned in at the last door before that one, and we found ourselves in an engineer's booth. A burly guy wearing a pair of headphones looked up at us, startled, from where he sat at an equipment console with more knobs and dials and buttons than I'd ever seen before.

"Johnny, what are you doing here?" the guy asked.

"We've gotta talk to Mr. Edwards, Bucky."

The engineer waved a hand toward the big window between this cubbyhole and the adjacent studio. On the other side of the glass, a handsome guy, also wearing headphones, sat at a console with a big microphone jutting up in front of his face. He was frowning at us. Hawaiian music played softly out of speakers on the walls.

"He's on the air, Johnny," Bucky said. "You can't disturb him."

I took out the leather folder again and opened it to show the badge. Bucky's eyes got wide, and on the other side of the glass, so did Webley Edwards's.

Edwards threw a switch on his console, and I heard him say, "Let those men in here, Bucky."

Johnny opened a small door into the studio. "I'm sorry to bother you, Mr. Edwards," he said as we went in.

"Who's your friend?" Edwards asked.

"FBI," I said, making my voice curt. "This is an emergency, Mr. Edwards. We have to take over your airwaves."

"They're the public airwaves. We just broadcast over them. A government agent ought to know that."

"Not my area," I said. "Johnny?"

He was sweating again. "Are you sure about this?"

"It's the only way," I said. "Mr. Edwards, if you'll break into the broadcast, then turn the microphone over to Mr. Fung here . . .'"

Edwards looked like he thought we were both crazy, but he couldn't bring himself to argue with the FBI badge. He shrugged and said, "All right. Get ready, Bucky."

A moment later, Bucky nodded from the control room, and Edwards pulled the microphone a little closer to him. The music stopped abruptly.

"This is Webley Edwards. We apologize for interrupting our broadcast, ladies and gentlemen, but we now bring you an important message from the federal government."

Edwards pushed his chair back and waved Johnny toward the microphone. Johnny hesitated, then leaned in and said, "Ladies and gentlemen of Hawaii, and all the ships at sea, this is an urgent announcement. A force of Japanese bombers and fighter planes is now on its way to attack Pearl Harbor and other targets on the island of Oahu early tomorrow morning. Please remain calm but take all necessary precautions to protect yourselves from this unprovoked act of war. I repeat, a Japanese attack force is on its way . . .'"

He ran through the spiel again, and I was proud of him. He sounded calm and sober and utterly believable. I knew that all over the islands, people were hearing the warning, people who might have otherwise died in the bombing but would now have a chance to live through it.

Edwards and Bucky were both staring in horror at Johnny as he spoke. Edwards turned to me and whispered, "Is this true?"

I nodded. "We got it practically from Tojo's mouth."

Johnny started going through the warning announcement a third time. I stepped out into the hall and walked to the end of the corridor, where there was a window. I slid the glass up and leaned out to listen. Air raid sirens shrilled in the distance, and the streets were filled with the honking of car horns. Even this high, I could hear people shouting. Honolulu was already in an uproar.

And yet it wasn't a panic. Oh, there might have been a little hysteria in the air, but by and large, people were reacting with relative calm to the news that they were about to be attacked. They would be ready for whatever came, I told myself. Out at Pearl and Hickam and Schofield, the word would be spreading as well. There was time for the fleet to get up some steam and get out of the harbor before the Jap planes reached it. Of course, they couldn't do that without orders, but with the news sweeping through the island the way it was, the men in charge wouldn't want to take a chance. They'd prepare for an attack then deal with the problems later if it didn't come.

I drew in a deep breath of flower-scented island air, not even thinking for once about what was in this for me.

Of course, it wouldn't hurt my business to be known as the private eye who'd saved Pearl Harbor . . .

I heard a footstep behind me and started to turn around, but then something heavy slammed into me and knocked me backward, through the open window and into empty air.

☆ ☆ ☆

I LET OUT a yell and slapped both hands on the sides of the window, catching myself just before I toppled out and fell to the pavement far below. I caught a glimpse of Hakashi's face, contorted with rage and hate, as he lunged at me again. I got a foot up in time to bury it in his belly. He stumbled backward, doubled over in pain.

A wrench of my arms put me back inside the window. I tackled the Japanese diplomat, knowing that once again he must have followed Johnny and me. He hadn't caught up to us in time to stop us from ruining the attack plan, though.

I hooked a couple of punches into his body, then he threw me off. I rolled across the corridor and came to my feet as he pulled a gun from his coat. Beside me against the wall was a tall, heavy glass ashtray with a bowl full of sand. I snatched it up and tossed it at him, catching his arm just as he pulled the trigger. The shot went wild, screaming past me.

More footsteps pounded in the hall. A harsh voice yelled, "Hold it! Get your hands up!"

Hakashi was in no mood to listen. He swung the pistol toward me again, and I hit the floor. Hakashi fired. More guns blasted in response, and as I looked up from the floor I saw him driven back by the bullets thudding into him. They knocked him against the window and he tumbled out, just as he had tried to make me do. Only instead of catching himself, he dropped from sight, and I knew he was going to make quite a mess when he landed.

Then somebody landed on *me,* and my hands were jerked behind my back and cuffs slapped on my wrists. I didn't care.

From the speaker mounted on the wall, Johnny's voice came as he continued to repeat the warning, and I knew that even if I got tossed behind bars, it didn't matter.

The Japs wouldn't catch us sleeping. We would be waiting for them, instead.

OF COURSE, the Japanese were listening to KGMB, too.

Their planes turned back, breaking off the attack and trying to reach their carriers, but by then our flyboys were chasing them and our battleships were steaming out to confront the Japanese fleet.

They fired the first shots, but we fired the last ones. That battle, north of the Hawaiian Islands on December 7, 1941, wiped out most of the Japanese task force. They had gone into the Philippines and attacked the marines on Wake Island at the same time, but they pulled out of those places fast enough when they found out the first battle of the war had been so disastrous for them. They had plans to attack American, British, and Dutch holdings all across the Pacific, but they had to scrap those ambitions and turn their attention toward defending their homeland.

We weren't in any mood to let them slink off, lick their wounds, and start getting ready for another sneak attack. Six months later, with the U.S. fleet, led by the battleship *Arizona,* poised outside Tokyo Bay, the emperor sued for peace.

Just as well we didn't have to bother very long with the Japanese. We needed everything we had that fall when the Krauts captured London and Hitler started making noises about invading New York next.

But that's another story . . .

As for me, well, the cops and the Feds didn't like the way Johnny and I had cut so many corners, but they couldn't argue with the outcome, and they couldn't throw a couple of genuine heroes in the clink. Johnny went to the mainland and did a guest shot on Jack Benny's radio show, playing a new houseboy, which didn't sit well at all with Rochester. I listened to the program. Pretty funny stuff.

Sue Worrell recovered from her wounds. It turned out she hadn't really had an affair with Hakashi, though not for his lack of trying. But she had strung him along until she found out what the FBI had recruited her to uncover.

Her stiff-necked husband divorced her anyway. What a maroon. But I'm not complaining, because that way I got to take Sue out to dinner when she was back on her feet. So it all worked out okay . . . until that business with the Nazis in London.

I should've known. You save the free world once, they expect you to do it all the time.

7

Path of the Storm

WILLIAM C. DIETZ

Once at the enemy, you should not aspire just to strike him, but to cling after the attack.
—Miyamoto Musashsi, *A Book of Five Rings*

PEARL HARBOR STRIKE FORCE, DECEMBER 5, 1941, 16:00

THE STORM WAS BORN over the warm waters of the Pacific near 12N 135W on November 29 about sixteen hundred miles southwest of Baja California. The depression began to gain strength the following day when it was reported by several merchant ships and one of the U.S. Navy's destroyers.

That's when the storm was named "Gabrielle," after a radioman's girlfriend. It moved west after that, continued to pick up speed, and was upgraded to a tropical storm at 13N 152W, or 470 miles SSE of Hilo.

Meanwhile, hundreds of miles to the north, a long gray wave, just one in what seemed like an endless train of such waves, rose like a miniature mountain then parted as the 27,500-ton *Kongo*-class battle cruiser plowed into its thirty-foot-high face. A welter of white spray exploded away from the ship's bow and flew back toward the stern.

The deck bucked and a two-foot-high wall of seawater sluiced along the side of the ship's superstructure to catch an unwary sailor from behind. The water pushed his feet out from under him, but he managed to grab a stanchion. The garbage can he'd been sent to empty rattled away, bounced off a 13.2-mm gun tub, and tumbled over the side.

A gunner, his body shapeless under a glistening oilskin, shook his finger. "You'd better go after that can or Cookie will have *you* for dinner!"

The sailor replied with a rude gesture, heard laughter by way of a response, and turned into the wind. It plastered his clothing against his body, dragged tears from the corners of his eyes, and doused him with cold salt water. The hatch was only ten meters ahead. It looked like a kilometer.

High above, standing on the wing that extended out from the enclosed bridge, Vice Adm. Chuichi Nagumo stared out to sea. On either side of his battle cruiser, the farthest ships lost against the ever-darkening skies, the rest of his fleet bucked and plunged. Not just *any* fleet, but what might be the most powerful fleet ever assembled. Six carriers, two fast battleships, two heavy cruisers, a light cruiser, and nine destroyers. All supported by eight tankers and supply ships.

Nagumo felt the ship lurch as she dived into another wave, waited for the hull to stabilize, and used the brief interlude to reenter the warmth of the bridge. The interior smelled of wet wool, strong tea, and stale cigarette smoke. His officers stood like statues, feet apart, their eyes on the spray-spattered windscreen.

The helmsman, both hands on the enormous wheel, spun the spokes to the left as a wave loomed off the port bow. The admiral pitched his voice to be heard over the sound of the wind, the creak of highly stressed metal, and bursts of static that leaked from the radio shack just aft of the bridge. "Send for Lieutenant Omato."

A rating scurried toward the hatch. Nothing was said, but every person on the bridge knew what the admiral was thinking. The storm could delay or even abort the all-important attack on Pearl Harbor. An attack that, if successful, would compromise American military power in the Pacific to such an extent that the United States would be forced to accept a negotiated peace while Japan continued to expand.

The deck officers were outwardly impassive as the lowly meteorological officer arrived on the bridge, pushed his glasses higher on his nose, and came to attention. He was nervous, as he had every right to be, and his voice shook. "Sir, you sent for me?"

"Yes," Nagumo replied, well aware that the bridge party was listening. "Have you noticed the weather?"

"Yes sir. I'm the meteorological officer, sir."

Someone sniggered but stopped when the steely eyed XO turned to glare at him.

"Yes," the admiral replied patiently, "that's why I sent for you. Tell me about the weather . . . how much worse is it likely to get?"

Omato struggled to formulate an answer. No mention of the storm had been made in the coded reports received from Japan, and given the need to maintain radio silence, he couldn't ask for help. Not that the Admiralty would necessarily have any relevant information to offer since they had very few resources east of the Hawaiian Islands. A submarine or two perhaps, but they spent a great deal of their time submerged and weren't able to offer more than localized reports. "I'm sorry, sir, I honestly don't know. My guess, and it's only a guess, is that we will encounter the worst part of the storm around 2100 hours tonight."

The admiral stared at the junior officer for what seemed like an hour, actually no more than a few seconds, then nodded his head. "Thank you, Lieutenant. That will be all."

Omato left the bridge, and Nagumo turned to the XO. "Maintain the same speed and heading. Call me if the weather worsens."

The ship's executive officer stood even taller. "Yes sir!" And he held the pose till the admiral had cleared the bridge. That's when he allowed himself to relax slightly and barked at the helmsman. "You heard the admiral! Steady as she goes."

The helmsman didn't blink. "Steady as she goes. Yes sir."

Signal lamps stuttered as darkness closed around the fleet and Nagumo's orders were relayed to the rest of his ships. Dawn remained a long ways off.

THE ISLAND OF OAHU, DECEMBER 5, 1941, 20:15

Most of the Pacific Fleet was in, and the Blue Girl was packed. The voluptuous mermaid occupied the better part of an entire wall and painted the entire room with her blue neon glow. She buzzed softly and seemed to float suspended within a haze of cigarette, cigar, and pipe smoke. Men in crisp white uniforms shouted for more beer, a dance tune blared, and a couple shuffled across the dance floor.

Marine Staff Sgt. Mike Moon eyed the crowd, liked the mix of uniforms, and looked forward to making a deposit in his steadily growing retirement fund. Something the burly noncom thought about more frequently of late. Three months, six days, and roughly twelve hours. That's when he would hit the magic twenty-five-year mark, kiss the crops good-bye, and head home to Montana. He'd buy some land, round up some cattle, and who knew? A wife? Kids? Anything was possible.

Moon's thoughts were interrupted as Corporal McKenzie, otherwise known as "Pockets," bumped the table, slopped some beer out of the pitcher, and sat in the adjoining chair. "I have what you're looking for, Sarge. A nice big deck ape, complete with his own flotilla of beady-eyed swabbies."

"Yeah?" Moon said. "Where?"

"Over there," the little marine answered, gesturing with his beer mug. "Under the weather hoist."

Any number of traditions were observed within the Blue Girl's sacred walls, one of which was to maintain a hoist of signal flags on one of the whitewashed pillars, or "masts," that supported the roof. Like most fleet marines with more than a single hitch under his belt, Moon could read most such signals and knew that a black box on a field of red signified a storm warning. *Two* such flags, one hung over the other, warned of a hurricane. The very thing that accounted for all the rain.

Of more interest, however, was the group of white uniforms gathered around the table directly below the flags. The man Pockets had selected was impossible to miss. His surprisingly small head sat atop a wedge-shaped torso. The carefully tailored shore rig was so tight the sailor had no choice but to keep his Camels stashed in a sock. The petty officer made an aside and his toadies laughed.

Moon took a sip of beer, waited for eye contact, and winked.

The sailor frowned, wondered if his eyes had somehow deceived him, and looked again. There was smoke, lots of it, and maybe that was the problem. No, the marine was blowing him a kiss!

Now, like remoras attached to a shark, the deck ape's entourage sensed his displeasure. One saw the kiss and was quick to comment. "Damn, Briggs, did you see that? The sergeant loves you!"

The petty officer stood with all the dignity of a mountain heaving itself off a plain, handed his hat to the toady on his left, and started across the room. Sailors scattered, someone yelled, "Fight!" and the bartender, a normally jovial sort, known as "Pops," groaned.

The bartender was reaching for the phone when a freckle-covered hand grabbed his wrist. Pockets shook his head. "Don't call the Shore Patrol yet, Pops . . . not unless it's absolutely necessary."

The older man hesitated. "Things cost money."

The corporal pulled a wad out of his pocket, peeled two twenties off the roll, and handed them over. "There you go, Pops, a damage deposit. Okay?"

The money vanished. "Okay, but keep it one-on-one, got it?"

Pockets nodded. "Got it. Semper Fi."

Pops replied, "Semper bullshit," waved the bar rag in a gesture of surrender, and turned to the shelves loaded with booze. Maybe, just maybe, he could pull the expensive stuff down before any chairs started to fly.

Moon sat back in his chair and watched the sailor wind his way across the room. He was a big one all right, with long arms and slightly bowed legs. "Well look what we have here," Briggs said. "A girlie boy all dressed up to look like a marine."

That, or something like it, was the cue Pockets had been waiting for. "Girlie boy?" the corporal objected indignantly. "Have you lost your fucking mind? Staff Sergeant Moon is 100 percent marine. . . . The kind who can kick your worthless deck-swabbing ass from one end of this bar to the other!"

The toadies now stood in a rough semicircle behind the petty officer. One of them, a seaman named Cristo, gave a snort of derision. "Would you like to put some money on that? Say ten bucks?"

"Ten? Hell, I'll put *twenty* on it," Pockets replied hotly. "And that goes for the rest of you mop pushers, too."

"Let's see the color of your money," a lanky torpedoman demanded, and Pockets obliged. One after another, bills were counted off the thick wad and given into the hand of an army sergeant for safekeeping. Had the sailors been less inebriated, and had they been a bit more knowledgeable regarding army insignia, they might have noticed that the seemingly avuncular noncom wore a Corps of Engineers insignia on one shoulder and the crossed cannons of the artillery on the other. But the small discrepancy was missed as was the wink that passed between the soldier and the corporal of marines.

"So," Briggs demanded heavily. "How do you want it, girlie boy? Sitting in a chair? Or up on your feet?"

"Up on my feet," Moon replied easily and rose from the chair. He stood six-two but was sadly out of shape. A pronounced pot hid the top half of his brass belt buckle. He swayed and was forced to grab a chair for support.

"Jeez," one of the sailors said, "look at the bastard! Briggs will lay him out in less than a minute! Hey, you! Put another ten on the bosun for me!" Others echoed the call, and *more* money flowed to the army sergeant, who obligingly tucked it away.

"The dance floor," Moon said thickly, "that's where I'll kick your ass."

Briggs allowed himself to relax. He'd been worried at first, concerned lest the marine turn out to be a genuine challenge, but there was no sign of that. He gestured for Moon to pass. "Lead the way, asshole—assuming you can transport that gut all the way to the other side of the room."

People laughed. Moon staggered and loosened his tie as he walked. It was off by the time he stepped onto the hardwood dance floor and turned to raise his fists.

Briggs expected, no *wanted* a toe-to-toe slugfest where his big knot-shaped fists could inflict the maximum amount of damage on his opponent's face. The face first and foremost, because that's where it hurt, that's where it would show, and that's where it would continue to serve as a flesh-and-blood testimonial to the petty officer's prowess.

The sailor's roundhouse right ran into an unexpected obstacle as Moon grabbed the petty officer's wrist, turned his hip inward, and reached up under his opponent's arm. That's when the NCO grabbed a fistful of jersey, used his hip as a fulcrum, and jerked the sailor off his feet. It was a simple throw, one every marine learned in basic, except Briggs had never been to basic.

Briggs hit hard, gave a roar of outrage, and bounced to his feet. Moon grinned and danced on the balls of his feet. "Had enough?"

Somebody laughed and that more than anything else brought blood to the petty officer's face. He landed a blow this time, a solid left hook, and the sailors hollered for blood as Moon's head snapped back.

But then, as Briggs prepared to follow with his right, something went horribly wrong. A rock-hard fist struck the ridge over his right eye. The heavy Marine Corps ring cut the sailor's skin, and the blood made it difficult to see.

The petty officer was game though, and made no attempt to touch the wound. He stepped forward, launched a quick flurry of blows, and felt at least two hit home. However, much to the deck ape's surprise, the soft gut wasn't as soft as it looked. Hard muscle lay just beneath the fat.

The combatants were about to go after it again when the front door burst open, and the Shore Patrol arrived. There were six of them, the exact number Pockets had suggested over the phone, and their uniforms were wet. Somebody threw a chair. The night-sticks started to rise and fall. The army sergeant, the one with the money, disappeared.

That's when Briggs, still intent on leveling his foe, took one last swing. It was a serious mistake. Moon, still hoping to make it out through the back door, brought a knee up into the petty officer's unprotected crotch.

Briggs was still falling, still screaming, when the baton struck the marine's head. That's when darkness fell. But later, *much* later, he would remember the ride to the brig, the rain, and the way it thundered on the truck's metal roof. The sound had a martial quality, like the drums in the Marine Corps Band, and the rhythm carried Moon away.

PEARL HARBOR STRIKE FORCE, DECEMBER 6, 1941, 07:15

The cabin felt like a cell. Admiral Nagumo had been called out twice during the night—each time with the news that the storm had worsened—a fact made obvious from the wild, almost impossible up and down movements of the ship. A *huge* ship, one of the most seaworthy in his fleet, which raised the obvious question: If the *Kirishima* was hard-pressed to deal with the storm—then what of the smaller ships?

Questions, hopes, and fears swirled like the storm itself as Nagumo stared at his watch, waited for the minutes to tick away, and left his cabin when he always did—at exactly 07:15.

A rating saw Nagumo in the corridor and took strength from his calm, seemingly emotion-free countenance. "He looked the way he always does," he told his shipmates later that day, "like a man with a stick up his ass."

All of the men laughed but still took comfort from the fact that not even the worst of storms could force their admiral to alter his daily routines.

Nagumo sensed something was amiss the moment he stepped onto the bridge.

The ship's captain, Akira Imai, appeared to be in mourning. The rest of them, including the navigator, chief gunnery officer, and fleet liaison officer looked similarly depressed. Nagumo kept his face expressionless. He strode to the windscreen, stared out through the spray-spattered glass, and said a single word: "Report."

The rest of the officers looked at Imai, who, as flag captain, had the responsibility of delivering the news. "Sir, the fleet remains on course . . . but we are running six hours behind schedule. There have been no ship sightings . . . and no suspicious radio traffic."

Imai cleared his throat. "There is some bad news, however. Two of the tankers are missing. The *Kaga* launched a seaplane, which was unable to find them. Perhaps they were blown off course, or suffered mechanical difficulties, but there's another possibility as well."

Nagumo kept his eyes forward. Focused on the point where the gray sky and the gray sea came together. "Go on."

"Lookouts aboard the *Zuikaku* reported a large ball of flame. It lasted for a full half minute."

There was silence on the bridge as the officers allowed their admiral to reach his own conclusions. Nagumo could see the encounter in his mind's eye. Two tankers, both off course, converging until . . . He could imagine metal slicing metal, fuel gushing outward, followed by the fatal spark. Yes, deep down, he knew the oilers were gone. So what to do? Could the fleet continue without them?

Nagumo did the mental math. At fifteen knots the fleet consumed fifty tons of fuel per hour. That equated to twelve hundred tons per day, or a tanker load every eight days. Of course prior to the storm his ships had been steaming at nearly thirty knots. The higher speed would triple fuel consumption to thirty-six hundred tons of fuel per day, or a tanker load every *three* days. Now, with only four tankers left, the Japanese admiral had a twelve-day supply of fuel.

Enough to attack Pearl Harbor and make it partway home. Once freed from the necessity to maintain radio silence he could request that tankers be sent to meet him. Would they be available, however? Especially given the nearly simultaneous assaults on Hong Kong, Singapore, the Philippines, and Thailand? Maybe, maybe not. All depended on the fortunes of war.

He could turn the Strike Force around, thereby abandoning the attack on Pearl Harbor, and shaming himself in the process, or proceed and risk putting his fleet into a vulnerable position on the return voyage. Neither option was especially attractive.

But what if there were a *third* way? A plan so risky, so audacious, that it would be worthy of a Nelson? What if he ordered the fleet to *increase* speed, put the Strike Force back on schedule, and attacked Pearl Harbor. But rather than disengage as planned, what if he put a landing force ashore? A force that could capture the fuel he required? Or, failing that, hold long enough for reinforcements to arrive?

Though not equal to imperial marines or regular army units, his sailors had received basic infantry training while in the Japanese equivalent of boot camp. Could they secure a beachhead? Hold it for up to five days? Maybe, *if* his fighters controlled the air and *if* the landing party had sufficient naval fire support.

Nagumo turned to his staff. A full five minutes had passed since the conclusion of Imai's report, and the officers were beginning to wonder if the admiral would ever speak again. He eyed them one after another. "The attack will go forward. However, rather than withdraw as originally planned, we will land and radio for reinforcements. Are there any questions?"

The officers had dozens of questions, and some doubted the wisdom of such a course, but none had the courage to say so. The matter was settled. The Strike Force would attack, land on American soil, and raise the Japanese flag.

TASK FORCE 8—U.S. PACIFIC FLEET, DECEMBER 7, 1941, 05:30

Hundreds of miles west of Oahu, having just delivered some planes to Wake Island, the ships of Task Force 8, which consisted of the carriers *Enterprise, Lexington,* and their escorts, began the long run to Pearl Harbor.

Squadron leader James T. Lockhart heard the dull rattle of his alarm clock, fumbled for the switch, and turned the device off. Then he yawned, swung his feet out onto the cold decking, and rubbed his eyes. This particular day promised to be like all the others. First, he would brush, shave, and shower. After that he would slip into a flight suit, grab some coffee, and visit the "met" shack. Once equipped with the weather forecast, the pilot would check the flight operation plan, drink *more* coffee, and down a fried egg sandwich. After that it would be time to brief his men regarding the day's training mission, take one hellacious pee, and head for the flight deck. That's where he would meet up with "Pistol Pete" Macklin, the petty officer who served as his gunner, climb into the single-engine Douglas SBD Dauntless, and head for the place he liked best: the wild blue yonder. It would be a good day, no a *great* day, and he would enjoy every single moment of it.

PEARL HARBOR STRIKE FORCE, DECEMBER 7, 1941, 06:00

Dozens of motors coughed then roared as the famous *Z* pendant broke out at the *Akagi*'s masthead. Chocks were pulled, lights flashed, and the deck crew cheered as each fully loaded plane fought its way up into the air. Some scraped the wave tops, a fighter crashed in the ocean, but the rest made it off. The first strike wave consisted of forty-nine Val bombers, forty Kates, and forty-three Zeros for cover.

Commander Mitsuo soon broke through the clouds into bright sunlight. He ran his fingers along the "thousand-stitch" good-luck belt fastened around his waist and turned his bomber toward the south. The target was ninety minutes away.

THE ISLAND OF OAHU, DECEMBER 7, 1941, 07:00

Pilot instructor Julie Lockhart forced herself to keep her hands and feet off the controls as her student kicked the L-2's rudder too far to starboard, brought it back, and paused at the end of the taxiway.

This was the worst part of teaching people to fly, the part where she handed the controls of her precious plane over to some half-baked playboy like Reggie Haines and could do little more than sit there while he manhandled the monoplane out onto the runway.

It was too early to drink, even for Reggie, so Lockhart was fairly confident that her student was sober. He ran the engine up, eyed the instruments, and tested the controls.

Then, with a thumb's-up from Lockhart, the student pilot released the brakes and opened the throttle. The little plane bumped along the ground, through a couple of potholes, gathered speed, and soared into the air.

The Taylorcraft L-2 was light, even with two people aboard, which meant that the Continental 65-horsepower engine had no difficulty pulling them up off the ground. It was noisy though, which served to keep conversation to a minimum.

Reggie might be a heel, but there was no mistaking the look of pure joy that took over his face. It was that, plus the need for fuel, that drove Lockhart to give lessons.

It was a bright sunny day, with miles of emerald green pineapple fields slipping by below, and the Pacific glittering off the starboard wing. Off to port, their tops wreathed in clouds, jagged mountains rose. They were volcanic in origin and made for a dramatic backdrop.

"All right," Lockhart said when the altimeter read four hundred feet, "you got her up here—let's see if you can put her back down."

Reggie didn't like touch-and-go landings, but he knew they were good for him. He put the plane into a wide, gentle turn.

Rogers Field quickly reappeared. It looked very, very small. Still, Lockhart knew it was at least *twice* the length of a carrier's flight deck. Was she good enough to put a dive-bomber down on a spray-slicked deck? The way her father, Comdr. James T. Lockhart, could and did? Yes, Lockhart believed that she was, not that she would ever get the chance to find out.

Reggie, oblivious to his instructor's thoughts, prepared for the final turn. If he could execute some perfect landings, maybe, just maybe, Julie would agree to have dinner with him. A rather agreeable prospect because, in spite of the lengths to which she went to disguise the fact, his instructor was both pretty and well put together.

Then, having fed her a few drinks, well, who knew? It was an amazing world and anything could happen. Especially if you were both wealthy *and* good-looking. Reggie completed the turn, lined up on the runway, and nailed the landing.

THE ISLAND OF OAHU, DECEMBER 7, 1941, 07:49

Comdr. Mitsuo Fuchida guided his bomber around the Kodakan peaks, took a look through his binoculars, and gave the necessary order. "Notify all planes to launch attack."

His radio operator obeyed and the famous letters "To To To" went out to all pilots (the first two letters of *Totsugeki,* or Charge!) and the first wave of torpedo bombers dropped out of the sky.

Moments later, as the lead aircraft swept over Battleship Row, a second prearranged signal was sent: "Tora! Tora! Tora!"

The signal meant that the surprise attack had been successful.

Admiral Nagumo was sipping a cup of tea when the news arrived, and he gave a single nod of approval. That, as the members of his staff knew, was as much praise as any of them were likely to receive.

While the torpedo bombers attacked the battleships, the first group of dive-bombers hit the tightly packed planes at Hickam Field. Explosion after explosion shook the ground as debris flew high into the air, smoke darkened the sky, and army personnel struggled to save what they could.

The sound of church bells blended with the wail of air raid sirens as the battleships *Oklahoma* and *West Virginia* were struck by multiple torpedoes.

The battleship *Arizona*'s forward magazines blew shortly thereafter, and a column of dark red smoke boiled high into the air. More than a thousand American sailors died within a few horrible seconds.

There was some good news, however, in that while the *Maryland,* the *Tennessee,* and the *Nevada* had sustained damage, all remained afloat. Reeling from the impact of the attack, but unwilling to submit, the navy fought back.

The men of the *Nevada* managed to bring her antiaircraft guns into action a little more quickly than some of the battlewagon's sister ships, but at least one of them had no idea what to do. Having just reported aboard, his sea bag still lying at his feet, Seaman Brad Hoskins stood and gaped as the battle raged around him.

Planes appeared, bombs dropped, and a series of explosions marched across Ford Island. Klaxons went off, orders were shouted, and men ran every which way. Though having just graduated from boot camp, Hoskins knew he should go to his battle station, but he hadn't been assigned one yet. That's why he was standing there, wondering what to do, when an ensign paused long enough to point at a nearby gun tub. "See that .50? See those planes? See what you can do."

The officer disappeared after that, and Hoskins, still attired in his white shore rig, climbed up into the gun tub. There had been one opportunity and one opportunity only to fire a .50 during training, and he hoped he remembered how. It took the better part of five long minutes to fumble the ammo locker open, pull the belt into place, crank a round into the spout, and aim the gun at the sky. A quick three-round burst served to confirm that the weapon was operational.

More confident now and determined to make a difference, Hoskins looked out over the battleship's stern. There, coming in from the port side, was a B5N "Kate." The sailor swiveled the pintle-mounted .50 to the right, squeezed the trigger, and watched tracers arc away. That's when he realized that by the time the shells arrived at the point he'd been aiming at, the plane had been there and left. A beginner's mistake. Hoskins used some of the vocabulary he had acquired during his stay in boot camp, made the necessary adjustment, and allowed the next Japanese plane to fly *into* his bullets.

It did, the prop flew apart, and the 1,000-horsepower Nakajima engine screamed loudly as the bomber hit the water, skidded forward, and did a full somersault.

Hoskins wanted to look, wanted to celebrate his victory, but that was when a 1,764-pound torpedo launched by another Kate struck the ship's bow and opened a forty-by-thirty-foot hole. The force of the explosion threw the sailor down. He got up, grabbed the .50, and pressed the trigger. The world was on fire.

THE ISLAND OF OAHU, DECEMBER 7, 1941, 08:05

Like most fleet marines, the soon-to-be-civilian Mike Moon could sleep through lectures on sexual hygiene, jungle downpours, and storms at sea. That being the case, he had little difficulty sleeping through the first minutes of the Japanese attack. "Pockets" McKenzie shook his shoulder.

"Moon! Get up! The Japs are bombing Pearl!"

The marine sat up, groaned as his head started to throb, and took a look around. The holding cell looked exactly as it had the last time he'd been a guest there. Green walls, cream-colored iron bars, and much abused steel furniture. The irregular *thud, thud, thud* of antiaircraft fire brought Moon to his feet.

A generous mix of sailors and marines were crowded around the cell's heavily barred window. Briggs, the petty officer who had been sacrificed to Moon's retirement fund, was not among them. He, it seemed, had been taken to a hospital.

Moon elbowed his way into the crowd, took a look at the thick column of smoke that poured up from the harbor, and turned away. Pockets was waiting. "What do you see?"

"Smoke, Pockets, a whole lot of smoke. Call the guard . . . let's see if we can talk our way out of here."

The corporal nodded obediently. "Sure, Sarge, what then?"

Moon looked surprised. "*Then* we're gonna fight. That's what they pay us for, isn't it?"

McKenzie nodded.

"All right then," Moon finished, "and get me some aspirin, too."

THE ISLAND OF OAHU, DECEMBER 7, 1941, 08:10

The little Taylorcraft L-2 had no radio, and due to the fact that both its occupants were focused on touch-and-go landings, neither of them noticed the Japanese planes until a Mitsubishi A6M2 bounced them from behind.

The only warning that instructor Julie Lockhart had was when two streams of 20-mm shells flew past the L-2's canopy and lost themselves in the cane fields below.

What Lockhart did next was part instinct and part training. Thanks to many hours spent in the cockpit with her father, she understood the importance of altitude. That's why she grabbed the controls and pulled the stick back as far as it would go. Reggie took immediate offense. "Julie, what the hell are you—"

The rest of the student's sentence was lost as the L-2 shook violently and the Zero shot past. "You'd better hold on," Lockhart advised grimly, "because this bastard plans to kill us."

And the Japanese pilot *did* plan to kill them. It was either that or suffer the contempt of his fellow fighter pilots. The fact that he had fired on a civilian plane and missed was more than embarrassing, it was shameful, and there was only one way to set things right.

Lt. Nagamo Shigeyoshi put his fighter into a wide turn. The small plane with the blue fuselage and yellow wings had a head start on him by that time, however, and was headed for the tall jagged mountain range off to the east. The fighter pilot followed.

Lockhart had flown the pass before—and her father had grounded her for it. Now, as the green-clad slopes closed around her, she performed a series of wingovers. Right, left, and right again. Tracers flew past the cabin, and Reggie flinched. "Holy shit . . . have you lost your mind? Land this thing before you get both of us killed!"

Lockhart grimaced as three slugs from the Zero's 7.7-mm nose guns punched holes through the port wing.

Reggie screamed as black volcanic rock raced at his face and passed out as Lockhart jerked on the stick and gave the rudder a decisive kick.

The L-2 entered a steep bank, Shigeyoshi followed, but he knew it was too late. In his eagerness to catch the trainer, the Japanese pilot had opened the throttle just a hair too far. Now, as Shigeyoshi fought the forward momentum generated by the powerful 780-horsepower Mitsubishi engine, the mountain pulled him in.

There was a reddish-orange flash, a boom that echoed off the surrounding slopes, and an avalanche of flaming debris. Chunks of metal were still falling, still shaking the foliage below, when the plane with the bright yellow wings shot out over Kaneohe.

Lockhart pulled a 360 to check her six, realized that the airstrip on the other side of the bay was under attack, and looked for a place to land. The pilot spotted a likely looking field, put the L-2 down, and bumped toward a storage shed. "So, Reggie, it's a good thing you want to fly. The Army Air Corps should have plenty of openings after this."

It was a perfect opening, a chance for the sort of snappy rejoinder that the playboy prided himself on, but Reggie was silent. His head rested against the instrument panel and the back of his khaki jacket was dark with blood. A quick glance confirmed that at least one 20-mm shell had punctured the plane's roof, drilled a hole through his seat, and struck Reggie from behind. Lockhart swore, felt for a pulse, but couldn't find one.

Sunlight glittered off something on the deck. Lockhart released her seat belt to reach it. The pilot knew what the object was even before she brought it up into the light. The flask wore Reggie's initials. Lockhart unscrewed the cap and took a swig. "Sorry, Reggie . . . You were a bastard, but you didn't deserve that."

So saying, the pilot opened the L-2's flimsy door, swung her boots down onto the ground, and walked away. A flight of enemy bombers passed overhead but Lockhart didn't bother to look up. Tears ran down her cheeks. Tears for Reggie, tears for others who would die that day, and tears for herself.

TASK FORCE 8—U.S. PACIFIC FLEET, DECEMBER 7, 1941, 08:40

Comdr. James T. Lockhart had landed and been pushed off to one side when he heard the news. It was delivered by one of the airedales who worked the flight deck. He had wide-set eyes, a pug nose, and looked as serious as any nineteen-year-old could. "Did you hear the announcement, sir? The Japs bombed Pearl Harbor half an hour ago! They sank the *Arizona* and a whole lot of other ships, too."

Lockhart's initial thoughts were for his wife and daughter. Martha would have been getting ready for church, and as for Julie, well, who knew? Still in bed most likely, or out at Rogers Field, tending her plane. He prayed both were safe.

They sent for him after that, and the squadron commander was soon consumed by the demands of his profession. William "Bull"

Halsey was pissed, *very* pissed, and wanted to strike back. Yes, the old man knew he was badly outnumbered, but he didn't give a shit. The moment the task force was within range, both the *Enterprise* and the *Lex* would launch their planes.

THE ISLAND OF OAHU, DECEMBER 7, 1941, 10:30

After a second attack at 08:40, a third air strike swept over Pearl Harbor even as three of Nagumo's destroyers, closely followed by two cruisers and the *Kirishima* herself, turned to port and entered the narrow passageway that led to Pearl Harbor. American shore batteries opened fire but were soon silenced by a well-coordinated air-sea attack.

The antisubmarine nets had been destroyed by the same Japanese minisubs originally assigned to attack the American warships within the harbor itself. Now, with the last potential barrier removed, it was clear sailing for Nagumo and his ships. The lead destroyer opened fire within seconds of entering the harbor proper.

The U.S. destroyer *Monaghan,* already damaged from backing into a burning fuel barge, was among the first to go as 120-mm shells hit her superstructure and a Japanese bomber put a torpedo into the ship's side.

The tender *Curtiss* was attacked next, followed by an ocean-going tug and a destroyer escort.

That's when the Japanese cruisers joined the fray. Their heavy 203-mm guns hit target after target even as their secondary armaments fired at anything moving, including ships, lifeboats, and trucks on the quay.

What already qualified as an unmitigated disaster had been transformed into a scene from hell as Japanese bombs rained down on heretofore undamaged ships and facilities. Three bombs intended for CINCPAC HQ landed to the east and hit the oil storage facility that Nagumo had ordered his pilots to spare. Explosions rocked the harbor, flames consumed the tanks, and precious fuel went up in smoke as the Japanese admiral watched in disgust. Later, assuming there was a later, the guilty pilot would be identified and punished.

Meanwhile, as one of the Japanese cruisers ran aground in the relatively tight quarters of the East Lock, the *Kirishima* made a slight turn to starboard and brought her enormous 14-inch guns to bear on the cruisers moored along the northwest flank of Ford Island.

The *Detroit* and the *Raleigh* had loosed their moorings and were getting under way when the Japanese battle cruiser bore down on them.

The Americans managed to loose one full salvo before the enormous shells, fired from less than two miles away, blew their ships apart.

Having successfully dealt with two of the American cruisers, the Japanese battle cruiser steamed on.

Strangely it was a submarine operating on the surface that put an end to the *Kirishima*'s mad rampage. It fired four fish, three of which struck the warship's side and exploded.

Later, they would talk about how the Japanese admiral stood unflinching as a piece of shrapnel tore the helmsman's head off— and how he remained expressionless as Captain Imai ordered his crew to abandon ship.

Though understrength, thanks to the fact that more than four hundred sailors had been inducted into the landing party, half of the *Kirishima*'s remaining crew were killed or wounded. Among those rescued from the harbor's oily waters was Admiral Nagumo himself. Still soaking wet, he wrote the message to Yamamoto in his own hand and ordered that it be sent.

It read: "Attack successful. Intend to hold Oahu. Request reinforcements." There was more, including the urgent need for fuel, but the first three sentences were most important. Would Yamamoto agree? Time would tell. Nagumo ordered tea.

THE ISLAND OF OAHU, DECEMBER 7, 1941, 10:35

Lt. Comdr. "Westy" Wells paused in front of the cell, waited for someone to bellow "Attention on deck!" and was rewarded by almost instant silence. He was a mustang, one of the rare individuals to work his way up through the ranks, and he was known for his colorful language. "All right, you scumbags," the officer growled, "you've heard the scuttlebutt and I'm here to tell you it's true. Not only did the Japs bomb the shit out of Pearl, but judging from the movement of their ships, the bastards plan to come ashore."

In spite of the fact that the men were supposed to be at attention, there were exclamations of anger and muttered threats. Wells nodded agreeably. "Sucks, don't it? Well, this is your lucky fucking day because somebody has to stall the shitheads while the doggies get organized and the civilians haul ass for the mountains."

Wells ignored the predictable groans and disparaging remarks about the army to wave a sheaf of papers. "Here's the arrest log for the past three days—and here's what I'm going to do with it."

A cheer went up as the naval officer ripped the forms to shreds. The brig rats were still cheering when a disgruntled guard unlocked the door and pulled it open. The officer grinned. "Now, I want the marine NCOs to step forward. The rest of you stand fast."

Moon looked at McKenzie and both men joined the half-dozen marines who made their way to the front of the crowd.

"Excellent," Wells said, "it looks like we have six NCOs. The rest of you will count off by sixes, join the appropriate squad, and file outside to collect your weapons. Any questions? Good. Now get your butts out there and kill some Japs!"

PHILIPPINE SEA, DECEMBER 7, 1941, 10:42

Thousands of miles to the west, on a Japanese aircraft carrier, an excited yeoman entered a compartment to find Adm. Isoroku Yamamoto playing a game of shogi with his staff gunnery officer.

The naval officer accepted the message, read it, and gave a grunt of astonishment. Nagumo had not only attacked Pearl Harbor from the air but entered the harbor with elements of his fleet and planned to hold it! Not the sort of thing he had come to expect from this particular subordinate—but war has strange effects on people.

The request presented something of a dilemma, however, since the battle group that best met Nagumo's requirements was already committed to Wake Island. The special landing force consisted of two light cruisers, four destroyers, and four transports loaded with imperial marines. While *six* tankers was out of the question, four was doable, and could be rerouted from other destinations.

But should he agree? The American stronghold on Wake Island was an important objective. Left intact it would leave the Americans with an important stronghold in the western Pacific. But Yamamoto was not one to dither over decisions, and he made the necessary call. Nagumo was about to hand Japan an even more significant victory than the one he'd been sent to secure and deserved whatever support he needed.

Orders were given, messages were sent, and ships turned toward the east.

Meanwhile, aboard the carrier *Akagi,* where Nagumo had established his flag, a message was delivered.

The admiral waited for the ensign to leave the compartment, double-checked to make sure that he was alone, and opened the envelope with trembling hands. It contained three words: "Request approved. Yamamoto."

Elsewhere, not twenty miles from where Nagumo sat, the message was decoded and rushed to U.S. Adm. Husband E. Kimmel. He read it, read it again, and slammed his fist down on the heavy oak desk. "Get this to Halsey! On the double!"

The Wave literally ran down the hall. Her heels rattled like a machine gun. The message was sent five minutes later.

TASK FORCE 8—U.S. PACIFIC FLEET, DECEMBER 7, 1941, 13:20

Squadron commander Lockhart joined the rest of Halsey's staff as they crowded around the long rectangular plot table. Cigarette and pipe smoke swirled like clouds over the carefully drawn ocean. The small flatbottomed ships looked like toys, but the purpose of the meeting was deadly serious.

Adm. Bill Halsey, sometimes referred to as "Bull" Halsey in the press, was in his prime. Having graduated from the Naval Academy in 1904 and won the Navy Cross during World War I, he was a naval aviator through and through. Never one to mince words, he went straight to the point. "Gentlemen, it turns out that Admiral Nagumo has some pretty sizable balls . . . Not only did the crafty bastard pick exactly the right moment to attack Pearl—it looks like he plans to put troops ashore."

There was a mutual gasp of surprise as the rest of the officers looked at each other in amazement. None had imagined that the Japanese fleet would linger, much less make plans to stay.

"So," Halsey continued, "we've got a problem on our hands, but a *good* problem, if there is such a thing. A reliable source informs me that Nagumo is short of fuel and *that*," the admiral continued, pointing to a small cluster of ships east of Wake Island, "is the relief force sent to bail him out."

Halsey paused to examine the faces around him. "Our job is simple," he said, "cut north, intercept the relief force, and destroy it.

"Then, with that accomplished, the task force will turn east, and engage Nagumo's fleet. Yes, I understand they have more ships than we do, but consider the facts: Nagumo's fleet is low on fuel, his planes have expended most, if not all of their ordnance, and thanks to the expeditionary force he plans to put ashore, the bastard will be short-handed as well. Not only do we have the opportunity to sink his fleet, but we get some measure of revenge as well."

One of the officers called out, "Remember the *Arizona!*" and Lockhart did.

THE ISLAND OF OAHU, DECEMBER 7, 1941, 16:20

Rather than put the naval landing force ashore on a more remote part of the coastline, where its presence would hardly be felt, Nagumo ordered them to land at Waikiki.

Yes, there was some light surf to contend with, but the approach was excellent, with plenty of room for his boats to make their way in side by side, a strategy that would force the Americans to defend a two-mile-long swath of beach. In addition, there were no shore batteries to speak of, no entanglements to slow his forces down, and once ashore the sailors should have little difficulty linking up with their counterparts in Pearl Harbor.

The timing was risky, given how late in the day it was, but Nagumo was adamant. To wait for dawn was to give the Americans a full night in which to organize, redeploy, and prepare for his attack. By striking immediately he hoped to drive them away from the coast and out of Honolulu. Then, with that accomplished, it would be a relatively simple matter to wait for reinforcements.

The key to Nagumo's plan was the fact that Japanese sailors were not only trained for land warfare, but the weapons and other materiel required to equip them were routinely carried aboard his ships.

Broadly speaking, the heavily reinforced landing party consisted of a headquarters group comprised of the commanding officer and approximately 50 support personnel, 8 rifle companies, each consisting of 1 officer, 7 warrant officers, and 292 enlisted men, plus the 500-man heavy-weapons unit. So, with the addition of 300 sailors spread across the communications, engineer, medical, supply, and transportation units, the total force had swollen to more than 3,000 men. The rough equivalent of three battalions . . . or 25 percent of Nagumo's command.

All of which meant next to nothing to the unfortunate Lieutenant Omato, who, in spite of his role as met officer, or perhaps because of it, had the dubious distinction of commanding the eighth rifle company, which, for some mysterious reason, had been assigned to hit the beach *first* and was therefore much more likely to take heavy casualties.

Omato looked left, right, and forward. There were a lot of boats, and he sought to take comfort from that. The more targets the Americans had, the better. The sailors were ranked along both sides of the metal lifeboat and looked strange in their helmets, green uniforms, and canvas leggings.

The met officer ducked involuntarily as what sounded like a freight train roared over his head. The 203-mm shell landed between two innocent-looking five-story hotels and sent a geyser of sand, rock, and lawn furniture high into the air.

More shells followed until explosions rippled the full length of the beach, some of the smaller hotels crumbled, and smoke poured into the sky.

That's when the Zeros began their deadly runs. They arrived one at a time from the south. Their 20-mm wing guns blew divots out of lawns, cut palm trees in two, and shattered dozens of windows. The fighters couldn't remain for long, however, not with the shortage of av gas, and were soon forced to leave.

The sight of the destruction made Omato feel better. *If* the Americans were waiting for him, and *if* they survived the bombardment, they would be frightened and confused. Easy meat for his hearty sailors.

A wave nudged the boat's stern, the helmsman swore as it veered to starboard, and pushed the rudder accordingly. Omato stood tall, pushed his glasses higher onto his nose, and hoped his commanding officer was watching. It seemed that war, when properly conducted, was just as glorious as it was supposed to be.

Meanwhile, on the top floor of a sturdy hotel, Staff Sergeant Moon, Corporal McKenzie, and a squad of "squids" lay huddled on the floor, prayed that the next 203-mm round would land somewhere else, and hoped the Zeros were gone for good.

A sailor named Dudley took a swig from the bottle, one of many "liberated" from the hotel's bar, wiped the opening with his sleeve, and passed it on. "So, Sarge, what's happening out there? Is it time to kill the bastards yet?"

"Not yet," Moon replied, squinting through the binoculars. "But real soon . . . Are you sure you know how to operate that thing?"

The .50-caliber machine gun sat crouched on the floor. The barrel cleared the windowsill by a good three inches with plenty of traverse. Dudley patted the weapon's well-oiled breech. "Are you kidding? Hell, Sarge, we've got plenty of these babies aboard ship. I could fire one in my sleep."

"Glad to hear it," Moon said, "because the bastards are getting close. Hear that?"

Dudley listened. The *crump, crump, crump* of 203-mm shells was farther away from the beach now. "Yup, they're shelling the bars."

"First Pearl and now this," Pockets said darkly. "They deserve to die."

Moon watched the first boat hit the sand, saw the helmsman struggle to keep his boat bow-on, and knew the others were waiting, too. All up and down Waikiki Beach, teams similar to his had been installed in the upper floors of the better-built hotels, concealed in crawlspaces, and hidden in palm-frond-covered pits. When a marine captain named Oliver gave the word, the entire lot would open fire. Those who could, at any rate, realizing that some were dead.

"Hold," Oliver said over his radio, "hold . . . hold . . . *now!*"

Moon gave the necessary order, heard Dudley open fire, and brought the M-1 up to his shoulder. The Japanese sailors, many of whom had been forced to exit their boats in three or even four feet of water, were like ducks in a barrel, especially from fifty feet in the air. The machine guns cut the sailors to shreds while well-aimed carbine fire found officers and noncoms.

The surf turned red with blood, *more* boats arrived, and *more* sailors tumbled out. Pinned at the water's edge and unable to move forward or back, Omato didn't have the foggiest idea of what to do. It was his radio operator, a plucky peasant from a hamlet outside of Sapporo, who told him what was needed. "Tell them to shell those hotels, sir. That's where most of the defensive fire is coming from."

Omato nodded, took the handset, and made the necessary call. Sixty seconds later, like a message from heaven, the first shell fell. It blew the front off a pink hotel, killed seven Americans, and triggered a withdrawal.

"Okay, boys," Oliver said over the radio, "you know what to do. . . . Leave the heavy stuff and pull back."

Moon relayed the order, waited for his team to vacate the hotel suite, and took one last look out the window. One of the Japs, what looked like a naval officer, was getting to his feet. He waved a pistol, yelled something to his men, and charged up the sandy slope.

Moon brought the rifle to his shoulder, aimed for the point where the officer was about to be, and took a deep breath. The weapon seemed to fire itself.

Omato felt a blow to his chest, and fell backward into the sand. The met officer had only one pair of glasses, and he wondered where they were. That's when he noticed the seagull, marveled at the graceful way in which it flew, and rose to ride the wind.

TASK FORCE 8—U.S. PACIFIC FLEET, DECEMBER 8, 1941, 14:00

It was a beautiful day. Only a few fluffy clouds marred the blue perfection of the sky, and the sun warmed the back of Lockhart's neck as the squadron leader peered down through the canopy of his Douglas SBD Dauntless.

"Pistol Pete" Macklin, who sat in the rear and looked out over his twin 7.62-mm guns, had a good view of the American planes, eighty in all, which flew in clusters to his left and right. There were two air groups. One from the *Enterprise* and one off the *Lex*. All could see the Japanese relief force by then and were eager to attack.

In order to coordinate the overall attack and ensure that the high-priority targets were hit, Lockhart had been named mission coordinator—a role that would force him to circle over the battle rather than participate in it. But orders were orders, and these originated from Halsey. The pilot spoke into his mike.

"Angel One to all squadron leaders . . . You know the drill . . . Forget the cruisers and put everything on the transports and oilers. And one more thing . . . drop a few bombs for me. Over."

There were a number of "Rogers," followed by a heartfelt "Tallyho!" as flight after flight of dive-bombers peeled off, lined up on their preassigned targets, and went in for the kill. As they came into range, puffs of black 40-mm antiaircraft fire appeared as if by magic, drifted sideways in the wind, and slowly came apart. Less visible, but just as deadly, was the 25-mm and 40-mm AA fire that slashed the sky.

As Lockhart circled the Japanese relief force, he actually felt sorry for them. With no carrier-borne fighters to protect them and only their AA guns for defense, the warships were sitting ducks. Just like the slobs at Pearl.

The dive-bombers went in one after another. Each plane carried a 1,600-pound bomb under its fuselage and two 325-pound bombs under the wings. Consistent with their orders, the SBDs went after the transports first, quickly scoring hits on two different vessels.

The first ship seemed to sag to port as hundreds of imperial marines struggled to launch boats and rafts. The second broke in half and sank within minutes. Most of her passengers went down with her.

Lockhart's Dauntless rocked back and forth as the wash from an exploding 40-mm shell hit the side of the fuselage. The mission coordinator barely noticed. His eyes were on the oilers, all four of which were making smoke and steaming untouched. "This is Angel One to all squadron leaders . . . Put some bombs on those tankers! Over."

Dozens of aircraft regrouped, swooped down on the oilers, and released their bombs. Others, racks empty, made strafing runs. Their 12.7-mm guns ripped through the ships' relatively unprotected superstructures, silenced their AA batteries, and in at least one case penetrated the deck. There was an explosion, followed by another until the entire tanker had been ripped apart. A patch of burning oil marked the spot where the tanker went down.

The other oilers followed, as did the transports, and two of the destroyers.

Finally, reluctant to let the surviving two cruisers and two destroyers escape, the bombers were ordered home. The relief force had been neutralized and, given the fact that Nagumo's fleet remained to be dealt with, Halsey would need every bomb, shell, and gallon of av gas he could lay his hands on.

Lockhart waited until all of his flock had turned for home, turned away, and followed along behind. Macklin, his fingers still on the triggers, scanned the sky.

THE ISLAND OF OAHU, DECEMBER 8, 1941, 16:30

Having received the news that the relief force had been destroyed, and lacking the time required for an orderly withdrawal, Admiral Nagumo had little choice but to divide his fleet into two separate battle groups. The first, under his command, would meet the American task force and send it to the bottom.

The second, under the command of Captain Imai, would remain off Oahu. He would provide the hard-pressed landing force with air cover and fire support for as long as he could, and then, depending on circumstances, pull them out or, if forced to do so, leave them behind.

Halsey, by contrast, had the easier task, thanks to the fact that the enemy had reduced itself by 50 percent and was short on sleep, ordnance, and fuel.

The stakes remained high, however, because in addition to the lives of his men, Halsey had the people of Hawaii to consider. *If* he failed, *if* he lost, Yamamoto might find a way to provide Nagumo with additional support and everything would be lost.

Initial contact was made not by the fleets themselves, but by their long-distance reconnaissance planes. The scouts, unarmed float-planes for the most part, typically got little more than a glimpse of the enemy ships before being forced to turn and run for their lives.

What happened next could best be described as an out-and-out brawl. The two fleets were still two hundred miles apart when they launched their planes. Both pursued similar strategies by sending bombers after the enemy ships and flights of fighters along to protect them. It wasn't long before Grumman F4F Wildcats were tangling with the Japanese Zeros in an all-out war to control the skies. The fighters turned, rolled, and dived as tracers etched lines between them. Some escaped but others seemed to stagger in midair, trailed thick black smoke, and spun out of control. Parachutes blossomed, or didn't, and planes hit the ocean.

The Japanese gained the upper hand at first, punching a hole through the U.S. fighter cover, and putting six Kates over the American fleet. One after another they rolled and dived. Of the six that attacked, two were destroyed by AA fire and one, for reasons that weren't clear, hit the surface of the ocean. Numbers four, five, and six were successful.

One plane hit the *Lexington*'s flight deck—exploding along with its bombs.

A bomb managed to punch its way through the *Enterprise*'s flight *and* hangar decks prior to exploding on deck four, where it started a fire.

There were shouts of elation from the *Akagi*'s bridge as the news came in, but the joyful noises were almost immediately lost in the rhythmic *crump, crump, crump* of steadily increasing AA fire as Commander Lockhart and his fellow bomber pilots bulled their way through the circling Zeros and came in for the kill.

Perhaps the battle would have lasted longer, perhaps it would have gone differently, had it not been for Lt. Peter Townsend, who managed to get past the Japanese fighters unscathed, release his 1,600-pound bomb at the perfect moment, and pull up out of his dive.

Nagumo, who was standing on the *Akagi*'s small islandlike super-structure at the time, actually saw the deadly cylinder separate from the plane's belly, tumble through the air, and hit the deck below.

There was barely enough time for him to think of his wife, to come to attention, and give thanks for an honorable death.

The ensuing explosion killed Nagumo, the carrier's captain, and most of the bridge crew. It also punched an enormous hole through the flight deck's three-inch steel armor, making it all but impossible for the *Akagi* to retrieve her planes. Some would land on other carriers, but many ditched at sea.

Upon Nagumo's death, command devolved to Capt. Tamon Kurita, who, as commanding officer of the *Kaga,* was more interested in trying to save his command from the results of Nagumo's adventurism than in trying to win what he saw as a nearly impossible victory.

That being the case, Kurita sought to disengage and eventually managed to do so, but only after heavy losses.

Those losses, combined with his controversial decision to abandon Captain Imai, the rest of Battle Group 2, plus the surviving members of the ill-fated landing force, left his reputation in tatters. He committed suicide two months later.

Meanwhile, on Oahu, Sgt. Mike Moon, with Pockets at his side, followed a group of dispirited POWs down a dirt road. Having been delayed at Waikiki, then attacked by elements of the army's Twenty-fourth and Twenty-fifth Infantry Divisions, the Japanese landing force had taken heavy casualties and soon been reduced to little more than groups of scared sailors hiding in cane fields.

"So," Pockets said, "I ran into Sergeant Wilkins over at Battalion HQ."

Moon raised his eyebrows. "And?"

"And I got him to cough up our share of the fight money," McKenzie replied. "All $674 of it."

The noncom nodded. "Good work, Corporal, the Mike Moon retirement fund thanks you as well."

"So, are you gettin' out?"

"What? And leave malcontents such as yourself to run *my* Marine Corps? Besides, there's a war to fight. I wouldn't want to miss the fun."

An army six-by-six rumbled past and left marines and POWs alike choking on the thick dust.

"Good point," Pockets said dryly, "and lord knows the Marine Corps is always a whole lot of fun."

8

The Fourth Scenario

WILLIAM H. HALLAHAN

THE JEEP DROPPED HARMON off at the main administration building. The whole Pearl Harbor Navy Yard spread out before him. Ships in navy gray everywhere he looked, and everywhere seamen and civilian workmen. A plane was taking off from Ford Island Naval Air Station across the loch. To the left, two ships in dry dock. Harmon got a glimpse of a falling shower of welder's sparks. Beyond were rows of towering oil storage units—a reminder that Pearl Harbor served as the navy's major refueling depot for the entire Pacific Ocean.

A soft sea breeze carried the smell of creosote and acetylene, fuel oil, diesel, and fresh paint. The sounds of hammering, riveting, voices, shrill whistles, bosun's pipes. Seabirds crying. From a multitude of mess halls and shipboard mess decks came the odor of the midday meal cooking, the same odor the world over.

Harmon showed the armed marine guard his navy ID and security clearance.

"Follow me."

"Yes sir."

"Don't call me sir, sailor."

Harmon followed him down the steps.

A chief radio operator waited at the bottom.

"Harmon?"

"Yes sir."

"Don't call me sir, Harmon. I'm Chief Tweed. I've been waiting for you. Come on." Harmon followed the chief through the door into a madhouse.

"Harmon," the chief said with the flap of a hand. "Welcome to the Dungeon. This is Station Hypo. Your home away from home. Spread before you is the Fourteenth Naval District's Communications Security Unit. Combat intelligence. You're very lucky. The air conditioning is working today." He sniffed the air as Harmon looked at the scene before him.

Men, crowded together, were moving restlessly back and forth—officers in khaki and enlisted men in whites. They were standing, sitting at desks, talking. Along one wall, radio operators wore headsets. In the center of the room, banks of IBM tabulating machines spewed sheets of perforated printouts. Tables held boxes of punch cards. Sailors fed the cards into the machines; other sailors sat at keypunch machines. The murmuring of voices, the ringing of phones. A strange mélange of odors: coffee, cardboard and ink, cigarettes, cigars, and pipes. And not a single window. Overhead, a pall of blue smoke. The restless, controlled urgency of the stock exchange in a plunging market.

The chief led him to the center of the huge room. On a desk to his right was a name plate: "Thomas H. Dyer, Lt. Commander." On the wall above the desk: "You don't have to be crazy to work here but it helps."

"Okay, Harmon. We have a first-class panic on our hands. Let me tell you what's going on and where you fit in. 'Kay? We do two things here. First, we track most of the ships of the Japanese navy by their radio signals. And second, by copying their messages and decoding them, we find out what they're up to. One radio signal; two purposes. Okay, now—" He pointed over to a group of officers.

"That's Lieutenant Commander Dyer at the desk. He's chief cryptanalyst and a bona fide genius. He's the only man I ever met who can do cryptanalysis for three or four days without sleep. The officer with him is Lieutenant Commander Joseph Finnegan, head of the Japanese translators. They say he can look at a blank sheet of paper and translate it. The man standing by the desk next to Mr.

Dyer is Jasper Holmes. He's professor of mathematics on loan from the University of Hawaii. You'd have to have a Ph.D. to understand what he does, but basically he keeps track of the movement of Japanese fleet units all over the Pacific by doing radio signal analysis. Very smart man. They are looking very worried now because we've lost contact with about thirty key Japanese warships. And that includes the flagship of the Japanese navy, *Yamato*—plus four Japanese carriers and a bunch of others. They've completely disappeared from our radio surveillance, so we don't know where the hell they are. We suspect they're getting ready to attack somewhere. And that means war. So Washington is screaming bloody murder. They want us to find those ships. And they want us to find them now. Understand?"

"I think so."

"You know how we find ships, Harmon?"

"Triangulation?"

"Bull's-eye. When you pick up a radio signal from a Japanese ship, you zero in on it from two separate points. You take the two directional signals, and where they intersect is where the ship is. That's how you can tell the location of the sender and then, as his ship moves, you can track him for direction and speed. That's what that Professor Holmes does—he tries to locate every Japanese ship in the Pacific by radio signals then tracks it. Okay?"

"Okay."

"The problem is, triangulation of radio signals is the only way we have of locating those Japanese warships. If they don't send radio messages, we can't track them. And for the last four or five days, they've buttoned up. Not one signal from them. They're in complete radio silence. No signals, no tracking, no messages to decode. So we don't know where they are or what they're doing. Capisce?"

"Yes."

"Okay. That's only one of the problems the Japanese have given us. Let me tell you about the other. Along that wall are the radio operators. That's where you're going to go. It's taken eighteen years to develop this team, Harmon. Every one of those operators is a specialist in Japanese Morse code. Just like you."

"Katakana."

"Yes, right. Katakana. What we do is listen in on Japanese naval radio circuits, and we copy down every sound they make. Then we turn the messages we copy over to the cryptanalysts, who try to decode them. And they've got a pretty good batting average. When they break the codes, the messages come out in Japanese, which they turn over to the translators, who put them in English so our top brass can read them. Okay? Now, each radio operator is listening to a different Japanese radio circuit. Each circuit has somewhere between ten and twenty radio stations. We're talking about hundreds and hundreds of Japanese radio stations. But only a few circuits are really important. Our operators have gotten so good they can identify many of the Japanese radio operators just by the sound of their 'fists.' You know what I mean?"

"Yes."

"And the king fist belongs to Admiral Yamamoto's chief radio operator onboard the Japanese flagship, *Yamato*. He sounds like he sends with a hammer. We have a nickname for him: Boom Boom. And the first time you hear him sending, you'll understand why. The *Yamato* is the key ship in this puzzle—but Boom Boom hasn't uttered a sound in days. So Harmon—with all those Japanese ships hiding somewhere and with Washington screaming at us—what you're looking at here is complete panic."

He led Harmon over to the radio circuits.

"Now here's the other panic problem. It's bad enough we can't find those ships. But to make matters worse, last Monday, December 1, at midnight, to be exact, without any warning, the Japanese navy changed the call sign for every cotton-picking radio station in the entire Japanese navy. Know how many there are? Thousands. To make things far worse, they shuffled their radio frequencies all over the place. So Japanese Radio Station A, which used to broadcast on radio frequency X, is now broadcasting on frequency Y with a new call sign we don't recognize. And that was only thirty days after they pulled the exact same thing on us. After thirteen years with no changes, they make two thorough call sign changes in a month. So we're sitting here trying to figure out what the new call signs are for each station and who's on what new frequency. As we begin to unscramble the mess, it dawns on us that we haven't heard any radio signals from thirty or forty key ships in the Japanese navy. Not a peep. And these ships are the cream of the Japanese navy. Not only haven't we heard from them. We haven't got the foggiest idea what their new call signs are. So they could be sending messages with their new call signs on a new frequency and we wouldn't know it's them. Capisce?"

"Wow."

"Wow is right, Harmon. So okay. You got the picture? We use Japanese radio signals for two reasons: to tell us where their ships are and what they're saying to each other. With radio silence, everybody in here's got a tight gut right now. We can't rest until we find Boom Boom."

He led Harmon over to another bank of radio receivers. "Now these radiomen are doing a separate operation. They're tuning through all the other frequencies on all the other radio bands, trying to find out if the Japanese navy has opened up a bunch of new radio frequencies. So far we haven't found any."

"Hey, Chief, what do you make of this?" a radio operator called out.

Tweed adjusted his earphones, plugged into a jack, and listened, frowning. "Yeah. We don't know what that is. Jason found the same thing yesterday. What do you think it is?"

"Don't know, Chief. Never heard anything like it before."

"It's not code," Tweed said. "It's not Morse. Maybe it's one of those new teletype frequencies." He shrugged. "As long as it's not Japanese Morse, I don't care. Come on, Harmon."

He led Harmon toward the group of officers who were pointing at a huge map of the Pacific on the wall and talking.

"Okay. That officer in the smoking jacket is the skipper here—Commander Joseph Rochefort. He wears that smoking jacket and slippers whenever that crazy air-conditioning system makes things down here really cold. He's probably busted open more Japanese codes that anyone else in the navy."

Chief Tweed walked up to him. "Sir, this is Harmon."

"Well, welcome aboard, Harmon. We can certainly use you. I understand you speak fluent Japanese."

"Yes sir." Harmon looked at Rochefort's tired eyes and two-day beard.

"Good. That's why you were sent to fleet radio school. That's why you were trained in katakana. You were raised in Japan?"

"Yes sir. My father was in the consulate service in Tokyo."

"You've spoken Japanese since childhood?" Mr. Finnegan asked.

"Yes sir."

Finnegan spoke to him in Japanese and Harmon replied.

"Excellent," said Finnegan. "Tell me, Harmon. Did you play all the Japanese children's games?"

"Japanese children's games. Yes sir."

"And you are an expert at *No.*"

"The Japanese board game? It's my favorite game, sir."

"That's fine. One of the Japanese coding officers we're up against is a master of *No,* and he also loves to put leaders in his encryptions using words from Japanese children's games. He knows that not many Americans are familiar with them. So maybe you'll be able to help us with that."

"Yes sir."

"Well, welcome aboard, Harmon," Rochefort said. "My God, you don't shave yet, do you?"

"No sir."

"I'm feeling old, Harmon. Old. Well, Chief Tweed will take you under his wing but be careful, Harmon, be careful. The chief can drink any man in the entire navy under the table then work without sitting down for thirty-six hours at a stretch. Don't let him teach you the wrong lessons."

Harmon walked back to the chief, who handed him a set of earphones.

"Okay, Harmon. Sit here. Plug your phones into that jack."

Harmon heard the Morse code chattering at high speed and felt his stomach knot.

"You're trained in the Japanese typewriter? Harmon? Right? Japanese typewriter?"

"Ah—yes."

"Okay. Log on. Type the time, GCT—in the left-hand column of the log sheet then your name and security number."

Harmon sat there with the Japanese typewriter in front of him and the earphones on and his mind went blank. It was the first time he had ever touched live radio. There was a roaring in his ears. After months of training he'd completely forgotten the Morse code. He couldn't read a dit. The bleating of the radio signals went whizzing by at ten thousand miles an hour. It might as well have been the squealing of a rusty pulley. Somewhere out in the vastness of the Pacific Ocean, a Japanese navy radio operator was sending a message in terrifying, relentless, unforgivably fast Japanese Morse code. And it was completely incomprehensible to him. His face exploded in cold sweat. In a panic, he began to stand up.

"Sit. Sit. Sit," said the chief, pressing a hand down on his shoulder.

"I—"

"It's okay. Okay. Sit down."

"I—"

"I know, Harmon. It's called 'buck fever.' Relax. You're just sitting in on Maxwell's circuit. And he's got everything under control."

Maxwell, at his left, smirked at him. "Scared the shit out of you, didn't it?"

"Yes!"

"We all went through that. Don't worry. It'll come back. You're only a virgin once."

"Yeah," Harmon said doubtfully. "It'll come back."

What came back was the memory of his deck swab from radio school. He had inscribed on the handle with an indelible pencil the dots and dashes for the entire Morse alphabet so he could refer to it as he swabbed the decks. And as he swabbed he had chanted: Didah is A—dadditditdit's B—dahdidahdit is a C.

And he remembered sitting in the classroom with the earphones on, copying each letter laboriously. And when Chief Chapman breezed into the classroom to the cries: "It's too fast! We can't copy it!" Chapman would plug in his earphones and on the blackboard with a piece of chalk would slowly write each letter then draw whiskers and eyes on it, tapping his toe waiting for the next letter. "Much too slow!" he'd say. Then he'd go over to the code machine and increase the speed and walk out of the classroom with cries of great dismay pelting his back.

Harmon took a deep breath and settled down. At last he recognized a Japanese letter. Then another. But many more went skipping by.

"Settle down, Harmon," Maxwell said. "It'll come to you."

Presently he began to get more and more letters. The Japanese radio operator had a nice fist. Precise. Crisp. Even spacing almost like a code machine. Harmon began to get word groups.

"What we're doing," Maxwell said, talking to Harmon while he was almost absent-mindedly copying those unfairly fast Morse signals, "is trying to link up these new call signs of these Japanese radio stations with the old ones they were using until the other night. I'm pretty sure I recognize this guy's fist, so I know his old call sign and I'm matching it up with his new call sign. If I'm right, I can pretty quickly identify the other twelve call signs he's sending to on this radio circuit."

Later Commander Rochefort came over and leaned down to look at Maxwell's transcription. "Ah! Five-digit units. Flag officer's code. Lot of it. Peachy."

"They've been sending it all morning, sir. They're really jawing back and forth about something."

Rochefort picked up several sheets of the copy and studied them. He looked at Harmon. "We've never been able to break this code," he said and walked away with the papers.

Maxwell commented out loud, "I've been doing this for three years, and I have to tell you something is up. I can feel it. But I'll be damned if I know what it is."

Twenty-seven hours later, with his mind whirling, Harmon came out of the Dungeon into a blinding tropical sunlight and stood in the midst of the teeming, noisy navy yard. He made his way back to the marine gatehouse where he'd hastily left his sea bag—it seemed like a year ago.

The marine on duty called the barracks master-at-arms, who arrived soon after in a jeep.

Gripping the sea bag and hammock by the lashings, Harmon bumped it up on one knee then hauled it up on his shoulder, feeling the great weight with each step. Down the center of his back was fatigue—last-ounce fatigue. All he wanted was a bunk and sleep. Sleep. He dumped the burden into the back of the jeep.

The MAA drove the jeep to a barracks then led Harmon up a flight of steps to the second deck.

"Put the hammock flat on the bedsprings then fold up the sides neat, neat, neat. Hear me? Put the clews, head and foot, on the hammock then spiral the lashing in a whirl in the center. Neat, neat, neat. Hear me? Then slide the hammock mattress inside a mattress cover and put it on the hammock and put your navy blankets folded at the foot like the rest of the bunks here. See? Neat, neat, neat."

"Sure. Just like boot camp."

"No, Harmon, worse than boot camp. Far worse. The officer who does barracks inspection here is the worst ball buster in the history of the United States Navy. I saw him unscrew a light bulb once and put his white gloved finger inside the socket, hunting for dust. For dust, Harmon. Inside a friggin' light bulb socket. And every swabbie here prayed he was going to electrocute himself. So don't run afoul of him, Harmon. Just don't do it. Stow your ditty bag and other gear in that locker. Neat, neat, neat. Got it?"

"Yes—neat, neat, neat."

"Mail call is four o'clock every afternoon." He turned as he parted. "Neat, neat, neat, or die, Harmon."

Harmon waited until the MAA was out of sight and fell face-down on the mattress. He slept without moving for six hours.

HE FELT a poke on his shoulder.

"We figured you died, Harmon," Maxwell said. "We forgot you're one of those ordinary everyday swabbies who actually sleep." Maxwell shook his head at him. "Forget sleep, Harmon. That's for civilians and dead people. You'll get all the sleep you can handle in the grave."

Harmon sat up. "They find you-know-what yet?"

Maxwell leaned forward and whispered. "Admiral Yamamoto telephoned Admiral Kimmel and told him he's hiding them in the Brooklyn Navy Yard. Let's eat."

"I smell apple pie."

"It's chow down on the mess deck, Harmon. Just follow your nose. Let's make it quick. All hell is breaking loose back at the Dungeon, and the chief is yelling for you."

Commander Rochefort stood in front of the wall map. "As nearly as we can calculate, there are at least twenty, maybe thirty capital ships out there hiding from us," he said. He pointed at a list pinned to the wall. "The key piece—Admiral Yamamoto's flagship—the *Yamato*—plus the four carriers—*Akagi, Soryu, Hiryu,* and *Kaga,* maybe two other carriers as well as all these others. They're still in total silence, so we still don't have the vaguest notion where they are and we don't even know their new call signs. If they do start communicating with each other, we won't even recognize them. And that smells to me like a task force moving secretly somewhere."

"How many of the new call signs have we identified?"

"More than half," Chief Tweed said. "Not too bad. Last time it took us a month. But if they pull another switch on us, they'll really put us in the deep six. My men are exhausted. And there's a hell of a lot of radio traffic out there."

"But not one of those new call signs belongs to any of these ships?"

"So far, no sir. Not one."

Rochefort looked at the wall map of the Pacific. "Where the hell can they be?"

It was now Friday, December 5, 1941. Adm. Husband E. Kimmel, commander in chief of the U.S. Pacific Fleet, looked around at the four naval officers sitting at his office conference table. Behind him, through the windows of his office, tied up at the first pier of Pearl Harbor, loomed the vast invincible form of his flagship, BB-38, the battleship *Pennsylvania*.

He handed out copies of two messages then nodded at Capt. Edwin T. Layton, his fleet intelligence officer.

Captain Layton picked up the first of the two messages.

"These are both from Admiral Stark in Washington addressed to Admiral Kimmel," he said and commenced reading: "HIGHLY RELIABLE INFORMATION HAS BEEN RECEIVED THAT CATEGORIC AND URGENT INSTRUCTIONS WERE SENT YESTERDAY TO JAPANESE DIPLOMATIC AND CONSULAR POSTS AT HONG KONG, SINGAPORE, BATAVIA, MANILA, WASHINGTON, AND LONDON TO DESTROY MOST OF THEIR CODES AND CIPHERS AT ONCE AND TO BURN ALL OTHER IMPORTANT CONFIDENTIAL AND SECRET DOCUMENTS."

Layton waited in silence as the others silently reread the words of the message.

Captain Lock, one of Kimmel's advisers, whistled softly.

Layton cleared his throat. "Second message," he said. "CIRCULAR TWENTY FOUR FORTY FOUR FROM TOKYO ONE DECEMBER ORDERED LONDON, HONG KONG, SINGAPORE, AND MANILA TO DESTROY THEIR

CODE MACHINES. BATAVIA MACHINE ALREADY SENT TOKYO DECEMBER SECOND. JAPANESE EMBASSY IN WASHINGTON ALSO DIRECTED DESTROY ALL BUT ONE COPY OF OTHER SYSTEMS, AND ALL SECRET DOCUMENTS. BRITISH ADMIRALTY LONDON TODAY REPORTS JAPANESE EMBASSY THERE HAS COMPLIED WITH MACHINE AND CODE DESTRUCTION."

They finished reading the two messages then sat back and waited.

"Here's another message," Commander Rochefort said. "It's a secret message from Tokyo to the consulate here in Honolulu. It orders the consul, Kita, to burn all his codebooks, burn all secret records of incoming and outgoing telegrams, and burn all other secret documents. When he finished the job he was ordered to wire back the code word *Haruna*. Last night Kita cabled Tokyo from here in Honolulu the single word *Haruna*."

The strain on their faces showed as they stared at him in silence.

"In addition," Rochefort said, "General Marshall in Washington has ordered the American military attaché in the American embassy in Tokyo to destroy all his codes. That's just in case Japan declares war and breaks into our embassy."

"Does that mean what I think it means?"

Commander Rochefort replied, "When a country destroys its code system it's almost a dead certainty that it's just days away from declaring war on somebody."

"Why?"

"Well, if you're just breaking off diplomatic relations with a country, you close your embassies but you still keep open your consulates. You don't burn your codebooks. The diplomats take their codebooks home with them. But if they burn them, it means they expect to invade another country who will immediately break into their embassies and consulates and confiscate their codebooks and code machines and start reading their top-secret mail. What the Japanese are doing is destroying everything, closing down their embassies and consulates and running like hell. And that includes Japanese embassies and consulates in Washington and London and—let's see the list—Manila, Hong Kong, Singapore, and Batavia. It can mean only one thing. War. And right now. Pronto."

"Yes, but where?" Admiral Kimmel asked.

"China coast?" Captain Lock asked. "French Indochina?"

"There's all of Southeast Asia."

"All that rubber and other war materiel. Japan has to make its next move there to get the materials it needs to make war. That's got to be their first move."

"Australia. That's where I'd put my money. They could be running their task force right down to the Solomons and into the Coral Sea."

"Is triangulation the only way to find those ships?" Kimmel asked.

"The only way unless some freighter spots them," Rochefort said.

Lock added: "Home waters. That's my bet. Just like the last two times. The Japanese are making another strike in Asia somewhere."

"What do you mean?"

"The last two times Japan invaded another country," Rochefort said, "they kept their carriers in home waters with complete radio silence—to defend the home islands in case of a counterattack."

Kimmel looked around. "So—couldn't that be the case here? All four carriers anchored in Yokohama Harbor? Comments, anyone?"

Rochefort was frowning at the floor and tapping a foot.

"Say something, someone."

"It doesn't strike me right," Rochefort said. "Something's very wrong. This isn't just their carriers. More than thirty of their key ships are out there somewhere, deliberately hiding from us. I'm not sure 'home waters' explains it this time. Something else is up."

"Something else?" Kimmel looked searchingly at Rochefort. "I need more than that, Commander. A lot more."

"Yes sir."

"Keep at it and bring me something more definitive. Something that will help me make an informed decision."

"Yes sir."

Rochefort watched the others packing their papers.

"Joe," Layton murmured to Rochefort. "Somehow, someway, you've got to find those carriers."

It was late Friday, December 5.

ROCHEFORT STOOD near his desk with a coffee cup in his hand, looking at the wall map of the Pacific.

"Japanese naval radio traffic is at an all-time high," Professor Holmes observed. "So we've managed to pinpoint the location of a number of their ships."

"But not the carriers."

"None of the twenty or thirty capital ships we're looking for. Not a peep." Holmes frowned at the map. "God. You could hide a thousand ships out there."

"And they could hit us almost anywhere," Commander Dyer said.

Rochefort turned the equation around. "I'll give you eight-to-five those carriers are not in their home waters."

"Then where the hell are they?"

"Assume the worst," Rochefort said.

"What's the worst?"

"I'm afraid to say."

AT 14:00, Chief Tweed pulled Harmon off the radio circuit and put him on the frequency search. "Not one," he said. "We haven't turned up one new frequency. I'm very suspicious. You've got fresh ears. See what you can find."

Tuning, tuning, tuning, listening for katakana. Crisscrossing the bands, periodically Harmon would pick up a station broadcasting those strange signals. Dah dah dah dah. For some reason he was intrigued by them. He felt he knew something about them but couldn't remember what it was. He didn't believe they were high-speed radio teletype signals.

Maxwell looked over at him. "Where did you hide those carriers, Harmon? 'Fess up."

Lieutenant Commander Dyer brought the civilian, wearing a business suit and necktie, over to Chief Tweed.

"Chief. This is Mr. Masters of the Hawaiian FBI, and he has an unusual problem. Commander Rochefort thinks you're just the man to help him."

"Hello, sir."

"Listen, I'm tracking this guy—a Japanese consular official in Honolulu. I know he's a spy, but before I cuff him, I need to know what he knows and who he's sending it to."

"Yes?"

"Well, my problem is I can't figure out what he's doing. He stands on the beach, looking out to sea with binoculars then he makes funny signs with his hands. I never saw anything like it before. It's not semaphore. I mean, he's not using flags or a flashing light. I'm here because I figure you people might know what he's doing."

"Like what? Show me."

"Like he's shaking his fist at the world. Then he holds up his hand like this—"

"You mean like 'Stop'?"

"Yeah. Like 'Stop.'"

"Okay."

"You know what it is?"

"Think so, sir. Sounds like 'palm fist.'"

"What's palm fist?"

"It's Morse code done with hand signals. The airedales use it."

"Who are the airedales?"

"Carrier-based aviation radio operators. When they fly in squadrons and want to maintain radio silence, they communicate with each other visually, with hand signals doing Morse code. Did you see this guy doing this? Like so?" Chief Tweed held up a fist and pumped it three times then held up a palm.

"That's it. Just like that."

"I just gave you three dits and a dah. The letter *V*."

"Oh. Like Beethoven's Fifth Symphony. Dit dit dit dahhhhh. The V for victory."

"Who's he communicating with?" the chief asked.

"Someone offshore. In a dinghy."

"Dinghy? How often does he do it?"

"Once or twice a week. Always about an hour before dusk."

"When is he going to do it next?"

"It should be today. This afternoon."

"I'd better go take a look. Okay?"

"You bet."

As he left, Chief Tweed picked up a pair of navy binoculars.

He returned to the Dungeon at 17:50.

"How'd you make out?" Dyer asked.

"He's signaling a guy in a boat, sir. All alone out on the water. My bet is he's off a Japanese submarine."

"What happened?"

"Good thing I went. As I thought, they were signaling katakana in palm fist. Our guy on the beach signals the one on the water. Very simple message: No CVs. Eight BBs."

"No carriers and eight battleships? Are there that many out there? Those spies know more about us than we do."

"Then the other guy on the water signs back."

"What did he say?"

"Where are the American carriers?"

Harmon was feeling fagged out. He'd been tuning and retuning for several hours. No one seemed to ever leave the Dungeon. Even when the radio operators were relieved by the next watch, they'd sign out on the log sheet, turn over the earphones to the next radio operator then, instead of running for the mess hall or the sack or liberty in Honolulu, they'd stand around with coffee and cigarettes, jawing, talking about call signs, code groups, and frequencies. They seemed to hate to leave.

His mind was drifting as he tuned. He ached for more sleep. But he found himself doing the same thing as the others. Sleepy as he was, he'd stand around, off duty, jawing, trying to remember where or when he'd heard a certain five-letter code group.

And no one was more amazing than Commander Rochefort. He could remember a strange code group from weeks before—which would send someone hustling through boxes of IBM punch cards, sorted by date and radio circuit, then rooting through the cards individually. Then: "Gotcha! Here it is, sir."

The Japanese navy used a number of codes from the simplest—designated PA-K2—to routine naval codes to the most difficult—the flag officer's code. There were also diplomatic codes and other codes used by the Japanese army. Station Hypo could read parts of some of these naval codes, but very little of the flag officer's code.

"Half an hour more, Harmon," Chief Tweed said to him. "Then I'll move you to one of the radio circuits. It's a ball breaker, isn't it?"

That's when Harmon heard the bleating. Strange signals. Like auditory pinpoints. Like an endless stream of visual pin lights. Dit-ditditditidit. He listened for a few moments, then retuned the frequency and retuned again, but it was unnecessary. The signal was almost an S-5 already with practically no static. Loud and clear and incomprehensible.

On an impulse, he turned on the radio receiver next to his, waited for it to warm up then tuned it to the other strange signal. Then he tried an experiment. He put two sets of earphones on his head, one tuned to each of the strange frequencies. Now he was more sure. He was getting a stream of irregular dits on one frequency and a stream of irregular dahs on the other. Yet he still couldn't read anything. He needed both signals to come through one set of earphones. Then he got up and from the shelf pulled down two small speakers and plugged them in, one in each receiver. Chief Tweed stood looking at him quizzically. Harmon now tried to balance the volume. He pushed the two speakers together. "Aha!"

"What've you got, Harmon?"

"Don't know. I'm getting dits on one frequency and dahs on the other. I'm trying to put them together."

"Mother of God!" said Tweed. "That's it! Wait! Wait! Wait! Maxwell! Maxwell! Quick! Quick! Quick! I want—now wait. How the hell am I going to do this? I want to splice both frequencies into one set of earphones. Maxwell, call those radio tech guys. In fact, call Chief Parsons. Tell him I have an urgent job for him. On the double."

The sound from the two speakers was carrying across the room and soon Lieutenant Commander Dyer came over.

"Hey," Maxwell shouted. "I know who that is! That's Boom Boom!"

Lieutenant Commander Finnegan came stepping quickly. "What's going on?"

"Harmon, you get an extra piece of pie at mess tonight," Tweed said. He turned to Finnegan. "Harmon's found Boom Boom, sir."

Now Commander Rochefort came over. And stood slowly shaking his head. "Clever," he said, "damn clever. Split frequencies. Harmon, I'm going to buy you a whole goddamn pie factory. Chief—"

"Yes. I know, sir. Seattle. Triangulate. I'm going to see Professor Holmes right now, sir."

"I'm right here," the professor said. "I need the number of those two frequencies. Now maybe we've at least found the *Yamato*."

Other radio operators gathered round and thumped Harmon softly with their fists.

"You done good, boy."

The three other radio watches were roused, and pretty soon Station Hypo was three and four deep in radio operators, cryptanalysts, translators, IBM keypunch operators—all talking, all skimming pages of previous transcripts, while a group of radio technicians were busy with pliers and friction tape and earphones. Chief Parsons himself had the back off two receivers and was busy rewiring them.

Everyone seemed to be smiling at Harmon.

"Four oh, mate, four oh."

"Hey Harmon, I'm going to take you into Honolulu into Lousy Lui's and buy you a beer two feet high."

"Beer? Harmon, I'm going to buy you a goddamn brewery."

When the headphones were ready, Parsons held them out to Harmon. "Start copying, son."

When he sat down at the circuit, everybody applauded. Beside his typewriter they'd put four cups of coffee and eleven packs of cigarets. "Sic 'em, mate."

Harmon looked up at Commander Rochefort. "I don't know what's going on here, sir. Boom Boom's not following any protocol. He's not waiting for go-aheads. None of the messages have priority designations, no source, no addressee. Just date and time groups and word counts between bits. And he's not getting any response. He's just sending one message after another without a break. It's just like Fox out of Washington."

"Don't like the sound of that," the commander said.

Chief Tweed approached Rochefort with a radio message. "From Seattle, sir," he said. "They finished the triangulation."

"And—"

"Bad news, sir. Boom Boom's not aboard ship. He's broadcasting from dry land right in Yokohama."

"Then who's he sending to?" Commander Finnegan demanded.

Rochefort nodded knowingly. "To his carrier. I see it now. Boom Boom is on dry land sending to his carrier out at sea. They outfoxed us. There's a task force out there, and Tokyo is communicating one way with them."

"I wonder how many others are on dry land."

"I bet they're all on dry land."

"You know what they've done? They've created a phantom navy, sending fake messages on the regular frequencies, while Boom Boom is feeding the real stuff to the real ships somewhere out at sea on these two new frequencies."

"Imagine all the stuff he's slipped by us. A whole week. While we're busting our humps decoding fake messages. He must be laughing his ass off."

"That means those missing ships have been sailing somewhere for a week without our knowing it."

"At least a week. More like ten days. In total silence."

Rochefort walked across the room toward the wall maps, calculating in his head. "If they sortied from a Japanese port on November 24—" He looked at his map. "Speed in knots times hours equals distance, right?" He reached a yardstick up on the wall map. "Huh."

"What?"

"They could be on their way to Pearl—"

"Pearl!" They gathered around the map. "Pearl Harbor?"

"And if so, by now they'd be less than two days' sail from us. There's where they'd be—right there—which would get them here sometime, let's see. Sunday morning."

"December 7."

"Yes. December 7."

They stood staring at the map.

"But a task force that large—with three or four carriers—someone should have spotted it. There are freighters from all over the world out there."

"But not if they're coming by the northern route. It's all endless storms up there. No freighter in his right mind would go that far north in the Pacific. The Japanese could have a fifty-ship task force crossing the Pacific up there, and nobody would see them except some Eskimos in kayaks."

With the yardstick he pointed a route from Japan heading north then east for Alaska then dropping suddenly south toward Hawaii. "They'd be right there about now. Just around the corner."

The three officers looked at each other. One exhaled sharply.

Rochefort went back to see Admiral Kimmel. "We can't rule out the possibility that a task force is on its way to attack Pearl Harbor."

"I keep querying Washington for direction," the admiral said. "I'd like a definitive statement, but all I get is platitudes. No damned help at all. Do you get the feeling that we're being kept in the dark?"

"Let me call the roll here, Admiral," Rochefort said. "First, there are dozens of their ships we can't account for. Second, they went to great lengths to fool us—putting their radio operators on dry land to send fake messages, creating a phantom navy. And at the same time they could have a strike force steaming somewhere in absolute silence. Third point—they've burned their codebooks in the embassies and the consulates around the world—in Hong Kong, Singapore, Batavia, Manila, Washington, and London, so we're sure they're just hours away from declaring war on someone. If it's us, what would they attack first?"

Kimmel nodded. "Sure. Pearl Harbor."

"One of the key questions they've asked their spies here in Honolulu is 'Where are the American carriers?' Why? What do they want to know that for? Because if they do attack Pearl Harbor, they've got to be sure to knock out our carriers so we can't counterattack theirs."

Kimmel nodded silently. "We don't have a single carrier in Pearl Harbor."

"Seems to me we're asking the wrong questions," Rochefort suggested.

"What do you mean?"

"We should be asking ourselves, what should we do if they're going to attack Pearl? Should we stay in port or should we slip all our ships out to sea?"

Kimmel nodded and drummed his fingers on his desk. "Okay. We can at least do that." He stood up. "Let me take care of that. I've got some homework to do."

LATE THAT afternoon, Admiral Kimmel summoned Commander Rochefort.

"I've got three scenarios on paper here," he said, drawing a sheaf of papers from a manila folder. He pushed a copy over to Rochefort.

"Scenario one: We do nothing. Let our ships sit right where they are. There are 86 ships in Pearl Harbor night now. Best estimates, the Japanese could hit us with 250 to 300 planes, and we could lose as many as 20 or 30 ships, including 6 battleships, a number of cruisers, light and heavy, more than a dozen destroyers. And up to 2,000 personnel. Our navy would be crippled and our navy yard would be in ruins. Both Hickam Field and the naval air station would also be destroyed. So we'd lose most of our planes to boot. Okay?"

"Yes sir."

"Scenario two: We send all our ships to sea. Now we have two different versions of what would happen if we did that. One predicts horrendous losses, practically our entire fleet and the loss of twenty thousand sailors. But most of my people disagree with that. They prepared a third scenario. They say, without the tremendous advantage of surprise, the Japanese planes would have a much tougher time of it. They would be running low on gasoline so they would have time for two or three passes at the most. If we send all our ships out of port, and disperse them properly, almost all of them will survive. With our planes swarming from Honolulu—navy and army from the naval air base and Hickam—we could fend off their attack. They won't have the tremendous advantage of surprise, and they will pay with the loss of many planes."

Kimmel let Rochefort study the three scenarios.

"Furthermore, Commander, my people agree with your time estimate. The Japanese planes could attack us as early as Sunday morning, December 7."

Rochefort nodded. "Tomorrow morning."

"Yes. Tomorrow morning."

"Perfect day to hit a God-fearing Christian navy. Everyone is either in church or sleeping off a hangover. Nobody on duty."

"I would certainly like some definitive evidence that they're coming here."

"Can't guarantee that, sir, but neither can I guarantee that they're not."

It was now late in the afternoon of Saturday, December 6.

Several hours later, Rochefort asked for an urgent meeting with Kimmel.

"I think I have the clincher, Admiral."

"Ah! You've found the carriers?"

"No sir. I have something else. This message was sent by cable by a Japanese consul officer here in Honolulu to Tokyo. Since they've burned their codebooks he had to use an old and primitive code: PA-K2. I could break it in my sleep. It's dated 6 P.M. Saturday, December 6, 1941—an hour ago. It's very short."

"Read it."

"ON THE EVENING OF THE FIFTH, THE BATTLESHIP *WYOMING* AND ONE SWEEPER ENTERED PORT. SHIPS AT ANCHOR ON THE SIXTH WERE:

NINE BATTLESHIPS, THREE MINESWEEPERS, FOUR LIGHT CRUISERS, TWO DESTROYERS. HEAVY CRUISERS AND CARRIERS HAVE ALL LEFT."

"Did you say *Wyoming?*"

"We think he mistook *Utah* for *Wyoming*. Otherwise his figure on the battleships is correct."

"But he's wrong about the cruisers. They haven't left. Look for yourself. I just checked the list. There are six light and two heavy cruisers out there plus twenty-nine destroyers, four minesweepers, eight minelayers, and three seaplane tenders."

"The next point he got right."

"What's that?"

"The second point he makes is, it appears that no air reconnaissance is being conducted by the fleet air arm."

Kimmel bristled.

"One last piece, Admiral."

"What is it?"

"This is a message Boom Boom—that is, Tokyo—sent to its carrier task force. We just decoded it."

"What does it say?"

"It says, 'There are no barrage balloons aloft at Pearl Harbor. And there are no torpedo nets protecting the battleships.'"

"My God."

Rochefort stood watching Kimmel staring out of his window at his flagship: the *Pennsylvania*.

"I can't stay in port and I can't sail out," the admiral said. "Damned if I do and damned if I don't. The nearest American aircraft carrier is days away." He seemed very much alone.

Rochefort waited. Which way, he wondered, was Kimmel going to go?

After chow Saturday night, Rogers and Maxwell took Harmon on his first liberty in Honolulu to buy him a special present. Christmas was coming and a few impatient shopkeepers had put up the first tentative Christmas decorations. As the bus moved, the thronged streets revealed Honolulu as an ethnic salad of the Pacific—a half million people: Chinese, Filipino, Korean, Hawaiian, and Caucasian with Japanese preponderating.

The Royal Hawaiian Hotel, four stories high with festive awnings and lit up like a cruise ship, was the first pink hotel

Harmon had ever seen. Next to it was the Outrigger Canoe Club, and adjacent were two other famous hotels, the Moana and the Halekulani. All of them spread along the edge of Waikiki Beach.

Honolulu had a huge Chinatown and also a separate red-light district. But most servicemen went first to the Army-Navy YMCA on Hotel Street.

Rogers and Maxwell took Harmon to Lousy Lui's bar at the end of Waikiki, which was filled with white hats. And there, over a beer, Maxwell looked at Harmon.

"Here's to you, mate, for finding Boom Boom." He and Rogers saluted Harmon.

"What do you think, Rogers?" Maxwell asked. "Shall we take Baby Face here to see Goldie?"

"Oh, good choice. Let's go see Goldie."

So they went into the red-light district to a cathouse, and when they got seated they ordered three beers.

Maxwell waved at an older prostitute—a Japanese woman with two gold teeth.

"'Allo, sailu boys."

"We brought you a little spring lamb, Goldie," Maxwell said.

"Nice." She stroked Harmon's cheek. "Like a peach. Nice boy. I going to be very good to you, nice boy. She pushed her fingers through his pale blond hair. "You name is Sleem," she said.

"Slim?"

"All Amelican sailu name Sleem. Listen, nice sailor boy, I think you alllll ready for a good time. You come with Goldie and I put you in heaven."

She laughed heartily with them.

"Hey, Harmon, you'll be in good hands," Maxwell said, "Goldie has single-handedly deflowered the entire Pacific Fleet."

"She's got notches on her bedboard," Rogers said. "Thousands of them."

"All by herself. And nobody helped her."

"Just don't give him a dose, Goldie."

"No dose here, sailu. Nice clean girls. Japanese and Haoles and Chinese. All very nice and clean. Navy doctor check us out all the time. You come, Sleem. We have a good time."

The shore patrol came up the steps—two of them, their heads rising up the stairwell as they climbed—then two more—then six. Behind them came six marine MPs.

One of the navy shore patrol raked his nightstick along the stair railings.

"Okay! Now hear this! Now hear this! All shore leave canceled. All liberty canceled. All naval and marine personnel are to report back to your duty station on the double."

The SPs in their white leggings and nightsticks on their webbed belts and black-and-yellow armbands began to go through the crowd, pointing at the stairs with their nightsticks. "All you swabbies, move your asses. Back to base on the double. All Liberties canceled. Haul ass, sailor."

"I've just come off a month's sea duty," said one.

"Stop. You're breaking my heart."

"I hate those Japs, screwing up my liberty."

"Tell it to the chaplain."

The SPs went up to the next floor and pounded on the bedroom doors with their nightsticks.

The three radiomen snagged a cab. Four others piled in with them, including a couple of ensigns from the battleship *Arizona*. They all hung on while the cab went racing back to base with its horn blowing.

A flowing river of white hats was streaming through the gates. The marines at the gates weren't even making a pretense of checking liberty cards. The gates stood wide open, and they waved all personnel to enter quickstep.

Maxwell jumped out of the cab even before it was fully stopped and made a dash for the radio shack. Behind him, Harmon and Rogers followed, running. Maxwell drew up short as he looked out over the bay.

"Holy cats," he said. "The whole friggin' fleet is leaving port."

The racket inside the Dungeon was thundering. Everyone was there; all the officers and enlisted men from all four watches, all talking. It was going to be a long, long night. But there still wasn't a sound from the missing Japanese ships.

"I wonder if this is a false alarm," Maxwell said.

The next morning at 07:55 the first wave of Japanese planes came calling. They found the navy yard almost empty and the sea around Honolulu alive with ships filling the sky with a nonstop anti-aircraft barrage. With no ship targets in Pearl Harbor, the planes attacked the navy's oil tank farms, and soon great writhing balls of fire roared into the air, accompanied by lofty columns of boiling black smoke. In minutes most of the navy's oil was burning.

The second wave of Japanese planes came an hour later. They turned their attention to the ships at sea. The skies were alive with airplanes. The older, slower American planes were no match for the Zeros, but they did distract them and soon there were planes from both sides falling from the skies.

Hawaii waited for the third wave. It never came. American reconnaissance planes reported that the Japanese fleet was sailing away westward.

By noon the navy called for a stand-down from general quarters.

The attack was over. And only a few ships were lost. Crew members were exultant. The Japanese attack was a failure.

Fires were still burning everywhere, particularly in the oil tank farms, which were flaming furiously, out of control. Everywhere people were running, many carrying stretchers. The sound of ambulance sirens still filled the air.

Rochefort found Admiral Kimmel standing in his office looking at the destruction and desolation of the navy yard while Captain Lock was reading the tally of lost ships.

"A destroyer, the *Quince*," Captain Lock said. "A minelayer, a laid-up submarine and two badly damaged battleships. One of them is the *Pennsylvania*, sir."

"How bad?"

"Extensive. But repairable."

"Casualties?"

"Fifty-seven men, sir."

"What else?"

"That's about it, sir. We may have bagged about forty of their planes. I don't see how they can claim a victory, sir."

The admiral was strangely silent. He nodded his head.

"Well, Admiral, they broke radio silence at last," Rochefort said. "They're reporting in full to Tokyo. Our hunch was right."

"We should have kept the ships in port," Kimmel said.

Captain Lock looked astonished. "In port?"

"Yes. In port."

"But—the tally—we would have lost many more ships, Admiral."

"It was that damned fourth scenario," Kimmel said, still looking out of his window at the fires in the navy yard.

"Pardon, sir? Fourth scenario?"

Kimmel turned. "There was a fourth scenario, Commander."

"What was that, sir?"

"The fourth scenario said that if the Japanese planes found the harbor empty, they would turn to secondary targets. The tank farms. And that's exactly what happened. They bombed every blessed oil tank." He turned fully to Rochefort. "Oil, man, oil. The navy runs on oil. And now we don't have a drop of fuel west of San Diego. You understand? Not a drop of oil between San Diego and Tokyo. Without those oil tank farms, the U.S. Navy is out of the Pacific for at least six months or even a year. Maybe more. And that's all the time the Japanese need to overrun all of Southeast Asia and pour into Australia while our fleet sits helpless in port waiting for the tank farms to be rebuilt. We may have to sue for peace."

He sat down on his desk. "Because of the fourth scenario, we may have just won the battle and lost the war against Japan."

Part 3

Alternate
Aftermaths

As a result of the attack on Pearl Harbor, the United States declared war on Japan.

The certainty of victory, however, was never a sure thing.

9

Victory at Pearl Harbor

BRENDAN DUBOIS

ALEX DWYER WAS AT his desk at the *Port Salinas Times*. The paper was a daily (except for Sundays) and covered Port Salinas and the surrounding small communities on this stretch of the California coast. At present Alex was working on the school lunch menu list for the next week. It was a dreary job, but one he didn't mind. He knew he was lucky to have a job during this recession, and having a job at a newspaper seemed to be the best thing in the world. Most of the time you worked inside, warm and comfortable, and you spent a lot of time on the phone. It was nothing like working outside in forestry or fishing. He had been at the job only four months—two months to go before his probation was up—and he did everything he was told. From obituaries to fishing reports to school lunches, he was glad to be here and looking forward to getting his journalists guild card when his probation was up. He was up to the Tuesday list. Most schools had macaroni and cheese on Tuesdays like it was some kind of plot.

The editor suddenly opened his office door and called out, "Alex! Come over here."

"Sure, Walt," Alex answered, grabbing his notebook and walking quickly across the small newsroom.

When he entered the editor's office, his boss, Walt Quinn, was behind his cluttered desk and motioned him to an empty chair. Behind Walt were large windows that looked over Memorial Park. The flags were snapping proudly in the strong breeze coming up from the ocean. Alex sat down, suddenly nervous about what might be going on, about why his editor had called him here. He thought he had been doing all right during this probationary period, but one never knew.

Walt coughed then announced, "I've got a story assignment for you. I was going to give it to Douglas, but he's out sick today. So I'll let you have it, but I've got to warn you, it's kind of sensitive."

"I'll be all right," Alex said. "Truth is, I'm getting kinda bored doing the lunch menus and fire department logs every week. I'd like to do something a bit more newsworthy."

Walt scribbled something on a piece of paper and slid it across the desk. "Here you go. Down by the pier. Noon today. There's gonna be a little ceremony, a wreath being tossed into the harbor. It's from the local chapter of the Pearl Harbor Survivors Association."

"The Pearl what?" Alex asked, writing in his notebook.

"Pearl Harbor. Jeez, don't they teach you kids anything in school anymore? Pearl Harbor. Exactly thirty years ago, on December 7. Great naval battle at Pearl Harbor in Hawaii between the American and Japanese navies. Get there and do a story about the ceremony. See if you can't talk to some of the vets. Be polite and nice and all that, but be on guard. They're getting old and they have funny thoughts about newspapers nowadays. Like most old-timers, they don't trust us."

"I'll be fine," Alex said, getting up from his chair.

"Oh, you'll be fine," Walt said. "But I want that story first thing this afternoon, before you leave."

"You'll have it, Walt," he said. "Should I take a camera?"

"No, no pictures necessary," his editor said. "Just a small little piece. A page or so of copy. That's it."

"Okay."

"Good," Walt said. "Now get to work."

☆ ☆ ☆

Within fifteen minutes Alex was at the small harbor of Point Salinas, wandering near another little park that was adjacent to the small body of water that eventually led to the Pacific Ocean. It was a cool day, even for southern California, and he wished he had enough money to buy a heavier jacket. And the thought of a new jacket made him again think of meeting the terms of his probation. This was a good job, not bad at all, and he hated the thought of being unemployed. Especially with the governor's announcing plans for involuntary work crews for those unable or unwilling to get a job, that is, if the welfare rolls didn't stop expanding. He looked out at the harbor and saw that most of the town's fishing fleet was out, which was a good sign. His dad and two uncles worked in the fishing fleet, and seeing the harbor empty meant full bellies and wallets when they came back.

The pier jutted out into the middle of the harbor, and it was wide and built with weather-worn timbers. Seagulls dived and floated above the pier, looking for handouts from the retired old men and young boys who fished from the pier day in and day out, in almost every kind of weather. He walked down toward the end of the pier and looked back, seeing a few Japanese tourists clicking away with their cameras. The few times he had been out on his dad's boat, he had enjoyed this view of the town, but he always felt seasickness coming on and couldn't look for that long. The town rose up the side of the wooded hills, mostly small homes and businesses in brick one- or two-story buildings. The main street led out to the state highway. A nice little town. And Alex had a secret desire to grow old here and maybe become the editor of the *Times* when his day came—if he made it through his probation and got a good recommendation from Walt.

But not if he didn't get the story. Where was this ceremony? Where were those veterans supposed to be? There were just a few people like himself, walking around, talking and looking at the view. He felt a little tingle of cold along his fingers. Walt was an easygoing guy most times, but he had a couple of hard-and-fast rules that nobody could afford to screw up. The first was to always make deadline. And the second rule was never to come back empty-handed from an assignment. Not once.

But suppose the veterans didn't show up? Would that be his fault? The clock chimed the noon hour at the town hall, and the cold tingle in his fingers returned. Where in hell was the ceremony?

Then, almost like it was planned, four people gathered at the end of the pier: a woman and three men. All of them were in their late fifties or early sixties. The woman had a paper shopping bag, and she reached in and pulled out a small wreath. The three men were wearing triangular garrison caps with faded gold-thread lettering. Alex came closer. The ceremony, such as it was, looked like it was going to take place after all. The woman's face was pale, and she looked nervous, as did two of her three companions. But one of the men, a stocky guy with a red nose, seemed to take his time. He unfolded a piece of paper and started talking in a loud voice.

"Today, December 7, a day which still lives in infamy, is remembered by us, the Port Salinas Chapter of the Pearl Harbor Survivors Association of California," he said, reading from the paper. Alex started taking notes as the man continued: "Thirty years after the dastardly and unprovoked Japanese attack on our forces in Hawaii and elsewhere, we remember those who fell, fighting for freedom and liberty. Three decades later, after that historical attack and battle between the United States and Japan, between the forces of good and evil, between democracy and dictatorship, we still remember. We must remember those sacrifices, for the sake of our children. And we shall never forget."

By now Alex saw that the shortest of the three men had reached into his coat pocket and unfolded an old American flag, one with forty-eight stars. Now he wished he had signed out a camera after all from the photo department. This would have made a great picture to go with the story. He kept on scribbling, noticing from the corner of his eye that most of the other people on the pier had drifted away. It looked like he was the only one paying attention, and suddenly he felt sorry for this pathetic little foursome. It didn't seem like anybody cared. The man with the loud voice said, "Now, three decades later, we salute our fallen comrades, who died in the name of freedom, and who most certainly did not die in vain. Grace, if you please."

The woman tossed the wreath into the harbor, and her three companions saluted. But Grace didn't salute. She folded up the grocery bag and walked away. The men kept the salutes for a long few seconds then stopped. They walked away as well, taking off their garrison caps, folding them up, and putting them away in their coat pockets. Alex hurried up to the man with the red nose. "Excuse me, sir?"

The man turned. "Yeah, what is it?" Without the cap, the wind was now playing tricks with his thinning white hair. His coat was soiled, and Alex noticed that patches had been sewn inexpertly on the elbows.

"I'm Alex Dwyer. With the *Port Salinas Times.* I was wondering if I could ask you a few questions."

The man laughed and called out to his friends. "Hey, Jack! Phil! Got an honest-to-God journalist here, asking questions. You think I should say any more?"

One of the men kept on walking, but the other stopped and threw back a word of caution. "Frank, if you had any sense, you'd go home. Don't waste your time with him. You know what reporters do, make up things and distort."

The man with the red nose looked like he had an attitude. He laughed again. "See, kid. That's the kind of advice I get. Just to walk away. So why don't I?"

"Because I'm doing a story, that's why."

"About this little ceremony? And why's that?"

"My editor told me to, that's why."

Frank shook his head. "I wrote three letters to the editor and a press release for the community news page, all about what you just saw. And nothing appeared. So that tells me your editor isn't that interested."

"Well, he was interested enough to send me," Alex said.

Frank slowly nodded. "Okay, I'll give you that. But why should I trust you? I mean, are you really going to do a story?"

"I am," Alex said, "and you can trust me. I'm a reporter, just telling a story. And I'll tell it right."

Frank seemed to think about that, rocking back and forth slightly on his heels. "Jeez, kid, I don't know . . . I've been burned a few times before, you know."

Alex said, "But not by me, right?"

That seemed to amuse Frank. "Yeah, you're right. Not by you. Okay, here's the deal. You can get an interview, but only if I get something in return."

"Sure," Alex said. "What is it?"

"Lunch," he said.

"Excuse me?"

"Lunch," Frank said louder. "It's a little past noon and I'm hungry. You buy me lunch, and I'll talk to you. Give you a nice little story. That sounds fair, don't it? I mean, you newspaper reporters, you have expense accounts, don't you?"

Alex thought for a moment. Yes, all of the reporters had expense accounts, but it was closely watched, both by Walt and by Tracy, the office manager, and they would chew you out if you tried anything funny. Like charging mileage for your personal car when it was cheaper to take one of the coastal buses. Alex had no idea how a lunch deduction would go through, but he remembered Walt's rules. Always come back with the story.

"Okay," Alex said. "Lunch. I'll buy, but I get to choose the place."

"Fair enough," Frank said.

Alex picked a small diner called Yoko's Place near the series of bait and tackle shops that serviced the fishing boats. Yoko was a retired Japanese woman who kept a number of high-school girls and boys in employ as short-order cooks and waitresses, but Frank didn't look particularly happy as they slid into a booth and looked at a menu.

"Couldn't pick any place other than this one?" Frank asked.

"It was close, and it was my choice," Alex said. "Am I right?"

"Yeah, yeah," Frank grumbled and looked again at the menu. A teenage girl in a pink uniform came over. Alex said, "After you," and boy, was he glad, because Frank—grumpy at some damn thing—ordered the most expensive item on the menu, a cheese-burger. Alex looked again at the menu, panicked that he might not have enough money to pay for the both of them. He ordered some ramen noodles.

Frank looked at him and said, "That's a hell of a lunch, some Japanese noodles like that."

Alex tried to keep his voice light. "I don't mind. Yoko does them right."

"Hah," Frank said, putting the menu away by a napkin dispenser and the salt and pepper shakers. "When I was a kid, cheese-burger like that would go for fifteen cents. Now look how much they're charging."

Alex placed his notebook on the table. "Was that when you were in the navy?"

"Sure it was," he said. "The Depression was still grinding along, but the prices were reasonable, you know? And we sure as hell didn't have a problem getting beef, that's for damn sure."

"Did you grow up here?"

Frank said, "Nah. Grew up in San Diego. Bummed around as a kid and then decided to join the navy. What the hell, that was what you did when you grew up in a navy town like San Diego. Went in as a green recruit. They turned me into a man, real quick. Eventually got assigned to the *California*."

Alex was confused, writing away. "I'm sorry, what did you say? You were assigned in California? Where? A base?"

"No, no, kid," he said impatiently. "The USS *California*. A battleship. And one of the prettiest battleships in the fleet, if you ask me. Spent a couple of years with her, and I never wanted to leave. That was a battleship navy back then, and battleships were the queens of the fleet. We even had a nickname for her, the 'Prune Barge.' Everybody was envious of us, 'cept maybe some of the flyboys off the carriers. But, ah, the *California*, she was gorgeous."

"And what did you do on the *California*?"

"In peacetime or wartime?" Frank said.

"Both, I guess."

"Okay," Frank said, clasping his hands together. "I was a quartermaster's assistant. No big deal, right? Just helping out the quartermaster, keepin' track of ship's stores and crap like that. Maybe do a little bookie action on the side. But during a drill—or the real thing—my duty was assisting a gunner's mate up on one of the antiaircraft batteries, up forward near the 'B' turret."

"And you were there, on December 7?"

The waitress came back with a plate and soup bowl. The bowl had a steaming portion of ramen noodles and bits of chicken and vegetables, but Alex found his mouth watering at the sight of the cheeseburger. With the recession and everything else, it had been a while since he could afford having beef. The older man picked up the cheeseburger and took a healthy bite.

"Mmm," he said around a mouthful. "Not bad. December 7? Sure, I was there, on December 7. Who in the navy wasn't? But you know, kid, we all had the feeling that something bad was going to happen with the Japs."

"Really? Why was that?"

"Christ, kid, don't you know anything about history? Anything at all? You go to college?"

"Sure I did," he said. "Pacific State."

"Whadja major in?"

"Creative writing and Asian studies." Alex took up a fork, spinning some of the noodles and spearing a piece of chicken. It was hot and tasted good, but the cheeseburger looked mighty fine . . .

"Bah," he said, taking another healthy bite of his cheeseburger. "Here ya go. Some history you didn't know back then. See, Roosevelt was president, and he was doing his damndest to get us into war with Hitler. The Japs was just a sideshow. You see, we had this economic and oil blockade against 'em, and we said, sure, we'd lift the blockade, the second you guys stop killing Chinese and pull back from Manchuria and Indochina. They had invaded all those places months and years earlier, and we didn't want 'em doin' it. Well, Christ, what Japanese government's gonna retreat from countries it had just conquered just to make Roosevelt happy? So they was running out of oil, and on that island, kid, there's hardly any oil they can call their own."

"Weren't there negotiations or something like that going on?" Alex asked. "Couldn't they have just cooperated?"

"Hell, yes, there were negotiations going on, but the Japanese, hell, they was running out of oil, and when you've got a big military machine like they did, bent on conquering all of Asia and the Pacific, they needed lots of oil. And they were gonna get it one way or the other."

"So what did they do?"

"Do? Hell, they was smart. They kept on negotiating, and while they were doin' that, they were preparing for war."

"And were the Americans doing the same?"

"Hah," Frank said, chewing thoughtfully. "That's when we got lucky. Nobody thought the Japanese would attack Pearl Harbor. It was way too far away. Later I read that people thought, hell, maybe Japan would attack the Philippines or the Dutch islands or whatever. But not Pearl Harbor. And we might have gotten whipped bad at Pearl Harbor, if it wasn't for a lucky car accident."

"Lucky?" Alex asked.

"Well, not lucky for the admiral, but lucky for us at Pearl Harbor. You see, by then, that was where our Pacific Fleet was stationed, including the *California*. And we had an admiral back then, real spit-and-polish guy, named Kimmel. Ran a tight ship, but you know what? That's what we didn't need back then. A tight ship with pretty sailors and pretty ships and everything squared away and polished. We needed an ornery and suspicious son of a bitch, which is what we got. And that brings me back to the accident. Ol' Admiral Kimmel is coming back from some official banquet or something when a drunk driver comes out of a side street in Honolulu and whales into him. Poor Kimmel ends up in the hospital with a broken leg, broken ribs, and he's in a coma for a long time. Well, ol' Roosevelt don't want his Pacific Fleet commanded by whoever, so he sends another admiral out, a guy named Nimitz. An old Kraut from Texas."

"So what happened on December 7?" Alex pressed, knowing that Walt wanted the story on his desk before the end of the day.

Frank shook his head, finished off his cheeseburger, and began wiping his thick fingers with a paper napkin. "The important stuff that happened, happened 'fore December 7. Nimitz came in, and he didn't like what he saw. There were hardly any reconnaissance patrols or anything, and he changed that right quick. Then he ran up against General Short, the army general in charge of defending Hawaii. Funny, huh, that the navy base was defended by the army, but that's the way it was back then. Word we heard later is that Nimitz was harping on Short to be more aggressive, more up-front in doing practice drills. We had a lot of leaves canceled and stuff, and let me tell you, we weren't very happy about that weekend."

"December 7 was on a weekend?"

"Yep, a Sunday. And what we heard is that a few days earlier, Nimitz got a message from Washington, saying negotiations weren't going anywhere with the Japs and that he should consider this a war warning. Which he did. I guess in the Philippines they didn't do much, but Nimitz harped on Short to put some of his units on alert, and all of us in the fleet—except for the carriers that were out on a mission—we had our leaves canceled that weekend. We was at battle stations, hour after hour, and on Sunday morning, that's when the little bastards attacked."

Alex heard someone cough. He turned and saw Yoko, the owner of the little restaurant, wiping down the countertop. She seemed a bit embarrassed, but if Frank noticed it, he didn't say a thing. He just kept on talking.

"It was a beautiful morning when the word came out that one of our destroyers had sunk a midget submarine that was trying to sneak into the harbor. And then this army radar station caught a flight of aircraft, comin' in. Man, you should have heard the bells and horns ringing. They was comin' in, comin' in hard, and man, we were waiting for them. It was wonderful."

Alex's hand was starting to cramp from writing so fast, but he didn't dare stop. This was fascinating, stuff he had never heard before, and he didn't want to miss a word.

"Go on," Alex said. "What happened next?"

"Well," Frank said, still wiping his fingers with the napkin. "Word came down that the Japs were coming, and we saw some of the aircraft, heading right to the harbor. Man, everything just lit off, like the biggest fireworks display ever. Every battleship moored along Ford Island, in Battleship Row, everything we had—.50-caliber machine guns, 5-inch guns, 1.1-inch pom-poms—they was firing away. Later, too, we learned that the army had some P-40s up there, and they managed to pick off some of the Jap dive-bombers. Oh, what a sight it was."

"Uh-huh," Alex said. "And you were firing, too?"

"You bet, kid, you bet. I was manning one of the .50-caliber machine guns, and we were just throwing up so much metal it was a miracle that anything could survive. But survive they did."

Then his voice slowed some. "Don't get me wrong. We were ready for 'em. We really were. But we took some hits. The *Arizona* took one right in the powder magazine and blew up. So did the *Shaw* and a couple of other ships. And Hickam Field and other places around the harbor were shot up and bombed. So we lost a few hundred guys, sailors and soldiers, no doubt about it. But we made 'em pay for it. Even the *California* took a torpedo. That was something, let me tell you. You could feel the whole damn ship shudder, but we were ready. All of our watertight doors and hatches were closed up tight, and they started counterflooding, to make sure we wouldn't capsize."

"How long did it last?" Alex asked, realizing that his lunch of ramen was getting cold, and not minding.

"Seemed like it lasted all morning long," Frank said, shaking his head again. "All morning long. They came at us in three waves, and you know, you gotta give 'em credit. The first wave had gotten shot up pretty good, but the other Japs kept on coming, like they didn't care. They sure were brave. Later we found out that they considered it an honor to die for the emperor. Can you believe that? Can you believe some American soldier or sailor deciding it would be an honor to die for Roosevelt? Like hell!"

Frank lowered his voice, leaned forward. "I thought Roosevelt was okay. But my buddy Roy McQuirk, he hated Roosevelt—him, his wife, even the guy's dog. McQuirk was from down South, nice and polite, but he was a killer when it came to the .50-cal. A real good shot, he was. He was the actual shooter; I just helped feed the damn thing with belts of ammo, one right after another. Hell, he fired that thing so much that morning I was sure the barrel would melt right there."

"Did you shoot down any planes?"

"Us? Hell, yes. You know, I remember one time, there was a torpedo bomber, coming right across the harbor, looking like he was ready to line up a shot at the *Oklahoma*. Roy lined up his gun and started blasting; I could even see the little spouts of spray where the bullets hit the water. There was shouting and screaming and all this pounding, but Roy kept right on, and he caught that little bastard. She started to smoke and flame and then she pinwheeled, right into Pearl Harbor. Cripes, what a beautiful sight that was. Funny thing was, the planes were all nice and silvery. They didn't even bother paintin' them with camouflage or anything, so you could see the rising sun insignia nice and clear. Boy, oh, boy, what a sight . . ."

Frank looked down at his hands, and Alex imagined that maybe the older man was fighting the battle all over again, pressing belts of .50-caliber ammunition into service.

Frank cleared his throat and went on. "After that torpedo plane crashed, Roy looked over at me, this crazed grin on his face. He said, 'Just like shootin' ducks back home. You gotta lead the little bastards.' I think we both laughed, but just for a bit, 'cause we had to keep on shooting. Then, after a while, the planes just stopped coming over.

That's all. The planes just stopped coming. And then we got word: the boilers had been fired up and we were ordered to sortie out."

"Sortie out?" Alex asked. "Why?"

"Why? Why!" The older man looked stunned at the question. "Jesus Christ, kid, the Japs came in and strafed and bombed and killed a lot of us *before* war was declared. It was a cheap, sneak attack, and we weren't gonna let them get away with it. No sir. Our battleships were gettin' ready to sortie out, 'cause it stood to reason that the Japanese fleet that attacked us was nearby. I mean, those were carrier-based planes that had attacked us, and we were ready to go out and kick some butt."

"Did it take long to leave the harbor?"

"Oh, a couple of hours, at least, but man, that was a sight," he said. "All around there were flames and smoke, big clouds of smoke rising up. And the poor *Arizona* was sinking, smoke billowing out of her, and some other ships as well. But one after another, the battleships, the queens of the fleet, we started sortieing out. First one out was the *Nevada*. Christ, what a sight that was, steaming out, her battle flags flying. And right after that, the other surviving battleships: the *Maryland*, the *Pennsylvania*, the *West Virginia*, and us. We all started steaming out. The other cruisers and destroyers did, too. We were going to group outside the harbor. You know, we didn't know then what was going on. We thought maybe the Japanese had an invasion fleet, too, with troops. We just didn't know."

The dishes were cleared by the teenage waitress, and Alex just nodded when she picked up his nearly full bowl of noodles. He would be hungry later on, but later on also meant finishing the story.

"Weren't you scared?" Alex asked.

"Sure, we were scared, but we were angry, mostly," Frank said. "I mean, there we were, in peacetime, on a Sunday morning, and we were attacked. Just like that. No war declaration or anything. So we were ready to pay 'em back with interest."

"I don't understand."

"Kid," he said, leaning forward. "Think it through. We had the battleships, most of 'em survived, and we were gonna go out hunting. That's what we were going to do. We were going to find the fleet that bombed us at Pearl Harbor, and we were going to sink 'em. I still remember Roy's saying, 'Just wait 'til those bastards get a taste of our 14-inch guns. Just wait.' Oh, we were in a fine fighting mood. We had taken a bit of a licking at Pearl, but we had beaten off most of the attacking force, and most of the Pacific Fleet was still in good shape. We were going to sortie out, meet up with the aircraft carriers that were coming in from Wake Island and Midway, and we were going huntin'. My, oh my, how excited we were."

"I can see why," Alex said. "So, what happened after your battleship left Hawaii?"

Frank looked skeptical. "You really don't know?"

"No, I'm sorry, I don't."

Frank rubbed his hands together. "Okay, kid, I'll tell you. But before I go on, you've got to promise me somethin'. Okay? You just remember this. Pearl Harbor was a victory, you got that? One of the greatest victories the navy ever had. We fought off a sneak attack and survived. You write that down, right now."

Alex did that, scribbling away in his notebook. Victory at Pearl Harbor. He even turned the notebook around to show Frank, who nodded with satisfaction.

"Okay. As promised. The rest of the story."

AN HOUR later, his head light from lack of food and from all of the information he had processed, Alex went back to the newspaper office and went straight to his desk. He grabbed a clean sheet of paper, rolled it into his typewriter, and typed in the slug at the top left-hand side: DWYER/PEARL HARBOR. He started flipping through his notebook and pounding at the keys. He knew that Walt had just asked for a small story, but he was hoping that he could make something longer and better, something that even Walt would want to run somewhere prominent. Hell, if he wrote the story as well as he thought he could, maybe Walt would change his mind and get some photographs. Maybe he would even convince Frank and his companions to get together again for a picture. Maybe even get Frank's companions to tell their side of the story as well, about Pearl Harbor and everything else.

Alex's fingers raced along the keyboard as he sketched out a story. He thought that maybe this one would free him up from doing lunch menus and all the other boring assignments that had come his way. Maybe this story would do it.

He kept on typing, enjoying the sensation of giving the story life. He flipped through the pages of the notebook, recalling what Frank had said, and the story came to life. This was the best part of reporting: taking raw notes and hammering the story together, like building a house with the raw materials lying at your feet. The writing went well and he was done before he knew it. He stacked up the sheets of paper, saw that he had written eight double-spaced pages. Lord, it was the longest piece he had ever written for the *Times.* And he was damn proud of every single page. He quickly scanned the pages, made a couple of minor corrections, and stapled them together. Alex got up and went into Walt's office. It was empty. He put the story down on the chair and then, feeling pretty good about the day, went outside to scrounge a snack to get him through the day.

WHEN HE came back from outside, a bottle of Coke and a bag of seaweed crisps in his hands, the door to Walt's office was closed. He thought for a second about tapping at the door, but no, better to let things rest. He sat down at his desk and munched the salty seaweed crisps, opened the Coke, and looked at the notebook again. What a story. What stuff he had learned. It had been . . . magnificent, almost, and he felt privileged to have written such a story.

What now?

He looked at the work remaining before him. Time to get back to the school lunch menus.

ALEX HAD made it to Thursday's menu when the door to Walt's office flew open and the editor shouted for the young reporter.

"Right here, Walt," he replied.

"My office," he said curtly. "Now!"

Alex got up, grabbing the notebook, and went in. Walt motioned to the chair, which he took. He sat still, not letting his back touch the rear of the chair. Walt slowly sat down, like everything in his joints had become stiff and painful. He sighed and picked up a sheaf of papers, which Alex instantly recognized.

"Your story?"

"Yes," he said. It seemed to be the safest thing to say.

"You sure? Anybody help you at all with it?"

"No sir, not at all," and he was tempted to add something proudly, like, see, I can handle the big stories, but something about Walt's tone was all wrong.

Walt rubbed at his face and said, "Two important things you need to learn about this business, if you want to make it to the end of your probation, okay? First, you were doing okay—before today. That's to listen to what your editor has to say and to do what he tells you to do. I told you to do a little piece, maybe five or six paragraphs. Not a goddamn opus, okay?"

Alex just nodded, realizing that he was in some serious trouble. Walt went on. "The second thing, which you obviously know nothing about, is to write the correct way. And this—" he said, tossing the story over to him, "—hasn't been written right, not at all."

"But it's the truth!' Alex said, leaning out of his chair. "Every word of it!"

"Really?"

"Really," Alex said.

Walt said, "Then tell me what this guy Frank told you."

Which is what Alex did. He went on for long minutes, telling his editor the story about what happened in the days after the attack on Pearl Harbor. It was like he was back in the small restaurant, listening to Frank . . .

☆ ☆ ☆

"So AFTER you and the other battleships left Pearl Harbor, what happened then?" There was silence. Alex looked up from his notebook, stunned to see tears glistening in the older man's eyes. Frank dabbed at them with a napkin for a moment. "Sorry," he whispered. "You know, it's been thirty years, almost exactly thirty years, and it still can get to me, you know?"

Frank coughed and took a breath. "Okay. Right after the bombing attack, maybe late morning, we were steaming out of the harbor, getting ready to hunt some Japs. Our first goal was to hook up with our carriers—the *Enterprise* and the *Lexington*—which were coming back from Wake Island and Midway with their own task forces. So we were heading out, ready to meet up with those two battle groups."

"But I thought you said the *California* had been torpedoed," Alex said.

"Sure, sure, but she was one tough battleship. And even with a couple of torpedo hits, with the right damage control and watertight doors, you can still fight. And believe me, kid, after that bombing that morning, after seeing the *Arizona* and *Shaw* get sunk, after we saw Hickam Field get shot up, we weren't in a mood to go into dry dock and get repairs. So we limped out with everybody else. Almost the entire Pacific Fleet. Man, I've seen old newsreel footage, showing them heading out to open ocean. What a magnificent sight."

Alex flipped another page over in his notebook. "How long before you met up with the aircraft carriers?"

"Less than a day," he said. "By then our reconnaissance aircraft had picked up on the Japanese task force. Six aircraft carriers, two battleships, two heavy cruisers, and nine destroyers. All heading back to their home islands. We were ready to fight, my God, we were ready to fight. And fight we did, until . . . until . . ."

Frank now looked down at his large hands, breathing hard again. Frank coughed and Alex asked softly, "How did the fighting go?"

"Stupid," he finally said. "We were so stupid and arrogant. We thought the mighty American white man, who hadn't lost a war ever since the country was founded, was going to take on these funny Japanese guys with buck teeth and thick glasses. We forgot—most of us, at least—that they were veterans. They had been fighting in China and Manchuria and Korea . . . Hell, about forty years earlier, they had whacked the crap out of the Russians, destroying their naval fleet. They knew how to fight. And us? We knew how to polish brass. We knew how to conduct fire-control drills. We knew how to polish shoes. We were a goddamn peacetime navy, with officers who had never heard a shot fired in anger. And when we finally caught up to the task force, they turned on us, they turned on us hard. Like we had been chasing a pack of rabid dogs. Christ, how they fought . . ."

Frank looked up, eyes glistening again. "We didn't have the air cover from the army. We didn't have the antiaircraft gun installations from the bases at Pearl. It was just us and them, and they mauled us bad. First to go was the *Enterprise* and then the *Lexington*. That was our air cover, right there. Sent to the bottom, with the surviving aircraft circling until they ran out of gas and had to ditch. Then the Japanese bombers and torpedo planes, those survivors who had refueled and rearmed after Pearl, came after us, again and again . . . until . . ."

Another cough, another dab of the napkin against his eyes. "I'm not too sure what got us, even today. The news is still mixed up about that battle, you know? But I did learn later that the Japanese had these long-range torpedoes, accurate as hell. We took three or four, and it was just too much. The *California* sank just after midnight, Tuesday, December 9. We lost hundreds. Lots of my buddies never made it out. I was lucky, being topside. I was able to make it into the water, and soon, as far as the eye could see, when the sun finally came up, there was just smoke and wreckage and oil slicks and survivors, bobbing up and down . . ."

Alex kept his eyes on his notepad as he kept writing. He felt he couldn't disturb this train of thought, this awful recitation of thirty-year-old memories. Frank coughed. "We thought when the sun came up, that it would get better, that we would be rescued, but it didn't happen, not for a long, long time. The sun was awful, beating down on us, and we started dying, one by one. Some guys had swallowed oil when they got in the water, and they choked and choked before coughing themselves to death. Other guys were burned or shot up or wounded, and they died, too. Then the sharks started coming around . . . Oh Jesus, the screams when the sharks got to a guy . . . I looked around, at all this wreckage and debris and death, and there it was, the mighty Pacific Fleet, sent to the bottom."

Alex didn't raise his eyes. "How long were you in the water?"

"Almost two days. By then guys were going crazy over the sun, and some fought each other over water bottles or bread. Eventually we were picked up by a destroyer, the *Ward,* and the decks were just filled with survivors. Thousands of us had died out there on the ocean. Thousands."

Now Alex looked at Frank, whose large hands were clasped together tightly, the knuckles white. "Funny the things you remember. After we got back to Hawaii and were hospitalized, there was this college professor, a guy who had been in the reserves and had been called up. He lost a leg, out there after the *Nevada* turned turtle and sunk . . . This professor type said it would have been better if we hadn't gone out after the Jap fleet. He said it would have been even better if the surprise attack had happened without us knowing about it. Can you believe that he said something like that?"

"Why do you think he said that?"

Frank shook his head, slowly unclasped his hands. "After a while, it made a crazy kind of sense. He said in the harbor, if the battleships were sunk, they could be refloated and refitted. Out there in the ocean, a sunk battleship was gone. Plus, during the attack on the seventh, our aircraft carriers weren't in the harbor, so they were spared. But in going after the Jap task force, we lost both of our carriers, and man, that was it. Our admirals and captains were mostly battleship sailors. You know? Thought that the naval battles in the forties would be like the naval battles from the First World War. Battleship versus battleship, slugging it out, horizon to horizon. They couldn't imagine what naval aviation could do, how much damage aircraft carriers could do with their bombers and torpedo planes."

Frank looked like he was trying to smile. "A few months later, when the navy evacuated from Pearl Harbor, our little fleet barely made it as a task force. Some subs, a few destroyers, support vessels. That was it. That was what was left of the Pacific Fleet, and when the navy left Hawaii, well, she was open for invasion."

Alex stopped writing, rubbed his fingers together. "What happened then?"

Frank seemed tired. "Ah, I've told you enough, kid. I think you've got enough there for a story, am I right?"

"Yes. Thanks for talking to me."

"No bother. And thanks for lunch. But one more thing."

"Yes?"

Frank reached over, tapped the notebook. "The truth. All right? You write the damn truth. Not like other newspaper guys I know."

Alex folded his notebook closed. "I promise. The truth."

☆ ☆ ☆

WALT STARED at him, and Alex felt extremely small. "The truth? He told you to write the truth?"

"Yes, he did," Alex said.

Walt picked up the story, started reading aloud: "'At noontime yesterday, a small ceremony took place at the town pier, marking something quite large, the beginning of a naval conflict between the Empire of Japan and the United States of America. Three veterans of the opening salvo of this conflict, which began with a unprovoked and sneak attack upon American naval forces at Pearl Harbor in Hawaii, remembered the deaths of their comrades with a small speech and the tossing of a memorial wreath into the harbor.'"

The pages went back down on the desk. Walt said, "You wrote this, right? You really wrote this?"

Alex shifted in his seat. "You know I did."

Walt said, "You like being a newspaper reporter?"

"I do. I really do."

"You looking to make a career of it? Are you?"

"If I make it past the probation period, I sure do, Walt."

His editor shook his head. "Well, you're about an inch away from not making probation. 'Cause you don't know how to listen to your editor, and you don't know how to write well. Here"—and Walt slid over a sheet of paper—"you read this aloud, and you tell me the difference. All right?"

Alex glanced down at the paper, looked back up at his editor. "What's this?"

"A rewrite. I took your story and wrote it the way it should have been done and the way it's going to appear in tomorrow's paper. All right? Start reading. I want to hear your strong young voice, Alex."

He cleared his throat, knowing his face was flushed with shame. "'At noontime yesterday, a small ceremony took place at the town pier, where a small band of ex-American naval personnel once again offered their apologies to the Imperial Japanese forces for their aggression thirty years ago against the natural expansion of the Greater East-Asia Co-Prosperity Sphere. In their remarks, they once again atoned for their actions against the Imperial Japanese forces and the emperor himself. At the end of the ceremony, a wreath commemorating the Japanese dead and honoring continued Japanese-American cooperation was tossed into the harbor.'"

Alex stopped reading, looked up at his editor. "But that's not what happened!"

Walt shrugged. "Who cares? That's what should have happened, and that's what we're going to report in tomorrow's newspaper."

"But I told that man I was going to write the truth."

"The truth?" Walt said, spreading his arms wide. "The truth? Were you here thirty years ago? Were you at Pearl Harbor in 1941? Were you? Did you learn anything like this from your teachers in high school or college?"

"No," he said miserably. "But Frank was at Pearl Harbor, and what he said—"

Walt pointed a finger at him. "What he said has almost got you fired, Alex. And what he said . . . if I had printed what you wrote, this story filled with lies and half-truths, by this time tomorrow afternoon you and I would be down at the police station, being interviewed quite vigorously by the polite gentlemen from the *Kempei Tai*. Would you like that?"

Alex felt his hands grow cold at the name of the secret police. Some mothers in town—but thankfully not his when he was younger—would tell their children, "Be good, or the *Kempei Tai* will get you."

"No, I wouldn't," he said.

Walt now smiled. "I didn't think so. Look. This wasn't a waste. It was a good learning experience. You've come right up against the balancing act a good reporter and editor has to do: report the news, but report the news responsibly. Understand?"

Alex nodded. "Yes, I do."

"All right. Look, take my rewrite, go back to your desk and type it up yourself. Then resubmit it, and we'll pretend you never did the other story. And if that guy Frank calls, all ticked off by what you did, send him over to me and I'll take care of it. Okay?"

Alex stood up. "Okay." He gathered up his original story and the rewrite. As he was getting ready to leave, Walt said, "One more thing." He motioned with a hand. "Your old story."

"What about it?"

"Shred it and burn the scraps, all right?"

Alex looked at his editor and then past him, out the window at the park, where two flags fluttered from two perfectly white flag-poles. The banner on the right was the white-and-red sun of Japan; the one on the left was the bear and rising sun of the California Pre-fecture. He remembered the old flag that one of the veterans had bravely and proudly displayed earlier at the pier. An old flag that existed only in memory and in a few history books.

"All right," Alex said, and he left Walt's office and went back to his desk. He looked down at his editor's rewrite and placed it aside. He then picked up his own story and glanced over at the far end of the office, where the shredder was.

Then he carefully folded his story in half, opened a lower desk drawer, and hid it way in back.

10

"I Relieve You, Sir"

BARRETT TILLMAN

SATURDAY, JANUARY 20, 1945

A JANUARY WIND WHIPPED off the Potomac and swirled around the White House, trailing vortexes of snowflakes and ambition in its wake. On the platform erected on the south portico, Washington's power elite prepared for the transition that many of the attendees could hardly accept.

The Chief Justice of the United States stepped to the microphone, turned toward the tall, slender president-elect whose wife held a Holy Bible. Never having held office, the son of a Minnesota congressman placed his left hand on the Scripture and raised his right. Before Justice Harlan F. Stone could begin the incantation, the public idol began reciting, his words brisk and fervent in the icy atmosphere.

"I, Charles Augustus Lindbergh, do solemnly swear that I will faithfully execute the office of President of the United States, and will to the best of my ability preserve, protect, and defend the Constitution of the United States." Then he added, "So help me God."

The twelfth chief justice of the United States extended a perfunctory handshake to the thirty-second president. "You realize, sir, that you are the first chief executive to assume the office during wartime. It's a heavy responsibility."

Lindbergh smiled grimly at the tacit challenge. Justice Stone
had served through three administrations since 1925 and could
scarcely believe that this, this . . . *aviator* . . . had unseated Franklin
Delano Roosevelt. True, the election was marked by bitterness and
controversy, and Lucky Lindy's stunning triumph was achieved by a
razor-thin margin in the Electoral College. But there it was: the
American electorate had turned out the man whom most of a
generation had regarded as the savior of the republic.

President Lindbergh declined to reply to the jurist. Instead, he
turned to embrace his wife, Anne, whose diary had overflowed since
the awesome news. That morning she had reread her entry for
November 7, 1944: "Charles has been elected president. My god,
my god! What will we ever do?"

Lindbergh warmly shook hands with his vice president, Gov.
Thomas E. Dewey of New York, whom many Republicans felt should
have had the nomination. "Lots of work to do, Charles," the veep
said under his trademark mustache. "There's a war to be won." Lindbergh squeezed once more.

"A war to be ended, Tom."

A lined, weathered face appeared beside the man of the hour. The
guest had been questioned by Capitol Police and Secret Service
agents who had never seen, let alone heard, of Walter Ballard. A
strong, bony hand reached across the vice president, and Lindbergh
earnestly grabbed it. "Slim, I don't guess I'll ever get used to calling
you Mr. President."

"I'll always be Slim to you, Walt. We've seen too much earth
and sky together."

Ballard shook his head, still unable to suppress his mirth. "I'll
hazard a prediction, Slim. Before long, barnstorming in those old
patched-together JN-4s will seem like the best time of your life."

Anne stood closer to her husband, grasping an arm. She did not
know Lindbergh's old flying buddies terribly well, but she knew
how much her husband thought of Walt Ballard. "The most important four years are just starting" she exclaimed, glancing up, for her
head barely came above her husband's shoulders.

"Yes ma'am," the flier agreed. "Slim's made a pretty good start
for himself: first solo across the Atlantic, Medal of Honor, best-selling
author, and now president of these United States at age forty-two."

"My birthday isn't for two weeks," Lindbergh observed. He knew that Theodore Roosevelt had been the youngest ever elected to the office at forty-two.

Roosevelt! Lindbergh remembered that the cousin of the great Teddy was on the platform. "Excuse me a moment," he said. He turned and strode to the front row where the defeated patrician sat in his wheelchair. Those who were present later said that they felt the chilly ambient air temperature drop another ten degrees. Lindbergh stood before the man he loathed and sensed the emotion's heartfelt return. Too many acrimonious words and deeds had passed between them over the past six years—the America First movement, opposed to FDR's occasionally illegal acts to save Britain in yet another European war; the president's vindictiveness in denying Colonel Lindbergh active duty in the capacity he could best serve. Still, it was in the national interest to provide a reasonably smooth transition. Lindbergh waited for Roosevelt to extend a hand, but the crippled New Yorker kept his gloves on. A slight nod of the head. "Mistah President," he said.

Lindbergh stood quietly for two heartbeats. He realized that people were watching. Looking down on his defeated opponent, he summoned his courage. "As you know, sir, I am an army man. But I believe that in the naval services the appropriate phrase is, 'I relieve you, sir.'"

A ghost of a smile crossed Roosevelt's lips. "You have the con, *Colonel.* Godspeed."

Lindbergh nodded curtly to Sen. Harry S. Truman of Missouri, FDR's running mate, then turned to his military aide, Army Air Force Brig. Gen. Casey Vincent. "Casey, remind the joint chiefs and the service secretaries that we'll hold a strategy meeting at eight tomorrow morning." Vincent nodded and disappeared.

In deference to the wartime situation, no inaugural parade would be held, but the airmen would not be denied. The growl of high-performance engines pierced the gray skies, and Lindbergh looked up. Pursuit planes and bombers from Bolling Field passed overhead, maintaining impeccable formation. They were trailed by dark blue navy planes, most flown by a youngster who fifteen years before had idolized Lucky Lindy, the Lone Eagle. Now he was their commander in chief. A few had already seen the presidential aircraft, a Douglas C-54 named *The Spirit of America.*

SUNDAY, JANUARY 21, 1945

Gen. George C. Marshall asked for a few minutes with Lindbergh before the new president's first official meeting. They stepped into an anteroom and the imperious army chief of staff dismissed the Secret Service man with a subtle head motion. He turned toward Lindbergh.

"Mr. President, before we proceed with other plans for the course of the war, there is something you need to know." Marshall licked his lips, contemplating how best to explain the nation's most closely held secret. *Well, he's a flier and evidently he understands something of science.* The chief plunged on.

"Since 1941 the army has overseen a top-secret project of immense potential. We call it 'Manhattan,' and its goal is to produce an atomic bomb." He allowed that information to sink in. He saw the dawning of realization in Lindbergh's eyes.

"How much?" the president asked.

"Money?"

"No, no. How much explosive power are we talking about?"

Marshall shrugged. "I'm afraid I am not qualified to discuss that end of it. I'm told that it's considerable—one bomb might destroy a city. My participation has been administration and funding. The officer you'll talk to is General Leslie Groves . . ."

"When can it be ready?"

"Well sir, I phoned General Groves yesterday, knowing that you would need details. He expects the first test this summer."

Lindbergh nodded, staring over the older man's shoulder with the five stars newly pinned to his epaulet. The general of the armies was twenty-one years older than his commander in chief, but Marshall surmised that the aviator was assessing technical aspects. He was right. "It'd be unusually large, and very heavy, wouldn't it?"

"Yes."

"That means a B-29 then."

"Correct. We have a tactical group already formed and training in Utah. General Arnold has the details for you."

"Thank you, General." Lindbergh motioned toward the door leading to the meeting room. Then he paused. "Oh, you said this is top secret. Who knows about it?"

"Well, sir, outside of the Manhattan Project itself, barely twenty people. Pres . . . Mr. Roosevelt, of course. But we've kept a very close hold. Not even Senator Truman knows of it."

Lindbergh allowed himself a wry smile. "The senator charged with oversight of military spending? Roosevelt's running mate?" He shook his head. "Why not?"

Marshall's gaze was level, looking up at the younger man. "Mr. President, he did not need to know."

"Well, General, my vice president does."

LINDBERGH FOLLOWED Marshall back into the meeting room and took a seat. He quickly glanced around the table, assessing the men whom he needed to bring about his goal—a goal that he knew many would oppose. Seated closest to him was Tom Dewey; next the secretaries of war and navy—Henry Stimson and James Forrestal. Both were Republicans tapped by FDR for their managerial skills and experience. Lindbergh decided to keep them aboard since he knew them as dedicated and competent; Forrestal had even been a naval aviator in the First War.

Of the other cabinet positions, Lindbergh was mildly satisfied. State: Edward R. Stettinius remained; he had presence. Treasury: industrialist Henry Kaiser was a decent choice. In any case, Morgenthau had to go; he'd been there nearly ten years and was much too concerned with "the Jewish question." Attorney general: another holdover, Francis Biddle had played a little role in the grand strategy, but he was nominally responsible for overseeing counterespionage.

On the military side, in addition to Marshall was Henry Arnold, an old acquaintance who headed the semi-independent army air force. *We'll see about that,* Lindbergh told himself. *America should have an independent air branch.*

Then there was Fleet Adm. Ernest J. King: tough, opinionated, almost studiously abrasive. Another aviator, though, and a submariner to boot—clearly well qualified to remain chief of naval operations. The U-boats had been defeated eighteen months ago.

Lindbergh leaned forward on the polished table, inhaled, thought to himself, *Here we go.* He let out his breath. "Gentlemen, many of you already know of my intentions for the conduct of the war. As I indicated in my inaugural remarks, I believe that we must seek an early end rather than outright victory over Germany. Tens of thousands of American lives can be saved."

He paused, allowing that sentiment to sink in. Secretary of State Stettinius, predictably, raised the first concern. He made an impressive presence, handsome and white-haired at age forty-four. "Mr. President, I am of course aware of your preference, and I wish to go on record as stating that we have briefly discussed this matter. But sir, this nation already is committed to the unconditional surrender of Germany. We have solemn pacts to that effect with Britain, Russia, and our other allies." The secretary of state paused for effect, adding, "As you know."

The president returned the diplomat's level gaze, the flier's blue eyes never blinking. "Indeed I do know, Mr. Secretary. But I know some other things as well." He held up one finger. "Tens of thousands of American lives are at stake; three or four times as many more will be crippled." A second finger. "Nazi Germany is on the ropes; we're coming out of the Ardennes offensive in even better condition than we went in." He glanced at Marshall. "Is that a fair assessment, General?"

The army chief bit his lip, nodded slowly. "Yes, yes it is. The Germans gambled heavily on what is being called the Battle of the Bulge. They made early gains but lacked the ability to sustain the drive. Their losses in men and materiel are considerable. Ours are heavy but are being offset fairly quickly. Hitler cannot possibly regain the initiative again. It's just a matter of time."

Lindbergh gave a faint smile of approval. *He doesn't like where I'm leading—probably doesn't like me. It doesn't matter.* "Within weeks, or a few months at the most, we'll be at the Rhine. Gentlemen, that is where I propose that we and the British halt our advance."

The Washington brain trust gave a collective gasp; heads turned and a few knuckles paled. Somebody—perhaps King—snapped a pencil. "You mean, just stop the war? Let Hitler go on running Germany?" It was Stettinius again. Clearly he had not bargained for a unilateral approach.

"No, not quite. What I propose, gentlemen, is an announcement that the Western allies will advance only as far as the Rhine, returning the occupied countries to their rightful owners. At that point, the German nation must decide whether to survive or perish, because if we and the Soviets cross those borders, then Germany will cease to exist. I know of the postwar plans to divide the country."

Henry Stimson, the elder statesman who had overseen the growth of the greatest army in American history, raised a hand like a schoolboy. "Mr. President, I daresay that nobody in this room disagrees with your aim of preserving American lives. But Hitler and his regime are criminals—the greatest in history. It is simply unthinkable to permit them to continue in power." He shrugged. "Besides, Stalin will have no part of it—nor, I think, will Churchill."

"Mr. Stimson, you are correct. But let's face facts. The British are dependent upon us and in no way can they prosecute the war alone."

"Some would say they did just that in 1940," Arnold offered.

"To a large extent, yes. It was a gallant effort, and it succeeded. But Hap, you know as well as anyone that it was completely different from now. The Battle of Britain was a purely defensive victory, won by courage and pursuit aviation and radar. But today, Britain has neither the manpower nor the logistics to defeat Germany on the ground."

Stettinius rapped on the table. "Mr. President, I must repeat: one of the core issues is bringing the Nazis to account. If we are seen to permit Hitler's gang to remain in power, the ramifications are vast and unknowable. It could easily lead to outright conflict with Russia."

Lindbergh literally shrugged off the suggestion. Some spines felt chills as a result. "Gentlemen, hear me out. I am not finished with my proposal. I suggest that we appeal to the German public's sense of survival: few Western troops on their soil, the bombing stops, relief supplies begin to flow. They must merely agree to cease hostilities and install a civilian government. Herr Hitler, Reischsmarshal Göring, and the rest will answer to an international tribunal."

"I'll be damned." It was King.

"Double damned." It was Forrestal.

"But it'll never work!" Stettinius was growing agitated. "Surely you don't expect Adolf Hitler just to step down and walk into a trial that'll surely execute him."

Vice President Dewey spoke for the first time. "Charles and I have discussed this at length, gentlemen. There's a German underground, and we know for certain that elements in the Wehrmacht welcome our plan. Even after the purges last summer, following the assassination attempt, there's an organization in place." He tweaked his mustache. "Frankly, I'd be surprised if Hitler and most of the others survive the event."

Warming to his subject, Dewey continued. "We also know it'll be a hard sell with part of the American public, but just think of it— thousands and thousands of families will be spared the agony of sons and brothers and husbands and fathers killed or maimed. Now, we believe that we can convince the Brits to come in with us. Churchill's an old warhorse, but he'll only be a wartime prime minister. We know from our London contacts that we'll have support in both houses of Parliament."

"That still leaves the Russians," Stettinius repeated.

Lindbergh stood—a conscious decision to emphasize his commitment. "Gentlemen, we are faced with two postwar situations: a Europe at least 50 percent controlled by the communist Soviet Union or a Europe resembling the status quo ante in 1939. Which do you prefer?"

No one replied, which is what Lindbergh expected. "Very well, then. We'll meet again tomorrow to continue this discussion. Meanwhile, I have a great deal of reading to do." He looked at the CNO. "Admiral King, I shall require some additional information from you. Good day, gentlemen."

MONDAY, JANUARY 22, 1945

Lindbergh buzzed his military aide, who despite the early hour responded on the loudspeaker with a crisp "Yes sir!"

"Bring me the Pearl Harbor files."

"Right away, sir."

The debacle that was America's most humiliating military defeat cried for investigation. Flipping through the folders, Lindbergh noted the summaries from the four hearings already held thus far. The Roberts Commission, headed by an associate justice of the Supreme Court, had clearly been a whitewash. It began barely after the smoke settled and the dead were buried, concluding in January 1942. The army and two navy hearings at least gave the impression of effort, each lasting several months in 1944. Two other investigations were still under way, run by army officers to determine how secret documents and code-breaking applied to the disaster.

With twenty-four hundred Americans dead and the Pacific Fleet a shambles, somebody had to pay. Therefore, the army and navy commanders in Hawaii became Roosevelt's scapegoats: Admiral Kimmel and General Short. Clearly they had been denied crucial information by Washington—allegedly to protect intelligence sources—and Lindbergh noted an almost incredible string of assumptions and arrogance. The so-called bomb-plot message was perhaps the most damning. He knew that U.S. intelligence was reading the Japanese diplomatic code called "Purple," dividing Pearl Harbor into grids. It was useless for anything but targeting—plotting—specific ships and other targets. Nowhere else in the Pacific Ocean received such treatment. As a former military aviator, Lindbergh recognized the significance—why didn't anyone else?

Then there were the back-channel reports he had heard from 1942 onward. He moved in celebrated circles, knew people and people who knew people. The Brits had known what was coming—apparently Churchill had phoned Roosevelt that the Japanese carriers were headed east! Evidently the Dutch knew; reportedly the Koreans and even the Peruvians—the Peruvians!—had indications. What in the hell went wrong?

Much as he sympathized with the disgraced commanders, Lindbergh noted disapprovingly the events of that Sunday morning. The destroyer *Ward* attacked and evidently sank a midget submarine an hour before the Japanese planes attacked, but still the enemy achieved surprise. Then the Opana radar station tracked a large formation—estimated at fifty-plus aircraft—north of Oahu, but the army decided it was a dozen bombers! Incredible. Just incredible.

Then there was the matter of Gen. George C. Marshall. Lindbergh instinctively distrusted the man. Oh, the chief of staff was capable enough—he'd built the modern U.S. Army as much as anyone and he was a hard worker. But Lindbergh had talked privately with reporters who received a briefing from Marshall a few days before the disaster, informing them off the record that Japan was about to strike. And why could the chief of staff not account for his movements that morning? The usual story was that he was out of contact on his regular Sunday horseback ride.

No wonder some Roosevelt haters were hinting at a conspiracy. It was common knowledge that he wanted America in the war to preserve Britain. After all, that was the basis of Lindbergh and Roosevelt's bitter acrimony dating from 1936. *We injected ourselves into the last war,* Lindbergh told himself, *and the Europeans only needed twenty-one years to start it again.* He wondered if perhaps the best thing that could have happened in the twentieth century might have been a German victory in 1914. Some property would have changed hands, things would have settled down in the Balkans, and perhaps there would have been no Bolshevik Revolution. It was all so clear: the global threat was communism, not fascism. Hitler and Mussolini had few adherents beyond their own borders. Why didn't Americans understand that?

Rear Adm. Clarence Darrow Burns sat beside King, a study in contrast. Lindbergh knew that the chief of naval operations was a self-proclaimed SOB who allegedly was so tough that he shaved with a blowtorch. Burns, his operations analyst, was suave and poised. Lindbergh looked at the two navy men and bluntly asked, "Gentlemen, I've read the files, but I need to know more." He paused for effect. "What really happened at Pearl Harbor?"

Burns obviously had been delegated by King to do most of the talking. "Mr. President, the best explanation we can provide is that the Japs got just about every break possible. They kept rolling the dice and coming up sevens." He spread some notes on the table before him. "As we analyze it, there were three main factors beyond the fact that they achieved complete surprise.

"First was the *Nevada*. She was the only battlewagon to get under way, but when those Jap dive-bombers sank her smack in the middle of the channel, she blew up like the *Arizona*. The rest of the Pacific Fleet was bottled up, and it took several weeks to clear a path. Even then, access was restricted until the following summer.

"Next, the Japs came back and hit us where it really hurt. They destroyed almost 80 percent of our fuel storage, which severely limited operations beyond Hawaiian waters. Those ruined tanks had to be cleared away, new conduits and pumps installed, and new tanks built. Combined with heavy damage to the sub base, we were just out of business . . . and that doesn't even take into account the poor performance of our torpedoes." Burns cast a sideways glance at King. "Some strategists feel that the failure of our submarines cost us the Philippines."

Lindbergh chewed his lower lip. "I've heard that the Jap commander didn't want to launch a third attack—the one that leveled our fuel farm."

Burns's reaction was mild astonishment. Unless the president had received an extremely fast briefing on that subject, somebody was blabbing. "Well, yes sir. Did you discuss signals intelligence with Admiral . . ."

"Let's just say that I know some people. Continue."

"Um. Yes sir. Ah, we began reading JN-25, the Japanese fleet code, a couple of months after the attack. We learned that Admiral Nagumo considered his mission accomplished after the first two waves and intended to break off and return to Japan. However, his air staff convinced him that with our carriers at sea, the best move was to sink them or hit their fuel supplies to keep them pinned in Hawaii. As it turned out, they pretty much had it both ways.

"Then, losing *Enterprise* to the subs and torpedo planes . . . well, we just didn't have anything left to throw at the Japs. It's still a minor miracle that *Lexington* survived, especially with all those marine scout-bombers on deck. They were going to Midway and . . ."

"Damn Bull Halsey." It was King, his tone acerbic as only the CNO could manage. "He was a fighter, no doubt about that, but he wasn't much of a thinker. What the hell did he expect to accomplish against *six* Jap carriers? It was damned bad luck that they found each other. He should've disengaged, preserved one-third of the PacFleet carriers, and come back to fight another day."

King stared at the desktop—actually, Lindbergh noted, the sea dog glared at it. "That's why we made him a dead hero. Otherwise we'd have court-martialed him."

Burns, visibly edgy, returned the conversation to its previous track. "Anyway, Mr. President, after 8 December we had exactly one carrier operating in the Pacific. *Saratoga* was loading planes in San Diego, but she was torpedoed by a Jap sub a month later. With *Lexington* also laid up for repairs, no battleships, and the subs practically useless, we had no meaningful way to strike back. We moved *York-town* from the Atlantic Fleet, and *Hornet* was newly commissioned, so General Doolittle's plan went ahead. You certainly know about that."

"Yes, Jimmy did a splendid job. But as I understand it, in the long run the Tokyo raid did us little good."

"Well, that's probably correct, sir. It goaded the Japs into capturing Midway, and we lost *Hornet* with *Yorktown* badly damaged. That was a squeaker—we missed getting the *Lex* and *Sara* to the battle by a few days. The Japs took Midway, of course, but it didn't do them a lot of good. As you'll recall, we recaptured the island in the spring of '43."

"Allow me to summarize," Lindbergh said. "We were forced into the defensive against Japan because it would take perhaps two years to rebuild our naval strength. The decision had already been made to concentrate on Germany, the main enemy, which suited Mr. Churchill's purpose anyway. Consequently, there's been a de facto cease-fire in the Pacific over the past three years, which doesn't sit well with the public."

King harrumphed.

"Yes, Admiral?"

"Mr. President, if I may I will speak candidly."

Lindbergh's eyes gleamed. "You do have that reputation, Admiral King."

"Yes. Well. Harrumph." King cleared his throat. "Sir, let's not dance around here. The fact that you occupy this office is partly due to the fact that the public was increasingly dissatisfied with Mr. Roosevelt's handling of the war. That is, apart from your objection to our becoming involved at all."

"Quite so."

"Mr. President, frankly . . . well, some highly placed people wondered if it was entirely coincidental that sensitive information about Mr. Roosevelt appeared when it did."

Lindbergh felt his neck reddening around the collar. He exerted some of the discipline that had kept him alive in more perilous times. "You mean a few weeks before the election. Go on, Admiral."

"Yes sir. After all, the German Abwehr was behind the so-called leaks. Admiral Canaris was quite astute in his timing, and he was brilliant in the way he released it via South American sources so neither you nor your campaign would be tainted. Most of the public did not mind the fact that their three-term president was crippled with polio, but many did resent that he concealed it for twelve years. And the press was complicit, no question. As for the . . . other . . . information, well, infidelity is hardly new in Washington. And the fact that the president's military secretary, an active-duty general, had been managing political events was more improper than illegal. But then it became known that the president had authorized a shooting war against Germany and Japan without bothering with Senate ratification, followed by the implication that Mr. Roosevelt conspired with the British to conceal prior knowledge of the attack . . ."

There were arched eyebrows and twitchy fingers in the room. Everyone present knew King's meaning: by themselves the individual revelations or accusations were nuisances. In combination they proved lethal. If anything, among some Americans Lindbergh's prewar statements about the Asian race now seemed less controversial in light of Pearl Harbor. Additionally, the Republican Party finally had pulled itself together. Robert Taft of Ohio was the other leading isolationist in the GOP camp, but party strategists felt that his influence and ability were better employed in the Senate. A team player, he subordinated his personal ambition to accomplish the mission of unseating FDR.

Lindbergh almost smiled at King's granite edifice. "Thank you for your candor, Admiral. It's what we've come to expect." There were grins and subdued chuckles around the table. "But there's something else to consider in all this. I may not possess a medical degree, but I do know something about the human body. I can say without fear of contradiction that Franklin Roosevelt had no business running for a fourth term. He's a man on his last legs in the most demanding position in this country. I predict that he won't last another six months; he certainly would not live out this term. Yet apparently he allowed his ego to override his intellect and his obligation to the interests of this nation. That is why I feel little regret in undoing some of the ill-conceived policies he established in this war."

The president rose to leave, and the powerful men assembled around him stood in respect for his office if not entirely for its occupant. As Lindbergh exited, the chief of the air forces heard something muttered by the secretary of state.

"How's that, Ed?" Arnold asked.

Stettinius slowly shook his white-maned head. "I just cannot conceive how a former stunt flier can manage this nation, let alone this war. Even one as accomplished as Lindbergh."

Hap Arnold pinned the secretary of state with an impish-peevish grin. The five-star general usually resembled an overage elf; now he seemed the pixie from hell. "Ed, don't you *dare* underestimate Charles Lindbergh. Like it or not, he's president of the United States and commander in chief of our armed forces. It's downright arrogant to regard him as a 'stunt flier.' Let me tell you something . . ." Arnold paused, then decided not to stalk around the table to Stettinius's side.

"Slim is one damn fine airman, which has absolutely nothing to do with his qualifications for office. But you and a lot of other people in this town need to get it out of your heads that the first solo flight across the Atlantic was some sort of damned stunt! It was a meticulously planned event that still could have gone wrong and cost that young man his life. That's why he's so damned confident and self-assured. You heard his campaign speeches—were those the ramblings of some throttle jockey? Have you ever heard a shade-tree mechanic use the language as he does?"

Stettinius began to respond, but Arnold cut him off. "Furthermore, Lindbergh is not some flash in the pan. He's representative of his generation—men like Doolittle and Byrd and Al Williams, who are superb fliers, highly educated people, well traveled with keen, analytical minds. Do you know of anybody else who's done what Slim did—his so-called stunt—and then devised life-saving surgical procedures with Dr. Carrell? Anybody who wrote a medical treatise like *The Culture of Organs*?"

Stettinius slumped into his padded chair. He seemed to deflate then rallied himself against the unexpected onslaught. "Hap, please." He gestured to the empty seat across the table. Arnold slowly resumed his place.

"Hap, all I'm saying is that there's never been anything like this situation. Not ever. And you cannot blame people who are concerned about Lindbergh's cozy relations with the Nazis. Now with this new proposal to leave Germany intact, it looks, well . . . like appeasement."

Arnold, hands folded on the table, pressed his chin to his uniform briefly. His knuckles went white, his face flushed. When he looked up again, his voice was ice. "I'm going to tell you people something that's not known. Slim didn't just happen to go to Germany and meet Hitler and Göring. He didn't just happen to visit their factories, interview their engineers, and fly their airplanes. He went there at the request of the Army Air Corps." Arnold allowed that fact to sink in. Its effect was electric in the room. "That's right. We knew that he could go places and learn things that nobody else could. But it had to appear that it was his doing. So he made the approaches; he established the contacts. He was playing the Germans like trout on a line. They thought they could convince him of their superiority even though—and we suspected—that it was part of their propaganda. To make the British and French fear their air force before it was a mature weapon.

"Slim Lindbergh accepted that thankless task even though he knew it would cause some Americans to lose their respect for him. But the information he brought back never made the papers." Arnold looked around the room, taking in the somber faces. "I wonder how many public figures in this city would risk their personal and professional reputations on behalf of their country."

TUESDAY, JANUARY 23, 1945

THE MEETING took up where it had left off two days before. Edward Stettinius sat back, inhaled, then slowly exhaled, staring at the tabletop. Finally he looked up. "For a moment let's assume that Germany accepts our offer. That still does not address the important aspects still outstanding—especially conditions within Germany and the criminal acts that have lasted for years. I mean, unless we physically occupy German soil, how can we bring Hitler and his thugs to account, let alone begin to redress atrocities such as the persecution of the Jews?" The diplomat spread his hands, palms up. "We have strong evidence that millions of people have been exterminated!"

Lindbergh drummed his fingers on the table, obviously nervous. "Yes, Mr. Secretary, I've heard the rumors and I've even seen some of the reports. But as you say, until we have independent verification, we don't *really* know what's happened there, do we?" He straightened in his chair, leveling his gaze at Stettinius. "You know, I have learned at great cost—to my family's great cost—something of human nature. I will not dwell on it, but the endless hounding by the press, the sensational treatment of my child's murder . . . I certainly do not deny the baser aspects of human nature." He thought for a moment. "But . . . I also know that the survival instinct runs deep within the human psyche. If even part of what we've heard is true, how can we credit it? For these monstrous acts to occur, it is necessary to conclude that vast numbers of people have been systematically slaughtered—with hardly one shred of resistance. How could millions of human beings cooperate in their own extermination? I repeat: How is that possible?"

Stettinius's voice raised an octave; pleading, supplicating. "Charles, my god! The Nazis have the power—they have the guns! Apparently they even have the consent of a large segment of the German population!"

The president managed to suppress the condescending tone he felt building in his throat. "Look around this room. Go ahead—take a look! Would *anybody* here stand by and watch his family, his very *race,* sent to oblivion without rising up, even bare-handed? Of course not! No matter what the odds, none of us would meekly submit to such barbarity—and there cannot be enough Nazis, enough guards, to outnumber the reported victims." He shook his head emphatically. "No, Edward. *No!* It is not logically credible. Therefore, we will proceed as I have outlined." He rose and scanned the cabinet. "Thank you, gentlemen."

After the conference, Vice President Dewey followed Lindbergh to the Oval Office. Dewey sat forward on the edge of his chair. "Mr. President, I concede that Germany *might* agree to your proposal. But there's a larger question—how will Stalin react? He's under no obligation to abide by what we do."

"That's right, Tom. He's not. Too many people in this country have conveniently forgotten that Stalin and Hitler signed a nonaggression pact despite the fact that they were bitter ideological enemies. Yet that didn't prevent them from invading Poland a month later and carving up the country between them. Less than two years later they were killing each other in large numbers."

Dewey nodded, uncertain where Lindbergh was leading.

"My point is, in no way may we rely upon the goodwill of Moscow. That is why we need to stop the communists where they are—preferably by convincing them that it is in their best interest to do so, before they rule the European Continent. Whatever Hitler's crimes, I still believe that a victory by Germany's European people would be preferable to one by Russia's semi-Asiatic Soviet Union. That's something that Roosevelt either accepted or ignored."

While Dewey was absorbing that statement, Lindbergh reached for the call box on his desk. "Mrs. Dundee, get me General Arnold. And have the *Spirit* put on alert at Bolling Field. Destination—Wendover, Utah."

Dewey could not contain his curiosity. "What's in Utah, Charles?"

Looking at his vice president, Lindbergh replied, "That young colonel named Tibbetts with the 509th Composite Group."

Dewey, who unlike Truman had been informed of the Manhattan Project, sat bolt upright. His eyes widened at the implication, and he heard himself utter the thought: *Oh . . . my . . . GOD!*

11

Beer, Betrayal, and Ho Chi Minh

DOUG ALLYN

BAD LUCK. THAT'S ALL it was. A stray round from a Japanese Arisaka 6.5-mm service rifle. A lousy inch one way or the other. The difference between life and death in Indochina.

Flying his L-4 Piper Cub at five hundred feet, Lt. Toby Bishop was scouting the Red River for Japanese barges. And finding them. Columns of them, linked by hawsers, being towed by tugs or hauled by human trains of coolies trudging along the riverbank.

The imperial forces were on the move. After easy victories in Burma and Thailand, the Japanese were shifting troops and supplies across Vietnam to reinforce their armies on the Chinese mainland.

It was obviously the beginning of a pincer movement designed to envelop and crush the ragtag remnants of the Chinese Nationalist army fighting under Generalissimo Chiang Kai-shek. The Japanese called it their Asia for Asians campaign. But apparently the Chinese didn't qualify, because the Japs had been killing them by the millions since the thirties.

Following their incredible success at Pearl Harbor, a raid that destroyed the American Pacific Fleet and its vital aircraft carriers, the Japanese had pretty much done as they pleased in the Pacific theater. With no American naval force to oppose them, the empire won smashing victories at Wake Island, Midway, and the Philippines. Malaya fell, then Burma.

And while their armies marched, their engineers were completing the Ring of Fire, a chain of fortified islands that girded the Pacific from the Solomons to the Aleutians: Tarawa, Saipan, Iwo Jima, and dozens more.

And with the ring nearing completion, they asked Roosevelt for peace talks.

They nearly got them.

Hawaii was practically defenseless against the Japanese navy. If it fell, San Francisco would be next. In Congress, the America First isolationists urged FDR to face reality.

The Axis victories at Dunkirk and Pearl Harbor proved that democracies had no business trying to defend the weak nations of the world. It was simple national Darwinism. A new age was dawning and only the strong would survive.

America would be best served by staying out of foreign wars. Let the Nazis keep Europe. Let the Japanese swallow China if they could. Build our defenses while the Axis powers are busy gobbling up their neighbors. Fortress America can negotiate with them from a position of strength when the fighting stops.

FDR admitted their arguments were both logical and perfectly practical. Of course, there was a minor point of national honor involved.

After the debate had raged for weeks, the president addressed Congress. With his "day which will live in infamy" speech, he asked them to declare war on the Axis. The vote was close, but in the end, lingering American anger over Pearl Harbor carried the day.

Declaring war was one thing. Fighting it was another. With no footholds left in the Pacific, America was reduced to supporting the Brits in India and the Nationalists in China.

For Lt. Toby Bishop, war was pure frustration. Losing friends, losing ground. Begging supplies and gasoline from the British air command at Lalaghat to fly routine reconnaissance missions over Indochina, keeping track of how quickly the Japanese were conquering Asia.

At least the river recon flights were relatively safe. Sort of. The freight barges had machine guns mounted in the bows, but their muzzles were trained onshore to keep the coolies in line. The boats had no antiaircraft batteries. Nor did they need any.

The Brits didn't bother to fly sorties over south China, and the Chinese Nationalists were hoarding their aviation fuel and battered planes to support their armies on the eastern front.

The only planes in daily contact with the Japanese forces were a scant handful of American recon fliers like Bishop. And they were harmless. Their little L-4 Piper monoplanes were unarmed.

Bishop made an official request to have his flight mechanic mount a Browning .30-caliber machine gun on one wing, but the Brit base commander at Lalaghat denied it.

"The Nips aren't bothering with air cover or flak over the convoys, Lieutenant Bishop. If you start shooting them up, Tojo will send a squadron of Zeros to put you out of business. If you want combat, try enlisting in the Chindit guerrillas, eh? They have all they can handle."

So Toby flew his daily flights unarmed. And unhappy. What the hell was HQ doing with all these pictures and reports, anyway? Wiping their asses with them? Any moron could see the score. The Allies were losing, Japan was winning, end of story.

Once China was conquered they'd turn on India, run the Brits out, and build a Fortress Asia in the Far East that would make Europe look like a playpen. They'd be invincible. Hell, they nearly were already.

But everything changed for Toby on December 7, 1943, the anniversary of the great Pearl Harbor raid. Flying a routine recon mission, he was photographing a column of supply barges on the Red River when a Japanese officer on a tugboat bridge started shooting at him. With his sidearm! A dinky little Nambu pistol.

Popping away, laughing with his friends, the casual contempt of the act pushed Toby over the edge. He'd had enough!

Opening the L-4's throttle, he pushed it into a steep dive, aiming the Piper's propeller at a river barge loaded with imperial troops.

Startled by the plane suddenly hurtling down at them out of the cloudy sky, some of the troops leaped overboard into the roiling water and flailed helplessly around the barge as their packs dragged them under, drowning them like rats. Ashore, the coolies scattered and ran for their lives, leaving the barge dangerously adrift in midstream.

Cackling at the mischief he'd caused, Toby kept the L-4 at wave-top level, blasting along the river at ninety knots, the little 65-horsepower Continental engine howling like the world's biggest Mix Master.

He buzzed two more barges, flashing over their decks, clearing them by inches, watching the terrified soldiers abandon ship while their officers cursed and shook their fists at him.

Damn! If he'd realized how much fun recon missions could be, he'd quit bellyaching about a combat assignment. He'd found the perfect way to fight the Japanese. Don't waste ammo on 'em. Scare the bastards to death!

Banking sharply, he was veering around the next river bend, with his wingtip only a foot above the silty foam that gave the river its name, when a slug ripped through his windshield! Plexiglas slivers stung his face, gashing his cheek as the wind whistled in through a tiny bullet hole the size of a dime!

Whoa! The troops on the lead tugboat were waiting for him! Urged on by the pipsqueak Lootie who'd started the shooting in the first place, the Japanese riflemen had formed a ragged defensive line in the stern, firing their Arisakas at him in volleys.

Toby never flinched. Imperial soldiers were notoriously bad shots and pulling up would only make him a bigger target anyway. Instead, he threw the throttle wide open, aiming the Piper directly at the tugboat's stern, five feet off the water, win or die.

And it worked. Facing the onrushing plane and death or dismemberment by its propeller, the soldiers broke at the last second! Throwing their weapons away, some dived overboard while the rest clambered over each other to get clear.

Too close! Toby kept the L-4 so low his landing gear slammed into the tug's wheelhouse, ripping away part of the superstructure, hurling it and the Japanese officer into the swirling waters.

Toby nearly followed him. Fighting to control the pitching aircraft, he barely avoided crashing into the trees along the riverbank, then juked hard to the east to avoid gunfire from the next column of barges.

Flying overland now at treetop level, Toby risked a glance backward. The river was littered with soldiers, some swimming, some floating, already dead. One of the barges had run aground, burying its prow in the muddy bank, dragging the column into the shallows, and effectively blocking the river.

Grinning with relief, Bishop eased the Piper's nose up, climbing toward the distant cover of the clouds. Aloft, without the constant blur of jungle shrubbery hurtling past, everything seemed to slow a bit. Time to shake his head at his own foolishness, take a deep breath and—smell gasoline!

Damn! The cockpit reeked of aviation fuel! He could see it, too, a fine mist blowing out of his right-wing tank, misting the cockpit window, coating the plane with high-test gas.

Luck. A dumb-lucky shot by a Jap rifleman who probably couldn't hit himself in the ass with a Ping-Pong paddle. Jesus, this couldn't be happening

But it was. The fuel gauge was sinking fast, and Toby was still a full two hours from the border. No way he could make it back to Lalaghat now. And if he came down anywhere near the river and the Japanese took him. . . . No. He'd suicide-dive the Piper into a troop barge first.

But not yet. Hauling back on the yoke, he powered the Piper into a steep climb toward the sun, trying for altitude, the higher the better.

Flicking on his wireless, he keyed a quick mayday in Morse code with his call sign and an approximate position. But even as he did it he realized it was hopeless. From this height all he could see was jungle—no clearings, no roads.

The Piper began sputtering, and he hastily switched it off. His fuel was gone anyway, and he didn't want a coughing engine to signal his troubles to the troops below.

After the constant din of the motor, the sudden silence was startling, ominous. The Piper nosed over and started down.

Fortunately the little high-winged monoplane made a fair glider. Keeping his line of descent as shallow as he could, Toby frantically scanned the ground for a place to land, any kind of an opening in the green canopy.

Smoke. Ahead and to the right. The east? A faint haze of smoke hanging above the trees. Japanese camp? Native village? Didn't matter. There might be fields nearby, somewhere to land. If he hit the trees he was dead. If he bailed out and the Japanese spotted him, he'd end up just as dead but a lot slower and more painfully.

Better to take his chances with the plane. And the smoke. Easing the rudder over, he swung the nose east, veering toward the haze. Even as he did so, he realized he'd never make it.

The turn had cost him too much airspeed. He was dropping faster now, the jungle canopy rushing up to meet him—and then he flashed over a clearing. Open fields. Rice paddies!

No hesitation. Toby hauled back on the yoke, throwing the Piper into an instant stall, dropping it like a rock into the opening. For a moment he thought he might actually make a fair landing. But he had too much airspeed. And then the fields were smaller than he'd thought. He was running out of room.

With the jungle rushing toward him, he braced himself and tried to veer off, but one of his wings hooked and then he was banging around in the cockpit like a pinball as the Piper cartwheeled through the mire and slammed into the trees!

Get the fuck out! Stunned by the crash, ears ringing, only half conscious, Toby's sole thought was to get clear of the Piper before the damned thing caught fire . . . or the Japanese found him.

Somehow he managed to get his safety harness unsnapped, kick the door open, and stumble out onto the muck.

The humid air and the stench of human fertilizer was so overpowering it nearly dropped him to his knees. He could see grass huts on the far side of the paddy. The smoke from cooking fires. Couldn't tell if the village was native or Japanese. Hell, he didn't even know what country he was in.

And it didn't matter. Anywhere short of India was Japanese territory now. The villagers must have heard the plane crash, which meant the Nips would be coming soon. He had to get clear of the wreck.

So far, he'd been lucky. He was shaken up but nothing seemed to be broken and the plane hadn't caught fire. If he could get a good start he could lose himself in the jungle before the Japanese showed.

He limped into the rain forest a hundred yards or so, stopped to check his compass. When he looked up he was facing gun muzzles. Two rifles in the hands of . . . he couldn't be sure. Asians? In khaki shorts and shirts, black scarves, rubber sandals, straw coolie hats. With bandoleers across their chests. Young. Scrawny. Probably still in their teens. Old enough to pull a trigger, though.

Toby's Smith and Wesson .38 was holstered under his armpit, but it might as well have been on the moon. The taller one motioned upward with his rifle. Toby slowly raised his hands. Damn!

"Parlez?" the youth asked.

Toby shook his head. He wasn't even sure what language the kid was speaking.

"Parlez vous Francais?" the boy insisted. His accent was strong but at least this time Toby got his drift.

"No," he said slowly, shaking his head for emphasis, pointing to himself. "No parley fran-say. American."

The boys glanced at each other, confused. But their guns never wavered. The guns. Their battered rifles weren't Arisaka, they were old Mausers, the kind the Chinese Nationalists used. Maybe these guys weren't working for the Japanese. "Mer-can?" the boy echoed.

"A-mer-i-can," Toby nodded, emphasizing each syllable, though he couldn't be sure if he was helping himself or signing his own death warrant.

"Rossvull?" the shorter one asked.

"Roosevelt," Toby agreed, nodding more vigorously. "President Roosevelt."

If the older boy was impressed, he hid it well. He slapped his chest, indicating Toby's shoulder holster, and held out his hand.

Last chance. Without his weapon he'd be helpless. Could he draw and fire before they did? No way. They might be young, but their eyes had the wary emptiness of seasoned fighters. One false move and they'd blow him out of his socks.

Reluctantly, Toby drew his .38 and passed it to the taller youth.

Frowning, the kid examined it carefully, as if he'd never seen a revolver before. Perhaps hadn't. Satisfied, he nodded. And handed the gun back.

"Rossvull," he repeated, pointing to Toby. "Padua," he said thumbing himself in the chest.

"Padua," Toby echoed, uncertain of its meaning. The boy's name? It must have been close enough. Motioning for Toby to follow, the youths turned and headed into the jungle.

Toby stood there a moment, dazed, shivering. He'd half expected the kid to kill him the moment he handed over his pistol. Or to bind his hands and sell him to the Japanese.

Apparently not. He had no idea who these guys were, but his luck seemed to be holding. Somehow he'd survived the crash. And since the two gunmen hadn't killed him straightaway, maybe they weren't going to. Maybe, just maybe, he was going to live through this after all.

Taking a deep breath, Lt. Toby Bishop holstered his revolver and fell into step behind the two young riflemen, following them to . . . wherever. He had no idea who they were or where they were going. But it was better than staying where he was. He hoped.

THE C-46 LURCHED, dropping a heart-stopping fifty feet in a half-second. Maj. Fletcher Patterson's stomach gave a similar lurch. Last time he'd checked, the Chinese Nationalist pilot had been flying the transport above the jungle at treetop level.

Unsnapping his safety harness, Patterson rose from the metal folding seat against the bulkhead. Using the overhead chute line to steady himself, he wobbled to the open cargo door to stare out into the night.

The windblast was horrific. Patterson guessed the pilot had the C-46's twin Pratt and Whitney radial engines revving near their maximum speed, but they weren't at treetop level anymore. They were well below it. The ChiNat pilot was rocketing along a riverbed only a dozen feet above the ripples, the glistening waterway stretching out ahead of them like a ribbon of moonlight.

Jesus H. Christ! What was this moron thinking? That they could make a parachute drop from ten feet at 250 knots?

Angrily, Fletch worked his way forward to the cockpit and tapped the pilot on the shoulder.

"*Wu bai chr! Wu bai chr!* Five hundred feet!" Patterson shouted over the roar of the engines, pointing down to indicate the minimum altitude for a night jump.

Unimpressed, the pilot jerked his thumb toward the rear of the plane. "*Dzwo sya! Syan dzai!*" He slapped his seat-belt harness for emphasis, telling Fletch to sit down and buckle up.

"*Wu bai chr!*" Patterson repeated, turning away. Couldn't make out the ChiNat's growled answer, but from grins he got from the

Chinese flight crew he guessed he'd been told to fuck himself. Or called a turtle's eighth egg, which was even worse. Fighting words under other circumstances.

Sighing, he settled back onto the seat and buckled up. Across the aisle Capt. Rene Beauchamps, his Free French liaison officer, grinned and held his open palm up beside his ear, the Chinese sign for crazy.

Crazy was right. The pilot was slowing down, lowering his revs, dropping his flaps. Jesus, they were too low already! He was going to drop them into the damned river! Which he did, five seconds later.

But instead of a watery crash, the C-46 touched down, bounced once, then made a perfect three-point landing, coasting to a halt on a long sandbar.

Instantly the flight crew sprang to life. Shouting and cursing each other in Mandarin, they began unstrapping the cargo and hustling it out the door.

Fletch and Rene piled out along with it. The ChiNat pilot was already pivoting the plane for takeoff as his crew scrambled back aboard.

Using his brakes to hold the plane in check, the pilot revved his engines to the max. The C-46 was shuddering so violently Fletch figured it was one second from shaking itself to pieces when the ChiNat cut it loose.

Blasting down the sandbar, the plane lifted off again, its undercarriage brushing through the bamboo as it disappeared into the dark.

Stunned by the speed of it all, Fletch and Rene looked warily around them, taking stock. They were stranded in the middle of a river. Somewhere.

Both men wore olive-drab allied uniforms and carried sidearms and Thompson submachine guns. Maj. Fletcher Patterson was the shorter of the two, a squat bulldog of a GI, red-haired, frecklefaced. Huck Finn in a helmet.

Capt. Rene Beauchamps was tall, slender, and sophisticated, with a tastefully tailored uniform and pencil-thin mustache.

"Well, looks like we're here, Captain," Fletch said dryly. "Any idea where the fuck 'here' is?"

"The Nam Yum River, I think," Rene said, "or maybe the Nam Oum. Possibly even the Red, though it seems too shallow for that. Welcome to French Indochina, my friend."

"I thought we were supposed to make a night jump somewhere near the guerrilla camp."

"So did I. Perhaps the camp has been moved. Or the pilot took a bribe to sell us and our supplies to the Japanese," Rene shrugged. "In this part of the world, nothing ever goes as planned, *mon ami*. Get used to it. And get down. We have company."

"Where?" Fletch asked, dropping behind a cargo crate.

"Along the far shore. Friendlies, I think. The Japanese would have started shooting already." Rene rose, lowering his weapon, waving his arm. *"Vietminh? Vietminh?"*

There was no reply, but a dozen men immediately slipped out of the bamboo on the shoreline, wading through the waist-deep water to the sandbar.

No uniforms, no insignias of rank. They were dressed in shorts, loose shirts, black scarves, and coolie hats. They all carried machetes, but three of them had firearms. Japanese service rifles with folding bayonets. Brand-new.

The leader, taller than the others and sporting a jagged scar at the corner of his mouth, bowed curtly to Rene, then touched his finger to his lips to signal quiet.

His men were equally silent. Quickly unloading the cargo crates, they divided the radios and bags of rice into manageable loads then waded back into the river without a word.

Ashore, they immediately struck out for the northeast with Rene and Fletch in the center of the column. Keeping to nearly invisible jungle trails, the Vietminh guerrillas stopped only a few minutes every other hour to allow the coolies to exchange or adjust their loads.

Dawn found them in rough country, rocky foothills with fair-sized mountains beyond. Though the going was much more difficult now, their pace never slackened.

At one point they heard an airplane approaching and immediately took cover. The plane passed to the south at the limit of visual range, but not so far off that they couldn't make out the rising sun on its fuselage.

It was 14:30 before "Scarface" finally called a halt, leading them off the trail to some shelter beneath a rock shelf by a small stream. Shedding their packs, the coolies untied their neckerchiefs. To Patterson's surprise, the scarves were sewn closed to carry rice. Each man carefully sprinkled a fistful into his palm and chewed it dry, washing it down with water from the spring.

No one spoke to Beauchamps or Patterson or approached them, but since a few of the coolies were conversing quietly in their own language, Fletch figured the silent march order had expired.

"Any idea where we are now?" he whispered as he eased down beside Rene.

"In the back country, perhaps fifty kilometers north of Hanoi. The guerrillas have a new mountain base called Tan Trao somewhere in the area. I'm fairly sure that's where we're headed."

"How far?"

"No idea."

"Can't you ask?"

"Ask?" Rene echoed.

"We're in French Indochina and you're supposed to be an interpreter," Fletch said, exasperated. "Don't any of these guys speak French?"

"These men are Nungs," Rene explained quietly. "Native tribesmen. Headhunters at one time. The equivalent of your American Indians, Apaches or Sioux. I wouldn't speak French to them, if I were you, my friend. It could get you killed."

"Killed? Why, for God's sake?"

"I've heard you speak French, Major. Your accent alone would be cause for justifiable homicide. In any case, the Nungs have never accepted French rule and don't speak any language but their own."

"Their rifles are Japanese," Fletch noted. "And they look new."

"Very perceptive," Rene nodded. "And since the Japanese would never supply Nungs with such weapons, we can assume they won them in battle or stole them. I just hope they don't decide they want ours as well."

The march resumed at dusk, climbing steadily upward through the foothills to the mouth of a long narrow canyon. Working their way into the pass, Fletch occasionally spotted sentries in the shadows above them, small dark men scarcely more than shadows themselves. He guessed there were many more he never saw.

After traveling through the night, they entered the village proper at noon the following day, a collection of rude grass huts on both sides of a mountain stream.

A few villagers turned out as they approached, but not to welcome them. They simply observed them in silence. If their arrival aroused any curiosity, the locals concealed it well. No one approached them or made any kind of a fuss. Apparently gunmen coming out of the jungle was a fairly routine business.

And soon they were almost alone. As they made their way through the town, Fletch noted their escorts were peeling off one at a time, returning to their homes without orders or permission, nor so much as a nod.

The last man remaining was the group leader, Scarface, who led them to a large hut at the center of the village.

"Tan Trao," he said, gesturing to the town. He pointed sharply at the ground, indicating they should wait, then strode off.

Fletch glanced at Rene, who shrugged, then both men looked around. Tan Trao was strategically in the middle of nowhere, nestled between two mountains, accessible only by the narrow trail they'd come in on.

"Good defensive position," Patterson noted.

"Better than you realize," Rene agreed. "The Nungs' weapon of choice is the crossbow. In many ways it's superior to the rifle in this terrain: accurate, deadly, and silent. They could have erased us at any point during the past ten kilometers and we would never have seen them. Couldn't even have returned fire. Still, they seem a bit more civilized now. In the old days we would have passed a wall of skulls at the entrance to the village. The taller the wall, the greater the tribe."

"Whose skulls?"

"Uninvited guests, I imagine. Not unlike ourselves."

"Very funny."

"Who's joking?" the Frenchman said mildly.

A moment later the Nung leader returned with two Asians. One was a pudgy little fellow in a white linen suit and a fedora. He smiled and bowed to them in welcome.

Surprisingly, the other Asian was wearing a standard-issue American uniform. He snapped to attention and saluted.

"Welcome to Tan Trao, gentlemen. I'm Sergeant Tom Chan, 544th Infantry, temporarily attached to the Vietminh, Nungs, or whatever you call this outfit. Glad you made it. Any problems on the way, Major?"

"None to speak of," Patterson said. "One Jap plane."

"Then you got lucky," Chan said. "I para-dropped in here with two other radio ops five months ago. I'm the only one left."

"What's the situation here, Sergeant?" Fletch asked.

"Tough. I was sent in to set up radio liaison with ChiNat forces in Kunming, but our radios aren't much use in these mountains. Not enough range. So we started going out with the Nungs against the Japanese, doing what we could."

"What happened to the others?" Rene asked.

"A mine got Corporal Liu. Jap sniper got Sergeant Ning."

"Liu and Ning?" Beauchamps echoed. "They were Chinese like yourself?"

"They were *Americans* like me, Captain," Chan said evenly. "I was born and raised in 'Frisco, grew up with Jack Liu. Some OSS genius figured we'd blend in with the locals. I guess he was right. Mines and snipers sure can't tell the difference."

"Sorry, Sergeant. I meant no offense."

"None taken, sir. Have you met Uncle Ho, the boss?"

"No," Patterson said, bowing politely to the guy in the white linen suit. "Introduce us."

"This isn't him, sir, this is General Vo Nguyen Giap, Uncle Ho's right-hand man. I don't think he speaks English, but I wouldn't bet my life on it. Nothing in this place is ever simple."

The door to the hut was draped with a Japanese army blanket. Chan rapped sharply on the doorpost. "*Ho Syansheng? Meiguo ren daule*" (The American is here).

A moment later the blanket was swept aside and a slender Vietnamese stood in the doorway. "How good of you to come so far, gentlemen. Please come inside. I am Ho Chi Minh."

Fletch's first impression? Ho's English was accented but surprisingly good. Didn't look like all that much, though. He was wearing the same khaki shorts and rubber sandals as his irregulars, and his uniform jacket had no insignia of rank. Slim as a riding crop, his face was gaunt but unlined. Only his silver hair and wispy gray goatee indicated his age, fifty-five or so. His eyes were the most striking thing about him: alert, optimistic, and very intense.

As they followed Ho inside, he noted that the old man seemed a bit unsteady on his pins, a suspicion that was confirmed when he eased carefully down in his chair at the small table in the center of the spartan room. The only other furniture was a small writing desk against one wall. The room beyond held a Japanese army cot with mosquito netting.

"Please sit down, gentlemen," Ho said. "Before we begin, I have gifts for you. First, though tea is customary in my country, in honor of our American guests . . ." He spoke in rapid-fire dialect to the Nung chieftain, who stepped into the backroom and returned a moment later with a brimming water bucket.

Reaching into it, Ho retrieved five bottles of beer. Opening them carefully, he passed them out to his guests. "Gifts from the Japanese," he said with a faint smile. "I hope the vintage is acceptable. We've aged it for a week."

Exhausted from his night march, Patterson's first instinct was to grab the beer and guzzle it straight down. But he caught the warning in Tommy Chan's eyes. And realized how expensive Ho's little gesture really was. The price of these small bottles had probably been paid in blood.

"A toast?" Chan offered. "To victory."

"Victory," the others echoed, raising their bottles.

"Here's mud in your eye," Fletch added, taking a long deep drought. Brewed from rice, the beer was sour and watery. And very, very good. Lowering his bottle, he realized Ho and Giap were both grinning widely.

"Mud in your eye?" Ho echoed. "What does this mean?"

"Um . . . you know, I really don't know," Patterson admitted. "It's just an old saying, that's all."

"Mud in your eye. A mysterious language, English. I have much to learn. But it will wait for another time. We have matters to discuss."

"That's why I'm here," Patterson agreed. "For openers, I need some information, Mr. Ho. How many men do you command and what weapons—?" He broke off as Ho waved him to silence.

"Before I answer, I have a much simpler question for you. Major, Captain Beauchamps is French, is he not? Why did you bring him here?"

"Indochina is my home, Uncle Ho," Rene replied. "I was born in Saigon and speak Vietnamese and Mandarin Chinese."

"He's here as a translator," Fletch added. "We had no idea what the situation was. Is there a problem?"

"I'm not sure. In Vietnam, the French are allies of the Japanese. I am most surprised you would travel with a French officer."

"Free French," Fletch corrected. "Perhaps a few of the French settlers in Saigon have been pressured by the Vichy government into cooperating with the Japanese but—"

"Pressured?" Ho said, arching an eyebrow. "The French in Vietnam were far better armed than the British in Malaya and Burma. They had twenty thousand Legionnaires in Saigon alone. Yet they offered no resistance to the Japanese. They welcomed them as Axis partners, gave them free access to the ports and railroads. Together they've seized so much of the rice crop that my people are starving to death by the thousands while French troops help the Japanese suppress Vietnamese freedom fighters."

"That's a bald-faced lie!" Rene snapped. "The Legion is confined to barracks in both Hanoi and Saigon."

"They were for a few weeks," Ho admitted. "Now they are in the field, fighting beside the Japanese. Ask Sergeant Chan."

"Chan's a Chinese, no matter what his uniform," Beauchamps countered. "After five months of living like a native he'll say anything you tell him to."

"Now hold on—" Chan began angrily, but Ho waved him silent, turning to Fletch. "As we have just met, I can understand that you might prefer to take the word of a fellow officer and friend over mine. Perhaps we can resolve this another way." He spoke sharply to the Nung chieftain, who stepped outside and returned with a young, blond youth in a tattered flight suit.

"This is my second gift to you today, Major Fletcher," Ho said. "May I introduce Lieutenant Toby Bishop. He was shot down over the Red River two weeks ago. My men brought him in last night."

"Major," Toby said, snapping a quick salute that Fletch returned. "Sweet Jesus, I can't tell you how glad I am to see you. Thought I was dead meat ten times over the last couple weeks. We must have ducked twenty patrols to get here. The guys who rescued me couldn't speak English—"

"What patrols did you see," Rene interrupted. "Japanese?"

"A few," Toby said, eyeing Beauchamps coldly. "But we saw more French than Japanese. I was even thinking about surrendering to 'em until we came on a village they'd just hit. The locals ran away before they attacked, but there was a hospital and, um . . ." Bishop swallowed. "The Legionnaires bayoneted the wounded, Major. All of 'em."

"You're sure they were French?" Ho Chi Minh pressed.

"I'm a reconnaissance pilot, sir. I damn sure know the difference between the Foreign fuckin' Legion and the Japanese army."

"Thank you, Lieutenant," Ho said. "You must be tired from your journey. Go with the Nung chieftain. We have food and a bed prepared for you. Rest now. You'll be leaving with Major Patterson when he goes."

"Major?" Toby asked.

"Go on, son," Fletch nodded. "We'll talk later."

"Yes sir." Toby saluted and followed the Nung out.

"That proves nothing," Beauchamps began.

"Put a cork in it, Rene," Patterson interrupted. "We're here to assess the situation, not argue local politics. Do you want Captain Beauchamps to leave, Mr. Ho?"

The old man considered a moment then shook his head. "No. I've been a guest of the French many times. Most often in their jails. Since he is your friend, he is welcome to stay, as all the French are welcome in Vietnam. As guests. Not as masters."

"Spoken like the communist you are," Rene snapped.

"*Captain* Beauchamps," Fletch barked, "I told you—"

"But he *is* a communist!" Rene insisted. "Ask him!"

"Oh, indeed I am," Ho conceded, "and a revolutionary as well. But above all, I am Vietnamese, Major. And as you said, we're not here to discuss local politics. I presume you want to know if I can be useful to you. Is this not so, Major?"

"Fair enough," Patterson nodded, sipping his beer. "How useful can you be, Mr. Ho?"

"Very," Ho Chi Minh said calmly. "I believe I can give you victory over the Japanese."

"Really," Fletch said, smiling at the small man's audacity. "And how will you do that?"

"Pearl Harbor was a grievous defeat for you. Your naval power in the Pacific was destroyed. You will rebuild it in time, no doubt, but while you rebuild, the Japanese will complete their Ring of Fire, the arc of fortified islands across the Pacific. Attacking these strongholds from the sea will be very costly."

"Maybe," Patterson admitted. "Do you have a better idea?"

"Attack in Vietnam instead," Ho said simply. "Ignore the Ring of Fire. There they are strong. Here they are weak. They even rely on the French for support. An obvious mistake. Help us overthrow them."

"Overthrow the Japanese?" Beauchamps snorted. "With a few Nung tribesmen?"

"And a million more Vietnamese," Ho nodded. "The British lost their holdings in Burma and Malaya because the people wouldn't fight for colonial masters. But they will fight for their countries and their freedom. As America once did."

"And after the fighting, who will rule, Uncle Ho?" Rene asked. "You?"

"Or another Vietnamese. That's what really troubles you, isn't it, Captain? Not that I am a communist or a revolutionary. But that I'm not a French lackey. Your allies will want you to attack the Ring of Fire directly, Major, spending your men on its beaches while the Japanese bleed China to death. So that afterward they take their colonies back."

"Isn't that what we're all fighting for, Mr. Ho?" Patterson asked. "To return things to normal?"

"Colonial empires are not normal, Major," Ho said flatly. "The tide of history is sweeping them away and those who swim against it will drown."

"Very poetic," Rene sneered.

"Then let us be practical," Ho continued. "If you attack through Vietnam, you have an open door into China. There you can join with Chiang Kai-shek's Nationalists to form an irresistible force, an army of millions that would sweep the Japanese back to their little island. Their Ring of Fire would defend nothing but empty ocean."

"An interesting idea," Patterson admitted.

"And afterward," Ho continued, "with Japan defeated, China on the mend, and the colonials gone, a free Asia could—"

"Free?" Rene interrupted. "Or communist?"

"Free to choose," Ho countered. "But whatever form of government we adopt, we will owe America a debt of honor we can never repay. For our freedom. America was a colony once, Major." Ho leaned forward, his eyes alight. "Help us to win our independence. Don't restore the old order. Remake Asia instead, in America's image."

No one spoke for a moment, then Rene sighed. "Can we return to reality, Uncle Ho? How many men do you actually have under arms?"

"At the moment, fewer than five hundred," Ho admitted. "With new weapons and equipment, we can field five thousand in a month, ten thousand in two, perhaps a hundred thousand in four months."

"And will they support an Allied offensive, wherever it takes place?" Fletch asked. "With no guarantees of . . . what comes afterward?"

"We'll continue to fight the Japanese whether you help us or not, Major. We'll fight more effectively with American weapons and training."

"Very well," Patterson said, rising. "I'll inform my superiors of your views, Mr. Ho. Sergeant Chan will be coming with me. We'll drop in a new team of radiomen with better equipment."

"Or not," Rene added.

"Take this with you," Ho said, offering a folded document to Patterson. "Forward it to your president, please."

Fletch scanned it, frowning. "The American Declaration of Independence? I don't—"

"It is the Declaration of Independence for Vietnam," Ho corrected. "I admit that we copied yours. What better example could we have?"

"You're a wily old snake, Uncle Ho," Rene said evenly, shaking his head. "We should have killed you when we had you in prison."

"At last we find a point of agreement, Frenchman," Ho said, his polite smile fading. "You're quite right. You probably should have."

BUCKLED INTO the C-46's metal jump seats as they wave-hopped their way back to Kunming, Rene realized Fletcher Patterson was staring at him from across the narrow aisle.

"What is it?"

"Just wondering," Fletch said. "You knew everything about Ho Chi Minh before we got there, didn't you? Knew he was a commie and a rabble-rouser. You even had him in prison for a while."

"We French have been in this part of the world a long time," Rene nodded. "We know it far better than you."

"Then I assume you also knew Ho spoke English, right? And since I didn't need a translator, Captain, why did you volunteer to come along?"

"To keep you from being taken in, *mon ami*. You Americans can be incredibly naive when it comes to Asian politics. You probably think you met a visionary today. Ho Chi Minh is just a crazy old communist dreaming in the jungle."

"You incredible asshole," Tommy Chan said quietly.

"Sergeant . . . ," Patterson warned.

"Fuck it, Major. Do you know how close Deschamps came to getting his head blown off back there? Maybe getting us all killed?"

"You overestimate Ho, Sergeant," Rene snorted. "He fears the French and rightly so. He wouldn't dare harm us."

"No? Well his Nungs aren't afraid of the French or much of anything else. I've seen 'em hang Japs upside down with their balls in their mouths as a warning. Foreigners all look alike to them. Even me. One word from that old man, and we'd be buzzard bait."

"I don't understand, Sergeant," Fletch said. "Ho seemed peaceable enough to me. What makes you think we were in danger?"

"That crack Captain Beauchamps made about killing Ho in prison?"

"It was only a jest, Sergeant—" Rene snorted.

"A joke? Five months ago the fucking Legionnaires executed Ho's wife in a Saigon jail! Couldn't catch him, so they killed her! By garrote. You didn't know that, did you, Beauchamps? I can see it in your face. I guess your superiors must have forgotten to mention it to you. Or maybe the French don't know this country quite as well as you think."

"Relax, Sergeant," Fletch said. "We're all on the same side here."

"I know," Chan grumbled, "that's what worries me."

☆ ☆ ☆

AFTER PATTERSON'S group left, Ho and Giap sat alone in the barren room as the shadows lengthened, sipping the sour dregs of their Japanese beer.

"What do you think the Americans will do?" Ho asked at last.

"Betray us," Giap said with a Gallic shrug. "The French and Americans are comrades-in-arms. Their generals are friends. When the fighting is done, the Americans will help their friends."

"You're a cynic, Vo Nguyen Giap. President Roosevelt opposes returning the colonies to their European masters. How could he justify giving Vietnam back to the French collaborators who fought for the Japanese?"

"And if he does?"

"Then we will fight them," Ho said simply. "And we will be free of them in the end. It will just take longer, that's all."

"If I'm a cynic, you're a relentless dreamer, Uncle Ho."

"Perhaps I am," the old man smiled, raising his bottle.

"Here's mud in your eye."

AUTHOR'S NOTE

Melodramatics aside, a meeting between Ho Chi Minh and an American OSS intelligence team (accompanied by a French officer) actually occurred during the dark days of the Pacific war.

After returning a downed American pilot, Ho made an offer much like the one described here, to use his country as a gateway into China and to remake Asia in our own image.

But as the raid at Pearl was only partly successful, the United States chose to attack the incomplete fortresses of Japan's Ring of Fire. Step by bloody step the Allies fought their way across the Pacific at a terrible cost.

FDR died before he could give Europe's Asian colonies the freedom he had promised. Instead, betraying our own national ideals, we returned those colonies to their former masters.

Temporarily.

Uncle Ho Chi Minh and his general, Vo Nguyen Giap, the one-time lawyer in the white linen suit, defeated the French, the Americans, and even the Chinese. But those victories were costly, and the war-shattered shell of a country that remains is nothing like the Asian America Ho envisioned in the jungles of Indochina in 1943.

If we had done as Ho suggested? Joined with the Chinese Nationalists, strengthened their army, and left a strong democratic government in China after the war? How very different the decades since might have been.

But that's another story . . .

D.A.

12

A Terrible Resolve

WILLIAM H. KEITH JR.

DECEMBER 7, 1941   1235 HRS

MITSUO FUCHIDA

RUBBER SHRIEKED ON TEAK deck planking. With flak damage to the wings and a severed control cable, Comdr. Mitsuo Fuchida's shrapnel-torn Mitsubishi Type 97 slammed onto the pitching deck of the flagship *Akagi,* the tailhook snagging the cable and jolting the aircraft to a precarious halt. It was just past noon on a gray and rain-streaked afternoon, a day to be forever remembered in the annals of naval history.

Designed as a torpedo bomber, the single-engine Mitsubishi had been reconfigured as Fuchida's command aircraft for the strike. Throughout the attack, his plane had circled high above Pearl Harbor as the strike's chief planner had made notes and taken photographs. His last view of the American base on that December morning would be with him always: battleship after battleship, moored two by two along Ford Island, wrecked and blasted, as towering palls of smoke billowed thousands of feet into the air to stain the bright morning sky.

Reaching up, he cracked the canopy over the observer's seat and slid it back, savoring the cold bite of the ocean air, heavy with salt,

with the mingled stinks of gasoline, oil, humanity, and the promise
of more rain. He felt again the heavy ocean swell swaying the carrier
deck beneath him. Off to port he could see the cold gray shape of
the *Kaga,* plowing ahead through the swell as she received the last
of her planes, and beyond her the carrier *Soryu,* the cruiser
Chikuma, and other vessels of the *Kido Butai,* the Carrier Striking
Force. The sight filled him with a swelling, irresistible pride.

As Fuchida clambered out of the observer's seat and onto the
aircraft's wing, a sea of men—sailors, mechanics, pilots, armorers—
surged across the flight deck to surround him, a cheering, shrieking
throng.

"Banzai! Banzai!"

Grinning, he stepped down off of the wing and onto the shoulders of two of the men, who paraded him across the deck in jubilant
procession. They put him down only when Comdr. Minoru Genda
pushed his way through the mob and blocked the way, a broad
smile on his face, his *hachimaki* still tied tight across his brow.
"Irasshai, eiyuu-kun!" he cried, grasping Fuchida's arms. "Welcome
back, hero!"

"Congratulations, Minoru. A splendid attack! Splendid!" The
youthful Genda had commanded the strike.

"We caught them asleep. This day will long be remembered in
the empire's history. A day to rank with Tsushima!"

"It will not be so easy next time, my friend," Fuchida said. "But
we must launch the next attack, and swiftly, before the enemy
recovers his balance."

Genda sobered. "There is talk . . ."

Fuchida's dark eyes narrowed. "What is it?"

"There is a rumor that there will be no second strike. Admiral
Nagumo and some of the staff officers—"

"Come with me!" Fuchida snapped. "There is no time to waste!"

The two pilots made their way through the crowd to the small
island on the port side of *Akagi*'s flight deck. The "Z" flag, he
noted, was no longer flying from the carrier's signal yard. Early that
morning, before the strike had been launched, Vice Admiral
Nagumo had ordered the hoisting of a signal flag identical to that
flown by Admiral Togo during the battle of Tsushima Strait thirty-
six years before, when Imperial Japan had defeated Russia and taken

her place as a modern naval world power. This entire strike had been code-named Operation Z in honor of that historic signal.

Vice Adm. Chuichi Nagumo was waiting for them on the bridge, the dour expression on his long and taciturn face evidence enough that he was expecting the two men. Rear Adm. Ryunosuke Kusaka, the burly chief of staff, First Air Fleet, stood at Nagumo's side as if ready to protect the diminutive fleet commander. Other staff and operations officers stood about the two like a small army.

"*Konichiwa, Chujosama,*" Fuchida said, bowing formally. "It is my honor to report that the first strike has been completely successful."

"I have heard the initial reports, *Chusasan,*" Nagumo replied gravely. "Your plan has surpassed all of our expectations."

"At least four battleships sunk," Fuchida continued. "At least three seriously damaged. And the enemy's air capabilities have been crippled. The seaplane base was in flames, as were all the airfields . . . especially Wheeler Field."

"Good," Nagumo said, nodding. "*Very* good."

"What of the enemy carriers?" Kusaka demanded. "We heard conflicting reports."

"I regret that the enemy carriers were not in port, sir."

"Ah." Nagumo nodded slowly. "We should see now to the safety of the fleet. The *Kido Butai* is still the heart of the Imperial Navy."

Then it was true. Nagumo had a reputation for being cautious, and he was exercising that caution now. He was calling off the attack after landing a single blow.

"Sir!" Fuchida said, giving another slight but deferential bow. "With respect, we must launch another strike immediately!"

"That is no longer an option, Commander," Nagumo replied. "The weather is worsening. And the enemy is now alerted to our presence in these waters."

"The American carriers will be hunting for us," Kusaka added. "And there is also the matter of refueling for the fleet. We must rendezvous with the tanker squadron to the north in order to take on fuel before the sea gets any rougher."

"Our luck thus far has held true. To press it further could well be disastrous," Nagumo said. "Now it is time to withdraw while we still can."

Fuchida felt a rush of disappointment. The first strike against the American fleet and army air assets in Hawaii, 183 aircraft launched in two waves, had resulted in a success unparalleled in the history of naval warfare. Disappointment was followed closely by anger and a fresh determination.

"Sir, excuse me," Fuchida said, "but there is a very great deal more we could accomplish, we *must* accomplish."

Kusaka responded with a sharp, indrawn sibilance, a hiss of anger. Nagumo looked at Fuchida coldly. "We have fulfilled our commander in chief's requirements for this operation in every particular, Commander Fuchida."

"We have crippled the enemy's fleet and air capabilities," Kusaka added. "Admiral Yamamoto's express desire in ordering this strike was to win a free hand for our operations in the western Pacific for six months. What you and Commander Genda have accomplished this morning guarantees us that time."

"Yes," Fuchida said. "We have done all of that and more, sir. But the base facilities at Pearl Harbor are still untouched. With another strike, we could . . . Wait. Look here."

At the chart table at the aft end of the bridge he pulled out a sheet of blank rice paper and a pencil and began quickly sketching. There was an enormous and highly detailed three-dimensional model of Oahu below in one of *Akagi*'s briefing rooms, but he needed to make his point now, to capture these men's imaginations before the opportunity was forever lost.

"Pearl Harbor," he said, roughing out an irregular outline, with a narrow outlet to the south. "Ford Island," he added, drawing an oblong mass in the south-middle of the harbor. Most of the battleships had been moored here, along the southeast coast of that island. "Opposite the line of battleships," Fuchida continued, indicating the southern coastline of the harbor, "is the main naval base and shipyard. Hospital Point on the west. Dry docks here. Aiea Bay up here, to the northeast. This strait between the base and Ford Island is the Southeast Loch.

"Now, right here . . ."—and his pencil tapped the rounded shoulder of land on the west side of the coast, where it opened into the strait leading south to the open sea—"at Hospital Point, I saw a large number of large oil tanks, painted white. It is my belief, *Chujosama,* that these are the fuel-oil storage facilities for the American fleet. They may well hold the bulk of the American naval fuel reserves."

"Yes!" Genda added, excitement sparking his eyes. "I saw those. They are easy targets, quite vulnerable."

"Since our primary targets were American ships and aircraft, none of our aircraft attacked those oil tanks or any of the other installations at the naval yard," Fuchida said. "Sir, if we can destroy those storage facilities, we may be able to block *all* American activity in the western Pacific for a year, perhaps more! Wouldn't that be worth the added risk?"

Kusaka puffed out his cheeks. "The losses to our aircraft and crews," he said, shaking his head, "would be terrible. We lost only nine planes from our first wave . . . but twenty from the second as the American antiaircraft assets began to respond. A third wave would fly into a devastating barrage."

"Sir!" Genda said. "My pilots are ready to return. They are *eager* to return! They are not afraid to do their duty."

"There is a difference, Commander Genda," Nagumo said quietly, "between duty and suicide."

"Sometimes the two are the same." Fuchida said. "It is *Bushido*." The Way of the Warrior.

"Lieutenant Fusata Iida has shown us the way, *Chujosama*," Genda said gently.

"Lieutenant Iida?" Nagumo said. "I don't—"

"Leader of the Zero squadron off *Soryu*," Kusaka said.

"Ah."

"Yes," Genda said. "Iida told his men before the strike that if they should find themselves unable to return to the carrier, they should crash into American ships and installations instead, to avoid capture. Every man in that squadron left their parachutes aboard their ship, to seal their pact.

"Lieutenant Iida was hit by ground fire after strafing Kaneohe. His Zero was losing gasoline. He signaled to his companions to return to the *Soryu* then turned back and dived his aircraft into the airfield."

"A brave man," Nagumo said.

"Yes sir. And every man in the air wing stands ready to meet his example, should that be required of them."

"It is *not* required of them," Nagumo said. "Brave men do not need to die when their duty does not demand it."

"*Ichi-mon oshimi no hyaku-zon,*" Fuchida said. It was an old Japanese proverb: one coin saved, a hundred losses. The Americans might have said penny-wise, pound foolish. "Sir, we have risked everything in dealing this blow against the Americans and have set in motion a train of events with an ending none of us can foresee. We can adhere to the letter of our mission orders and delay the American war effort for six months. Or we can strike the enemy again and *again,* if need be, finish the job we have started this morning, and offer to the emperor a victory worthy of Admiral Togo and Tsushima!"

Nagumo's eyes narrowed, his face hardened. Fuchida knew that he was treading perilously close to insubordination with the implied unfavorable comparison between the vacillating Nagumo and the heroic Togo. A word now from Nagumo, and Fuchida's career would be over.

But against that was honor and the knowledge that victory, *complete* victory, was now within the *Kido Butai*'s reach.

"Enough!" Kusaka snapped. "The risks are far too great. We would have to refuel and rearm all of the aircraft . . . and to load the Nakajima Type 97s with bombs, since torpedoes are useless against shore installations. And we still do not know the location of the American carriers. If a carrier strike were to be launched against us while we were rearming our planes, the carrier flight decks would become an inferno. We could lose . . . everything!"

"With respect," Fuchida said, bowing, "I suggest that our torpedo planes and half of the fighters be held back as insurance against the appearance of the American carriers. The Nakajimas can be rearmed with torpedoes later, against that possibility." Kusaka started to speak, but Fuchida pressed on, determined to have his say, whatever the consequences. "But the Aichi Type 99s and the Mitsubishi Type 97s should be rearmed with bombs and sent on a third strike with the remainder of the Zeros protecting them, specifically targeting these fuel storage tanks.

"*Chujosama* . . . another opportunity like this may never be presented to us! We *must* strike again, a killing blow, or we run the risk have having merely angered a deadly foe when we might instead have won the final victory!"

For a long and deadly moment silence hovered over the bridge. Fuchida, breathing hard, his fists clenched at his sides, waited to hear the verdict. He would not, could not push the argument further. As it was, a refusal by Nagumo now meant Fuchida's disgrace. He would have to retire, perhaps even take his own life.

The concept of ritual suicide, of *sepuku,* was deeply ingrained within the philosophy of the Warrior's Way. Still, there was no official sanction for the wholesale suicide of fighting men sent into combat against impossible odds. While planning Operation Z, Fuchida had seriously considered the possibility of a deliberate one-way mission . . . but he had been argued out of the idea by the officers on his staff. The time might come when the country needed to trade an airplane and its pilot for an enemy ship, but that time was not yet.

With a total victory at Pearl Harbor, that time might never come at all. . . .

"Sir," Kusaka began. "We should withdraw as planned. We—"

Nagumo cut him off with a wave of his hand. "Enough," he said. "Enough. *Chusasan* Fuchida is correct. Give the orders, please. We will launch another strike."

Several of the other staff officers present nodded, and there was a murmur of agreement. Fuchida felt a momentary dizziness and reached out to catch hold of the edge of the chart table. *Hai! Banzai!*

"But may the gods help us all," Nagumo continued. "There is another proverb, you know . . . *Nama-byoho wa o-kega no moto.*" It meant, roughly, that crude tactics resulted in severe loss.

"Yes sir," Genda said. "And to that I answer, *Koketsu ni irazumba koji o ezu.*" To capture a tiger cub, in other words, to win something valuable, one had to enter the tiger's den.

They were literally risking all on another throw of the dice.

"Well, we will see which proverbs prevail this day," Nagumo said quietly, "*if* we survive it."

DECEMBER 7, 1941   1745 HRS

TAKASHIGE EGUSA

Approaching from the south, Lieutenant Commander Egusa pushed the stick of the Type 99 dive-bomber all the way forward, watching as the target—one huge, squat, white-painted cylinder surrounded by many identical cylinders—swiftly grew to fill the simple cross-hair bombsight mounted on the cowling of his plane. The Aichi D3A bounced and trembled with the concussion of flak bursts in the sky to either side. Tracer rounds were floating up from the ground in unending streams of color, and the air was thick with the dirty black smudges of antiaircraft fire.

To the north, it looked as if all of Pearl Harbor was engulfed in roiling, billowing clouds of greasy smoke, but Egusa noticed none of the spectacle, none of the flame-shot horror. He could see only the fuel storage tank in his bombsight, larger now, enormous, filling the width of his windscreen. Savagely, he yanked the bomb release and felt the Aichi jolted upward as its 500-kilo bomb swung clear of the aircraft's belly and shrieked earthward.

Pulling back on the stick now, Egusa wondered if he'd waited too long, wondered if his downward slant was going to carry him into his target . . . and then as the G forces drained the blood from his head and brought him perilously close to blacking out, the nimble dive-bomber nosed up, shuddering, as an explosion erupted beneath and behind. For a terrifying moment, Egusa wondered if he would be able to maintain control of his aircraft . . . and then he was flying low and straight, north across the southeastern loch.

"Did we hit it?" he shouted back over his shoulder at Tanaka, his rear-seater. "Did we hit it?"

"I can't see anything but smoke and flame!" Tanaka shouted back. "Smoke everywhere! I think the whole tank farm is ablaze!"

"They burn even better than battleships!"

In fact, several of the battleships nestled along the southern coast of Ford Island were still burning after the morning's attack. One had rolled over completely, and another, which had gotten under way during the first strike, had run aground not far from the narrow entrance to the harbor. One large battleship, the *Arizona,* had exploded; only her upper works were still above water, her massive foremast tilted drunkenly to one side, and most of what was left of her superstructure was still surrounded in sheets of flame. The water itself appeared to be on fire, as oil on the harbor's surface blazed away. Dozens of boats and small craft moved among the stricken behemoths like water beetles, ferrying personnel, plying fire hoses on burning wreckage, or simply seeking to escape this new and devastating onslaught.

As expected, the American antiaircraft defenses were far more deadly this time around, as if they'd been waiting for the return of the imperial air armada that had savaged them that morning. Flak bursts thundered and popped on all sides. Streams of antiaircraft wove patterns of drifting, burning stars across the smoke-choked sky, converging on each attacking aircraft within reach. Everywhere he looked, Egusa saw the smoke trails of Japanese planes that had been caught in the ferocious barrage. Ahead and to the right, he saw a Zero in flames, arcing down to smash into the water close to the funereal pyre of the *Arizona*.

As he roared across the water, Egusa saw several lines of tracer rounds arcing toward his plane from ships and batteries ashore, seeking to claw him out of the air. Banking hard to the left, he roared low above the western end of Ford Island then angled west across the narrows toward the Waipio Peninsula.

Still circling, he turned south, lining up with the channel leading to the sea. Opposite Hospital Point, however, as he passed again the battered, grounded *Nevada,* a double sledgehammer blow rocked his Aichi violently to the right. Glass exploded all around him from behind as part of the canopy shattered. Instantly, smoke and thick, hot oil began streaming back from his cowling, washing over his windshield and making it almost impossible to see. His engine was missing, sputtering, threatening to quit at any moment. He knew in that instant that he would not survive this battle.

"Tanaka!" he yelled. "Tanaka! We're hit bad!"

There was no answer from the rear seat. Twisting around against his shoulder harness, he saw his bombardier-navigator's head lolling against the shattered canopy, wearing a scarlet mask of blood.

It didn't matter. The entire dive-bomber group had elected to emulate the heroic Iida on this strike and left their parachutes on board the carrier. He began searching for a suitable target.

He found it in the fuel storage tanks behind Hospital Point. Several of them, struck by bombs from his aircraft and others, were burning furiously, but more than half were untouched. Their orders before launching on the afternoon assault had been clear: ignore the ships in the harbor unless they were the missing American aircraft carriers. Concentrate instead on the shore installations, the naval yard and dry docks, and most especially, on those impossible-to-miss storage facilities.

Nursing his fitfully sputtering engine, his oil pressure dropping to nothing, Egusa pulled his Aichi dive-bomber around to the left and pushed the stick over, lining the aircraft up as well as he could with the dimly glimpsed oil tanks all but lost in the smoke.

Fire licked at his legs from the burning engine, but he scarcely noticed. It was all he could do to hold the stricken aircraft steady on course as gunfire from the ground rattled and burst and exploded all around, as his wings bucked and shuddered, as more rounds slammed into the D3A, shredding the tail and left wing.

Egusa was screaming as his plane cartwheeled into the center of the oil storage tanks, erupting into a blossoming, sky-devouring gout of brilliant orange flame.

SEPTEMBER 2, 1945   0912 HRS

ISOROKU YAMAMOTO

As he walked across the quarterdeck, the admiral leaned against the railing and looked down at the gray waters of the harbor. A whaleboat was approaching from the south, motoring across from 1010 Dock, closely escorted by several smaller craft. Within the boat, which flew an American flag, were several men in uniform and one small figure in civilian clothes. Adm. Isoroku Yamamoto felt a powerful stirring in his chest, at his throat. They were here. It was very nearly time. . .

Straightening up, he looked about the expanse of the harbor, the shipyards and buildings, the cloudless, crystal blue sky overhead, the blaze of the morning sun in the east. Yamamoto was, quite frankly, somewhat surprised that he'd lived to see this day. He'd long had a premonition that he would not survive this war, a war for which, from the beginning, he'd had grave misgivings.

This war had been launched at the army's insistence; the generals had forced the confrontation with the United States in order to continue their war in China and to secure free access to the material bounty of Indonesia and Southeast Asia, especially rubber and oil.

But the navy had prosecuted the far-ranging campaigns from Malaysia to Hawaii, from Australia to the Aleutians. The army had begun this war. The navy had finished it.

His misgivings had been deep and rooted in practicality. Since long before the war, when he'd been the navy's vice minister, he'd warned his peers and his superiors repeatedly that any war with America would have to be won with a single quick, decisive thrust, that a prolonged war against America's industrial might was certain to end in Japanese defeat. So outspoken had he been that his chief, Navy Minister Mitsumasa Yonai, had sent him to sea as commander of the Combined Fleet in the summer of 1939 just to keep him safely out of the reach of ultranationalist assassins.

He stood now on the quarterdeck of the immense imperial battleship *Yamato,* anchored off the navy yard at Pearl Harbor. He was immaculate in his full-dress uniform whites. Members of his staff and other naval officers gathered in hushed, solemn groups to observe this long-awaited ceremony. All around him were the marks of the final Imperial Japanese victory in the Pacific. Most of the rusting hulks of Battleship Row remained where they'd settled to the harbor's shallow bottom on that clear December morning less than four years before. Much of the navy yard had been cleared of wreckage, but the dry docks were still half buried in a tangled forest of fallen masts, toppled cranes, and the shattered, bomb-torn hulls of the battleship *Pennsylvania* and the destroyers *Downes* and *Cassin.*

The Japanese flag flew high from a mast over 1010 Dock, east of the dry docks. Just beyond, the skeletal wreckage of the immense fuel storage tank farm remained as mute testimony of the disaster that had overtaken the American fleet. The victory, Yamamoto thought, the *real* victory, had been won there . . .

He flexed his hands, sheathed now in dress white gloves. The gloves masked the fact that he was missing two fingers . . . lost when he was a young ensign at the battle of Tsushima. That naval action, too, had determined the ultimate victor of a war.

The whaleboat was approaching *Yamato's* port side now, drifting up to the floating pier attached to the bottom of the long, suspended ladder leading up the immense vessel's gently curving hull. A boatswain snapped orders, and Japanese sailors in dress whites stepped up smartly to draw the boat close and make it fast, then coming to attention and saluting as the boat's passengers began to disembark and file up the swaying ladder.

The strategists, the armchair tacticians back in Japan, still argued over Nagumo's wisdom in launching a second strike on that December day four years before—a third wave of aircraft to pound the already battered American installations on the island of Oahu. The attack had been fearfully expensive. In the first strike, in the morning, twenty-nine aircraft had been downed from the two waves, not counting one Zero that had crashed in the predawn twilight while launching. In the afternoon attack, another fifty-eight aircraft had been shot down by savage antiaircraft fire, and many more had been lost while trying to find Nagumo's carriers in the darkness, high winds, and rough seas as they returned. In all, casualties had totaled more than 50 percent; among the dead and missing were the immortal Genda, leader of the attack, and Fuchida, the air fleet's overall commander and the tactical planner for Operation Z.

More aircraft had been lost the following day, when search planes from the carrier *Enterprise* had finally spotted Nagumo's force. Fortunately, only the *Enterprise* had been within striking range; in the lopsided battle that followed, one, at least, of the American carriers had been so badly hit by Nagumo's torpedo bombers that she'd been sunk by an American destroyer the next day. Another victory . . . but a perilously dangerous one. If the Americans had been able to assemble an all-out airborne strike against the *Kido Butai* on December 8, the war in the Pacific might well have ended very differently.

So . . . had it been worth it? The sacrifice? The martyrdom of some of Japan's finest fliers? Yamamoto was a practical man, not given to sorties of imaginative fancy, and he rarely tried second-guessing his own decisions. Still, the facts of history now suggested that the war had been won that December 7 afternoon with the destruction of those oil storage tanks. That alone had been worth the sinking of any ten battleships, worth even the destruction of the entire Pacific Fleet. After the morning strike, the American fleet had been crippled, yes, but they still possessed four aircraft carriers. Most of the ships destroyed or damaged were old ones, in any case, and the American industrial capability was more than up to handling an aggressive rebuilding program that would swiftly have outmatched Japan's capabilities. Unless Japan could have won an armistice within a few months of Pearl Harbor, six at the most, she would have inevitably found herself in a long and grueling retreat across the Pacific, fighting a foe appallingly superior both in numbers and materiel.

No one on the planning staff had imagined, however, that those oil storage tanks at Hospital Point had held every drop of reserve fuel for the American fleet. When those tanks had erupted in a thundering volcano of flame with the heroic Egusa's dive-bomber strike, the Americans had had no choice but to pull their fleet operations back to the American West Coast.

Unable to use Hawaii as a staging area for operations, the Americans had been critically restricted in all of their operations, forced to assume a strictly defensive posture, sortieing out of their bases at San Diego, San Francisco, and Seattle, but unable to logistically support deployments into the western Pacific. Fuel shortages had probably contributed to the American naval defeat off Dutch Harbor in early June 1942, when two of the carriers missed at Pearl Harbor, the *Lexington* and the *Yorktown,* had been sent to the bottom by Nagumo's carrier strike force.

There'd been no stopping the avalanche of Japanese conquest after that. Repeated carrier strikes against Oahu had frustrated attempts to rebuild, attempts hampered in any case by the necessity of supplying all naval operations in and around the Hawaiian Islands by tanker. Tiny Midway Island, snapped up as a diversion in Yamamoto's far-flung Aleutians campaign in 1942, had become the staging point for a much more ambitious operation, the invasion of the Hawaiian Islands in October 1944.

Hawaii was now the far eastern bastion of the Japanese Empire and the final nail hammered into the American defeat. For the past year, Japanese engineers had been hard at work clearing away the debris of the original Pearl Harbor attack and beginning to rebuild, but had still barely begun the monumental task. It might be years before the naval facilities here were fully restored and operational.

The American officers and the lone civilian stepped off the ladder and onto *Yamato*'s quarterdeck, stopping as boatswain pipes squealed and the imperial naval officers awaiting them saluted. Words were exchanged, and a staff officer escorted them down a long double row of Japanese sailors.

A long table decked out in a green cloth, with folding metal chairs on either side, had been set up on a red carpet for the formal ceremony, but Yamamoto walked past the table to greet the visitors.

The civilian, Yamamoto realized, was old, shrunken and wizened, looking too small for the formal morning coat, vest, and top hat he wore. Behind him were two American naval officers, admirals, to judge by the gold on the sleeves of their whites, the bills of their caps, and the boards on their shoulders.

"Welcome aboard, gentlemen," Yamamoto said in English. A phalanx of interpreters stood ready to one side, but the admiral needed no help from them. He'd attended college at Princeton University many decades ago and was proud of his knowledge of the language. "I am Admiral Yamamoto."

"Admiral Yamamoto," the civilian said stiffly, "I am Cordell Hull. These are Admiral Husband Kimmel . . . and Admiral Harold Stark."

"I am honored to meet you. I know all of you well by reputation, of course."

And so he did. Hull was the former American secretary of state under Roosevelt. He'd retired after Roosevelt's death last spring but had been brought out of retirement as a special envoy for this meeting. Kimmel had been Yamamoto's opposite number in the American fleet in 1941, the commander of the American Pacific Fleet. Stark had been Kimmel's immediate superior, the chief of naval operations.

Both Kimmel and Stark, Yamamoto knew, had been under an official cloud since Pearl Harbor. Blamed for the general unpreparedness and poor internal communications that had led to disaster on December 7, Kimmel had been relieved of command. Stark had not been relieved, but he had been reassigned to the European theater in what many saw as a frenzy of finger-pointing in the wake of the Japanese attack. Both men had been repeatedly investigated by various boards and commissions seeking to fix the blame on someone, on *anyone,* after Pearl Harbor.

Yamamoto was intrigued by the fact that both men had been assigned to this deputation . . . or had they volunteered? To come here, of all places, to sue the empire for peace, must surely be the gravest of humiliations.

And Cordell Hull . . .

The former representative from Tennessee was well known worldwide, a diplomat who'd done much to ease the tension between the United States and a Latin America prickly over recent American violations of their sovereignty. He was known to be a strong and outspoken advocate of a so-called United Nations, a kind of international assembly to replace the old, failed League of Nations once this war was finally over. His name had even been raised in some circles as a possible future recipient of the Nobel Peace Prize.

Yamamoto wondered if this ceremony today would enhance Hull's reputation or leave him perceived as a traitor by his countrymen. The decision to do what these three were doing here on the deck of Imperial Japan's mightiest battleship could not have been easy or taken lightly and had caused considerable dissent within the United States.

"I am delighted you have come here today, Mr. Hull, gentlemen," Yamamoto said. "It is not easy for you, I know. But . . . perhaps we should begin."

Hull pulled a gold pocket watch from his vest pocket and examined it closely. His hand, Yamamoto noticed, was trembling. "Yes," Hull muttered. "Yes, indeed. We're running a bit behind schedule. We should begin at once."

Aides showed Hull, Kimmel, and Stark to their seats on one side of the table, while Yamamoto took his place on the other, opposite Hull. Adm. Matome Ugaki, once Yamamoto's chief of staff and now commander of all imperial naval air assets, sat at his right. His current chief of staff, Rear Adm. Takajiro Onishi, sat at his left, and other staff officers and officials stood in massed ranks at his back.

"Mr. Hull," Yamamoto said gravely, "I am authorized by my government to discuss with you the terms leading to an immediate cease-fire in the Pacific and an armistice between the United States and the Japanese Empire."

Hull looked again at his watch. "I'm afraid, Admiral Yamamoto, that we are here under more or less false pretenses. We did not come to arrange an armistice . . . not, that is, unless you agree to *our* terms."

Yamamoto drew in a single sharp, hard breath. "It seems to me," he said quietly, "that you are not in a position that would allow you to dictate terms. Our navy has outmatched yours at nearly every turning. You have been unable to maintain your logistical lines between North America and Australia, not enough to matter, at any rate. Your Douglas MacArthur has been fighting valiantly under impossible conditions in Queensland, but he has been unable to dislodge our forces there.

"And . . . I should also tell you that orders have been given to resume carrier air strikes against your cities in California and Washington, should we fail to reach an agreement today. You must see that your position in the Pacific is hopeless, and that further loss of life would be—"

"Excuse me, Admiral Yamamoto," Hull said. "I don't mean to be impertinent, but time is *very* short. We are not going to agree to a cease-fire, not on your terms, at any rate."

"We want you out of Hawaii," Stark said with rude bluntness. "*And* out of the Aleutians. And we require an immediate cessation of hostilities against all of our allies in this conflict."

Yamamoto kept his face poker-player blank. "You overestimate your position, Admiral Stark," he replied. "True, the Nazi Reich has been destroyed. Your 'Germany first' strategy worked admirably to bring Hitler and Mussolini down. And quite frankly, there are many of us within the imperial military who feel some relief at their passing. They were untrustworthy allies, dangerously overextended and insanely greedy.

"However . . . consider your own allies. England is in ruins. The Soviet Union has been devastated by four years of war and has suffered many millions of casualties. Your own people . . . how much longer will they want to continue this costly, vicious war? The rationing? The shortages? The casualty lists? We patrol off your West Coast almost at will. We have bombed your western cities. Our carrier strikes have closed the Panama Canal, further restricting your fleet operations. We are beyond your reach, separated from you by an ocean embracing half the planet. How could you possibly—"

A light appeared in the southern sky.

Yamamoto thought at first that a photographer had taken a picture using a strobe flash—a grave breach of protocol—but then he realized that the flash was continuing, a fierce, white glow in the sky behind the tangled ruins of the fuel storage tanks and the navy yard, as bright as the sun at noon.

Yamamoto glanced at his watch. It was 9:25.

Gradually the glare died, and as it did clouds appeared to materialize out of the fading light. Yamamoto rose slowly, staring at the cloud, which appeared to be rising sluggishly above the horizon, still in complete silence. The ranks of officers nearby began to dissolve as men stared, pointed, whispered among themselves, and shaded their eyes. Even the three Americans stood up so that they could better see past the crowd.

"My God," Kimmel murmured. "My God in heaven."

"What . . . what does this mean?" Ugaki said. "What *is* that?"

Yamamoto was watching the Americans. Kimmel appeared awed. Stark bore an expression of sheer joy. Hull seemed even older and more shrunken, as though his worst fears had just been realized.

"Mr. Hull?" he asked. "What is happening?"

Hull met his eyes with a bleak expression. "Admiral Yamamoto, an American B-29 has just dropped a single bomb of very special design, a *uranium* bomb, on elements of your fleet on patrol south of Oahu."

"What did he say?" Onishi demanded. Yamamoto translated.

"A single bomb?" Ugaki said, incredulous. "Impossible!"

As if in reply, a low, steadily swelling thunder boomed in the south. Yamamoto realized that the sound of that titanic, incredible explosion had only now reached them after . . . how long? He glanced at his watch again. Two minutes had passed. The sound would have crossed . . . what? About twenty-five miles in that time. And that accorded well with the current position of Vice Adm. Takeo Kurita and his Third Fleet, guarding the southern approaches to Oahu.

The thunder continued to roll. The palm trees ashore stirred as if in a hot, ghostly wind. Yamamoto felt the battleship's deck heave beneath his feet, as if the distant blast had sent a shock wave rippling out through the ocean to be felt as far away as Pearl Harbor. The wind intensified, setting the signal flags on the mast high overhead snapping and clattering, and still that awesome cloud climbed into heaven, spreading now at the top like an immense mushroom.

"What is this?" he demanded. "What do you mean by 'uranium bomb'?"

"I'm afraid I don't understand the specifics," Hull said. "And I wouldn't be able to explain them to you if I did. Suffice it to say that that explosion out there was the equivalent of the detonation of something like twenty million tons of TNT."

"What kind of fools do you take us to be?" Yamamoto said. "No aircraft could carry a twenty-million-ton bomb—"

"The bomb's design utilizes physics rather than chemistry," Stark said. "It's not that much larger than an ordinary bomb, but it is millions of times more destructive. Just one of those could destroy a fair-sized city."

"But . . . delivered by a bomber? It is three thousand miles to the American West Coast! That is far beyond any bomber's operational radius! And what is left of your carrier force has been bottled up in California for months now."

Hull nodded. "You are quite correct. Even the B-29 cannot fly three thousand miles out . . . and return. But a one-way trip . . ."

"One way! A suicide attack? That is . . . barbaric!"

"Come now, Admiral," Kimmel said. "Your own pilots have sacrificed their lives. At Pearl Harbor, one of your pilots deliberately crashed his aircraft into those fuel storage tanks over there."

"The code of Bushido demands exceptional sacrifice at times," Yamamoto said. "And a samurai is always ready to sacrifice his life, if need be, for his emperor, his mission, or his honor. Our pilots deliberately sacrificed themselves when their planes were hit, and there was no alternative but to surrender.

"But to make suicide a deliberate part of the mission? To order men to their deaths? That is unthinkable, a monstrous sacrifice of life!"

"Admiral Yamamoto, those air crews are volunteers," Stark said. "Every one of them. We had way more volunteers than we could accept. All they wanted was a chance to hit you people where it hurts."

"What are they saying?" Ugaki demanded. "What are they saying?"

Yamamoto told him then gestured for one of the translators to come closer and keep Ugaki and Onishi informed.

"Suicide attacks!" Ugaki said, shaking his head. "Such an inhuman disregard for life!"

"They are desperate," Yamamoto replied. "If we were backed into such a corner, we might consider the same."

"Never," Ugaki said.

"To trade one airplane and its crew for a ship?" Onishi said. "Or a dozen ships? Or a city? It makes sense, in a viciously commercial sort of way."

"But I fear the war has taken a new and more horrible turning," Yamamoto said. He looked at Hull, eyes cold as he shifted back to English. "This . . . this act shames your country, Mr. Hull, and your government. To attack us in this way under the guise of discussing armistice . . ."

Hull's aged face hardened. "Yes? And might I remind you that four years ago your ambassadors, Mr. Kurusu and Mr. Nomura, arrived in my office one hour *after* your planes began attacking Pearl Harbor? Continuing their charade of peace negotiations, attempting to prevent war between your country and mine. You have damned little room in which to talk about shame, Admiral!"

Yamamoto considered replying that that incident had been an accident, an unavoidable delay, but decided not to mention the fact. He had argued against the stratagem of continuing negotiations until the last possible moment, knowing how such apparent treachery would be perceived by the United States. Japan had a long history of using every weapon in an attack. At Port Arthur, Admiral Togo's torpedo boats had gone in against the anchored Russian fleet before a declaration of war had been presented. Sometimes, military necessity outweighed the niceties of formal protocol.

And yet, when the result was to inflame the enemy beyond all reason, inflame him to the point that he was capable of such an atrocity . . .

Years before, Yamamoto had voiced his fears about the attack on Pearl Harbor. "I fear all we have done is to awaken a sleeping giant and fill him with a terrible resolve."

Osoroshii ketsui. A terrible resolve indeed, to use and deploy such a weapon by such means. . . .

"The detonation of that one bomb," Hull went on, "will have destroyed much of your fleet. It is a warning and a demonstration of this device.

"I must tell you now that a second aircraft with a second bomb is already en route. If I do not radio your acceptance of our terms by"— he looked at his watch once more—"by two o'clock this afternoon, that's four and a half hours from now, the second bomb will be dropped on another target."

"What target?"

A shrug. "This island. This ship."

Yamamoto's eyes widened. "You would not bomb Pearl Harbor!"

"Why not?" Stark said. "*You* did."

"Our intelligence tells us that your Third Fleet headquarters is now located here," Hull went on, "and that you are working toward completely repairing and rebuilding the harbor facilities here. You must understand that we cannot stand by and allow you to build a major naval base here. Unfortunately, the city of Honolulu will also be destroyed. It's just good that we evacuated most of the civilians last year, when it became clear you planned to invade."

Yamamoto looked again toward the southern sky, where the mushroom cloud towered ominously above the horizon, somewhat indistinct behind a curtain of haze. "We know your plane is coming. We will be ready for it."

"I doubt that. The B-29 flies higher than your antiaircraft can reach, higher than any of your fighters, even, except for a very few . . . the Tony, the George, and that new rocket-powered interceptor of yours, the *Shusui*. A copy of the German Me-163, isn't it? But we also know that you don't have any of those based in Hawaii. Why should you? As you said, Hawaii is outside of the B-29's operational radius."

Yamamoto knew that Hull was correct. B-29s based in China had raided the Japanese home islands several times in the past year. Called "*B-san*" by those who'd witnessed the attacks, they had an operational altitude of nine or ten thousand meters, which the army's Type 1 fighter—the Americans called it "Tony"—the navy's *Shinden,* or "George," and a few others could just barely reach. Even then, they could not hold that altitude, for any banking caused them to slide and fall.

A *B-san* raid here would be completely unopposed.

"If you bomb Oahu," Yamamoto said, "you must know that you three will die as well. We cannot bring a battleship the size of *Yamato* to steam in so few hours."

"Of course," Kimmel said with a dark grin. "We were hoping to nail this baby. We consider our own lives . . . expendable."

"But why? Why throw away your own lives?"

"To convince you that we are serious," Hull said. He shrugged, his eyes on the mushroom cloud far out at sea. "And perhaps to complete the circle of our own lives. Pearl Harbor has haunted all three of us, you know. There is a certain satisfaction in coming back here this way, to the beginning . . . and to the beginning of the end."

"The end of what? The war?" He gestured at the cloud. "That changes nothing!"

"No? I think it does. Think about one of those rising above Tokyo. No country, no city on earth will be safe ever again."

"Your B-29s can only make it as far as Hawaii, and only when the crews throw away their lives."

"Admiral, that cloud out there represents a whole new way of waging war . . . of *thinking* about war. From now on, war is going to be the domain of the scientists, the physicists, the push-button boys." He sighed. "It won't be much longer. Your German friends had a new weapon you may have heard about . . . the V-2? A rocket that could lob a one-ton warhead over two hundred miles.

"Now, two hundred miles isn't much compared to the Pacific Ocean, but our scientists say there are ways of extending that range, maybe even of reaching halfway around the world. In Germany, we captured a number of plans for new secret weapons the Nazis were working on. There was one, the brainchild of a rocket scientist named Sanger. He suggested putting a kind of rocket plane on top of a bigger version of the V-2. It was called the A-10, and the idea was to boost the plane high enough and fast enough that it could travel all the way from Germany to the United States and deliver a bombload on New York City.

"Just imagine one of Sanger's rocket planes coming over the imperial palace one morning and dropping one of these uranium bombs. It would only take one. . . ."

"We can already reach Japan from China," Kimmel put in. "Or the Russians might let us base aircraft in Siberia. The Japanese home islands will never be safe again."

"Then we will build uranium bombs of our own."

"I'm sure you will," Hull replied. "I'm sure you will. And city after city will vanish in white hellfire. Admiral, we're looking at the end of the world here. But you can stop it."

"How?"

"Radio your government. Tell them what you've seen here. Have them negotiate, really negotiate, a balanced peace. We want Hawaii and the Aleutians back as well as some of our other territories in the central Pacific, like Guam, Wake, and Midway. We want you to withdraw your forces from Australia and from India. I imagine the Philippines will be negotiable and possibly Indonesia and Southeast Asia as well. But the fighting must stop immediately. If you continue this war of aggression, of conquest, we will use this new weapon. You must believe this."

Yamamoto was silent for a long moment. "You do not really understand the Japanese character, Mr. Hull. What you ask is not possible."

"I suggest you make that call to Tokyo, sir. Tell them what you've seen, what you've heard. You have . . . a little less than four and a half hours."

Yamamoto gestured to some imperial marines standing at attention nearby. "Take these men below!" he snapped in Japanese. "Lock them away!"

Kimmel and Stark struggled when the guards grabbed their arms. "What is the meaning of this!" Stark yelled.

"You have violated the principles of the Geneva Convention, using a flag of truce in order to launch a sneak attack. You are no longer protected under diplomatic immunity and must now be considered prisoners of war."

"Tell your people in Japan what you've seen today, Admiral," Hull said. "Tell them, or it's all been for nothing. They won't be able to begin to guess what happened to you or your fleet."

"Take them away," Yamamoto growled.

He spent a long time looking at that towering cloud, now reaching halfway to the zenith, as the ranks of white-uniformed officers and men dispersed. Any disappointment they may have had over the abrupt cancellation of the day's ceremonies was obviously replaced by wonder and speculation about that ominous pillar rising in the south. A whole new way of waging war.

"Did you feel it?" Ugaki said at his side.

"Eh? Feel what?"

"That blast of hot wind. A storm wind. It made me think of the *kamikaze*."

Yamamoto grunted assent. The kamikaze, the divine wind, was the name for the storm that had destroyed a Mongol fleet bent on conquering Japan in 1570. Here was a kamikaze of another sort, defending the American homeland.

"Where will this end, Ugaki?" he asked.

"In death, Admiral. All things end in death. The question is whether or not that death is honorable."

Yamamoto made his report to Tokyo but received no immediate reply. The operator at imperial fleet headquarters merely acknowledged the transmission and told him that a reply would be forthcoming.

He did not say when, did not comment on Yamamoto's description of the new weapon, and did not mention the Americans' deadline.

An hour passed. Then two. Preparations were made to get the *Yamato* under way, but as Yamamoto had intimated, it would be hours before the huge battleship's cold boilers could be brought up to steam. A third hour passed, and still there was no word from Tokyo.

Yamamoto went to the battleship's radio room and sent another message, demanding to speak with someone, anyone, in authority. "The war minister!" he yelled. "Put me through to the war minister!" He knew Gen. Korechika Anami well, knew him to be an honorable man. If Yamamoto could convince him of the seriousness of what had happened . . .

"That," the distant radio operator replied, "would be difficult."

And Yamamoto knew in that moment that the decision was his and his alone. Japanese formality frowned on blunt refusals; if something was difficult, it was almost certainly impossible. If Anami was not available to speak with Yamamoto, to convey a message to the chiefs of staff or the emperor himself, it was because Anami *chose* not to be available.

Yamamoto could not negotiate with the Americans, not on these terms. He didn't have the authority. Still, he could send the required radio message that would abort the attack on Pearl Harbor and begin preliminary talks, at least. If Tokyo decided to disavow him and his actions, that was their right. He would have to tender his resignation and then, in the honorable tradition of a samurai, commit *sepuku* for having transgressed his authority. But Hawaii would be spared, as well as the lives of many thousands of his men.

He thought again of his old premonition, his belief that he was fated not to survive the war. Such premonitions, he now realized, were nearly always correct.

Meiyo shi. Death with honor.

He could not yield to the Americans' demands. He would *not* treat with them for peace at the point of a gun. He could not, not to save his life, not to save the lives of every one of the men under his command. Isoroku Yamamoto was known throughout the navy as the god of war. To capitulate to a threat, however serious, was to dishonor himself, his family, his nation, his emperor.

A single plane with a single bomb? How could that be considered a threat? No one in the home islands would understand.

The two o'clock deadline passed. The entire island was on full alert, and aircraft patrolled the skies overhead. Radar. One of the new wonder weapons of this new age of scientific warfare probed the skies, searching for any sign of the enemy.

At just past three, Yamamoto was in his office cabin when an urgent shout from outside brought him up on deck. A ship was moving into Pearl Harbor, limping slowly in a pall of her own smoke up the channel past Waipio Point.

It was the *Akagi,* the venerable flagship of the First Fleet, Nagumo's flagship at the original attack on Pearl Harbor. The vessel had been transformed . . . horribly.

Akagi had begun her career in 1920 as a 42,000-ton battle cruiser, but as a result of the provisions of the infamous Washington Naval Treaty, had been converted to an aircraft carrier. She looked now as though she'd reverted to her cruiser role. Her flight deck had been peeled up and back, ripped away leaving only jagged metal behind. Her flight deck island, masts, antennae, all were gone, and a dozen fires guttered in the wreckage. Her smokestacks—an unusual design element that had them pointing out and down on the starboard side to vent smoke clear of the flight deck—had been torn off as well, and dirty smoke billowed from the rents in her hull.

Boats sent across to the shattered *Akagi* returned with survivors' tales. The carrier had been four miles—*four miles*—from the center of the midair blast that had ravaged the First Fleet. Half of her crew was dead, hundreds terribly burned, blinded, deafened. The survivors had jury-rigged auxiliary steering gear below decks in order to guide her to safety inside Pearl Harbor, where the ocean swells could no longer threaten to turn her turtle.

Yamamoto thought about the supposed safety of the harbor and managed a bitter smile.

An officer came to him on the quarterdeck and reported that steam was up. The *Yamato* was ready to sail. He nodded. Perhaps there was yet time.

Thirty minutes later, *Yamato* slowly rounded Hospital Point, steering south toward the open sea. An air raid siren sounded ashore. . . .

"It seems that war will never change, Onishi," he told his chief of staff. They stood together on the *Yamato*'s port bridge wing— Yamamoto, Onishi, and Ukagi—feeling the hot breeze from the sea in their faces. The sky to the south was brassy, overcast, and strange. Overhead it was a cold and crystalline blue. "The weapons change, but men continue to lock themselves into the old patterns of hatred, vengeance, ignorance, and death."

"With weapons this horrible," Ukagi said, "perhaps we will learn how to live without war."

"They said that about the machine gun," Yamamoto replied. "I am more concerned that we will learn how to live without honor. If a weapon exists, it will be used, sooner or later. That is the way of things. I fear the Americans will use this kamikaze weapon of theirs to drag us down, even if they are destroyed as well. I am glad I will not live to see such a world."

Far off, on shore, the heavy *thud-thud-thud* of antiaircraft cannon sounded like the pounding of hammers. Nearer at hand, machine guns joined in the clatter.

He looked up. A single white contrail was scratching itself slowly across the blue sky, high above the dark gray puffs of exploding shells.

A lone aircraft . . .

I fear all we have done is to awaken a sleeping giant and fill him with a terrible resolve.

And then the sky flared in a dazzling white light, devouring the sky.

Postscript

December 7, 2001: A Classroom on the American Continent

December 7, 2001

A Classroom on the American Continent

ALLEN C. KUPFER

I THINK THERE'S BEEN a lot of nonsense written over the years about Pearl Harbor. On this sixtieth anniversary of the Pearl Harbor incident and as a student of Japanese ancestry, I really resent the lies that have been perpetuated about my ancestors."

"Lies? What lies, Takashi? Are you gonna sit here in this class and pretend that the Japanese didn't attack Pearl Harbor? Do you think any of us—especially the professor up there in front of the class—is gonna swallow that?"

"I never said the Japanese didn't attack Pearl Harbor."

"Then what are you saying?"

"I'm saying that my people were provoked into it."

"Provoked? You must be joking. It was a savage attack that was totally uncalled for. Thousands of Americans lost their lives."

"That was your own fault for being unprepared. American leaders ignored the warning signs. They were ignorant and lazy. And that's not even to mention the corruption in your armed services."

"Oh, is that right? I guess the fact that the Japanese military was aggressively muscling into China and endangering half of Asia is a fact we should ignore. The United States gave the Japanese warning."

"The U.S. put a strict embargo on oil, Feeney. That was too harsh an ultimatum. The imperial army had no alternative but to respond militarily."

"Oh, bullshit . . ."

The professor sat upright in his seat. He was prepared to address any breaches in the laws of classroom debate and decorum.

"Oh, sorry, Professor . . . I forgot about the foul-language rule. May I continue?"

The teacher smiled and nodded his head. Debates were useful, he thought to himself. They helped foment new ideas.

And conversation and debate must always be present, especially in the classroom.

"What is there for you to say, Feeney? There's no way you can win this debate. Again, I assert that Japan was not to be blamed for the attack on Pearl Harbor. The oil embargoes and the vicious attack on Japanese soldiers in Manchuria in 1939 justified the Pearl Harbor bombing."

"Oh for God's sake, Takashi! You're not going to bring up that oh-so-convenient myth again, are you?"

"It is *not* a myth. The oral historians have long told of—"

"Oral historians!! . . . Oh, forgive me, Professor. No offense meant. But oral historians are human, after all . . ."

"Professor, he is not allowed to interrupt like that, is he?"

The instructor glared at Feeney. Feeney took notice.

"Sorry, Professor. Sorry, Takashi. I will abide by the rules of debate."

"The oral historians have told of the slaughter of hundreds of Japanese soldiers *and* Manchurian civilians by secret American troops in 1939. Several of these invaders were killed. They were not Asian."

"The U.S. government has consistently denied that those troops were American."

"They weren't Asian, Feeney. If it wasn't the United States that sent those troops, then who was it? Holland?"

The professor leaned back in his chair, obviously appreciating the quip.

"That's a good one, Takashi. You made the class laugh. Even the professor is laughing. But there's still very little evidence that those were U.S. troops. Oral historians aren't totally reliable sources. No disrespect meant, Professor."

"Where do you get your information from, Feeney? Television? The Outlaw Internet that spreads misinformation faster than any other medium known to man? Other than the oral historians like the professor here—who has memorized and retained the information from over thirty written texts on the history of the Final World War—one can only consult the SAATs for reliable, accurate, unbiased historical accounts."

"The *Selected and Approved Texts* are not the gospel truth necessarily."

The professor rose to his feet for the first time since the debate began.

"Well, I didn't really mean that, Professor. They are accurate. It's just that they . . . well, they . . ."

The teacher decided not to censure Feeney. After all, if debates lead to new ideas, the old ones will fall by the wayside. Facts will be replaced by "ideas."

"More important, Feeney, the SAATs also report that the ships at Pearl Harbor were scheduled to attack Japan the following week. So the attack on the Americans was a defensive move. You should pay more attention to SAATs."

"But . . . my grandfather told me about the Final World War. He was there at Pearl Harbor. He told me there was never any planned offensive, and he never heard of any U.S. troops in Manchuria."

"Was your grandfather a high-ranking officer, Feeney?"

"Well, he was a captain."

"Then he probably wasn't in a position to know, was he?"

"I . . . I don't know. But I do know he wasn't a liar. And until the day he suddenly disappeared—I was thirteen years old when that happened—he insisted that the whole Pearl Harbor incident was manipulated by the . . ."

The professor took a step toward Feeney.

"Who?"

"Never mind, Takashi. Forget it. I just think the attack on Pearl Harbor was savage."

"But not quite as savage as the attack on Hiroshima."

"Hey, I thought this debate was about Pearl Harbor."

"If you had read your instructions more carefully, Feeney, you'd know it's about Japanese-American offensives during the Final World War. But of course, not being of Japanese ancestry, you would want to focus only on Pearl Harbor."

"Well, fine. If Japan hadn't threatened that attack on San Francisco, Truman never would've decided to drop the bombs on Hiroshima and Nagasaki."

"Speaking of myths, Feeney, that's a good one!"

"Are you saying San Francisco wasn't threatened? It's all in your precious SAATs, Takashi. Take a look."

"The SAAT reports are radically different from what I have been told by my family."

"Are *you* now calling the SAATs wrong?"

"I . . . I'm . . ."

The professor turned his eyes to Takashi. He wondered if Takashi had the nerve to proceed where Feeney didn't . . . or wouldn't: to blatantly deny the accuracy of the SAATs.

"I suppose I'm saying that . . ."

"Yeah, what, Takashi? Huh?"

The time for the debate was over. The professor pointed at his watch, and another student, who had been appointed to do so, called for final statements.

"Well, Professor, obviously Feeney and I have different views of things. I guess that's obvious. I suppose all I can say is that history is never cut and dry."

"I agree with Takashi, Professor. Even though we are fortunate today to have oral historians and SAATs to refer to and *not* all the conflicting and confusing views of history that once existed in books and other media, history still sure is hard to understand."

Satisfied, the professor dismissed the class. Takashi and Feeney shook hands on the way out.

When the classroom was empty, Professor Schenker sat contentedly thinking. After only a few generations, little memory of Germany's participation in the war remained. And not a single student of this generation—not even those who had family members involved in the conflicts—even suspected that German troops had invaded Manchuria in 1939 nor even fathomed how Hitler's intelligence officers had manipulated Truman into bombing two Japanese cities into oblivion before Truman himself was secretly assassinated.

Through careful means and subtle manipulations—and more violent, dramatic actions when absolutely necessary—the oral historians in conjunction with the government had successfully edited the facts of history. This editing process, Schenker knew, was necessary to sustain long-lasting peace.

Never again would there be a "world" war.

Grinning, Schenker appreciated the beauty of it all. These students and their parents actually *believed* they were still living in a thriving American democracy, even though their freedoms were slowly, methodically being taken away from them and replaced by pseudo-freedoms, like this meaningless classroom debate. These students had left the room thinking their voices and opinions were important. And all they remembered about Pearl Harbor, and in fact, all of what was now referred to as the Final World War, were the United States–Japanese skirmishes.

Schenker closed his briefcase and sighed. He had a long night in front on him. It was once again his turn to convert the government version of historical fact into another volume of a SAAT. He was looking forward to this new volume. Its topic: how the German Alliance of 1945 ended the war by sending its peacekeeping forces into both Japan and the United States. And how the alliance helped the U.S. government "restructure" itself after the war to end all wars.

Appendixes

Appendix A

Pearl Harbor, December 7, 1941

A Timeline

ROLAND GREEN

Midnight, December 6

More than 300 miles north of Oahu, the Imperial Japanese Navy's *Kido Butai* (First Air Fleet) steams south at 26 knots. The most powerful carrier force in the world consists of:

6 fleet carriers (*Akagi, Kaga, Hiryu, Soryu, Shokaku, Zuikaku*)

2 fast battleships (*Hiei, Kirishima*)

2 heavy cruisers (*Tone, Chikuma*)

9 destroyers

8 fast tankers and supply vessels

The *Kido Butai* carries 423 carrier-based aircraft and 13 reconnaissance seaplanes. The carrier-based aircraft consist of Mitsubishi A6M2 Type 00 fighters (the famous "Zero"), Aichi D3A1 Type 99 dive-bombers ("Val"), and Nakajima B5N2 torpedo and level bombers ("Kate").

27 Japanese fleet submarines are deployed around the Hawaiian chain and between the islands and the American West Coast. The 5 boats of the Special Attack Group have surfaced and are beginning their run toward Pearl Harbor to launch two-man midget submarines. The midgets are intended to penetrate the harbor under cover of the air strike.

At Pearl Harbor are 94 ships of the U.S. Pacific Fleet:

8 battleships (*West Virginia, California, Maryland, Tennessee, Nevada, Arizona, Oklahoma, Pennsylvania*)

2 heavy cruisers (*New Orleans, San Francisco*)

6 light cruisers (*Honolulu, St. Louis, Phoenix, Helena, Raleigh, Detroit*)

29 destroyers

1 gunboat, 9 minelayers, 10 minesweepers, and 24 assorted auxiliaries

Of the 3 Pacific Fleet carriers, *Enterprise* and *Lexington* are at sea and *Saratoga* is on the West Coast.

None of the moored battleships have torpedo nets, in spite of the British torpedo attack on the Italian fleet at Taranto in November 1940. Pearl Harbor is believed to be too shallow for aerial torpedoes, and nets would restrict ship movements and seaplane operations.

At 7 airfields around Oahu, the Hawaiian Air Force (U.S. Army) and the navy have 268 combat and many utility aircraft. Only 169 of the combat aircraft are modern—the army's P-40 fighters, A-20 light bombers, and B-17 heavy bombers; the navy's F4F fighters, SBD dive-bombers, and PBY flying boats—and not all are serviceable. In addition, the army planes are disarmed and clustered for protection against sabotage.

0116–0333, December 7

The 5 midget submarines are released from their mother ships, 7 to 10 miles off the entrance to Pearl Harbor.

0300 (0830 in Washington, D.C.)

In Washington, U.S. Army Intelligence decodes the fourteenth part of instructions to the Japanese ambassador, indicating an end to negotiations, as well as further instructions to deliver the complete message at 1300 (0730 in Hawaii). This heightens the fear of Japanese military action, but American attention remains focused on danger to the Philippines and the British and Dutch possessions in Southeast Asia.

Aboard the carriers of the *Kido Butai,* the mechanics begin final preparations of the planes of the first wave. The carriers lack the deck space to launch an adequate single strike.

0342

Minesweeper *Condor* sights what is believed to be the wake of the periscope of a submerged submarine 1½ miles off the entrance to Pearl Harbor.

0357–0435

Patrol destroyer *Ward* searches for the alleged submarine but finds nothing.

0415

An army radar station at Opana on the north shore of Oahu goes on the air. This is an experimental installation, largely used for training, but it can search out to 130 miles.

0458

The antisubmarine net at the entrance to Pearl Harbor is opened to allow *Condor* to enter. To accommodate other ship movements, it remains open until 0846. This allows at least one midget submarine to enter Pearl Harbor.

0530

Cruisers *Tone* and *Chikuma* launch reconnaissance seaplanes, one for Pearl Harbor, the other for the alternate fleet anchorage at Lahaina Roads.

Aboard the *Kido Butai,* the airmen finish breakfast. Visibility is marginal, and the carriers are rolling 11 to 15 degrees. A peacetime exercise would be canceled.

0550

The carriers turn into the wind at 24 knots. The weather delays launching the first strike at least 15 minutes.

0610

The first wave begins launching: 180 of the 182 aircraft launch successfully. One has engine trouble on deck, another crashes into the sea (the pilot is rescued). The first wave consists of:

> 49 "Kates"—horizontal bombers, each carrying one 1,700-pound armor-piercing bomb converted from a 16-inch artillery shell

> 40 "Kates"—torpedo bombers, each carrying one aerial torpedo with special attachments to allow it to be dropped into water less than forty feet deep

> 51 "Vals"—dive-bombers, each carrying one 550-pound bomb

> 43 "Zeros"—fighter escort

The first wave launches in less than 15 minutes. To form the combat air patrol over the carriers, 39 fighters are also launched or alerted.

0620

The first wave forms up and turns south toward Oahu. The *Kido Butai* turns south at 24 knots. Mechanics and deck crew raise the planes of the second wave to the flight decks. It is now daylight.

0628 (1158 in Washington, D.C.)

The War Department encodes for transmission a message to all Pacific commands: "Japanese are presenting at one P.M. eastern standard time today what amounts to an ultimatum also they are under orders to destroy their code machines immediately. Just what significance the hour set may have we do not know but be on alert accordingly. Inform naval authorities of this communication. Marshall."

Atmospheric conditions prevent transmission to Honolulu. Instead of going by navy channels, the message is sent at 0647 Honolulu time by commercial teletype.

0630

The supply ship *Antares* sights a "suspicious object" off the entrance to Pearl Harbor and reports it to the patrol destroyer *Ward*.

0637

Ward sights a submarine trailing *Antares*. It does not resemble any American submarine and is in a restricted area.

0640

Ward goes to General Quarters.

0645–0646

Ward attacks the submarine with gunfire and depth charges and claims a sinking. So does a patrolling PBY.

0648–0652

Radar stations (including Opana) pick up several blips to the north of Oahu.

0651–0653

Ward sends two messages reporting her engagement with the submarine. The second and more definite one reads: "We have attacked, fired upon, and dropped depth charges upon submarine operating in defensive sea area."

Ward is then occupied with intercepting, halting, and turning over to the Coast Guard a fishing sampan also operating in the restricted area.

0702

The radar station at Opana, still on the air for extra practice, picks up an unusually large blip 136 miles to the north. The operators estimate it at 50 planes. They notify their commanding officer.

0705

The *Kido Butai* turns into the wind and commences launching the second wave. This wave consists of:

54 "Kates"—horizontal bombers, carrying either two 550-pound bombs or one 550-pound bomb and six 130-pounders

78 "Vals"—dive-bombers, carrying one 550-pound bomb

35 "Zeros"—fighter escort

Of these 167 aircraft, 167 successfully take off.

0712

The duty officer at headquarters, Fourteenth Naval District, receives *Ward*'s message. He takes it seriously. Because of repeated false alarms by sea and in the air, however, higher-ranking officers keep requesting confirmation.

0715

The commanding officer at Opana says that the large blip is a flight of B-17s, coming in from the mainland. By this time the blip shows a distance of 88 miles. The radar operators decide to keep tracking, to test their radar.

0733

The RCA teletype office receives the War Department warning and gives it to a messenger headed for the district that includes army headquarters at Fort Shafter. It is not marked "Priority."

0738

The two scout planes report that the Pacific Fleet is not in Lahaina Roads, where it could be sunk in deep water. It is at Pearl Harbor, but no carriers are present.

0739

The Opana radar operators go off the air after losing the blip at 20 miles to ground scatter from the surrounding mountains.

0748

The first Japanese shots of the attack are fired as fighters and dive-bombers attack the naval air base at Kaneohe, northwest of Pearl Harbor. One of the first casualties is the base fire truck. Of the 36 PBYs based there, only the 3 out on patrol end the day intact.

Nearby, at Bellows Field, the army takes the warning telephone call as a practical joke for several critical minutes.

0749

The strike commander gives the attack order. Due to misunder-stood signals, the torpedo and level bombers attack simultaneously rather than allow the slower and more vulnerable torpedo bombers to hit first.

0753

Satisfied that the Japanese have achieved surprise, the strike commander sends the signal for a successful surprise attack: "*Tora! Tora! Tora!*" ("Tiger! Tiger! Tiger!").

0755–0800

The first Japanese aircraft are not recognized as an attacking force. Even after the bombs start falling, people on the ground think it is an unusually realistic exercise.

When responsible officers recognize the Japanese insignia, they signal: "All ships in harbor sortie" and "Air raid Pearl Harbor. This is NO [or NOT a] drill!"

The torpedo bombers' attack concentrates on the anchored battleships. In rapid succession they hit:

West Virginia—6 possibly 7 torpedoes. She lists heavily but effective damage control keeps her from capsizing. She sinks at her moorings but is later salvaged and rejoins the fleet in 1944. The *West Virginia* enters Tokyo Bay with the victorious Allies in 1945.

Nevada—1 torpedo forward. She suffers extensive damage but maintains effective antiaircraft fire.

Oklahoma—3 torpedoes. She promptly lists to 35 degrees from uncontrollable flooding. "Abandon Ship" is ordered.

California—2 torpedoes amidships. Because many watertight spaces are open for inspection, serious flooding begins immediately.

The torpedo bombers also hit the light cruisers *Raleigh* (1 torpedo, for major damage) and *Helena* (less damage, but the torpedo explosion ruptures the seams of the minelayer *Oglala*, which is moored alongside *Helena*). Japanese pilots accidentally attack the target ship *Utah* (a former battleship), hitting her twice. She begins to capsize.

Dive-bombers attack both the navy air base on Ford Island and the army bases at Hickam and Wheeler Fields. The Hickam Field barracks suffer heavy damage. Bombing and strafing attacks devastate closely parked aircraft.

0800–0810

The high-level bombers attack with armor-piercing bombs. They hit the battleships *Tennessee* and *Maryland* for minor damage.

Several bombs hit the battleship *Arizona*. One inflicts fatal damage, igniting black powder stored forward, which touches off the forward magazine. The resulting explosion completely wrecks the front half of the ship. Although she takes no torpedoes, *Arizona* is a total loss and loses more than 1,100 of her crew.

Arizona's survivors try to fight fires and rescue wounded shipmates, not abandoning ship until 0832. Some of the battleship's guns are salvaged for coastal defense batteries, but she herself remains where she sank. In 1962 the remains are converted into a national memorial.

The repair ship *Vestal,* moored alongside *Arizona,* takes two bombs as well as damage from the explosion.

0810–0820

The flight of 11 B-17s from the West Coast arrives in the middle of the attack. The planes are unarmed, and the crews at first mistake the Japanese aircraft for a welcoming committee or war games. People on the ground think the B-17s are Japanese planes and open fire. The B-17s land, but 1 is destroyed by strafing after it reaches Hickam Field.

Oklahoma takes 2 more torpedoes on her armor belt as she capsizes. She comes to rest nearly bottom up; hundreds of men are trapped below—32 of them will be rescued through holes cut in the ship's bottom. Others will survive nearly two weeks before running out of air. The ship herself is a total loss, but the hulk is salvaged in 1944 to clear the harbor. In 1947 she sinks while under tow to the West Coast for scrapping.

Utah capsizes. Some trapped men are rescued, but the ship is never salvaged.

A flight of 18 SBD dive-bombers from the carrier *Enterprise* arrive without warning, because the *Enterprise* group was under radio silence. Japanese fighters or American antiaircraft shoot down 5; the 13 survivors land at either Ford Island or the marine base at Ewa Field.

The citizens of Honolulu, seeing smoke and hearing explosions, wonder what is going on.

At 0817, the destroyer *Helm*, the only ship under way at the beginning of the attack, becomes the first ship to leave Pearl Harbor. She immediately sights, fires on, but does not sink, a midget submarine.

0820–0830

The conclusion of the first wave's attack. Americans aboard ships not under attack are busy with damage control, rescuing survivors, and bringing power and ammunition to the antiaircraft batteries. Aboard the heavy cruiser *New Orleans*, a chaplain urges the crew to "praise the Lord and pass the ammunition."

Burning oil from the sunken battleships spreads across the surface of the water, endangering swimmers, the swarm of rescue and fire-fighting craft, and ships still afloat. These include the battleship *California* and the fully loaded tanker *Neosho*.

At the air fields, survivors are manning their battle stations and trying to salvage or disperse aircraft, fight fires, operate antiaircraft batteries, and get fighters off the ground. The only field not attacked is the emergency strip known as Haleiwa Field, with a detachment of P-40s. Pilots assigned to Haleiwa use the lull to reach their planes.

Just before 0830, the destroyer *Monaghan* gets under way. Japanese pilots continue to bomb and strafe targets of opportunity. Between 0830 and 0835 the last planes of the first wave withdraw. They have lost a total of 9 aircraft—5 torpedo bombers and 4 fighters—all to antiaircraft fire.

0830–0855 (The Lull)

At 0837 *Monaghan* sights a midget submarine in the harbor.

At 0840 the battleship *Nevada*, endangered by burning oil from *Arizona*, gets under way, backing unassisted out of her berth. She negotiates the channel beside Battleship Row.

At 0842 the tanker *Neosho* backs out of her berth by the oil storage facility and steams toward the navy yard.

At 0844 the *Monaghan* attacks and sinks the midget submarine by gunfire and ramming. She runs aground in the process but backs clear and gets safely to sea.

At 0854 the Japanese second wave begins its attack.

0900

The principal Japanese targets at Pearl Harbor are the navy yard and the battleship *Nevada*. All the airfields, except Haleiwa, also suffer further attacks.

Dive-bombers swarm over the *Nevada*, hitting her with 6 to 10 bombs and starting severe fires. She is ordered to beach herself to avoid being sunk in the main channel.

Bombers attack Number One Dry Dock, which contains the battleship *Pennsylvania* and the destroyers *Cassin* and *Downes*. The two destroyers are hit immediately.

Also bombed and set on fire, in a floating dry dock, is the destroyer *Shaw.*

American fighters are now in the air: 5 from isolated Haleiwa Field, 3 from Bellows Field, and 4 from Wheeler Field. They lose 4 pilots and 5 planes but claim 10 kills.

0905

The captain of the *Pennsylvania* orders the dry dock flooded to fight severe fires in *Cassin* and *Downes*. The battleship is hit twice, causing minor damage.

The second wave meets heavier antiaircraft fire. One of the victims, a dive-bomber, crashes into the seaplane tender *Curtiss,* which is later hit by a bomb.

Shell fragments and dud shells fall on Honolulu, causing casualties and property damage.

0910

The *Nevada* runs aground. The current soon pulls her back into the channel.

0930

Cassin and *Downes* sink in the flooded dry dock. They are later salvaged and rejoin the fleet in 1943.

An explosion aboard the destroyer *Shaw* blows her bow off, producing a famous and spectacular photograph. She and the dry dock sink, but both are salvaged and returned to service.

0931

The light cruiser *St. Louis* gets under way. On her way out, she will engage and probably sink a midget submarine.

0935

The last Japanese planes of the second wave depart, except for the strike commander, who remains to observe until 1000.

The Japanese have sunk or damaged 18 ships and destroyed or damaged 347 aircraft. However, only 3 of the ships and 165 of the aircraft are permanent losses; 80 percent of the damaged aircraft are salvaged. American casualties include 2,403 dead and 1,178 wounded.

The Japanese have lost 29 planes and 5 midget submarines. But only 1 ship of the Pearl Harbor attack force will survive the war.

0940

Tugs help *Nevada* to ground herself permanently and fight major fires.

1000

The minelayer *Oglala* finally capsizes. She is eventually salvaged.

The light cruiser *Raleigh* fights a successful battle against capsizing by jettisoning topside weights.

The battleship *California* is temporarily abandoned because of the danger from burning oil. She will finally settle into the mud on December 10 but will be salvaged and rejoin the fleet.

1010

First planes of the Japanese first wave begin landing.

1047

Recovery of the first wave is complete. One pilot is mortally injured in a landing crash. Several planes with landing or battle damage are pushed overboard.

Among the commanders, a lively debate rages. Should they attempt a third strike, to finish off damaged ships and destroy irreplaceable support facilities, such as the oil depot and the navy yard's machine shops?

1130

The second wave begins landing.

The light cruiser *Phoenix* leaves Pearl Harbor. In 1982, as the Argentine *General Belgrano,* she will be sunk by the British during the Falklands War.

1214

Recovery of the second wave is complete.

1300

Among the Japanese commanders caution has prevailed because of the danger of missing the essential refueling rendezvous and the fear of the American carriers, whose whereabouts are unknown.

The *Kido Butai* begins its withdrawal to the north

Afternoon

Hawaii is at war. Rumors run wild, including claims of a third Japanese wave, amphibious and parachute landings, an enemy fleet just offshore, sabotage by Hawaiians of Japanese descent, and attacks on the West Coast.

Martial law is declared and civil defense efforts join the military in the recovery effort.

Enough ships sortie from the harbor to form a surface task force. Surviving aircraft are sent out on searches—almost uniformly in the wrong direction.

2045

Trigger-happy gunners mistake 6 F4F "Wildcat" fighters from the *Enterprise* task force for another Japanese attack. "Friendly fire" shoots down 3 of the Wildcats, killing the pilots as well as inflicting casualties on the ground.

Periodic outbursts of firing continue until after midnight.

> *What I have achieved*
> *Is far from a grand slam,*
> *Let me in all modesty declare.*
> *It is more like*
> *A redoubled bid just made.*
>
> > —Isoroku Yamamoto, commander in chief of the combined fleet, on Pearl Harbor, quoted in Stanley Weintraub, *Long Day's Journey into War*

> *Yesterday, December 7, 1941—a date which will live in infamy—the United States was suddenly and deliberately attacked by naval and air forces of the Empire of Japan.*
>
> > —Franklin D. Roosevelt, president of the United States, on Pearl Harbor

Appendix B

The Diplomatic Subtext of the Pearl Harbor Attack

PAUL A. THOMSEN

U NTIL DECEMBER 7, 1941, MOST Americans had not taken the empire of Japan seriously. U.S. policymakers felt they could handle the Japanese Empire and negotiate an equitable conclusion to the ongoing "China Incident." Neither side desired a lengthy Pacific conflict, but by failing to achieve their fullest diplomatic measures, the battlefield became the extension of each nation's flawed diplomacy. Japan's leaders believed that the attack on Pearl Harbor would achieve a secured Asia, but they also feared that America's largely untapped industrial and military might could soon be mobilized against the resource-poor island nation. The Japanese military inflicted heavy damage at Pearl Harbor, but ironically, lacking the Hawaiian-based American sailors' unwitting sacrifice, the United States would have been hard-pressed to join the Allied forces against the Axis powers across the Pacific and the Atlantic.

On the morning of Friday, November 28, 1941, an American carrier task force had departed the safety of its new home port of Pearl Harbor, Hawaii, for the open seas. (Their absence was dutifully noticed by Takao Yoshikawa, a spy under diplomatic cover for the empire of Japan, and conveyed to his superiors as part of an ongoing research project formulated by Adm. Isoroku Yamamoto.) A Japanese attack on the United States had been considered a last resort by the imperial cabinet of Emperor Hirohito and Prime Minister Konoye Fumimaro, but years of brinkmanship between the

Pacific powers over the Japanese Empire's expansionist Far East activities and a rapidly depleting stockpile of natural resources had brought the two Pacific Rim neighbors to a critical juncture.

Fearing an unfavorable shift in the region's balance of power, U.S. President Franklin D. Roosevelt played the only card his isolationist nation would allow—measured diplomacy. The Roosevelt administration condemned Japan's earlier annexation of Manchuria and 1937 invasion of China for jeopardizing the region's free trade, but the Americans could do little more. Though longtime supporters of China's efforts against communism, the American public, nestled in the false security of isolationism since the end of the First World War, chose to deny decisive action against Japan's "China Incident."

Roosevelt knew America's naval facilities at Pearl Harbor would play a pivotal role in settling his country's overseas capitalistic endeavor, and a show of naval force in the Pacific, it was thought, might encourage the Japanese to end their aggressive territorial aims. In 1938 the president had wrung from a begrudged Congress a $500 million increase to the defense budget and subsequently authorized the relocation of the Pacific Fleet command from its headquarters in San Diego, California, to Pearl Harbor. In July 1940 Roosevelt similarly approved a Two-Ocean Naval Expansion Act, soliciting the production of a fleet that, when added to the bulk of U.S. naval vessels already patrolling the Atlantic and Pacific, would far surpass the Japanese fleet within a few years and hence, he thought, would further wordlessly encourage the Japanese to settle the Asian crisis.

Roosevelt was wrong.

Manipulated by the maneuverings of several Japanese militant xenophobic organizations that were united in leading their nation into war against the Western powers, a bloody nationalistic crusade had been launched against influential peace-minded military men and politicians in Japan. With the demise of six prime ministers between 1912 and 1941,[1] the installation of anti-West militants—including Prime Minister Konoye Fumimaro and War Minister Gen. Hideki Tojo, the silence of their new emperor, and the complicity of

---

1. Len Deighton, *Blood, Tears, and Folly: An Objective Look at World War II* (New York: HarperCollins, 1993), 513.

Japan's industrial power, the Zaibatsu—Japan's radical factions had indeed succeeded in bending their nation toward achieving their closely held dream of *Hakko-Ichiu* (The Whole World Under One Roof) with Japan at its center.

By the early 1930s the Japanese nation, schizophrenically led by both the imperial cabinet and the military, had already seized key territories from Russia, Korea, Manchuria, and Northern China. Calculating that China would capitulate to their expansionist desires as others had, Japan's army moved against Eastern China. While China's factional army was in retreat, the territory's agrarian stores and Indonesia's beckoning oil fields were secured, making Japan independent from the feared West.

With the European powers immersed in the more immediate concerns of recovering from an economic depression and the rebirth of totalitarianism (in the forms of militarized social nationalism called Nazism and Italian fascism), it fell to the United States to intervene on behalf of capitalist Asia and its Western counterparts. Blinded by the prejudiced trappings of European elitism, the American nation initially held little interest in Asia and its island chains, but in the later half of the eighteenth century, with the country's westward expansion, the United States had advanced into the Pacific Rim.

The United States' dubious methods of expansion and the European powers' corruption of China had, in part, spurred Japan into adopting a panic-driven policy against the Western nations. The island nation accelerated its own technological armament revolution and amassed the world's largest fleet. By the late 1930s an equally impressive if often uncontrollable army had won a number of battlefield victories. An American ambassador to Japan reported, "Japan today is one of the predatory powers; she has submerged all moral and ethical sense and has become unashamedly and frankly opportunist, seeking at every turn to profit by the weakness of others. Her policy of southward expansion definitely threatens American interests in the Pacific."[2]

For months Roosevelt had worried about implementing his nation's severest peacetime measures: economic sanctions. The

2. James MacGregor Burns, *Roosevelt: The Soldier of Freedom* (New York: Harcourt Brace Jowanovich, 1970), 20.

president questioned whether the imposition of sanctions against the Japanese Empire would actually serve the best interest of the United States. Secretary of State Cordell Hull had been meeting with the Japanese ambassadors and special envoys since the onset, with little success, as the Japanese refused to acknowledge America's concerns for trade in the region. Like the president, however, Hull believed a settlement could be reached with the Japanese without resorting to drastic economic measures.

Others among Roosevelt's cabinet were in violent disagreement. Secretary of War Henry Stimson, Secretary of the Treasury Henry Morgenthau Jr., and Secretary of the Interior Harold Ickes lobbied heavily for an early embargo, warning the president, "There will never be so good a time to stop the shipment of oil to Japan as we now have."[3] Trusting his secretary of state and the State Department to evaluate Japanese trade relations on a day-to-day basis in light of ongoing negotiations, the president hoped the precarious position would be suitable encouragement to induce Japan's Prime Minister Fumimaro to acknowledge the new U.S. stipulations of withdrawal from China and the reinstatement of free trade.

Congress reinforced the president's position when, on July 2, 1940, it passed legislation placing several strategic materials, previously exported to Japan, under the restriction of a day-to-day licensing system. Twenty-four days later, having received little reaction from the Japanese save several formal protests, Roosevelt ordered a broadening of the licensing system to include aviation fuel, lubricating oils, high-grade iron, and steel scraps to Japan (a direct economic attack on Japan's war-making industries and industrialized economy).

An embargo by the United States would have starved Japanese foreign trade and virtually eliminated the industrialized island nation's most essential import: oil.[4] The order had been a calculated warning to Japan that America would not allow Asian aggression to go unchallenged. Carried with it was the implication that a full embargo would hurt them more than the West, should such acts of

---

3. John Toland, *Infamy: Pearl Harbor and Its Aftermath* (Garden City, N.Y.: Doubleday, 1982), 255.

4. I. C. B. Dear, ed., *The Oxford Companion to the Second World War* (New York: Oxford University Press, 1995), 607.

aggression continue. The audacious move, however, only hastened the demise of peace. Across the Pacific, the Japanese imperial cabinet was undergoing a fundamental restructuring to deal with America's audacious and (in Japan's eye) arrogant quasi-trade war.

Prime Minister Konoye had long since acknowledged the potential usefulness of an unrestricted supply of oil, especially in light of the recently placed limited U.S. embargoes. Taking the rapid acceleration of American naval power in the Pacific as a threat to Japanese security (with a striking similarity to America's previous opening of trade relations with Japan in the nineteenth century) and, hence, fearing an American military retaliation (inaccurately estimated as inevitable), the Japanese saw the potential of once more being brought humiliatingly to heel. Tacit alliances with greater powers, Konoye and the imperial cabinet knew, would be necessary. Designating Matsuoka Yosuke as his foreign minister, Konoye sent the former head of the Manchurian railways to meet with the enemies of their presumed adversaries, Nazi Germany and the Soviet Union. Foreign Minister Matsuoka returned with Adolf Hitler's and Benito Mussolini's Tripartite Pact (promising, among other tenets, to come to Japan's assistance should the United States make war against the Japanese) and a treaty of nonaggression with Joseph Stalin.

By signing the Tripartite Pact, the Japanese had, in the view of the American administration, thrown themselves over to Hitler's agenda of blitzkrieg warfare. The United States had already announced several large loans to aid Chinese leader Chiang Kai-shek's rebel army and had enacted an embargo on all forms of iron and steel scrap after Japan next invaded Indonesia, but to no beneficial results. Addressing the nearly deaf, glass-eyed Japanese ambassador, Adm. Nomura Kichisabura, Roosevelt railed, "From every viewpoint this action was contrary to the interests of Japan; that Hitler would rule over every country if once given the opportunity, just as he is today rolling over Italy and other countries which had trusted him."[5]

If Japan were to broaden Hitler's war of aggression across the Pacific, America, Roosevelt believed, would have no choice but to

5. Gordon W. Prange, *Pearl Harbor: The Verdict of History* (New York: McGraw-Hill, 1986), 166.

ensure Japan's place as "the ultimate loser."[6] With the diplomatic dialogue between Japan and the United States in atrophy, Roosevelt ordered Hull to engage in a new dialogue with the Japanese government. Hull sent a note to Tokyo, asking for Japan's position. It inadvertently arrived in the middle of a power struggle within the imperial cabinet.

Foreign Minister Matsuoka's attempts at reasonable negotiations had essentially ended before they had begun. During the intervening months Matsuoka had been labeled emotionally unstable by his colleagues and was dismissed as Prime Minister Konoye reformed his cabinet for the third time to deal with the apparent American threat. "The Japanese wish to conclude the negotiations between United States and Japan quickly, and yet, at present the negotiations do not go further than a general understanding," reported a British diplomat, observing that the two nations were working at cross purposes. "On the other hand, the United States is carrying out delaying tactics and is resorting to trickery in every phase of the adjustment of diplomatic relations. It is foolish to miss the present chance by adopting a cautious attitude without understanding Japan's true intentions or her pressing internal situation."[7] And things were about to get worse.

Isoroku, the adopted orphan of the Yamamoto family, had been reared by the Japanese navy and served in the navy throughout the Russo-Japanese War. Attaining the rank of admiral and serving several positions (navy minister, chief of naval aviation headquarters, and commander of the combined fleet), Isoroku Yamamoto had vainly tried to contain his nation's political extremists. Failing that, Yamamoto worked to prepare for his empire's survival against his reckless superiors and their audacious plans against the American "Arsenal of Democracy." In 1940 Yamamoto laid before his superiors a contingency plan to their diplomatic efforts, utilizing innovative tactical assets of carrier-launched torpedo dive-bombers to decimate the American fleet in one swift blow. Yamamoto knew

---

6. Prange, *Pearl Harbor,* 166.

7. Military History Section Headquarters, United States Armed Forces Far East, eds. Political Strategy Prior to the Outbreak of War: Japanese Monograph No. 147. 1445. http://sunsite.unc.edu/pha/monos/.

America could marshal its industrial might and decimate the sizable Japanese navy given enough time. The admiral hoped there would be enough time to successfully force the United States into a negotiated surrender.

Despite its initial lukewarm reception, Yamamoto persisted. Word of his plan quickly reached the ears of the prime minister and his advisers. After careful consideration, a budget and facilities were allocated for the plan. The operation was considered a research project until negotiations with the United States reached an impasse, only then would the "go-order" be given to execute Yamamoto's plan on the bulk of the American fleet, ironically relocated to Pearl Harbor (one of Roosevelt's symbolic Pacific Rim deterrents to war). Takao Yoshikawa and his fellow spies were dispatched to the Hawaiian target soon thereafter.

The prime minister had not been happy about the Pearl Harbor plan, code-named Operation Z. Konoye sensed both the end of his career and, should his final gambit fail, the beginning of unrestricted military control over domestic and foreign policy. After much deliberation among the ministers, they answered Secretary of State Hull. Japan would withdraw from China as soon as the "China Incident" was settled. They promised not to attack anyone. They desired to keep only a token force within China, if the United States would end its assistance to Chiang Kai-shek and lift its embargoes on the island nation. More startling, however, Prime Minister Konoye also offered to meet Roosevelt midway in the Pacific to negotiate an end to the crisis without the necessity of military involvement. The prime minister would then return to Japan, garner the emperor's support, and present the military with his own ultimatum. War Minister Tojo grudgingly supported the move, but he did not trust the Americans.

Roosevelt was taken aback by the bold proposal. Encouraged, the president presented the idea to his staff. His Far Eastern advisers balked at the idea of meeting the Japanese unless the administration's major Asian questions were settled well in advance of any meeting. Reading the gathered intelligence from Magic (intercepted and deciphered Japanese cables) and having watched Asia as long as he had, Hull distrusted Konoye's ability to rein in Japan's military should an agreement be reached. As a grim result, the president, following his secretary of state's line of reasoning, tabled the decision.

Prime Minister Konoye had failed. He resigned on October 16 and was replaced by, it was said, the only man capable of keeping the army on a short leash, War Minister General Tojo. The emperor immediately ordered the new prime minister to return to a "blank page" diplomatically. When questioning whether the United States would attack Japan, navy chief of staff Osami Nagano told his new prime minister: "There is a saying, 'Don't rely on what won't come.' The future is uncertain; we can't take anything for granted. In three years the defenses in the South will be strong and the number of enemy warships will increase."[8] When asked when it was possible to go to war, Nagano shouted: "Now! The time for war will not come later!"[9]

Prime Minister Tojo decided to give the negotiations one last chance. If a very amicable arraignment failed to be reached by midnight on November 30, Tojo explained, Japan's future would be in Yamamoto's hands. With few perceived viable options remaining, the others agreed. Shortly thereafter, the gathering of reluctant militants agreed they would present a proposal calling upon the Americans to recognize a restoration of the status quo of Asia prior to July. Additionally, neither nation would advance on Southeast Asia or the South Pacific, Japanese troops stationed in China would be removed, and the United States would assist Japan in acquiring resources through the Dutch East Indies as well as export one million tons of oil annually to the island nation.

Roosevelt and his advisers turned back every Japanese diplomatic advance in favor of their own proposals. The United States offered to restore economic relations (including some oil and rice immediately), introduce the Japanese to the Chinese for negotiations, but declined to take any part in the talks if Japan would send no further troops into Asia, agree not to invoke the Tripartite Pact if the United States were to enter the European war against the Axis, as well as six other points.[10] Though decidedly favorable, the Japanese ambassador refused to send the terms to Tokyo. With the military nearing the precipice of readiness, an advantage it might never have again

8. Burns, *Roosevelt*, 154.

9. Ibid.

10. Ibid., 156.

(Yamamoto's Operation Z had been secretly laid before Japan's leadership during the prior week), Prime Minister Tojo knew there would never be a better chance to drive the United States into submission. As a result, the deadline passed without resolution.

On December 1, Prime Minister Togo gathered his advisers at the imperial conference, saying, "At the moment our Empire stands at the threshold of glory or oblivion."[11] The plan would proceed without delay. To maintain secrecy regarding Yamamoto's now committed forces driving toward the U.S. Pacific Fleet's Hawaiian stronghold, Tojo communicated to the ambassadors in the United States that negotiations would continue until December 8, Tokyo time. After the transmittal of a fourteen-part letter from Emperor Hirohito to President Roosevelt (the first half was immediately passed on to the president, but the second half would arrive on the morning of December 7, Washington time), Japan's ambassadors would be instructed to break off diplomatic relations. The empire would then declare war a half-hour before the first torpedoes were scheduled to disturb the still waters of Pearl Harbor.

A slow typist in the Japanese consulate in Washington delayed delivery of the emperor's completed response. By the time Ambassador Nomura arrived at Cordell Hull's office with the final section of their emperor's letter, unknown to the ambassadors, the attack had already been under way an hour. When the Japanese arrived, Hull, muttering "scoundrels and pissants,"[12] immediately turned Nomura back out the door as he consulted with others over the smoldering results of the Roosevelt administration's myopic and misguided diplomatic venture. As the last of the Japanese spies went to ground and the United States carrier task force rushed back to Pearl Harbor at flank speed, launching its fighters to repel the burning port's attackers, the Japanese militant leadership celebrated their diplomatic failure.

---

11. Ibid., 158.

12. Paul Johnson, *Modern Times: The World from the Twenties to the Nineties* (New York: Harper & Row, 1983), 395.

THE ATTACK on Pearl Harbor need not have happened. Both powers erred in evaluating their adversary's intentions. While the United States had been traditionally driven by expansionist capitalism, when faced with the more immediate prospect of a National Socialist Europe, the Roosevelt administration held little regard for the Asian continent's internal affairs. The American economy was not dependent upon income deriving from trade with either China or Japan. From an economic point of view, America could have easily ignored the expansion of the Japanese Empire well into 1942 or possibly 1943, but from the Roosevelt administration's perspective, Japan's acts of aggression against Manchuria, China, and Indonesia had shown little regard for Western conventions of civility and diplomacy. This point of view was only reinforced by the apparent American threat-induced devolution of the empire's domestic governments from a peer-ruled society to a quasi-dictatorship.

Since the onset of the invasion of China in 1937, Japan's militarist leadership had been reacting to a perceived Western/American threat to its sovereignty. Similar to Adolf Hitler's desire for "breathing room" and later Joseph Stalin's call for a buffer zone from the West in annexing Poland, Japan had coveted mainland China as a bulwark against future Western intervention and, more important, as a largely untapped cache of natural resources beyond Western economic control. With the great powers of Europe already at war and America seemingly craven with isolationism, the majority of the Japanese leadership felt that the occupation of China and Indonesia would enable Japan to become a world power. However, distracted by their long-term goal of forging a Greater East Asian Co-Prosperity Sphere, Japan's cultivated xenophobia and sense of national insecurity predisposed the country's leaders to no other course of action than leading the island nation into a direct confrontation with the United States and its Western allies. Furthermore, by initially and erroneously projecting Japan's insecurities onto the American isolationist populace and then later erroneously projecting their own aggressive notions onto the United States' reactionary arms buildup, the Japanese leadership repeatedly failed to take advantage of the Roosevelt administration's proffered concessions.

Likewise, had Roosevelt not relocated the Pacific Fleet to Pearl Harbor, deemphasized the scheduled production of American naval vessels as a forerunner to his diplomatic overtures, and taken special measures to conceal the personal feelings of White House advisers Henry Stimson, Henry Morgenthau Jr., and others toward the island nation as Cordell Hull had, Prime Minister Konoye and the imperial cabinet would have been less pressured to concede ground to the military in the wake of the "China Incident." The prime minister may well have been able to win the emperor's confidence in a dealing with America without securing Hitler's and Mussolini's Tripartite Pact. Devoid of the Nazis' and Fascists' shadows, both Pacific Rim powers might have been able to successfully conclude a tacit concession-filled agreement. Having already prioritized his nation's resources to fight the pending threat of National Socialism in Europe and its wolf packs prowling the Atlantic, Roosevelt could have easily turned a blind eye to Japan's Asian actions until such time as they directly threatened the United States and its Pacific Rim assets of the Philippines, Guam, and Hawaii.

The United States had failed to properly perceive the hard-line militarism of imperial Japanese leadership. The Roosevelt administration and its military advisers had initially dismissed the Japanese Empire's actions as limited in scope and confined to the western Pacific Rim. Their policies of measured diplomacy and implied projected naval prowess had accelerated the rise of Japan's militant factions, quickened the island nation's necessity to find alternative means of obtaining raw materials and natural resources in China and Indonesia, and hastened the demise of any hope of a mutually benevolent agreement with the resignation of Prime Minister Konoye. Furthermore, the United States' failure to perceive the Japanese Empire as on par with the United States not only blinded Roosevelt to the dual nature of Japan's civilian and military leadership, but, despite the acknowledged numerical naval superiority of the Japanese, the United States also relegated the Japanese to a subordinate status both as a world power and as the preeminent South Asian nation-state.

Still, the United States–Japanese diplomatic failure and the ensuing attack on Pearl Harbor indirectly served one of the Roosevelt administration's aims. Spawning dozens of theories over the years, some have theorized that the president of the United States had purposely sought war with Japan in order to foster a declaration of war against the Nazis (a notion over which Roosevelt had been struggling with Congress and his isolationist population for months). Yet America declared war against Germany only after Hitler had declared war against the United States one week after the Japanese attack on Pearl Harbor (a move Hitler need not have made, which validated his seemingly one-sided Tripartite Pact agreement with Japan and also served to bring about Nazi Germany's demise far earlier than it might have happened).

Had Hitler not declared war on the United States, Roosevelt would have been hard-pressed to find popular support for a two-front war against the Nazis and the Japanese in the wake of Pearl Harbor. Furthermore, had neither Japan sought nor Hitler offered the Tripartite Pact agreement, Roosevelt and Hull would have been given greater latitude in brokering a deal with Konoye, a move that might have brokered an agreement between the two Pacific Rim neighbors and subsequently forestalled the ascendance of General Tojo and the militants.

Should cooler heads and clearer minds on both sides of the Pacific have perceived their neighbors oppositely or been less driven than the other, the Allied powers might have had to wait until 1942 or years later for the United States to shake off its isolationism and join their forces against the Axis. In that time, with the fragile lifeline of American commerce to the besieged island of Britain stretched thin across the Atlantic by Nazi submarines, it is quite possible that Germany could have redoubled the blockade of Britain and starved the United Kingdom into a weakened state of defense. With drastically limited offensive capabilities, some among the British might not have thought capitulation an acceptable solution. Furthermore, with a delayed entry of American forces into the war, had the United Kingdom survived, the Allied powers may well have allowed the Nazis to more properly prepare their defenses for an Allied invasion of North Africa, the soft underbelly of Italy, and the eventual invasion of the continent of Europe. The death toll would have most certainly been higher, the battles longer, and the chance of total victory slighter.

Appendix C

The Realities of an Alternate Pearl Harbor

WILLIAM R. FORSTCHEN

IF EVER A WAR was started based upon profound misassumptions about the opposition, Japan's decision to take on America in 1941 is a classic example.

Defeat in war usually comes about because an aggressor either misreads his opponent and his intentions, such as Saddam Hussein's belief in 1990 that America would not intervene in Kuwait, or because an opponent is thought incapable of serious resistance, with Napoleon in Spain or Hitler in Russia as classic examples.

Japan completely misread not just America's commitment to a presence in the Far East, but also the American willingness to fight a bitter and protracted war to maintain that presence and gain revenge as well. Few in Japan realized just how dangerous the "sleeping giant" truly was.

To understand why the Japanese misread the American position, and to better consider the possible alternate outcomes of their fateful attack on Pearl Harbor, a consideration of the history leading up to the "day of infamy" would be helpful.

Japan was one of the few nations that successfully resisted the great wave of European imperialism that started in the sixteenth century. When Portuguese merchants and missionaries reached Japan, the warlords of that island kingdom quickly perceived the threat but realized as well the need to adopt European technology to resist that threat and at the same time to settle their own internal squabbles.

Thus, by the early seventeenth century, Japan could field an army equipped with modern artillery and shoulder weapons that was capable of taking on the mightiest of European powers. Backed by this high-tech arsenal, a unified Japan slammed the door shut on Europe for more than two centuries.

By the middle of the nineteenth century the paradigm shifted due to the industrial revolution. Steam-powered ships and modern armies outfitted with repeating rifles were an irresistible force, and the rulers of Japan saw that the barred gate would have to come down, the new technology embraced, and societal changes undertaken if Japan was to survive.

Less than forty years after their start toward modernization, Japan shocked the world when it soundly defeated a European power, Russia, in the 1904–5 Russo-Japanese War. To the Japanese this war, fought for imperialistic reasons, was their debut on the stage of international power and colonial expansion. It should be noted that the opening attack in that conflict was a surprise Sunday morning assault on Russia's main naval base in the region, followed later by an overwhelming victory against the Russia Fleet sent from the Baltic at the battle of Tsushima. Many of the officers who planned Pearl Harbor, Isoroku Yamamoto among them, were young cadets and officers in that conflict.

The move toward overseas imperialism was not just a matter of prestige, it was believed as well to be a question of national survival. Japan is singularly blessed as an island nation totally unsuited to support an industrial revolution. It is nearly devoid of all crucial natural resources, especially oil, high-grade iron ore, rubber, and even arable land to support a burgeoning population.

The Japanese believed that their outstanding triumph in the war against Russia had granted them a place at the table of international deal cutting. The problem, however, was that they had reached the table after all the cards had been dealt, and in the twentieth century moral qualms were beginning to emerge regarding the naked land-grabbing imperialism of previous centuries, especially when the new player was Asian.

Nevertheless, Japan gained recognition as a military power to be respected. Theodore Roosevelt's Great White Fleet was dispatched in large part as a demonstration to the Japanese of America's increasing commitment to the Pacific. Furthermore, a new base was developed at Pearl Harbor for the American fleet, and even the construction of the Panama Canal was undertaken in large part for the strategic purpose of facilitating the movement of that fleet if war should ever develop in the Pacific.

On the eve of World War I, when the British withdrew nearly all naval assets from the Pacific to concentrate against Germany, an understanding was reached with Japan that it would now be the "cop on the beat" to help protect British interests. This was yet another signal that Japan could consider itself to be an equal with the Western powers. Japan even declared war against Germany in World War I, took part in several minor actions in East Asia, and joined in combined allied efforts against the Soviet Union in 1918.

Thus its delegates arrived at Versailles believing they came as equals. That disastrous conference, which set Germany on the path to another war, set the stage as well for all the anguish that would unfold in East Asia across the next sixty years.

The Japanese delegates were shoved to one side and returned home with a clear message that cooperation with the Western powers would forever leave them at the back of the bus. It was at this same conference that a young Ho Chi Minh was literally thrown out the door and into the waiting arms of the Soviets.

By the late 1920s the Japanese position in relationship to America and Britain was hardening. American fleet maneuvers in the Pacific were seen as war games directly aimed at Japan, which in fact they were. By taking advantage of the chaos in China and the Soviet Union, it could be said that Japan fired the opening shots of World War II in 1931 with its military occupation of Manchuria, a long-sought-after prize due to its rich iron and coal reserves.

The Japanese truly believed that their efforts in China were nothing more than an imitation of British and French imperialism of centuries past. Modern technology, however, played against them, for the brutalities of eighteen-century conquests had gone unrecorded, but the barbarism of Japan's invasion of China and its medieval-like destruction of Nanking were seen in movie theaters and picture magazines around the world, thus hardening global public opinion, especially in America, which saw itself as a protector of China.

Here is the crucial dividing line in the crisis between Japan and America. Japan saw its imperialism as a continuum, that the strong of the world had a right to such actions and the American-British reaction was racist. Such things, when done by the French in Indochina, were accepted, but when done by the Japanese, they became unacceptable. It was at this time that a crucial decision was reached that in itself is worth an alternative history study. The Japanese warlords had essentially divided into two schools, referred to as the Northern and Southern schools. The Northern saw that the path of expansion should be into Mongolia and Siberia at the expense of the Soviet Union. The Southern school argued for expansion into French Indochina and the Dutch East Indies.

The Northern school lost the national debate for three reasons. The first was a disastrous miniwar fought in eastern Mongolia against a combined Soviet-Mongol army. The Soviets appeared to be incompetent fools when fighting Finland in the 1939–40 "Winter War," but in the East their superior armor and Mongol mounted units devastated the Japanese invaders. The Japanese were routed and driven out. It is an unknown war in the West, but in Mongolia the memory of it is still strong and a great source of national pride.

The second factor was the Nazi triumphs in Europe. France and Holland were occupied, and the French administration in Indochina went over to the Fascist side. England, though still holding out, was hard-pressed, and the tantalizing prospect now appeared that perhaps India itself could be taken.

The third factor, however, was perhaps the most crucial of all, and that is the premise with which this essay opened, the misassumption one culture holds about another.

Most of the planners of the Southern school held America in contempt. America was viewed as a decadent society, mired in economic depression, addicted to pleasure, and as one leader put it, befuddled by "Negro Jazz." Some even believed that the American West was as they saw it in cowboy movies, untamed, with Indians still conducting raids on cavalry outposts.

The few who tried to argue against this were mainly Japanese who had studied at American universities, traveled across the country, and understood its sheer size and industrial potential.

The Southern school argued that an opportunity that Asians had dreamed of for centuries was at hand: the expulsion of white

European imperialists from the East. The fact that one form of imperialism would be replaced with another that was far more brutal didn't matter. Japan could create an empire even vaster than the one the Nazis were already creating.

The only barrier to the fulfillment of this dream was America.

Here now is another point of misassumption, and it is the American interpretation of World War II. The Roosevelt administration approached that global conflict as a true global conflict, believing that America's enemies were ultimately bent on the country's total destruction. That might have been true with Germany, at least in relationship to their long-term planning, but it was never the intent or even the wildest dream of the Japanese warlords. American propaganda films and poster images of German and Japanese troops linking up somewhere near Denver, the way American and Soviet troops would meet eventually on the Elbe, was never even a remote consideration.

The Southern school saw its impending war with America as global in scale but ultimately limited in its final intent, even if those goals did encompass nearly a third of the world.

The grab would be south and west, not east. French Indochina (which actually was the trigger point for the decision to go to war when America imposed an oil embargo after Japanese occupation in the summer of 1941), the oil-rich East Indies, India, and China were the real targets. If the Nazis defeated the Soviet Union, then Siberia might be added in as well.

The American-occupied Philippines and perhaps the Hawaiian Islands were on the list, but San Francisco and Los Angeles were never a consideration. When contemplating alternate histories, this point is essential: Japan never dreamed of going "all the way." Contrastingly, after Pearl Harbor, the American goal was to make the rubble bounce in Tokyo.

The Japanese battle plan for this limited war was as follows: first and foremost, take out the American fleet. The Japanese had pretty well figured out America's Orange Plans, that is, if war started, our fleet was to sortie in support of our troops in the Philippines and then hunt down the Japanese fleet and destroy it. The attack on Pearl Harbor was therefore to be a preemptive strike to take out the U.S. fleet first. Ironically, this approach was a fulfillment of the

American naval prophet Alfred Thayer Mahan's most basic principle: the enemy fleet should always be the first target in war.

Step two would then be the "run and grab" operation that the Japanese war planners believed would last for at least six months and perhaps a year. America, reeling from the initial defeat, would take months to mount a counteroffensive. Meanwhile, the Japanese would take the East Indies, the Philippines, Singapore, expand out in China, cover the Australian flank by taking New Guinea and the Solomons, snatch Burma, and perhaps even move toward India with the hope of triggering a rebellion. These occupied areas would be protected by an outer defensive ring of interlocking strongpoints, airstrips, fortified islands, and forward naval bases.

The oil, rubber, steel, and food from the captured provinces would flow back to the home islands, industrial output would soar, and the fleet would be expanded for phase three: the second encounter with America. A few optimists hoped that America would bow out after the first defeat, but few expected it. Drawing on their memory of the Russo-Japanese War, when the Russians sent their Baltic Fleet halfway around the world to its doom, the Japanese assumed the United States would mount at least one strong counterstrike by pulling resources from the Atlantic. It might hit as early as the middle of 1942; the optimists were hoping it wouldn't come until 1943.

That battle would be fought along the outer edge of this new empire, where more than a million troops, thousands of land-based planes, six to eight carriers, and a dozen battleships would be waiting. The 1905 battle of Tsushima, which had decided the Russo-Japanese War, would happen yet again. The white imperialists would be destroyed . . . and then sue for peace. In fact, there was a second battle like Tsushima. It is known as the battle of Midway.

But in those days of dreams and planning back in the summer of 1941, the key assumption was that after a second disastrous defeat, weak, decadent, jazz-addicted America would crawl away, sit humbly at a peace conference, and acknowledge the Japanese conquests. There was to be no conquest of California. No march on Denver. It was to be a war fought on a global scale for limited goals.

There were a few who warned against this misassumption, men such as Yamamoto, who understood that Americans tended to link warfare not to the traditional concept of power and land acquisition, but rather to moral absolutes. A war fought for moral absolutes must be won absolutely. It was for this reason that Yamamoto insisted that war must be declared before the strike at Pearl Harbor. Given the American sense of "fair play," the Eastern tradition of starting a war with a preemptive strike would serve only to unify the enemy, a result far outweighing any gain of an immediate tactical advantage. Failure to follow this strange Western custom would result in an outraged America turning the conflict into a holy crusade, which is exactly what happened.

It is with that background in mind that the reality behind alternate histories of Pearl Harbor should be considered.

WHEN IT comes to alternate histories of the attack on Pearl Harbor, consider the four scenarios that a number of historians have speculated about:

1. The Japanese launch a third air strike on December 7 to take out the oil depots and dry docks.

2. The three U.S. aircraft carriers based at Pearl Harbor are engaged within twenty-four hours after the start of the war and sent to the bottom.

3. The Japanese send in a landing force, either as a suicidal spoiling force to ensure the total destruction of military facilities on the island or in a bid to occupy this crucial strategic position.

4. This possibility, although not directly related to Pearl Harbor, is an action that I have personally wondered about: Why did the Japanese fail to launch a strike against the Panama Canal? Such an attack was planned in the closing days of the war, a remarkable effort to be carried out using giant submarine aircraft carriers, but the subs were recalled and sunk while trying to get back to Okinawa. Half a dozen planes, a suicide mission if need be, sent to destroy the main lock controlling the water level in the canal, could have taken that vital connection out of action for a year or more.

The failure to launch the third strike on the morning of December 7 is truly one of the great "ifs" of this battle. Total surprise had been achieved in the first strike, and though the second wave did suffer a higher rate of casualties, the Japanese still maintained full air superiority over Oahu. The Japanese task force commander, however, stunned by success, did not want to throw away a winning hand by gambling on a third strike. Since the three U.S. carriers were not caught at Pearl Harbor and had not been located, there was a lingering fear that perhaps a trap was being set and it was time to withdraw.

It's a curious decision, since one of the primary goals of the strike on Pearl was to take out the carriers. It shows, as well, one of the myths regarding the Japanese approach to the war, that they were more carrier-oriented while America was still dominated by battleship admirals. In fact, it was the Japanese who doctrinally leaned toward battleships far more than American planners did. They viewed the strike on Pearl Harbor as a nearly complete success since the U.S. Pacific Fleet of battleships had indeed been sunk. Risking their fleet to take out the oil tank farms and the carriers was not seen as being prudent or effective. More than one American naval officer, however, believed that all that had been achieved was the sinking of a fleet that was already obsolete, thus clearing the way for the carrier admirals to take over.

If the Japanese had indeed gone back for a third strike and smashed the dry docks and oil tank farms, the subsequent American war effort would have been seriously hampered. Nearly a year's worth of fuel for the fleet was stored on Oahu. Its destruction would have meant the diversion of precious tankers that were ferrying fuel along the East Coast, tankers that the Germans were sinking at a phenomenal rate. A genuine fuel crisis would have severally impacted American operations in the Pacific for at least a year or more.

The dry docks, used throughout the war, were crucial for the quick turnaround of ships damaged in battle. The loss of these facilities would have meant towing ships all the way back to the West Coast for repairs.

If this alternative is conceded to the Japanese, that they successfully launch a third strike and millions of gallons of fuel goes up in flames and the dry docks are flooded ruins, then the second alternate comes into focus: the destruction of the three American carriers based at Pearl. Assume that, during the third strike, a Japanese scout plane, sent out beyond Pearl to cover the attacking force, spots the American carriers. Late in the afternoon a fourth strike is launched, this time against the carriers (which actually did steam into Pearl the following morning since they were low on fuel), and it succeeds in sinking all three ships. Gone are the valiant *Enterprise* and the brilliant Adm. William "Bull" Halsey, which were the backbone of U.S. naval efforts in 1942.

Here is a battle with success much greater than what had been achieved in the first two strikes at Pearl. There would now be no American carriers in the Pacific and no fuel, and the port facilities would be destroyed. Thus there would be no battle of the Coral Sea, no Midway, no counteroffensive starting at Guadalcanal in August. The six-month free run for the Japanese would have turned into a year or more.

Add the third and fourth factors. A convoy loaded with a division of imperial marines and escorted by half a dozen destroyers and cruisers invades Hawaii during the evening of December 7. The mission is to strike hard into the burning wreckage of Pearl Harbor, take out the troops stationed at Schofield Barracks, and then hold on. If possible, repair some of the facilities to provide support for Japanese subs, which could then operate along the California coast.

As a variant, perhaps the destruction of the dry docks and oil reserves would not have taken place. If a scout plane spotted the carriers before the third strike was launched against Oahu, the armament could be changed, the attack launched against the U.S. carriers, the landing force on Oahu secures a truly operational base. Once resources have been freed up after the conquests in the Dutch East Indies, Malaysia, and the Solomons, more troops would be sent to relieve this spoiling force. Possession of the oil stored on Oahu would have nearly doubled the strategic reserve for the Japanese fleet in the Pacific.

The landing operation would most likely have met with a frightful level of success. The imperial marines were a hardened lot, with plenty of combat experience in China, a force that would have torn apart the stunned naval personnel and garrison troops on the island.

The prospect of a Japanese base at Pearl would have created a nightmare for the U.S. Navy. Even with limited salvage efforts, Pearl could have been used as a sub base, projecting the highly capable Japanese submarine force all the way to the West Coast while, at the same time, denying the base for American sub operations against the Japanese merchant fleet. Long-range Japanese scout planes could have flown nearly to the American coast and back, tracking U.S. naval movements and creating a near constant state of panic.

Finally, add in the Panama Canal scenario. The real plan that the Japanese came close to launching in 1945 was to send half a dozen torpedo planes from a submarine aircraft carrier (the largest sub ever built up till the "boomer" ballistic missile carriers). The strike would hit the primary lock that regulated the vast reservoir that maintained water level throughout most of the canal. Its destruction would have sent a tidal wave–like flood into the central part of the canal, followed by a rapid drop in water level that would have stranded traffic. If the first plane successfully hit that lock, the others would take out other locks. In short, a total nightmare. Repairs might have taken a year or more.

All ships transferring from the Atlantic to the Pacific would be forced to go around South America, adding eight thousand miles to the trip, sailing through the German sub–infested waters between Africa and Brazil.

All of this seems to add up to a sure win for the Japanese. The U.S. Pacific Fleet is gone, Pearl is occupied, American ships are forced to make the dangerous, arduous, and expensive run around South America just to reach the West Coast. With Pearl occupied, all operations would have to be staged out of San Francisco or Seattle. The rare Japanese sub moving along the West Coast might instead have turned into wolf packs. Panic would have ensued, and precious divisions that were in actuality committed to North Africa and Australia would have to be deployed to defend the West Coast against invasion.

The early relief effort launched in the spring of 1942 to buttress Australia would have been unthinkable, and chances are that the Japanese would have placed troops on the north coast of that continent, creating a panicked response from the Australian and New Zealand governments, something that would impact the British campaign against Erwin Rommel in North Africa.

Looks like Japan is on the way to winning the war.

Doubtful; in fact, impossible.

The reason for this comes down yet again to the fundamental differences in how American and Japanese societies viewed the war. Japan perceived it ultimately as a limited conflict designed to create an empire. Though they attempted to dress it up with a shoddy propaganda campaign, claiming that theirs was a war of liberation against white imperialism, those who suffered under their occupation quickly learned that one master had been replaced by another who was far worse.

America, on the other hand, saw the war as a conflict between democracy and totalitarianism in both Europe and Asia. Though Japanese plans were not aimed at total global conquest, Americans were convinced that that was indeed the intent, that the Japanese and Germans were determined to take everything.

Next was the outrage over the sneak attack on Pearl. The word *infamy* will forever be linked in the American psyche to Pearl Harbor and December 7. The attack was seen as a moral outrage, a "dastardly" stab in the back, and the only response was the total annihilation of the perpetrators. An early indicator of this was the fact that the United States had gone to war in 1917 over the issue of unrestricted submarine warfare and bitterly denounced the Germans for this same issue throughout 1940 and 1941. Before Roosevelt had even asked Congress to declare war, the U.S. Navy had issued orders for American subs to commence unrestricted operations, sinking all Japanese shipping, civilian and military, on sight and without warning.

Finally there was the underlying difference regarding each country's perceptions as to the purpose of war. Americans have always tended to view war as an aberration, the breaking down of an orderly process into disorder that disrupts the free flow of a capitalistic system. They believe that one tends to win economic advantage through the "warfare" of capitalism; actual combat and the spilling of blood are resorted to only for national defense or in defense of certain moral absolutes.

The American Civil War is a classic example. Both sides perceived the war as a breakdown of the orderly process of the republic. The Union first cast its cause as one of a moral crusade to defend the ideal of the republic, but toward the end of the conflict, additional strength was added by redefining the war as a moral crusade to end slavery.

The Spanish-American War, which in reality was nothing but a naked land grab, nevertheless was sold to the American public as a moral crusade to free the oppressed of Cuba. When the land grab extended into the far Pacific, the freeing of the Philippines from oppression became an issue as well, although when the Filipinos took us at our word and demanded independence, Americans fought a bitter five-year campaign against the nationalists in a truly forgotten war that cost ten times as many casualties as the Spanish conflict.

American distaste and cynicism over World War I came directly from the fact that it was ultimately perceived as a war that achieved only limited aims, that was political in origin, and that was manipulated by corrupt politicians at its conclusion. No moral high ground was won. The rallying cry of making the world safe for democracy was, within a year after the end of the war, openly ridiculed by a disgusted public.

Thus America's entry into a war with Japan after a real or alternative-history attack on Pearl Harbor would be exactly the same: a rising up of a nation unified in its rage and moral indignation. The additional defeats in the alternate scenarios would have only added fuel to that fire. A Japanese occupation of Hawaii, and not just a couple of frozen islands in the Aleutians, would have triggered a national fury. And given the typical methods of Japanese occupation, photographs and films of Japanese atrocities smuggled out of Hawaii would have ignited an unquenchable lust for revenge.

The first step would have been the defeat of the Japanese fleet somewhere in the waters between Hawaii and California. This would be a battle sought by both sides. The Japanese would believe that victory in such a battle would end the war; American planners would approach it as but the opening move in a march that would end only in Tokyo, no matter what the cost. Mass production of the *Essex*-class carriers kicked into high gear in 1942. In the historic conflict, America outproduced Japan at a ratio of well over six-to-one in heavy carriers, but more important was the production of planes and pilots, where Japan never stood a chance of catching up.

It should be remembered also that, throughout the war, the effort against Japan was viewed as a secondary front. From the very beginning, Roosevelt and Churchill insisted that Germany was the key enemy, even though American passions against Japan ran far deeper. The reason for this is obvious now, but it was realized by only a privileged and rather frightened few back in the dark days of 1942. Then it looked as if Germany might win the war, that Russia might bail out, and worst of all, Germany might be on the edge of developing operational nuclear weapons. Given those fears, Germany had to be defeated first, even if it meant delaying actions against Japan until the late 1940s.

Had the Japanese secured a total victory against the American and British forces in the Pacific, the Allies' priorities would have remained generally the same, although one could see at least a partial redistribution of resources to the Pacific front to retake Hawaii as quickly as possible. Even if an alternate battle of Midway, now the battle of Hawaii, was yet another Japanese victory, the Allies would undoubtedly have built another fleet of carriers and done it again and again, until they finally got it right.

Logistically a battle for Hawaii would have been in America's favor, with America's ability to return to the islands being far greater than the Japanese ability to hold it. By no later than the middle of 1943, the islands would have been under U.S. control again, and the Japanese fleet would have been in retreat.

Given the atrocities committed by the Japanese in any territory they occupied, there's no doubt what returning Americans would discover upon the liberation of the Hawaiian Islands. Such a discovery would have fueled a national desire for revenge and for pressing the war to total victory.

At about the same time that the Allies would finally retake the Hawaiian Islands, the damage to the Panama Canal would have been repaired and a flood of materiel would pour into the Pacific. The entire strategic approach of the United States might very well have changed at this point. In the historic war, America engaged in a two-pronged offensive with the marines and navy cutting across the Central Pacific while the army under Douglas MacArthur came up through the southwestern Pacific. By the end of 1943 the China-Burma-India (CBI) theater of operations would receive enough support for limited offensive operations as well.

This undoubtedly would have changed. There might very well have been a battle of northern Australia to push the Japanese off the continent, but after retaking Hawaii the move would be on to slice straight toward Japan, the action in the southwest Pacific and in CBI taking a back seat.

The end result would be the same as the actual war, although perhaps lasting into 1946.

By late 1945 U.S. forces would have seized a forward base, perhaps through the historic route of taking Tinian, perhaps driving straight on to Iwo Jima and Okinawa, and once those bases were secured, the rain of bombs would have started. Historically, American scientists produced three atomic weapons in 1945: one was used as a test and the other two were dropped on enemy targets. The difference this time would be that one or perhaps both bombs might have been dropped on Tokyo. Given how this alternate war would have run, it's fair to assume that U.S. planners would have been even more ruthless in seeking revenge. Use of additional atomic weapons in 1945 had actually been a bluff after Hiroshima and Nagasaki; American forces did not have enough fissionable material for a third bomb until late 1945 and had only several such weapons by the spring of 1946. If Japan had tried to hold out, those weapons would have been used without hesitation.

The Soviet Union would have entered the conflict as well and perhaps even jumped onto mainland Japan ahead of American forces, something they had every intention of doing in the final weeks of the actual conflict. It must be remembered that the humiliation of the Russo-Japanese War was only forty years in the past, and Stalin would have loved to preempt America in the settlement of the Pacific War.

So the end result of an alternate Pearl Harbor would remain a defeated Japan. Their raid on Pearl Harbor, when viewed dispassionately, was without a doubt one of the most audacious and brilliant tactical successes in the history of warfare. On a strategic and political level, however, it was an unmitigated disaster for Japan.

Yamamoto was right when he declared, "I fear that all we have done is to awaken the sleeping giant." No matter how much more was added to that day of victory for Japan, even to the capturing of Hawaii, the sinking of our carriers, and the crippling of the Panama Canal, all Japan had achieved was to stir the American nation into a righteous anger that would not be appeased until the final victory had been won.

Acknowledgments
and Contributors

Acknowledgments

"Introduction: When Interesting History Makes Bad Hollywood" by Brian Thomsen. Copyright © 2001 by Brian Thomsen.

"The Sumter Scenario: A Time Wars Story" by Simon Hawke. Copyright © 2001 by Simon Hawke.

"The Secret History of Mr. Churchill's Revenge" by Tony Geraghty. Copyright © 2001 by Tony Geraghty.

"Cain" by Jim DeFelice. Copyright © 2001 by Jim DeFelice.

"Pariah" by Ed Gorman. Copyright © 2001 by Ed Gorman.

"Green Zeros" by R. J. Pineiro. Copyright © 2001 by R. J. Pineiro.

"The East Wind Caper" by James Reasoner. Copyright © 2001 by James Reasoner.

"Path of the Storm" by William C. Dietz. Copyright © 2001 by William C. Dietz.

"The Fourth Scenario" by William Hallahan. Copyright © 2001 by William Hallahan.

"Victory at Pearl Harbor" by Brendan DuBois. Copyright © 2001 by Brendan DuBois.

"'I Relieve You, Sir'" by Barrett Tillman. Copyright © 2001 by Barrett Tillman.

"Beer, Betrayal, and Ho Chi Minh" by Doug Allyn. Copyright © 2001 by Doug Allyn.

"A Terrible Resolve" by William H. Keith Jr. Copyright © 2001 by William H. Keith Jr.

"December 7, 2001: A Classroom on the American Continent" by Allen C. Kupfer. Copyright © 2001 by Allen C. Kupfer.

"Pearl Harbor, December 7, 1941: A Timeline" by Roland Green. Copyright © 2001 by Roland Green.

Contributors

Simon Hawke has been writing professionally for more than twenty years. He has published over sixty novels, among them the popular Time Wars Series, The Wizard of Fourth Street novels, and The Reluctant Sorcerer trilogy. His latest book, *Mystery of Errors,* is available in hardcover from Forge Books. Hawke lives with his wife and stepson in Greensboro, North Carolina.

Tony Geraghty is the respected author of the nonfiction military books *Who Dares Wins,* a history of the British Special Air Services Regiment; *March or Die: A New History of the French Foreign Legion;* and *Brixmis,* the story of British espionage during the Cold War. A veteran paratrooper, he lives with his wife, author Gillian Linscott, in England.

Jim DeFelice's recent techno-thrillers include *Brother's Keeper* (2000) and *Havana Strike* (1997), both currently available in paperback from Leisure Books. His first novel, *Coyote Bird,* was reissued in paperback by Leisure in February 2001. DeFelice has also written more than a dozen works of fiction and nonfiction for young people, including an A&E biography of the Beatles published by Lerner Books in 2001. He lives with his wife and son in Upstate New York and can be contacted by e-mail at JDchester@aol.com.

Ed Gorman has been called "one of the most original crime writers around" by *Kirkus* and "a powerful storyteller" by Charles Champlin of the *Los Angeles Times.* He works in horror and westerns as well as crime and writes a number of excellent short stories. To date there have been six collections of his work, three of which are straight crime, the most recent of which is *Such a Good Girl and Other Stories.* He is probably best known for the Sam McCain series set in various small towns in Iowa during the 1950s ("good and evil clash with the same heartbreaking results as Lawrence Block or Elmore Leonard"). He has also written a number of thrillers, including *The Marilyn Tapes* and *Black River Falls,* the latest being *The Poker Club.*

R. J. Pineiro is the author of several techno-thrillers, including *Ultimatum, Retribution, Breakthrough, Exposure, Shutdown, Conspiracy.com,* and the millennium thrillers *01-01-00* and *Y2K*. His tenth novel, Firewall, will be published in February 2002. He is a nineteen-year veteran of the computer industry and is currently at work on leading-edge microprocessors, the heart of personal computers. Pineiro was born in Havana, Cuba, and grew up in El Salvador before coming to the United States to pursue higher education. He holds a degree in electrical engineering from Louisiana State University, a second-degree black belt in martial arts, a pilot's license, and a gun permit. Pineiro has traveled extensively through Central America, Europe, and Asia, both for his computer business and for his writing. He lives in Texas with his wife, Lory, and his son, Cameron.

In a full-time writing career that has spanned a couple of decades, **James Reasoner** has written in virtually every category of commercial fiction. His novel *Texas Wind* is a true cult classic, and his gritty crime stories about contemporary Texas are in the first rank of today's suspense fiction. He has written many books in several ongoing western series, including the *Faraday, Stagecoach,* and *Abilene* novel series. His other work includes The Civil War Battles Series published by Cumberland House and The Last Good War Series published by Tor Books.

William C. Dietz has published eighteen science-fiction novels, the latest of which is called *By Blood Alone* (a sequel to *Legion* and *The Final Battle*), three *Star Wars*–related novellas, and five short stories. He grew up in the Seattle area, spent time in the navy, graduated from the University of Washington, lived in Africa for six months, and has been employed variously as a surgical technician, news writer, college instructor, television director, and public relations manager. Dietz lives in the Seattle area with his wife, two daughters, and two cats. He enjoys traveling, snorkeling, canoeing, and not surprisingly, reading.

William H. Hallahan has written ten suspense novels and several nonfiction histories plus a number of shorter works. His first mystery novel was nominated for the Edgar Allan Poe Award and his fourth won it. His history titles are born out of the research he has done for his novels. Everything is connected to everything else and nothing is wasted. Over the years he has consumed many a beer in many a pub "what-ifing" Pearl Harbor scenarios.

Brendan DuBois is the award-winning author of several short stories and novels. His short fiction has appeared in *Playboy, Ellery Queen's*

Mystery Magazine, Alfred Hitchcock's Mystery Magazine, Mary Higgins Clark Mystery Magazine, and numerous anthologies. He has received the Shamus Award from the Private Eye Writers of America and has been nominated three times for an Edgar Allan Poe Award by the Mystery Writers of America. He's also the author of the Lewis Cole Mystery series—*Dead Sand, Black Tide,* and *Shattered Shell.* His most recent novel, *Resurrection Day,* is a suspense thriller that looks at what might have happened had the Cuban Missile Crisis of 1962 erupted into a nuclear war between the United States and the Soviet Union. This book received the Sidewise Award for best alternative history novel of 1999. He lives in New Hampshire with his wife, Mona.

Barrett Tillman is the author of four novels—one of which, *Hellcats,* was nominated for the Military Novel of the Year in 1996—twenty nonfiction historical and biography books, and more than four hundred military and aviation articles in American, European, and Pacific Rim publications. He received his bachelor's degree in journalism from the University of Oregon in 1971 and spent the next decade writing freelance articles. Tillman later worked with the Champlin Museum Press and as the managing editor of *The Hook* magazine. In 1989 he returned to freelance writing and has been at it ever since. His military nonfiction has been critically lauded and garnered him several awards, including the U.S. Air Force's Historical Foundation Award, the Nautical and Oceanographic Society's Outstanding Biography Award, and the Arthur Radford Award for Naval History and Achievement.

Doug Allyn is an accomplished author whose work regularly graces annual collections of best short fiction stories. His work has appeared in *Once Upon a Crime, Cat Crimes Through Time,* and *The Year's 25 Finest Crime and Mystery Stories,* volumes 3 and 4. His stories of Talifer the wandering minstrel have appeared in *Ellery Queen's Mystery Magazine* and *Murder Most Scottish.* Allyn's story "The Dancing Bear," a Tallifer tale, won the Edgar Award for short fiction for 1994. His other series character is veterinarian David Westbrook, whose exploits have been collected in the anthology *All Creatures Dark and Dangerous.* He lives with his wife in Montrose, Michigan.

William H. Keith Jr. is the author of more than sixty novels, nearly all of which deal with the theme of men at war. Writing under the pseudonym H. Jay Riker, he's responsible for the extremely popular SEALS: The Warrior Breed series, a family saga spanning the history of the Navy UDT and SEALs from World War II to the present day. As Ian

Douglas, he writes a well-received military–science fiction series following the futuristic exploits of the U.S. Marines in combat on the moon and on Mars. A former hospital corpsman in the navy during the Vietnam era, many of his characters, his medical knowledge, his feel for life in the military, and his profound respect for the men and women whose lives are on the line for their country are all drawn from personal experience.

Allen C. Kupfer is the author of the novel *Double Crossfire* and several short stories. He teaches composition, literature, and film at Nassau Community College on Long Island, New York.

Roland Green is a persistent writer of fantasy, science fiction, and book reviews. His most recent book is *Voyage to Eneh*. Green lives in Chicago with his wife, Frieda Murray, daughter, Violette Green, and a cat named Thursday. None of them has auburn hair or freckles.

Paul A. Thomsen is a freelance researcher and writer. Having received his master's degree in history from Brooklyn College in 1996, he has also served as a research associate and archivist for Joseph A. Califano Jr. and the Benjamin J. Rosenthal Library of Queens College and performed specific assignments for various book packagers and publishers. Thomsen's articles have appeared in *American History* magazine, *World War II* magazine, and *The American Intelligence Journal,* and the upcoming book *Alternate Gettysburgs*. He resides in New York City.

William R. Forstchen was born in New Jersey in 1950. He was educated by Benedictine monks and graduated from Rider College in Lawrenceville, New Jersey. He taught history for ten years and ran workshops on creative writing in Maine. In 1989 he returned to graduate school at Purdue University, where he gained a master's degree in European history. He is currently finishing a Ph.D., specializing in nineteenth-century American military history. His first novel, *Ice Prophet,* was published in 1983, and since then he has written many others. He has also written numerous short stories, fiction for young adults, science articles, and a number of guest editorials, including a publication with the *Chicago Tribune*. Forstchen has always enjoyed traveling and has ventured to Russia and visited a fair part of Europe. Other interests include scuba diving, cycling, travel by train, pinball machines, classical music and historical reenactment as a private with the Twentieth Maine Volunteer Regiment.

DATE DUE
